West of Paradise

Also by Gwen Davis

NOVELS

Naked in Babylon
Someone's in the Kitchen with Dinah
The War Babies
Sweet William
The Pretenders
Touching
Kingdom Come
The Motherland
The Aristocrats
Ladies in Waiting
Marriage
Romance
Silk Lady
The Princess and the Pauper
Jade

POETRY

Changes
How to Survive in Suburbia When Your Heart's in the Himalayas
American Woman Loose in the UK

PLAYS

The Best Laid Plans
The Women Upstairs
Who Is Sylvia?

West of Paradise

Gwen Davis

St. Martin's Press
New York

A THOMAS DUNNE BOOK.
An imprint of St. Martin's Press.

WEST OF PARADISE. Copyright © 1998 by Gwen Davis. All rights
reserved. Printed in the United States of America. No part of this book
may be used or reproduced in any manner whatsoever without written
permission except in the case of brief quotations embodied in critical
articles or reviews. For information, address St. Martin's Press, 175
Fifth Avenue, New York, N.Y. 10010.

Design by Nancy Resnick

Library of Congress Cataloging-in-Publication Data

Davis, Gwen.
    West of paradise :   a novel / Gwen Davis. — 1st ed.
       p.   cm.
    "A Thomas Dunne book."
    ISBN 0-312-18678-9
    I. Title.
    PS3554.A9346W47   1998
    813'.54—dc21   98-5328
                                                                     CIP

First Edition: May 1998

10   9   8   7   6   5   4   3   2   1

For Gary L. Bostwick, Esq., who told me,
"Not the ghost of Swifty Lazar, not the Buddha himself,
should stop you from writing this book."
Well, they didn't, but they tried.

And for Jamie Lee Curtis, without whom . . .

Contents

Dramatis Personae	ix
A Celebrity Funeral	1
A Party at Wolfgang Puck's	18
A Snowflake in Hell	39
By Hook or by Crook	57
Rats	77
A Stalker's Daisy Chain	97
Special Occasions	114
Incidental Music	135
Last Lunches	157
Building Bridges	176
People Who Live in Glass Houses	194
Burning Bridges	214
Will the Real Larry Drayco Please Stand Up	227
Paradise East	249
And the Winner Is . . .	267
Afterword	285

Dramatis Personae

(In Order of Appearance)

LARRY DRAYCO—a dead Producer

KATE DONNELLY—a would-be Writer

WILTON SPENSER—Actor/Dope Dealer

SARAH NASH—Author of a Hollywood exposé

ARTHUR FINSTER—a scrofulous Publisher

FLETCHER McCALLUM—Dealmaker/Lawyer

WENDY—an ex-Duchess

SAMANTHA CHATSWORTH—West Coast Editor

ALGERNON REDDY—Philosopher/Guru

RODNEY SAMETH—a reclusive Director

DARCY LINETTE—Studio Head/Good Guy

MORTY SCHEIN—Clothing Manufacturer

JAKE ALONZO—Movie Star

LILA DARSHOWITZ—Relative of the Deceased

CHARLEY BEST—a once Top Attraction

BRANDY—a Bimbo

HELEN MANNING—the number one Female Star

LINUS ARCHER—an aging Enfant Terrible

VICTOR LIPPTON—a major Player

NORMAN JESSUP—just as major

CHEN—Mrs. Lippton

CARINA—Jessup's Fiancée

PERRY ZEMMIS—a Fool

ALEXA DE CARVILLE—a Mistress

TYLER HAYDEN—a Pure Soul

MEL BRYNNER—an Agent

ASHER PFALTZ—Hollywood Historian

MORGAN CRAIG—a Graduate Student

RALPH ROBERTSON—Interviewer/Lecher

HALLOWELL VINCENT—Private Detective

BOBBY SHORT—an Entertainer

BINKY DANFORTH-SMYTHE—a Bounder

LORI—a New York Literary Agent

Special Guest Star:

F. SCOTT FITZGERALD—a dead Writer

You will always need the favour of the inhabitants to take possession of a province.

—Niccolo Machiavelli, *The Prince*

West of Paradise

A Celebrity Funeral

$\mathcal{M}$arilyn Monroe was there, and Natalie Wood, and Dorothy Stratten, the murdered centerfold, beneath an embittered message to the world left by her lover, near the slaughtered daughter of the writer who still covered the courts in search of a justice that seemed never to prevail for victims, and Darryl F. Zanuck with a hot brass plate on his grave, the Hollywood version of the eternal flame, and next to him the wife to whom he had been so brazenly unfaithful, and some few feet away, Armand Hammer in his own mausoleum, a contemporary Capulet. It was a wonder any room remained in the cemetery.

The place was less than a quarter of a New York City block wide, and space was at a premium. Workmen had removed Peter Lawford from his niche in the white-marbled wall when his widow failed to keep up the payments. Those who still put flowers in the tiny vase by Marilyn's crypt—just around the corner—took satisfaction from that, since well-documented gossip made it Lawford's fault that she was there at all, the original introduction to the Kennedys having been made by him.

But the bodies interred at Pierce Brothers in Westwood, behind the movie theater complex fronting it, were truly chockablock. Non-celebrity couples, even rich, had to make arrangements to be buried one atop the other. So it rather surprised Kate, who in her research about Hollywood had learned about that cemetery, that the funeral for Larry Drayco was being held there. From what she had read in

1

the obituaries he was without family that anyone knew of, or even close friends who'd deserted him, as they had Dean Martin, laid to rest a while before in the crowded sod, amid sobbing eulogies from those who hadn't spoken to him for decades.

Kate didn't belong at the funeral. She crashed it as some would an Oscar party. Isolated in the unique way people could be in Los Angeles, where the only real crowds were on the freeway, she was desperate for company. Recently arrived in that spread-out city, she had had no opportunity to make friends. There were no casual meeting places. People got together only by design. It was the social equivalent of job opportunity: you couldn't get an assignment unless you had done something before. You couldn't really connect with people in L.A. unless you already knew them.

Believing the lore, she had been certain Hollywood would mean rubbing shoulders with celebrities. And they *were* visible, in the same way movies were, always around, but not genuinely accessible. Not to talk back to you, not to touch, like the romance on the screen that life rarely provided.

She had come to Los Angeles in the hope of being a writer. She already *was* a writer in her mind, and in the piles of half-finished manuscripts, and in the will of her father, who'd left her enough insurance to underwrite a beginning, giving her in death what he hadn't been able to in life. So she was free to pursue her dream, for a little while anyway, taking two afternoons a week to go to the library and help someone else pursue her dream, a Hispanic chambermaid who'd never learned to read, and longed to. So Kate worked with her and taught her, and they became, in a way, friends. But there wasn't anyone who would ask Kate to her home, or feel comfortable being invited to Kate's, or give her a real feeling of connection. So even in doing good, Kate's isolation was intensified. She was ready to give her soul for a friend.

Coming into the chapel, Kate felt a rush of genuine exhilaration. So many famous people, none of whom she knew, all of whom she felt she knew, none of them knowing her. In the short time she had lived there, she had found no one to confide in but an agent. And he was hardly courting her confidence, suffering her more than appreciating her. Her honesty seemed to embarrass him, a direct contradiction to the way he operated. She had called him once in a crisis and he'd put her on hold.

So she was at sea on the almost empty pavements, where the celebrated sometimes roamed. To walk down streets where Alec Baldwin carried his dry cleaning, sit at sidewalk restaurants where Julia Roberts suffered aloud about whether to cut her hair, and not be able to interact, was a shroud on Kate's outgoing spirit. She had things to say to these people, these luminous beings whom she knew from *Vanity Fair* were as lonely as she. She had read of Larry Drayco's death and the planned proceedings as though it were an invitation. Finally, a kind of Welcome Wagon, the mortuary version. What harm was there in her going, really? It wasn't as if he could say she hadn't known him.

It was an unaccustomed audacity on her part, masquerading among strangers, especially since she did not yet fully know who she herself was. As a young, aspiring writer, she had fallen in love with F. Scott Fitzgerald, and through him had cultivated a love of things that were out of reach. His last obsession had been this town and its industry, Hollywood as the glowing amplification of the golden siren who'd destroyed him. As though his dream were a fallen standard, Kate had picked it up, ready to bear the flag across the battlefield, in a war fought for no true cause.

"Are you on the bride's side or the groom's?" whispered a familiar-looking man she couldn't quite put a name on, one of those nondescript supporting players in TV movies that the solitary pretended they didn't watch.

She guessed he was being sardonic. But as she didn't know him, she wasn't sure, and suppressed a smile.

"It's all right to laugh, trust me." He had lively brown eyes, lightly shaded at the corners with awnings of skin. He was busily checking out everyone coming in, looking past Kate even as he spoke to her, with a barely detectable lisp. "Did you ever do business with Drayco?"

"No."

"Are you a relative or a former lover?"

"No."

"Then you're in no position to say this isn't a laughing matter." He held out his hand, still without exactly being there, his attention focused on the possibility of someone coming in who mattered more to him than even he did. "I'm Wilton Spenser."

"Kate Donnelly."

There was in his handclasp a kind of sincerity. It was not a strong grasp, but it felt as though his fingers, at least, were trying to make real contact. She experienced a wave of relief: he was funny, and he didn't know she didn't belong. It was the closest she had come to communication since arriving in Los Angeles.

The chapel was filled with the subdued buzz surrounding the solemn celebration of death, made somehow alluring because of those in attendance. Kate recognized the established stars. Tight in their ranks moved the recently deposed duchess, who was giving her title to a new line of clothes. Behind her, but not with her, as he seemed to be with no one of this world, walked Algernon Reddy, gingerly, with a cane. This philosopher, writer, and once guru of the psychedelic seekers was now ingesting the process of dying as he had mushrooms in the sixties. Rodney Sameth, the reclusive director who made his home on the Isle of Wight where his money was, had apparently overcome his phobia about flying in order to attend.

Present also was the studio head everybody loved whom nobody could say a bad word about, with the mate about whom no one could say anything good. Most of the people there were unknown to the general public. But Kate had seen their pictures in the trade papers and carefully filed them in her brain: studio executives, producers, entertainment lawyers, as powerful as the clients they represented.

Most noteworthy among those was tall, somber, balding Fletcher McCallum, who had been on the front page of the *Wall Street Journal* a few days before, brokering a giant industry merger. Kate had seen McCallum depicted in the paper only in caricature, a pen-and-ink sketch. But the jut of his jaw was unmistakable.

"Fletcher!" said a short, round man with dreadlocks that appeared to be extensions woven into his hair. He wore Armani glasses, sun lenses attached to their tops and flipped up at the moment to reveal albino eyes, a gray that was eerily translucent. His smile was wide and pointy-toothed, a light film around the enamel and gum line, as if he had not bothered to brush. It seemed to Kate a contemptuousness past confidence, as though he didn't concern himself with other people's sensibilities. He held out his manicured

4

hand to the attorney, the half moons of his nails glowing pale pink, the only part of him that looked really clean.

McCallum ignored the offered hand and pointedly looked away. "Is that any way to treat a client?" the short man said.

"There's a letter in the mail to you, Arthur. The firm will no longer be representing you or your publishing company."

"For what reason?"

"It's all in the letter."

"Oh, come on. You can be straight with me."

"If you insist." McCallum drew a breath, and the massive jaw seemed to grow. There was a pugnaciousness to it that seemed almost prosthetic, as if he had implanted in his chin a wedge that said, Don't mess with me. Leading with his jaw, McCallum spoke. "Because you're a fraud."

"That's *slander!*" Even as he said it, Arthur Finster looked exultant at having gotten under such important skin.

"Worse than that, you do it knowing you're a fraud."

"I think I'll sue."

"Go ahead."

"Okay. Will you represent me?" Finster grinned darkly, a troll with luminous eyes, and slipped into a seat a few rows away.

The minister, a former child star now with the liver freckling of age, stepped to the microphone at the podium. Kate had read a facetious article about his getting the call one day on the set of an MGM movie, when the studio still had sets and "more Stars than there are in Heaven." All that, the piece went on to say, had vanished under the reins and reigns of various incompetents, the prideful motto disappearing along with sections of real estate sold off to the Japanese. Now, the article added, there were few MGM stars who weren't in Heaven, except Katharine Hepburn, and, arguably, those grounded in Forest Lawn.

Even that kind of great Hollywood tradition, the old-time funeral, was apparently over. No one these days would drive, even in limousines, as far as they had for Clark Gable, buried next to Carole Lombard, a gravestone's throw from a private movie theater, one of the prior perks.

There had been no question of Larry Drayco's being interred at Forest Lawn. It was all the head of Marathon Studios had been able to do to cull a respectable crowd for a place this convenient, and then only by promising a lunch afterwards at the new Wolfgang Puck's.

"Friends," intoned the minister, "we are gathered here this darkly sunlit morning . . . " The talking subsided. "Friends," he began again, "we are gathered to honor a most unusual man—"

There was a loud clattering of high heels. Everyone turned. Darkly radiant in black, Helen Manning swept noisily by, like a preened, exotic bird, feathers jutting from a boa drawn around her honey-skinned shoulders. Her phoenix eyes, so labeled by the writer-painter Bunyan Reis in his birthday piece on her in *Life* magazine, glowed amber, a shade darker than her hair. They slanted at angles to the sides of her head, flaring like rebirth from the ashes, as her career, like her many loves, had done. The dress she wore ended just below her knees and looked painted on her body, her remarkable breasts and thighs distinguishable beneath the satiny cling.

The ensemble by Vera Wang, recently featured on the cover of *W,* was sleekly suitable for daytime, though the glossy raven feathers looked out of place. But whose place was it, this side of Marilyn Monroe? Kate wondered. Who was there, alive, besides Helen Manning, who had that kind of glamour, the ancient Scottish word that meant to "cast a spell"?

"Oh." Helen seemed surprised at having caused such a stir, chagrined at interrupting the proceedings. Her black gloved hand moved to her darkly outlined cupid's bow mouth, from which issued her little-girl voice. "I'm so sorry."

She moved down the aisle, head bowed as if in remorse. Silky blond hair drawn back into a knot at the base of her perfectly shaped skull, she made her way to the front of the chapel, ignoring those who signaled vacant places in the rows she passed.

"To honor a man," the minister went on, looking at Helen as though awaiting license to continue, "who has meant so much to the motion picture industry."

What Larry Drayco had meant, as most of those present knew, was major scandal in a business where no one thought another, saltier scandal possible. In the argot of gossip—the official language of Hollywood—he had fucked the town's most impressive women, and fucked over most of its men. But he'd always failed up, as the expression went, moving on to more exalted positions in bed and in the boardroom. Even when he'd actually broken the law, he'd gotten off scot-free, becoming the head of a better studio than the one he'd embezzled from. It was as though the town, like the judge who'd suspended his sentence, couldn't do enough to make him feel better about getting caught.

"Larry Drayco has given us . . . " Here the minister began listing his many credits. Behind him, an auburn-haired harpist who'd been Drayco's sponsor in Narcotics Anonymous, to which the judge had remanded him for his cocaine habit, played the themes from his movies. There were snatches of familiar melody, strung together on the strings. As the harpist strummed the most moving strain from the song that had won the Academy Award the year Drayco couldn't, having been ruled out by his confreres because of his behavior, Helen Manning rose and started to sing. The lyrics were curiously apt, dealing with a love that was stronger than death. The sound of her childishly clear soprano struck such an honest note that the minister was silenced without seeming offended.

Others started to sing, and then, the minister himself. He had a deep voice, a bass baritone, that made the song into a hymn. As music could transform, the scene changed to one of reverential solemnity, where several people seemed genuinely moved. Some wept openly. Was the sadness for Larry Drayco, Kate wondered, a black sheep transfigured by death to scapegoat? Or were the tears they shed for themselves? As little experience as she'd had in her young life with funerals, she knew people usually grieved for a number of things: what they had lost, that they were left behind, that they would not be left behind forever. Their own mortality, really.

One who seemed determined to live forever sat just in front of Kate: Charley Best, the biggest star of the fifties. His face was still oddly cherubic, his skin miraculously unsallowed in spite of years of admitted alcohol and drug abuse. But the scars behind his ears were ill-concealed by his curly brown toupee. The platinum blonde with him wore an outfit that looked like Frederick's of Hollywood, a store that specialized in ready-to-wear for Heidi Fleiss–type professionals. It was a rubber dress, ebony for the occasion, pumping up her breasts like expectations. She started to sing along with Helen, her voice a *Playboy* magazine squeal. It was an out-of-date, out-of-style bimbo kind of sound, like her look. She seemed unconscious at a level that superseded stupidity, totally unaware, as though no one had told her Hugh Hefner had gotten out of his pajamas, married, sired a new set of children, and put toy fire engines in his front hall. Charley Best looked delighted at the awful impression she was obviously making.

"The coffin's closed," Charley turned and whispered to Wilton. "How can we be sure he's dead?"

"The same way we know you are," Wilton answered.

"To be insulting . . . " murmured a painfully thin woman with a modified Mohawk, brown hair barely more than fuzz along the sides of her head, with heavily moussed high scarlet spikes down the center. The width and size and steel blue of her eyes would have been exquisite in a softer face. As it was, they looked trapped in the wrong person, trying to figure out a way to escape. " . . . is not the same as being clever."

"Your editor should have told that to you," Wilton said.

The chapel, like the service, was nondenominational, no crosses, Jewish stars, or obtrusive stained glass. It was a simple, tasteful structure with polished wooden benches, a model of understatement except for the lavish floral displays and the people who were getting up to make speeches. Speaking, like reading, was a skill that was not much practiced in the town, except at black-tie dinners honoring the accomplished and occasions like these where accomplishments were at an end. Reading had become a low-echelon occupation, with young people doing "coverage" for studio heads and producers, a few sentences summarizing what writers had taken years and thousands of words to express. But there was no one to do that for speeches, with the exception of Army Archerd, who could be counted on to sympathetically synthesize the tributes in *Daily Variety* the next day, the only columnist in town who was nice to everybody.

All this Kate knew, although she knew no one, being an assiduous researcher who'd had plenty of alone time to dissect a society. And a society it was, without question: not one that might have engaged fully the mental capacities of a Jane Austen but one that might easily have seduced her had she been alive to be celebrated by it. To be feted as the winners always were. Not a society based on breeding or education or land—although the real estate holdings of the heirs and stockholders of Disney were enviable—but a society where Success was the key. Success here meant grosses, which meant money, which meant people wanted you, and that, in her spinster longings, Jane Austen would have surely understood. Just as Kate, for all her wit and wish for detachment and objectivity, understood. Understood to the marrow of her bones as she read every week—for the purposes of her studies, she assured herself—the glossy giveaway paper called *Beverly Hills 213*, all the while trying to convince herself she wouldn't have wanted to be at all those parties. Her bibliography also included the trade papers printed on slick paper, *Daily Variety* and *The Hollywood Reporter*, and an even slicker magazine, *Buzz*, that acidly scoffed at the industry while, like Kate, longing to be embraced by it. Every day she read the *Los Angeles Times*, torn to shreds monthly by *Buzz*, which seemed to have an unnamed insider within the *Times* organization as potent as the one who had spied on the Clinton campaign, and become "Anonymous."

The chapel was silent now except for the sultry voice of a television actress who had been one of Drayco's few avowedly loyal friends. She addressed the coffin in wry tones, chiding him for dying as though he'd been a sitcom that had been canceled.

"It used to be that she knew where the bodies were buried," Wilton whispered about the actress to Kate. "Now the word is that she finds them."

It had been in that morning's *Times* that a woman friend, the one who stood now acerbically raging, had gone to Drayco's house when he failed to answer his phone, and discovered his lifeless body. They had attended the same party two evenings before, where she had noted that he seemed depressed. Though the coroner was to rule out both the rumored drug overdose and suicide, there was still a patina of sensationalism over the proceedings. Few seemed to believe that Larry had simply died. The actress recounted funny tales of him, making him seem warmer than the vision the general public had. She spoke of his generosity of spirit, which, according to Wilton's whispers, no one was aware of but her.

"She is unfailingly loyal to friends," he murmured, "and fabulous in intensive care wards. They're starting to call her the angel of death."

"Have you no shame?" said Sarah, fingering her Mohawk.

"You're rich on the blood of others," said Wilton. "Why don't you buy me some?"

"Who is that woman?" Kate whispered to Wilton, of the person with the dinosaur back on her head.

"Sarah Nash."

"That's Sarah Nash?" Kate felt a flood of excitement. She had read Sarah's bestselling book about Hollywood, and heard, beneath the barbs, the voice of a genuine writer. Fettered by her own innocence and affection for the naivete that had been Fitzgerald's, Kate attributed a questing spirit and vulnerability to anyone who could put words together. "I thought she'd be older."

"She *is* older. She sold her soul to the devil. Mike Ovitz was still an agent at the time and made the deal."

Sarah Nash was one of the few California writers whom the New York literary establishment took seriously, and was well reviewed, welcome at Elaine's, probably accepted by Gay Talese. At the same time she struck fear and loathing into the movie industry, the kind of panic that prevailed when people had both the capacity to wound and make money.

The press, with the exception of Army, a writer from *The Hollywood Reporter,* Larry King, and Samantha Chatsworth, the studiedly chic West Coast editor of the high-line New York magazine *East,* were kept outside the chapel. Even now they were being held off by security men. They stood behind a temporary barrier wheeled in for celebrity funerals, next to a permanent barbed wire fence put in place after the third time someone had scaled the wall after midnight in an attempt to steal Marilyn's brass nameplate.

People still came through the open gates by daylight and took flowers from notable graves. Kate had witnessed such thefts on her way to the chapel. In Natalie Wood's case flowers had been replaced by potted plants, chained and bolted to the metal covering her portion of earth, bearing the legend left by R.J., "More than love." It saddened Kate, beyond the too-early, long-ago death, that a surviving lover could not even give a gift of flowers in this souvenir-crazed city without suffering additional loss.

"They had a lot of names for that big guy," the woman delivering the eulogy was saying, in the style of vanished sportscasters, her full-lipped mouth twisting in a wry smile. "And some were pretty dirty. But I tell you no one ever had a better friend."

"That's because she's an actress," said Wilton. "Even she doesn't know what she's really feeling."

"You're an actor," Kate said.

"Only sometimes."

"What else do you do?"

He did not respond. He looked uneasily at Sarah Nash.

"Why so shy about yourself, Wilton?" Sarah muttered.

"Why don't you tell her? Or do we have to wait for your next memoir, where you hang the rest of the town by the balls?"

"There's nobody left after what Arthur Finster just published."

"Maybe you could expose Arthur."

"Maybe," Sarah said. A look of mischief softened her too-thin face, making it seem fleetingly girlish. "I'll check with my lawyer."

"And now," said the minister, looking at the list of speakers. "We will hear from Larry Drayco's longtime associate and co-producer."

A pallid, gray-haired man with thyroid eyes moved to the platform. In a halting voice, he began to speak, reading from a piece of paper a prose reworking of Gray's *Elegy in a Country Graveyard*. He paused, swallowed, his enormous Adam's apple bobbing visibly. "God rest you, pallie," he said, rapping his knuckles gently on the coffin.

"Knock, knock, who's there?" cried an enormously fat woman in a pew across the aisle, getting to her feet. "Nobody!" She took an audible breath, loud as she was, as if the mere act of standing, with that heft, had taken all the air out of her. "You're a bunch of empty phonies. Where were you when his stock got low and he needed real friends?" She had Pillsbury Doughboy skin, pasty, with puffed cheeks, great sacks of flesh atop her eyes, bags below them. She looked to Kate to be the only older woman at the funeral who hadn't had plastic surgery. Her ankles were conspicuously swollen above worn leather shoes. "Talking about him like you cared about him. Most of you didn't even know his real name."

"Darshowitz," Wilton whispered. "That's probably his mother, Lila. The one person on the planet he was truly afraid of."

One of the ushers went over to calm the woman. "Get your hands off me, you fairy," Lila said.

"From Queens, you know," murmured Wilton. "They haven't heard yet there's a new vocabulary."

"The interment will be private," the minister said quickly, and raced from the microphone.

$\mathcal{N}$othing in his life so became him as the leaving of it." Wilton pinned onto his lapel a little sprig of violets twisted around a green-wrapped pipe cleaner that a woman handed him as he exited the chapel. "As Kenneth Branagh might have said."

"Where's your car?" Kate had parked her Saab by the Sanctuary of Peace, a white-marbled crypt wall-to-wall with slotted, cremated tenants.

"I came by cab. One never knows when one might bump into one's Destiny, and ought to be without a way of getting home." He pulled the stem of his violets, arranged it so the tiny nosegay sat more neatly on his olive drab corduroy jacket. "I think they got this idea from Elizabeth. Now *there* was a woman who knew how to bury people. I remember when Laurence Harvey left us, and she arranged a ceremony where grown men wept not on cue."

"Would you like me to drop you someplace?" Kate asked.

"Aren't you coming to the lunch?"

"I don't really know any of these people."

"Nobody knows them but Gore Vidal and he's got too much taste to examine them."

"Hey, Wilton!" Linus Archer sprang from behind the open gate to the Sanctuary of Tranquility. His hair was close-cropped and silver, the grin on his angular, sharp-nosed face still boyish and cocky, as though he were smugly pleased he could continue to surprise people with sudden entrances and the ability to spring. He was close to sixty now, Kate guessed. His career spanned over four decades, only the early films less than memorable, while he was still trying to portray likeable people. "The mantel of Jimmy Dean," a Hollywood historian had written, "has fallen on Linus Archer like a Boy Scout tent." It had taken him a lot of years to untangle himself, emerging as the villain he had been born to play. Perhaps, from the talk, not just in the movies. "What do you think really killed Larry?"

"I heard it was an aneurism."

"Well, sure, that's the official line. But let us not forget his own M.D. OD'd. And there *is* the book."

"Book?" asked Kate.

"You're pretty cute. Have I ever been married to you?" asked Linus. His heavy, still-thick eyebrows pulled together, forming one straight line over his nose, as though he were really trying to remember. His hazel eyes, small-pupiled, were at once searching and blank.

"She's new in town," Wilton said.

"I just moved here from—"

"Then you don't know about me," Linus interrupted. Origins seemed no longer of interest to him, since he had overcome his own.

"No, I don't," Kate lied, setting aside her usual honesty. Judging from this morning, a little duplicity worked wonders. Though she had no firsthand knowledge of these people, she intuited the enormity of their egos. Like cats, they were more likely to try and cozy up to what they saw as indifference.

"You didn't catch my interview on A & E? You didn't see the cover of *GQ*?"

"Linus likes to talk in initials," Wilton said. "It makes him think he's in Washington."

"Hey, those guys like to think they're in Hollywood."

"Aren't they?" Kate asked.

"Not just another pretty face," said Linus. "You sure we haven't been married?"

"She isn't your type," said Wilton. "She thinks."

"I've been with women who think."

"Not the ones who wrote the book," said Wilton.

"What book?" asked Kate again.

"We're instituting a class action libel suit against Harbinger Press and Arthur Finster," Linus said. "Fletcher McCallum is handling it for us. Can you believe Arthur publishing that book, the creep?"

"I heard he has notarized affidavits from the hookers and the madam. Lie detector tests."

"They're going to find him with his cock in his mouth," said Linus.

"Strapped in black leather?" Wilton said.

"I'm not into bondage," said Linus, fuming. "That's a fucking lie!"

"Affidavits," Wilton said archly. "Lie detector tests."

"Finster should be strung up just for killing the trees to print that shit. Can you believe the writing? 'He put his hot hand on my tight buns.' "

"I don't think it's being bought for the prose."

"*Nancy Drew and the Hidden Screw,*" Linus said contemptuously. "I wish Larry was still alive so he could join in the suit."

"Talk is he was reading it when he died. They found him naked on the toilet, with the book open on his lap to the chapter about him."

"Maybe we could add wrongful death to the lawsuit. The stuntman's widow on my last picture got five mil. But we'd have a hard time proving he wasn't drugging. Everyone thinks he OD'd."

"A bubble burst in his brain."

"You weren't supplying him?"

"He wasn't using anymore."

"Right. And O.J. never did crystal meth."

"I don't think we should be talking about this here," said Wilton, looking around at the crowds coming out of the chapel.

"We should have a wake at Larry's house. I know where he kept his stash."

"He no longer did coke."

"A pop in the brain from what he was reading?"

"Only because he couldn't get to the kitchen to put a knife through his heart."

*S*o is that what you do?" Kate said, as she drove her car onto Wilshire Boulevard. "You're a drug dealer?"

"Only for friends," Wilton said. "It started during the Screen Actor's strike. So many actors were losing their houses, I knew I needed a second career."

She adjusted her rearview mirror and caught a glimpse of herself. She looked a little too wide-eyed for someone twenty-seven, her chestnut curl–capped face with its faint, barely detectable lines starting at the corners of her chocolate eyes slightly too eager, as though she were still taking creative writing courses at Stanford. "Aren't you afraid of getting caught?"

"I'm afraid of being poor. And my friends are afraid of being bored and empty. It's a charity I perform, really."

14

"What if they overdose?"

"I don't deal anything low grade. No crack. And nothing really hard."

"You don't think cocaine is hard?"

"Not in this town. Cocaine is easy. If they didn't get it from me, they'd get it from someone who didn't care about them, and that could be fatal."

His smile was guileless, his expression amused, tolerant. Now that she looked at him carefully, Kate realized he was older than her first impression. His haircut, flat-topped, military, made him look youthful, athletic, as his trim, long-legged body did. His hands were graceful, a musician's hands they looked to be, only the high, blue veins on the backs of them indicating age. He was tanned a George Hamilton brown, as if not being good-looking were more to be feared than skin cancer.

"So now you know about me," Wilton said. "What about you? What do you do besides give lifts to the slightly stoned?"

"You're on cocaine?"

"I never do cocaine. Do I look stupid? I just took a little hit on a joint to take the edge off the morning. The sting out of funerals. Tell, tell."

"I'm a writer."

"Low man on the town totem pole," said Wilton. "Writers don't count for shit here, unless they eviscerate people like Sarah Nash did and make themselves into bigger celebs than the people they destroy."

"What about this book that Linus was talking about, that Larry was reading?"

"It isn't anything you have to *read*. It's just something you move your lips to while the girls go down on you. Writers are beneath contempt here, and contempt is the janitor. Did you hear the joke about the Polish actress who wanted to be a movie star, so she slept with the screenwriter?"

"I don't write screenplays. I'm trying to write a book."

"Why would you move here to write books?" A black Jeep Cherokee cut in front of them. Wilton opened his window. "How very four-wheel and macho!" he shouted at the driver.

The man raised his middle finger. "*Soooo* articulate." Wilton closed his window. "Why L.A.? You could live anywhere."

Dark green fronds, like cheerleaders' pom-poms urging the team to victory, waved from the tops of tall, gray-barked palm trees lining the wide boulevard. The fanlike stirring surges of color softened the white and gray stone of the high-rises on either side, their windows a cool, jewellike mint green. In the distance the white peaks of the San Bernardino Mountains sparkled with perfect clarity, snow-capped after the recent heavy rains. It was one of those rare, crystal days in Los Angeles that swept doubt away along with the smog, rid the mind of earthquake, fire and flood, made people wonder why they considered living anywhere else. It would have been truthful for Kate to say she really liked the place, hungered for what it could offer if she succeeded.

But there had been her PhD thesis and the oral report before the committee. The words were still stored in her, easily remembered, and Wilton was obviously bright. "As a young romantic," she tried not to seem to recite, "a would-be writer, I fell in love with F. Scott Fitzgerald. Not just his writing. His life.

"I always imagined if I had been his love instead of Zelda, I could have saved him. Saved him from drink, saved him from his lack of belief in himself. Talked him out of his conviction that there were no second acts in American lives. Given him a second act. Here, in the place where his life ended. The last frontier of the American dream, where things still happen Overnight." She capitalized the word with her inflection. "Instant love, instant recognition, instant table from the headwaiter. Where he wrote his last book, but only a fragment. *The Last Tycoon.*"

"You going to finish it for him?"

"I wouldn't presume to try. But the fascination he had with the prototype of the Hollywood producer, the character of Monroe Stahr . . . "

"He had Irving Thalberg for a model. A genius. A visionary. An infant industry that had magic. And you've got this prick."

"How do you know there wasn't some aspect of Larry Drayco's life that was memorable? 'Action is character,' Fitzgerald said. Maybe Drayco once did something . . . meaningful. An act that ennobled his life."

"You're not a romantic. You're delusional."

"Maybe I could find it. What made him matter."

"Like redeeming social significance in pornography?"

"It's worth a try."

"And I thought I was the one who was stoned," said Wilton. "Turn left at the next intersection."

A Party at Wolfgang Puck's

The parking attendants at Wolfgang Puck's were as good-looking as some movie actors. Some movie actors were as good-looking as parking attendants. And for good reason: they had once been them. Harrison Ford had been a carpenter, so a raft of carpenters still had the dream. Demi Moore had come from a trailer park. Anything was possible.

The parking attendant who opened the door for Samantha Chatsworth, West Coast editor of *East,* was a cast-off lover of Norman Jessup, the town's most powerful producer. Norman had never promised him anything, as he never promised any of them anything. Still, it was a little humiliating for the parking attendant to open the door for a woman he had sat on the right of at a black-tie dinner party when he was in favor. But since he was now in a different kind of uniform, she didn't recognize him, so he didn't have to worry.

"Be careful with the Rolls," she said.

"I'd be careful even if it was only a Porsche, ma'am," he said, despising her.

As she did not look at or hear him, and since feeling what other people felt was not her strongest suit, the moment was lost on her. Most moments that would not make good stories for the magazine or photo opportunities or a little good late-night gossip were lost on her. And her focus right now was strictly on the duchess, helped from the other side of the limo by an even better-looking attendant than the one helping Samantha. The Silver Cloud Samantha had succeeded in promoting for the duchess pulled away as a swarm of photographers descended.

The shoes the former duchess wore, though no longer Cinderella's slippers, were Manolo Blahnik, their straps snapped by one alert paparazzi who knew that unusual shots of Wendy were at a premium. So far, there had been no glut of her toes. She was dressed in the dark, dark, dark blue that was this season's fashion substitute for black, unless one was in genuine mourning.

The duchess was not. She had known the fallen producer only from a dinner party he paid a great deal to her favorite charity to attend, one of the few there who hadn't toadied or fussed, so she'd liked him. The scandalous tales that broke out like a fever within hours of his death, along with the vilifying chapter in the book, had made her decide to go to his funeral. She knew firsthand what cormorants fed off idle talk. In her own way, she *was* grieving, if not for him, for the death of decency. For a lost time when people left each other alone.

"I'm still not sure I should have let you come," Samantha said, in a British accent that outstripped the duchess's.

"He was generous to the children's hospital," the ex-duchess said in a gentle tone, but with a slight edge to it, concluding that argument. Strength, like knowing exactly what to wear, had come unexpectedly to her, and she was still trying it on.

Photographers continued to take her picture, from every conceivable angle, shouting "Your Highness! Your Highness!"—a term that no longer applied. Bureaus and worldwide services had an insatiable appetite for her photo. But in this environment, her looks seemed a little plain, almost homely. She could not hold a physical candle to movie stars, whom Americans had made their aristocracy, as they had made politicians into movie stars, if for only one Kennedy season. Since there was no royalty in America, films had given the nation the closest it could come to lineage. So, when an indisputable blueblood fell into the place, no one knew quite what to do, besides invite her to everything.

"Samantha!" Wilton cried, as he got out of his car, waving. "Here's someone you have to meet!"

The slender blond woman smiled tolerantly, already having at her side the only one at the event who really mattered, and continued to steer the duchess through the crowd like a prize float in the Rose Bowl parade. But she did make a step in Wilton's direction, since she found him amusing, a word she had learned to use rather than *fun*.

"This is Kate Donnelly," Wilton said, proprietarily, and put his hand to Kate's waist. "She's F. Scott Fitzgerald's granddaughter." He pinched Kate into silence.

"Really," Samantha said, obviously impressed, and gave her her card. "You must call me. We'll lunch." She turned to introduce the duchess.

"Why would you tell a lie like that?" Kate whispered, as though there were degrees of lies. In spite of his pinching her into silence, once past the shock, she'd been moved to dispute him. But as she'd already transgressed by being in a place she didn't belong, she'd kept quiet. And the card with its raised lettering felt good in her hand. *East* magazine, it said. The best magazine in the country.

"It's not a lie, it's a fable." Wilton edged his way into the main room of the restaurant. "This whole town is filled with fabulists. They don't even know what they're making up." He grabbed an hors d'oeuvre from a passing tray and popped it into his mouth. "You're only as good as your last picture, and you haven't made any."

Past his bantering mouth she could see Norman Jessup in deep conversation with Victor Lippton, the tobacco heir, who'd just taken over Cosmos Pictures. And not a moment too soon, the wags had noted, what with Congress uncovering amounts of nicotine doctored to keep smokers hooked, and Jesse Helms having to seem friendly to Vietnam to try and help the tobacco industry. Lippton had shaved off his beard since coming to Hollywood, but Kate still recognized him from the leonine mane of golden hair and the exquisite woman on his arm, the wife said to be even richer than he was, the daughter of a Hong Kong billionaire.

There was a stunning woman with Jessup as well, the fashion model Carina. Their engagement had been announced in a very social way in *The New York Times,* besides the trades.

"You want to find out what you need to know for your book," Wilton was saying, munching, "leave your credits to me. People will only accept you if they think you're somebody."

He took her by the hand and whooshed through the proceedings as though lightened with helium, slightly above it all, nodding, smiling, taking stock of those attending. "What a pity Mavis isn't here to cover the funeral. She would have given it an A."

"Mavis?"

"A gossip columnist who used to rate parties. Her husband left her for another man. She felt so vulnerable she stopped being vicious, lost her power, and fell mortally ill. No one even visited her in the hospital but her hairdresser, a genuine act of allegiance since she'd lost most of her hair. She died. *Nobody* came."

"Perry!" he called out to a well-known agent. "I want you to meet someone. She has an unpublished manuscript by her grandfather, F. Scott Fitzgerald, that would make a terrific movie!" He pinched her again.

"Fitzgerald!" Perry said. "My favorite."

"Kate Donnelly, Perry Zemmis. Agent, producer, former studio head, manager, Father of the Year . . . "

"Ease up," Perry said, and ran a big hand through a shock of silvering black hair. "This ain't my funeral."

"Were you close to Drayco?" Kate asked.

"Not so close that he could sting me," said Perry. "Kate Donnelly, huh?" His black eyes, flat, took her in, Rolodexing her name. "What's the story?"

"It's sort of a sequin to *The Last Tycoon*," Wilton said, and chuckled. "Really, it's a sequel, but in this town . . . "

"I meant the personal story," said Perry, the eyes suddenly taking on some depth, little flecks appearing like lights around his irises, x-raying her. "Are you involved? Married? Divorced?"

"She's new in town," Wilton said.

By the bar, Charley Best was talking to Sarah Nash. Already Kate had picked up the darting attention of the local residents, though her eyes stayed fixed on Perry. But she could hear Charley's voice, grainier than it had been when he was in his prime, the number one box office draw.

"I had the best time of anyone. I was King Kong. I have no complaints," he was telling Sarah.

"How unlike you. No whining. So self-effacing."

"You better explain to Brandy what that means." He turned to the buoy-breasted blonde. "Sarah was a producer once, but now she's gone all literary."

"Do you know what literary means?" Sarah asked Brandy.

"It means you knew Swifty Lazar," the blonde said.

"And you thought I liked her for her body," beamed Charley.

"You good with kids?" Perry asked Kate. "My wife is the greatest with kids. Unfortunately she can't have any of her own, but we've adopted five—"

"They're crippled," Wilton said.

"Where you been living, on the moon?" Perry said, annoyed. "They're not even called handicapped anymore. Crooks in Washington are now referred to as 'ethically challenged.' "

"Perry knows a lot about Washington," Wilton said. "Along with Father of the Year, he's been named West Coast Political Coordinator of the Decade. That means he's raised and contributed enough money so that if his candidate gets in, he's up for ambassador."

"Mere speculation."

"What country?"

"Tonia was hoping Italy, but I'd settle for Holland."

"Greenhouses that grow grass along with tulips. Open bars that sell hash," said Wilton dreamily. "The French are highly critical of the Dutch, you know. All the Froggies do is set off bombs in the Pacific, sabotage Greenpeace, and have a right wing that's worse than Germany's."

"I'll try not to ask for Paris," Perry said. "Fitzgerald. What a great writer. A shame he blew his brains out."

"That was Hemingway," noted Wilton.

"But they were very good friends," Kate said quickly, already understanding the politics of the land was appeasement.

"How good a friend could he have been, that he wrote Fitzgerald had a little dick?" Perry asked.

"You read *A Moveable Feast*?" Kate said, astonished.

"I saw the coverage. We were thinking of using the title for a movie on Wolfgang."

"Puck," translated Wilton for Kate. "This is his restaurant."

"Some writer, that Hemingway," Perry mused.

"I remember in my youth," said Wilton, "I was in Charley Best's pool with Swifty Lazar, and Hemingway had just published 'The Dangerous Summer' in *Life* magazine, about the rivalry between

Ordonez and Dominguin. And I asked Swifty if he had read it, and he said, 'No, but I saw the bullfights.' " Wilton laughed.

"What's funny about that?" asked Perry.

"Like, 'No, but I saw the movie.' "

"You find it comical to be on the inside? You wouldn't have beat your ass to Pamplona if you were invited?"

"I wasn't saying . . . "

"He's frequent flyer mileage–challenged," said Kate.

"Quick. I like quick," Perry said, standing up to his full height now, so he could lean over her. "I forgive him because he's with you."

"Forgive me for what?"

"For being insensitive to Fitzgerald's having a little dick."

"I heard that Jake Alonzo has none at all," said Arthur Finster, the publisher, hovering behind them, eating an hors d'oeuvre.

"Is he here?" Kate asked, trying not to seem too excited.

"Why would you care, when he has no dick?" Perry asked.

"He's a fabulous actor," Kate said.

"You think he can act like he's fucking?" asked Perry.

"Arthur, why don't you publish a book about the size of movie star dicks?" asked Wilton.

"We were going to incorporate it into the hooker book, but it seemed a little tasteless."

A little of what Wilton was drinking shot out of his nose.

*B*y the buffet table, Norman Jessup prepared a plate of hors d'oeuvres for the reed-slender Carina, spooned some caviar into her mouth. "What a touching display of bisexuality," Sarah Nash observed.

"You better get off his case," advised Charley Best. "He doesn't make a good enemy."

"He didn't make that good a friend," said Sarah, sipping a Singapore Sling the color of the center path of her hair.

"Funny. That's what he says about you. How much did that trial cost him?"

"Court costs and lawyers' fees. He could afford it."

"He isn't a man who likes to lose."

"He isn't a man," said Sarah. "A shame he's still pretending."

"You still shouldn't have outed him in print. No wonder he sued."

"That wasn't what he sued for. Truth is a defense in libel. All I had to do to prove he was gay was produce a few of his squeezes. There's one parking cars outside."

"So what was the suit then, exactly?"

"I don't want to talk about it." Sarah looked suddenly old, the punch gone even from the combative scarlet of her spikes. "It took years out of my life."

"But you won."

"Nobody wins in a lawsuit but the lawyers."

"Just tell me what it said on the subpoena. I'm thinking of sending Brandy to law school."

Sarah gulped her drink. "Fraud and breach of contract."

"You had a contract not to blow the whistle on him?"

"He claimed we had an oral contract."

Charley snickered. "Well, as Sam Goldwyn said, 'An oral contract isn't worth the paper it's written on.' "

*O*n the far side of the buffet table Rex Hanson, producer of most of the glittering successes of the fifties, stood untalked to, his face a mask of ill-concealed grief, his toupee more of a wiglet. It had been decades since he'd made a film, years since anyone who could green-light a project had even asked him to lunch. He was a man who had made not just movies, but careers. He did so by giving other people an endless supply of style, while he himself had the grace and generosity of spirit not to mind that he was rather bland. He had put a whole studio in the black. A few of the people who ran that studio were still in power. But he couldn't get them on the phone. The only one who returned his calls, and always on the same day, was Darcy Linette, the current head of Marathon, a woman who not only knew how to play the game, but made people feel they mattered, and kept all her friends, even when they were no longer—as they said in Hollywood—bankable. Rex was no longer bankable.

Gazing into the crowd that exemplified the full extent of his loss, he stood white-faced and frail at the edge of the gathering, tears glistening on his cheeks. Another good friend of Darcy's, a once-powerful gossip columnist who'd lost her clout because she wasn't shallow enough to be manipulated, proved to be far more intelligent than anyone expected, was good to her parents, and interested in God, made her way to Rex and touched his shoulder consolingly. "I'm so glad to see you," she said, kindly. "A real producer. A man who loved movies. A fan. You're a vanishing breed, Rex."

He wept openly now, his thin shoulders wracked with sobs. She embraced him.

"I didn't realize you were so close to Drayco."

"I couldn't stand the son of a bitch. I only came as a favor to Darcy. I knew she'd have trouble pulling a crowd."

"Then why are you crying?"

"Dead, he has a better chance of making a deal than I do."

*W*hy is Algernon Reddy here?" Kate asked Wilton. Among her other reading materials to acquaint herself with the culture of the city, sub- in certain cases, was the *L.A. Weekly,* an underground publication that had profiled him. He was no less vocal about the fact that he was grievously ill than he'd been about his drug usage, except that in this case there was no chance of going to jail. "Was he friendly with Larry?"

"He's friendly with Death," Wilton said. "Maybe he's here to remind us that the Reaper isn't that Grim. Or maybe he's reminding himself."

"He's still very handsome." Kate noted the fine jut of jaw, starkly angular cheeks beneath piercing blue eyes.

"In the sixties he was known as Ever Reddy," Wilton said. "He had this legendary cock that hung to his knee, and the word was he could do it for days. Longer than Rubirosa. Such things are not listed in the *Guinness Book of Records,* but they have been chronicled by Harold Robbins, under fictional names of course. Then Algernon found God and this heiress who subsidized him."

"Are you Kate Donnelly?" a husky voice said behind her.

The hairs on the back of Kate's neck stood on end at the sound as she recognized the voice. "I'm Jake Alonzo," he said as she turned. A genial smile softened the slightly battered face, the jagged nose that had once been part of a profile that made him too handsome for anything but romantic leads, the dark eyes set on reconstructed cheekbones. Somehow, the spectacle of that shattered face, no matter how cleverly put back together, rendered him even more appealing, evincing as it did that male beauty could be just as fragile and evanescent as a woman's, especially when coupled with character flaws. The tree he had slammed into at the base of the Hollywood Hills had a plaque on it now, part of a prepaid pilgrimage for fans who couldn't afford to go to Paris to visit Jim Morrison's grave and weren't quite sure where Kurt Cobain was buried. They celebrated Jake's being alive, the fact that drugs had nearly killed him but missed. The darkness that had obviously been inside him was now evident in his face, getting him better, more shadowy roles. He held out his hand.

She took it. It was warm.

"I heard you were here," he said.

"Me? *You* heard *I* was here?"

"F. Scott Fitzgerald's granddaughter," he said. "The greatest regret of my whole career is that Redford made *Gatsby*."

She felt touched by the fact that even with the heavy turn his career had taken because of the transformation in his face, Jake imagined he could play an innocent. He never stopped making movies now. But if he essayed being a hero, it was always one who was slightly askew, scarred by circumstances as his skin would be if the town wasn't crowded with plastic surgeons. Skilled as they were, they hadn't been able to bring back the perfection. "You could make it again," she said.

"What was he like, old Scott?"

"I never knew him," she said, grateful for being able to speak that truth, at least.

"I'm a little too beefy for the part, even if they would consider doing it over. I always imagined Gatsby like Fitzgerald himself. Slender. That lost, blond, glazed blue-eyed look. Dark men can't do that."

"You could do anything," she said, believing it, accepting along with him that he could seem as ingenuous as before.

"Maybe I could thin down like De Niro fatted up for *Raging Bull*. Wear contacts. Become an alcoholic." He looked at the mineral water in his hand. "You could disappoint me, and then I could blame you."

"Disappoint you how?"

"Turn out to be an airhead. No substance."

"I'll try not to do that," she said.

"I bet you couldn't even if you wanted to."

"But I could disappoint you in other ways," she said, wondering why she felt on the verge of tears. She had not realized that a man like Jake Alonzo could be vulnerable in other than physical ways, open to disillusion, or that someone like Kate herself—or what he thought Kate was—was capable of doing him in. Just being there had taken a gouge out of her emotionally, frazzled her with the unreality of the situation. What seemed like only a moment before she had been the Little Match Girl, nose pressed against the bakery window. Now she'd been shot through the glass, straight into the cakes and breads, the fragrance of freshly baked dough in her nose. It would have been overwhelming even without this, this actor admired by everyone, including her. This man who had publicly denounced his own weakness, healing on the inside while his face did, looking at her like something might really be possible between them.

She wanted desperately to set him straight, clear the air, dispense with the lie, and have him admire her for her honesty. Her hands clenched into fists. She felt something cutting softly into her palm. She looked down and saw the card from the woman from *East* magazine, looked up and saw Jake Alonzo's eyes. Really interested. How perceptive was he? With all the women in the world who were throwing themselves at him, would he bother to take the time, have the curiosity to find out who she was, if he didn't already think she was somebody?

"What other ways?" he asked.

The question hung on the air, unanswered. She couldn't risk it.

"Hey," Linus Archer said, bobbing up to them, a Coke in his hand, conspicuously nonalcoholic, still in its bottle. "What are you doing moving in on my territory, Jake?"

"Your territory?"

"She's my ex-wife."

"Is that true?" Jake asked.

"I never met him before today."

"My next wife then."

"She's too young for you."

"No one's too young for me. I'm in my prime. They celebrate me in Paris."

"No one said the French were smart about everything," Jake said.

"I hear you're Hemingway's granddaughter," Linus said.

"You hear wrong."

"He was my hero." He set down his Coke, took the scarf from his neck, and making it into a miniature cape, did a miniature veronica. "Toro! Toro!"

"Takes one to know one," Jake said.

"Are you interested in this putz?" Linus asked Kate.

She could feel herself blushing.

"Well?" Jake said.

A moment passed. "Who wouldn't be?" she said. An honest answer.

"Okay," said Linus. "You've made your choice. But you'll be sorry." He whispered in her ear, as he went by her, quoting. " 'It was a hell of a way to be wounded.' "

*T*here was a commotion by the doorway. "Don't give me that shit," a raucous woman's voice yelled out. "I'm the only one who really belongs here." Lila Darshowitz pushed her way past security, and burst into the room. "Who do you have to double-cross to get a drink around here?"

A waiter came over with champagne and chardonnay. "I like red," she said churlishly.

"I'll get it for you," he said, and backed away.

"Doesn't this place have a bouncer?" Wilton came over to Jake and Kate, taking the two of them in. His eyes sparkled, avuncular, pleased.

"You can't keep Drayco's own mother out of his funeral," said Kate.

"Larry would have. The only reason she got in is that he's dead," said Wilton.

"I'll be right back." Jake indicated his empty glass. "Can I get you something, Kate?"

"I'm fine," she said.

"You certainly are," beamed Wilton, as soon as Jake was gone. He started singing, like Ethel Merman, the introduction to a Sondheim-

Styne song. "I had a dream . . . " He stopped. "But it wasn't *this* good. This *fast*." He hugged her around the neck. "I'm so proud of you!"

"Why?"

"You're going to find out for sure what everyone only speculates about."

It took her a minute to understand he was saying that Jake Alonzo wanted to take her to bed. Did he? Could she risk disappointment with him if the rumors were true? Could she put aside her own duplicity, which she found to her chagrin she was starting to do? "He heard the Fitzgerald thing. I have to tell him."

"You tell him *nothing*," Wilton said. "He's obviously taken with you."

"Not who and what I really am."

"So what? We're all just the shadows on the wall of Plato's cave. People don't want to know the truth: it's the illusion that captures them. The illusion that they think is the truth. Illusion *is* truth in Hollywood."

"What are you two buzzing about?" Perry Zemmis came back over to them.

"Plato's cave," said Wilton.

"I remember that place," said Perry. "It was where everybody went to fuck."

"That was Plato's Retreat," said Wilton, disgusted.

Perry waved the correction away. "It's not like we can risk going anymore, whatever it's called. It's the same reason they had to close the bathhouses."

Lila Darshowitz walked past them, a glass of red wine in both hands. A little of it had already spilled down the front of her dress, which was not exactly funereal, black being only a part of the print. The rest was white and a fuchsia that nearly blended with the wine spill, but not quite. The print seemed to exaggerate her already enormous form: breasts the size of pumpkins and a stomach that was girdled to no effect, other than to push a roll of fat above her waist. She was a two-fisted drinker, finishing the glass in her right hand and heading for the buffet table.

"What a slob," said Wilton.

"I feel sorry for her," said Kate.

"How long have you been in Los Angeles?" asked Perry.

"Two months."

"You'll get over it," he said.

Lila took a plate. People made a wider circle around her than they seemed to be making around Arthur Finster. Only Sarah Nash, piling her plate high with salad and pasta, seemed unperturbed at standing next to him. "So much for the rumor that you're anorexic," said Arthur.

"So much for the rumor that you can't pronounce words of more than one syllable," Sarah said. "I heard you followed Brandy into the ladies' room and offered her a contract on a book exposing Charley Best."

"Actually, it was the men's room," he said, biting into a miniature pizza. A string of the cheese hung between his teeth and the crust in his hand. "I think she's a transvestite."

"Are there no depths to which you won't sink?"

"At least I don't betray my friends," he said.

"That's because you don't have any."

There was a huge tray of guacamole molded into the shape of a Mexican hat, a bowl at its base filled with blue corn chips. "Is it all right to eat this?" Lila Darshowitz asked no one in particular.

"Only if you're not kosher," said Arthur.

"Where's that guy with the wine," Lila said, loading her plate, spooning the chunky green paste into her mouth in what would have been fistfuls, had she used her hands.

"Garçon!" Arthur snapped his fingers in the air. A waiter headed for them, bringing a tray with wine.

"You're being pretty solicitous . . . " Sarah murmured under her breath, " . . . for a guy who murdered her son."

"He OD'd, and the whole town knows it."

"He was clean," Sarah said.

"He was a driven man with compulsive habits." Arthur ate another pizza, licked his fingers, took another. "Materialistic and greedy."

"And you're here to make the world a better place. A safe haven for literacy."

"At least I didn't publish O.J. books. Or juror books. Or Faye Resnick books."

"Only because Michael Viner got there first."

He drew himself up to his full height, which was still eight inches shorter than Sarah's. "I am in competition with no one."

"You're forgetting Sleepy, Dopey, Grumpy, and Sleazy."

"I like red," Lila said to the waiter. "Save yourself a trip. Bring two." She handed him her empty glass, then wolfed a calzone. A piece of the spinach fell on her dress.

"That poor woman," Kate observed from where she was standing. "She's spilling things all over her dress."

"How can you tell?" asked Wilton.

"I really have to talk to her."

"What for?" asked Perry.

"I have a project. An idea."

"What about the unpublished Fitzgerald?" Perry said. "When can I get a look at that?"

"Never," Kate said.

"Aw, come on. You're just playing hardball. Trying to make me more interested. Well, it's working." He put his hand on her shoulder. She took it off.

"Okay," he said. "What's your price?"

"There is no price," she said.

"How about if I optioned both of them. Grandpa's and yours."

"You don't even know what mine is."

"So tell me."

"She's going to examine the life of Larry Drayco," Wilton said. "Search it out for meaning."

"Forget it," said Zemmis, and went to get a drink.

*M*ortimer Schein, who was shortly to produce the duchess's clothing line, felt awkward at parties, especially this one. There was no question it was a party. *Entertainment Tonight* and the E cable channel were both covering it, even though someone was screaming at their minicams that they had no respect.

Mortimer, or Mort, as he was called by his friends, who were mostly still in New York and East Hampton, had come to the funeral because he'd played cards with the dead man. That was a kind of bond, even though Mort suspected he'd cheated. Larry Drayco couldn't help stealing: it was in his character, or lack of same, as Mort's mother might have said. Once one of the men in the regular game, a producer, had come in raving about a new book he'd read in galleys and announced that he was going to buy the rights. Drayco excused himself to go to the toilet, called the agent who represented the author, and made a deal from the bathroom.

So he couldn't help being a shit, even when pretending to take one. Still, there had been something stylish about him, like a highwayman. And Mort always admired style.

He'd come to the funeral because that's what a nice guy did when he'd known a guy. Besides, *she* might be there. He longed, more than getting out of the rag business, to be in a place where he could look at her, and just watch her move, and not be under pressure to talk. He knew he had nothing to say to her really. She was a blueblood. His own blood was Jewish, and he was nervous about that, as he would have been even if there hadn't been a Pat Buchanan. But to be in a room with a genuine duchess, this particular duchess, even if she was divorced from the title, all the while he hungered to be near her, was almost more than Mort could bear.

"Duchess Wendy," he said, bowing as she passed him.

"Morty," she said gently. "I told you. I'm not allowed to use the title anymore except on our clothes."

"It's not good enough for you anyway. It should be Princess. Queen, maybe. Goddess." His face and neck shone bright red.

"Why, Morty. I've never heard you talk so." Her hair was dark and softly waved, close to her skull, marcelled as it would have been in the era she better belonged in. "I thought you only spoke cuts and fabrics and prices."

"I've had a little champagne. Can I get you some?"

"Yes, please."

He hesitated for a moment. "I should give it to you in a glass slipper."

She looked away. "Glass slippers aren't all they're cracked up to be."

*I*t had been noted that because of their fashion model washboard slimness, Carina, Norman Jessup's fiancée, and Chen Lippton, Victor's wife, looked strangely alike, in spite of facial dissimilarities.

Chen was markedly Chinese, round-faced and black-eyed, while Carina, whose origins were South American, had a pointed chin, and almond-shaped, brilliantly sea-green eyes. But they both had thick, dark hair, blunt cut to the jaw, and incredibly slender bodies. And of course they both dressed in the highest of high-fashion clothes.

The Lipptons, newly come to the scene as they were, set an example of elegance and fidelity, which Norman Jessup and Carina voiced every intention of following. So it pleased Norman that the women not only complemented each other physically, but genuinely seemed to like each other. He encouraged Carina to take Chen shopping and whatever else it was that women did when they were not joining their mates for dinner. And the four dined together at least once a week, two of the town's great power couples, which they were now considered, since the women, in their way, had as much potency as the men, as one could see clearly from how often they appeared in W.

The Jessup-Carina nuptials were planned for October, to be held at the Hotel Bel-Air. Carina had already asked Chen to be her matron of honor. Norman had as best man lawyer Fletcher McCallum, who had stood up for him under all the important circumstances of his life, including the odious lawsuit. So he couldn't have Victor Lippton as his best man. But he *would* be among the groom's men, knowledge of which had sent everybody in town clamoring for invitations, trying to politick their way in. The guest list was already fuller than the cemetery in Westwood, presenting some problems for the hotel, which could accommodate only a hundred and fifty guests. Norman had suggested he could perhaps build an annex for the occasion, as Larry Drayco had redecorated three meeting rooms of a Vegas hotel for one of his weddings.

The Lipptons, Jessup, and Carina, or as they were known now, the Beautiful Four, were so affable they usually did everything at a similar pace, including leave parties, or a funeral like this one, at the same time. But because Norman, like many others at the event, wanted to show his affection for Darcy, who'd organized it, he stayed longer than the Lipptons.

So he was there when Lila Darshowitz threw up all over herself and had to be carried to the ladies' room. And he was there when the E reporter and crew, having run out of stars, trained their camera on Carina and asked to interview her.

"You'll have to call my office," he said, "and speak to our publicity director."

"But we were hoping for a spontaneous . . . " said the tiny blonde who'd majored in communications, holding her microphone in his freckled face.

"You'll have to call my office," he said. And that was that.

There was an authoritative but innocent nobility in his carriage, as though Tom Sawyer had grown up to be Abe Lincoln. He looked very much the country boy he wasn't, with his great thatch of strawberry hair, cowlick, and freckles, an image added to and made more convincing by a kind of "down home" accent. That had been developed since the trial, where he'd spoken much too quickly, and said far more than had benefited him. Panic had stripped him of his customary confidence, and he'd turned into a blunderer, spilling over as he hadn't since he was a boy. So he'd slowed himself down with a deliberate drawl. Too late to save him from the jury verdict, but maybe in time to save him from ever making the same mistake again, including trusting a woman like Sarah Nash.

It was his fault for ever believing her, that she'd leave him out of the book. It was his fault for telling her who was screwing whom, who was taking what drugs, who embezzled, who covered up, really believing they had an understanding she would not involve him. She had been his buddy. The last bitch he'd ever buddy up to. She had proven once again, too late, that women were the enemy. He would never let one close into his life again. Except of course Carina. But she was another story.

"Well, well, well," Sarah Nash said, coming over to them at the buffet table. "If it isn't the pseudocouple."

"You've got brass balls talking to me," Norman raged. Carina pulled at his elbow.

"Better brass than none at all."

"Let's go," Carina said, softly.

"She's not chasing me out of anyplace," he said proudly. "She's the one who had to leave the country. She's the one who had to hide. Who still has to hide from all the people who despise her."

"But you're the one who lost the lawsuit."

He drew himself up to his full, Lincolnesque height. "In the long run you failed to damage me," he proclaimed, as his lawyer had tried to tell him ever since the trial. "Homosexuality is openly accepted in the civilized world—"

"And its own little Mafia in Hollywood," Sarah said.

"I wonder if a woman can be found with her cunt in her mouth," murmured Linus from the sidelines.

Norman inhaled deeply, as his meditation teacher had taught him. "All of that is beside the point now." He put his arm possessively around Carina. "I have fallen deeply in love with this exceptional woman, and she is soon to be my bride. You'll understand if you're not invited."

"Oh, I understand all of it," Sarah said. "Really I do. I've been studying Kraft-Ebbing, which still sets a good standard for sexual deviation."

"Deviant only to you, who has to hire beach boys to make love to you."

"Like you've never paid anybody."

"Not ever in my life. Anyone who was with me was with me because they wanted to be, and never got a cent from me."

"Which is why some of them are now parking attendants."

Darcy Linette came forward, looking as soft as her job was hard, tall and honey-haired, with the same long hairdo that had served her since college, when she learned that appearing girlish made a bright woman less threatening to men. "Please, people. This is a solemn occasion. Don't turn it into a brawl."

"Why don't they just step outside," goaded Linus. "Gunfight at the Wolfgang Puck Corral!"

"In the long run you have failed to damage me," Norman recited again to Sarah. "My life is fuller than yours will ever be." He hugged Carina close. "I have turned myself around through therapy."

"Well, I wish you every happiness," Sarah said icily. "But I think it's Carina who'll have to turn herself around, so you can pretend she's a boy."

He reached over with his long-fingered, freckled hand, took Sarah by the back of her neck, and shoved her, facedown, into the guacamole. "All *right!*" cried Linus, right fist shooting into the air, a victory salute.

Sarah came up sputtering. Waiters ran over with napkins. She wiped the bilious clumps from her face, pulled them from her spikey hair.

"That color is really becoming," Norman drawled. "Now you look like you do on the inside."

"You won't get away with this," Sarah muttered. "I'll get even with you, you pervert creep."

"Miss Nash," Carina said very softly. "You've already done your worst to Norman. There's nothing more you can do."

"That's what you think," Sarah said, and headed for the ladies' room.

On the pink satin chaise near the makeup console, Lila Darshowitz lay on her back, a wet towel against her mouth. "Are you all right?" Kate asked, bringing another towel.

"Why should you care?" Lila said.

"I just do." Not the moment for the genuine reason to this woman either, sick as she was, still half retching, Kate assured herself. Compassion was in her act, and as Fitzgerald had said, action was character, so if the act was compassionate, so was she. She wasn't just being self-serving, she was positive.

"I'm sick," Lila said, and turning on her side, retched again, this time into the towel.

"Do you have a way of getting home?"

The reddened, heavily lidded brown eyes tried to take Kate in, as they filled with tears. "I don't have a way of getting anywhere." She shook with self-pity, her great, obese body heaving with sobs. "Oh, Larry. Larry. Why'd you ever come to this shitty place?"

"You want me to call you a cab?"

"Okay, I'm a cab." Lila tried to laugh. "That was one of his jokes."

"I'm really very sorry for your loss," Kate said, wondering what some of his other jokes were. Maybe that had been Drayco's saving grace, humor. Maybe he had once done something really funny, something healing. Laughter was the best medicine, went the old homily, and it was true. Kate wasn't just a fan of Fitzgerald's, but of movies as well. She loved Preston Sturges's work, got the message he'd proclaimed quite clearly in *Sullivan's Travels,* that comedy was man's salvation. Larry Drayco hadn't made any comedies as far as Kate knew. But maybe he'd done something genuinely loving once, making someone laugh.

She knew she was reaching. Nobody at the funeral seemed to feel a sense of genuine loss, except this poor jellyfish of a woman.

Sarah Nash burst through the doors, talking to herself, murmuring obscenities, uttering future programs of revenge, carom-shooting threats. She put her head under the faucet, started to wash the guacamole away, filling the sink with shades of putrescent green.

"Did I do that to you?" Lila asked, embarrassed, half sitting.

"What happened?" Kate said.

"That queen has messed with me for the last time," Sarah said.

I hate it when these occasions turn ugly," said a columnist from *The Hollywood Reporter.* "Though it does make for better copy."

"Well, I have something positive you can put in your column," Perry Zemmis announced. "I've just bought the *sequin* to *The Last Tycoon.*"

*W*here did you disappear to?" Jake Alonzo asked Kate, when she came back.

"I was with Larry Drayco's mother. I'm taking her home."

"But I wanted to take *you* home." He looked genuinely disappointed.

"I'm sorry," she said. "I have to go get my car."

"Can I take you to dinner?"

"Not tonight. She really needs somebody." It was a good excuse, a selfless one, while calming her fears of his discovering her deception. Or her discovering . . . what? Was she so shallow that some physical deficiency of his would impact her? Wasn't she more moved by him *because* his face was no longer too beautiful?

"May I call you?"

"Of course," she said, and gave him her number. Wherever it was going could wait for another time.

"Are you nuts?" Wilton followed her out to the parking lot. "You blow off Jake Alonzo for that blowsy drunk?"

"We don't know that she's a drunk. She's upset. Understandably. And Jake said he'd call."

"These people have a short attention span," Wilton said. "You have to strike while his iron is hot."

"It's the black Saab," Kate said to the parking attendant, handing him her ticket, not looking at Wilton, not looking into herself, really. Not allowing herself to feel what was actually there. She was in no hurry to find out about Jake. In spite of the dangers of the era, this wasn't high school, or an age when you said "Not yet." Not to a movie star. Not to Jake Alonzo.

"He likes me for something that isn't true," she said to Wilton, not needing to share with him that there was something less than genuine in her. Not needing to share it with herself, really, trying to sidestep it even in her own mind.

"What does it matter, as long as he likes you?"

"I like him, too. Too much to play off a lie." That much of the admission was completely sincere. She did like him. What was the word he had used about her? *Substance.* Yes. That was it. He had unexpected substance. But what if it turned out he didn't have it where a woman expected it? What if the truth about him was as disappointing as the lie about her?

Two attendants were helping Lila out of the restaurant. She hung between them, a multicolored disaster area, her swollen ankles draping over the edge of her tight-fitting shoes, feet not quite maneuvering the concrete.

"Besides," Kate said, as the good-looking parking attendant opened the door of her car, and the two waiters loaded Lila onto the seat, "she's my source material."

*I*n the shadows of the restaurant, Norman Jessup watched a tidied-up Sarah Nash head for the front door, her makeup washed off with the guacamole, so she looked almost fresh-faced, if you didn't know better. He moved into a palmy alcove, empty of people, and took out his cellular phone. Dialed. "She's leaving now," he said softly, into the slat of a receiver. "Follow her."

A Snowflake in Hell

*D*riving west into the sun in its afternoon blaze, down Sunset to Pacific Coast Highway, Sarah Nash had the disconcerting feeling there was someone after her. Paranoia had been one of the side effects of publishing the book. Writing had been an incredible high for her, finding out she had the talent to survive independent of the people she vilified. Taking them on, she had known full well she was closing doors. But she'd had nothing to lose: the doors had already been slammed shut. That she'd had to turn on Norman, in addition to everybody else, when she still really liked him, was something she didn't allow herself to think about.

She'd had to hide out, quite literally, for a time after she'd become a bestseller. A lot of people would gladly have given her the same chance as her title: *A Snowflake in Hell*. She had lived in secluded five star hotels in Europe, Australia, Asia, registered under aliases, bathed in luxury, but drying off with eczema on her skin, little pimples of anxiety. Fear that someone might find her.

The process server did. The suit from Norman Jessup, though she had expected it in a way, still came as a terrible shock. She had thought his shame would be greater than her guilt, that he wouldn't want to draw more attention to *Snowflake*, already a sensation. She imagined his attorney would tell him not to press the issue of libel, since all she had to do to win was prove his homosexuality. She'd been right about that. He didn't sue for libel. He sued her for breach of contract and fraud.

They had been close friends. Or at least as close friends as a woman could be with a faggot, which she uncharitably considered him now. He had told her everything about everybody, including who was into bestiality. Some of the information truly blew her away, as jaded as she thought she was. From her wildest forays into pornography, usually whipped through while mellow with freebased cocaine, she had known about women who smeared their vaginas with beef extract and then let their lap dogs at it, shepherds with their sheep, Catherine the Great purportedly dying when the horse she was fucking fell on her. But never had she imagined men having animals up their asses. And the poet thought custom could not stale the infinite variety of Cleopatra!

All of it Norman told her with the express understanding she would shield him as the source, and reveal nothing about Jessup himself. But her publisher insisted the book needed jazzing up, that she had to come up with one or two even bigger names than the hundreds she'd already dropped and ground into earth. So she went back on her word, *allegedly* (her lawyer had drilled the word into her) betraying Norman, giving him up as Judas *allegedly* had, making her *allegedly* Faustian bargain.

He took her to court. He had gotten the best trial lawyer in Hollywood through Fletcher McCallum. She found one in Santa Monica, where, in spite of the proximity to the motion picture industry, reality still abounded. Hers had used various legal ploys that put the trial on delay. The court calendars were full. After some stomach-churning years, where she'd broken into a sweat at the sound of her doorbell for fear it was another subpoena, they went to court. She remembered it all too clearly.

By the time the verdict came in, even those who had little or no interest in the law or that star-spangled phrase "freedom of the press," were riveted. The case had everything: sex, scandal, a powerful protagonist, a patently brilliant woman (she had proved it to the bastards, and *in print*), as well as drama's most captivating elements, fury and revenge. *Jessup v. Nash* seemed less a breach of contract suit than breach of promise. He was like a lover scorned.

"She betrayed me," Norman Jessup said, not for the first time, even as Sarah's lawyer rolled his eyes heavenward so the jury could see he was about as fed up with the refrain as they had to be.

Oliver Crowley, the defense attorney, was a tall, fair-skinned man with wheat-colored hair and eyes so light it was surprising the darkness they could give off when they flashed with contempt, as they did now. But he was careful to make sure his back was to the judge. "Please answer the question."

"I don't remember what it was," said Jessup.

"I don't wonder," murmured Crowley, so low that the judge might not hear his disdain.

"Objection," said William Arnold, the plaintiff's lawyer, older by decades than his adversary, but no less energetic.

"Well, if your client would stop making speeches—"

"Mr. Crowley, I must warn you," the judge said.

"I'm sorry, your honor. But I'm sure all our patience is wearing a little thin."

"I'll determine how forbearing we must be. Would the clerk read the question?" Usually the judge dozed through civil cases, but this one had kept even him awake.

"How soon after Miss Nash's book appeared did you become ill?" Part of the damages Jessup had sued for were based on his claim that he had been thrown into a crippling depression, suffered physical ailments, and become incapacitated because of what she had written.

The expression on Jessup's freckled face was absent the jauntiness that had characterized his opening testimony, nearly four weeks before. There were sunken pockets below his high-boned cheeks. "Before it was even published. Someone at one of the book clubs slips us early looks at manuscripts . . . like . . . advance men in armies."

"Telling you where the battles are going to be waged?"

"In a way. Alerting you to books you might have to fight over."

"Well, you certainly picked up your cue," said Crowley.

"Objection!" Arnold said, at the very moment the judge made his admonition.

"Mr. Crowley . . . "

"I apologize. Please continue," he said to Jessup, with a veneer of politeness.

"She swore to me I would be no part of the book. That she would leave me out of it. That was the only reason I consented to give her a lot of the information."

"Information?"

"The insider stuff that nobody knew."

"And you were willing to spread that gossip?"

"Your honor," Arnold said.

"Don't make me warn you again, Mr. Crowley."

"What would account for that generosity?" Crowley said.

"She was on her ass. Nobody would make a picture with her, because she spelled trouble. I tried to make her a part of some of my deals, because that's the kind of friend *I* was. But nobody would come near anything I had if she was attached. Her only hope was that book. She gave me her solemn promise . . . " His hands started to shake. "When I read the galleys, I had to be hospitalized. They thought it was a heart attack."

"A heart attack?" The hospital records had been submitted during the discovery preceding the trial and showed Jessup had been treated for gastroenteritis.

"Well, I got diarrhea, too." He furrowed his brow.

"What else besides diarrhea?" Crowley said it a little scornfully, like the television commercials that ask "Do you mind if I say a few words about . . . diarrhea?" and a viewer wants only to throw a shoe at the set and scream "Yes!"

"I couldn't sleep. I still can't. I've lost more than twenty pounds. She betrayed me. She made me think if she said anything about me, it would be sympathetic."

"You were not trying to promote yourself personally? You are not a publicity seeker?"

"Objection!" William Arnold was dressed in a well-cut, pin-striped blue suit, a typical Grand Old Man attorney, with just a touch of color in his lucky tie, the one he always wore the day before the case would go to the jury. He usually won.

"Sustained."

"I want to answer anyway," Jessup said, ignoring the hand signals from his lawyer, who angled himself so neither the judge nor jury would see. "I don't need any publicity."

"And yet you have a publicist, a whole department of them on staff."

"That's to promote my pictures."

"You have no wish for self-promotion?"

"I don't need it."

"Aren't there little gates outside the complex you have at the studio, with some kind of brand above them, with what you claim is your family seal?"

"That's decor," said Jessup. "Decor is a very important part of Hollywood history. David O. Selznick had his name hanging in the breeze, like a shingle. I got shingles from her, too. All around my waist. I couldn't breathe. Her book nearly strangled me."

"Can we get him to stop making speeches, your honor?"

"Just answer the question," said the judge.

"Yes. There are gates."

"And what purports to be a family seal?"

"I come from a very good family," said Jessup contentiously. "My mother also had to be hospitalized."

"In response to your young companion's hanging himself?"

"He was unstable," Jessup said. "Actors in this town commit suicide all the time. There's a lot of pressure. Competition."

"Not because you threw him out?"

"That was months before. Sarah made it seem in her book as though it had been the same day, as if I had killed him. She ended the chapter on me on that terrible note. She betrayed me. She let me believe nothing of my life would be between the covers. And then she made it read like I killed him!"

"I didn't even know about that kid when I started the book." Sarah was on her feet. At the time she had an ordinary haircut, subdued on the outside, as she tried to be on the inside. But the press, focusing on the two combatants as much as the trial itself, had labeled her surprisingly colorless, the less interesting of the two, with Jessup the one with the passion. So her lawyer had agreed that if she wanted to show emotion at some point, it might be a good idea. Just not to overdo it.

"Any further outbursts," the judge said, "and I'll hold you in contempt."

Sarah sat back down.

"She made it read as though I had driven him to it," Jessup said. "I wanted to be invisible. She agreed I would be. Instead she held me up to ridicule . . . "

"Do you deny you boasted to Sarah Nash there wasn't a man you couldn't have?"

"Your honor." William Arnold half stood.

"It wasn't a boast," Norman said.

There were seven women on the jury and five men. It was, unusually, a highly educated jury, the defense team having gone for as much intelligence as possible, since the issues of breach of contract and fraud were complex. Jessup had crowed of his accomplishments and standing in the community sufficiently through the trial that the jury's patience appeared to be wearing thin. Everyone was tired. Even the court watchers, those retirees who spent their days at the courthouse in Santa Monica rather than watch soap operas, seemed relieved when Jessup was excused from the stand, and the judge called a recess. These were in the months before the televised Simpson affair, which turned a trial, even more than baseball, into a national pastime.

It had not been Crowley's intention to finish with him quite yet. But the words "It wasn't a boast" seemed to hang on the air, suspended, underlining the vanity of the man. And after all, it was Santa Monica, where in spite of AIDS benefits, supposed progress, and political correctness, a rose by any other name was still a pansy. It felt to the lawyer like a good place to end it.

"There's just Sarah Nash's final cross left," said a reporter into one of the three adjoining pay phones in the marbled corridor outside the courtroom. The case involved celebrity and so was of interest to the whole country. So there were two other reporters from the area, another from Chicago, one from *The New York Times,* one from *The Washington Post.* In addition, there were several magazine writers. There was no one from the publishing house that had printed Sarah's book. Arnold had left them out of the suit, since there was no way they could be said to have breached a personal contract. The publisher considered it circumspect not to have any representatives at the trial itself, as they were holding back a great reserve of Sarah Nash's voluminous royalties in case anyone else should decide to sue and include them. But a few of the young men in the courtroom were whispered to be part of the publisher's legal staff, quietly observing the proceedings.

"Then the closing arguments," said the reporter into the phone. "The instructions to the jury, and, depending on how long they take to get to their verdict, maybe we can get it into the Sunday edition."

"No real courtroom theatrics," said the reporter on the next phone. "Everybody's pretty worn down."

*S*arah Nash had dressed differently for this last day of the trial. Throughout the proceedings, her clothing, like her demeanor, had been restrained, businesslike, rather drab, with only the occasional hint of courtroom flair, a scarf of some softness or color at her throat. That swanlike arch of neck was all that seemed assailable, naked as it was, revealing her alabaster skin. Everything else was lightly powdered over or obscured, from the steel blue of her wide-set eyes, shielded by the bought-for-the-occasion glasses, to her sizeable breasts, boxed into conventional career clothes, Brooks Brothers for women. It was a persona her attorney had worked very hard with her to present, the jury needing to put aside any prejudice it might have against an admitted cocaine and alcohol abuser, who had found restraint, self-esteem, and everything but God in the cleansing act of writing her book. Her shoulders were so broad as to seem androgynous, an image that would have been fortified were it not for the slenderness of her waist. Her hair, at the time still lustrous and dark, hung in a page boy just below her resolute, one might have said stubborn, jaw. Her nails were blunt and buffed. As character- ized as her writing was by sharp wit, only the dimple that appeared occasionally to the side of her tight-held mouth indicated any humor. Throughout the trial she had appeared very much the serious author, just incidentally a Recovering Everything, and woman.

Today though, as she entered the last phase of her cross-examina- tion by Jessup's attorney, she wore a light-blue coatdress, with a but- toned self-belt at the waist. Her breasts, which had seemed almost bound during the trial, looked opulent, the full fall in between made discreetly indistinct by the fashionable scarf tucked into her décol- letage. It was finally clear that a woman sat there. Her generous mouth, loosed from its tense moorings, relaxed into an unaccustomed smile, as William Arnold asked her if it was not true that she deeply disliked Norman Jessup.

"Absolutely not. I really loved Normie." Her glasses were perched atop her hair now, in Jackie Kennedy fashion, so she seemed less the driven career woman she had been depicted as in various publications, than a fortyish female who'd probed unexpected depths to become a writer.

"Was it not your intention to vilify him? To break your contract?"

"There was no contract," she said. "And as for . . . allegedly vilifying him, I left out a lot he said that was more offensive than anything I used."

"Did you not give him your word . . . an oath?"

"Lacks foundation, your honor," said Crowley. "There is no evidence that—"

"Withdrawn. If you 'loved' him, why would you invade his privacy?"

"Privacy?" Sarah said. "He was more public about his leanings than anyone since Oscar Wilde. Didn't you ever have lunch with him?"

"Why would you make him sound so callous?"

"They were his own words." She did not quite look at Jessup. All through the trial they had avoided each other's eyes. ("I thought she was my friend," he had keened, over and over during his testimony. "I spoke to her as my friend. She betrayed me.") "All of them his own words."

"Did you include what Jessup might really have wanted to say?"

"There isn't room in a book for everything Normie might want to say. There isn't room in a whole library."

One of the jurors tittered. Sarah's attorney, his shoulder angled so the judge could not see the gesture, raised his hand in warning, almost imperceptibly shook his head. No sarcasm, he had cautioned her at breakfast. Everyone was already aware of how clever she was. They had all read the book. And no real display of wit. Jurors didn't like uppity women. Remember Jean Harris, he'd counseled her. Juries didn't favor bright women, as prejudiced as they still might be against gays. Juries liked deviant men more than women who thought they were smarter than anybody, especially if they were.

"And yet you say you liked him."

"I did like him."

"Wasn't your ending his chapter as you did, with the suicide, a deliberate and malicious attempt to defame—"

"Objection." Crowley was on his feet. "This is not a libel trial."

"Will counsel please step forward," the judge said. "I have warned you both for the last time," he said very softly, as they stood before him.

Arnold tightened his tie, stepped back, and readdressed the witness. "Miss Nash, why did you end the chapter with that revelation?"

"There wasn't anything Normie hadn't told me about himself, from his sex life to his educational background to his much-too-early potty training at the punishing hands of the mother he's now so concerned about. He never stopped talking. The only thing he kept silent about was the boy who hanged himself. I found that out on my own. It seemed to make a point."

$\mathcal{M}$y colleague will tell you that Sarah Nash damaged this man's career and hurt his health, ladies and gentlemen of the jury," Oliver Crowley said in his closing argument. His gray suit was quite rumpled now, a hard-working contrast to his adversary's impeccable tailoring, as his emotional style was to the older man's reticence. "I will have no further chance to rebut him. So I ask you to listen very carefully and hold in mind what I'm telling you now.

"Norman Jessup has lost none of his power. He is simply a man who has lost some weight. A man who could not control his other appetites, even with a young boy who was obviously unbalanced. His cravings are exceeded only by his hunger for publicity, his yearning for self-promotion. He brought this suit for the same reason he talked to Sarah Nash, soliciting more celebrity.

"He says Sarah Nash and he had a contract. That she invaded his privacy. You've heard him. I believe you see without any help from her how little privacy he chooses to have. He is, by his own proud admission, publicly, a philanderer. And not exactly as we're used to them. Should such a person receive damages? They say that virtue is its own reward, ladies and gentlemen. Let it be the same with corruption."

$\mathcal{T}$here was a quietly impassioned closing plea from William Arnold, about a man's home being his castle, sanctified, with those who are invited in as friends honoring that autonomy. "Now he has no place to hide," Arnold said. "Sarah Nash has pillaged his sanctuary, taken from him an altar where he could speak as a penitent to a priest, the privileged relationship, the trust that is implicit between friends. He trusted her.

"Like one of the Indians who don't want you to take their picture because it will rob them of their souls, he has had his soul violated. Secrets he wanted to share *only* with his intimates, published without his permission and *with* her assurance that he would be protected. She has taken his most precious goods, his privacy, his very identity, and put them out in public. A betrayal all the more shocking because she masqueraded as his friend. But this was how she planned it from the beginning. And for his humiliation, his hurt feelings, this *fraud,* he should be compensated, though no amount of money can ever restore what she has taken away.

"There was between these two people an implicit contract, a solemn oath. Sarah Nash was not simply Norman Jessup's friend, she was his supposed ally. And she betrayed him. A similar case, MacDonald versus McGinnis, was tried before a jury here in Los Angeles. A journalist betrayed a convicted murderer, promising he would take his part if given access to personal material. Instead, he turned against him. The lie, the betrayal, was reprehensible, even though people condemned what that murderer might have done.

"I tell you this because no matter how liberal or enlightened you may be, there is still a tendency to discriminate against a homosexual. But surely no matter what his style of life, or acts, they cannot match those of a convicted murderer. And yet this murderer had been betrayed. He had an understanding, an implicit contract, and he was betrayed. As Norman Jessup was betrayed.

"There are no moral judgments in play here. There is simply a question of one's word. When a witness touches that Bible and swears to tell the truth, the whole truth, and nothing but the truth, if he lies it is perjury. When a trusted friend swears she will honor and respect . . . well, I have but one word to describe it." Arnold teetered on the brink of speaking, and then fell onto the word, almost gasping it. *"Judas."*

He was silent for a long moment. "I ask you to award my client ten million dollars."

*T*he judge gave his instructions. The jury returned with its verdict. "We find for the defendant," the foreman said. They awarded Norman Jessup nothing.

*A*fterwards in the almost deserted courtroom, as Arnold packed up his exhibits, sorrowfully drawing strings around mounted blowups of documents, Jessup sat ashen-faced in the corner of the first row. "I can't believe it," he said, his voice grating. "I just can't believe it. She ruined my life, and it costs her nothing."

"It cost her her lawyer's fees," Arnold said. Remarkably, his hair was not yet white, and the pomade he used to slick it back and down made it seem as dark as it had been in his long-ago youth, when he'd gone into law because he thought it meant justice.

"I could have strangled her, calling me Normie like that on the stand. By a nickname. Like she really had affection for me."

"It's over. Let it go."

"I should have won."

"No question about that. It was as good a closing argument as I've ever given. I have something at stake in this, too. I don't like to lose. But in the long run the jury believed she didn't damage you. Homosexuality is openly accepted in the civilized world."

"Ha!" Jessup said.

"I'm telling you as a *friend* as much as your lawyer, in the long run you haven't been damaged. You must see that. If you don't now, you will. You are still a powerful and productive man. Let it go."

"I can't. I can't let her get away with looking me in the face and then betraying me. Crucifying me."

"This has already taken up years of your life, not to mention the money." Arnold said. "You have to move on."

"Oh, I intend to." Jessup got to his feet, color coming back into his cheeks, the light returning to his eyes. "Indeed, I will move on. But perhaps not exactly in the way she expects."

*   *   *

*O*ne of the few who'd remained unobtrusive in the courtroom had been a representative of Sarah's publisher. He'd reported to her that last exchange. So ever since the trial she'd been looking over her shoulder, expecting that Norman might be after her. Some time had passed, and she'd finally worked up the courage to come back to Los Angeles. There was no question she was a snowflake in Hell. But a snowflake without the drugs she'd genuinely tried to get off of, and without booze to anesthetize her loneliness. There was nothing to blur the fact that she was, in her way, a woman without a country. She'd grown weary of gypsying. There was nowhere else she really belonged.

Not that she belonged here, even with a secret hideaway. Even with the place on Topanga Canyon so secluded and gated and riddled with alarm systems that nothing could get to her but the next earthquake, the next mudslide, or any of the natural disasters that courted those who stubbornly clung to this apocalyptic place. No one knew where she lived except for a small cadre of her remaining friends, a few new friends from the publishing world who admired her audacity, her writing style, and even more the number of books she'd sold. And, of course, the realtor who'd sold her the property, under oath. A stronger oath than the one Sarah had *allegedly* given to Norman Jessup. This one stated in writing, drafted by her lawyer, that if ever the realtor revealed the whereabouts of Sarah's gated home, the realtor herself would have to pay what remained of the mortgage and return the down payment. So Sarah knew she could count on the realtor's loyalty, anyway.

And still, she had the feeling, as she drove up the twisting, inhospitable road, that someone she didn't want to know where she was might know where she was. "Just because you're paranoid," her dentist had said to her, years before she had reason to be, "doesn't mean someone isn't after you."

She drove behind the barrier of hedges, tree-high, that she'd had installed so no one could see her house from the road. She closed the electric gate, operable only from inside her car or inside the house, and stopped for a moment. A little Volvo went by, a young man at the wheel.

She didn't recognize him. No one she'd made an enemy of could possibly drive a Volvo. She gave a deep sigh of relief, and realized she hadn't been breathing. She pulled into her high-security garage, put in her private code, unlocked three locks, and went inside the house.

She bolted the door behind her and rubbed behind her right ear, one of the nervous habits she'd developed since the suit started. Her finger felt sticky. She looked at it. Fucking guacamole. The bastard had made her green behind the ears.

Well, she wouldn't stay that way long. She hadn't been that innocent even when she was an innocent, and now that she was far from innocent—though they'd failed to find her guilty—there were no lengths she wouldn't go to to get even with Jessup. There had to be more she could find out about him. If he'd kept one secret, there were others to be uncovered. Maybe even more sinister than the suicide. Old lovers never mentioned, strangely out of his life. The dancer he'd lived with for years. What had become of him? What was his name? Paulo. Paulo something-exotic.

She went to the phone and called her researcher in New York and told him to get on it.

*T*he young man at the wheel of the Volvo that had passed by Sarah's house was breathtakingly beautiful even in profile, sitting down. That was how he'd first been seen when Norman Jessup found him, meditating on the beach in front of Jessup's Malibu home. He'd had his eyes closed and his large, graceful hands placed on his kneecaps, exposed through the fabric of his deliberately worn-out jeans. He'd looked very much like a golden-lashed angel, maybe one carved out by Michelangelo, complete with radiant curls that circled his head like a white-yellow halo. When Jessup greeted him and he'd stood up to his full height, it was no longer one of the artist's cherubs he resembled, but his statue of David. He was six foot three, an inch taller than Jessup himself, with a chest that seemed about to burst his shirt. Norman wished it would.

"I'm so sorry," the young man said. "I didn't realize this was private property. I didn't mean to trespass."

"I forgive you your trespasses," Norman said. "What's your name?"

"Tyler Hayden."

"Norman Jessup," he said, extending his hand, waiting for the name to register on the kid. It seemed not to. He felt mildly annoyed. "You're an actor, of course."

"No," Tyler said.

"What do you do?"

"Still trying to work that out," Tyler said.

"Would you like to come up to the house for a little lunch? I've invited some interesting people."

The interesting people were all men. They had seen the boy on the beach and sent Norman down to corral him. All of them thought they knew all the beauties in town, even from behind, or especially from behind, but none had seen this particular broad, tanned, muscular back before. Their numbers included Bunyan Reis, by his own appraisal the most interesting painter-writer since William Blake, but a better conversationalist. Gil Besoin was also in attendance. The producer of television comedies, he was considered funnier than anything he'd managed to get on the air. There was a gay black actor from New York, Hoover Coolidge Gray, long past his prime. But Norman liked to show he did not practice ageism any more than racism. There were also a few young numbers who didn't have much to say, but that wasn't why they were there. And into their midst came Tyler Hayden.

"My God," Bunyan exclaimed, when he saw him. "Aphrodite rising from the sea. Penis on the half shell."

"I don't think I can stay," Tyler said.

"Control yourself, Bunyan," said Norman. "I apologize for Mr. Reis."

"Apologize for yourself," Bunyan said. "It was not *I* who was publicly disgraced, *and* in Santa Monica. They might at least have held the trial in Santa Barbara, where we could have gone horseback riding afterwards."

"Are you the writer Bunyan Reis?" Tyler said.

"And the painter," said Bunyan.

"I've read everything you've written."

"Well then, you're one up on me," said Bunyan. "I just write it and let other people read it. Have to save the eyes, you know." He had thinning white-silver hair, the same color as the beard he had recently grown in the event of a transplant, and silver eyes he coordinated with all his clothes. "I would like to paint you." He narrowed his eyelids. "In oils."

"I thought you had given up painting," Norman said.

"I didn't mean on canvas," said Bunyan.

"You've got a lot of yellow," Tyler told him. "I'm surprised. I thought you'd be all violet."

"Excuse me?"

"Your aura," Tyler said. "Violets are the most creative. The people who have come here to be the full expression of themselves and inspire others."

"Well, you've got that right," said Bunyan, dazzled. "What's yellow?"

"The eternal child."

"Oh, my. You must have been speaking to Mum. She's on the other side. Can you do that?"

"Everybody can," said Tyler, his blue eyes luminous, laughing at them, at the same time reassuring.

"Can I get you something to drink?" asked Norman.

"You have bottled water?"

"Is there any other kind?"

"I'll just have some bottled water."

"Bring him a case!" Bunyan shouted to the houseboy. "More, more, you exquisite creature. What other colors do you see?"

"That's it. You're strictly a yellow-violet."

"And what am I?" asked Gil Besoin, sucking in his enormous belly, which hung over his running shorts.

"Fat," Bunyan said.

"Don't be bitchy. You'll frighten him away," Norman said.

"I can handle it." Tyler looked at Gil. "You're yellow and violet too, but with a lot of green."

"What's green?" Gil asked.

"Money. Mental. You really like using your mentality to make money."

"Otherwise you'd never have gone into television," Hoover said.

"One must survive. Not all of us have Jesse Jackson in our corner," said Gil. "Are you married, beautiful boy?"

"No."

"Will you marry me? We can do it at the Bel-Air and preempt Norman and Carina."

"I'm dying to see her. Absolutely perched on the edge," Bunyan said. "When's she coming out?"

"In a couple of weeks," Norman said.

"I don't mean to be charitable," said Bunyan, "but I do wish you nothing but well, after that awful ordeal."

"Thank you," said Norman.

"How that vile Sarah could say that on the stand, comparing you to Oscar Wilde." Bunyan snorted. "If anyone is to be compared to Oscar Wilde, it is I. 'I have put only my talent into my work,' " he quoted. " 'My genius I have put into my life.' *I* have put my genius into both, but unfortunately I have only a mild case of genius. My talent is virulent."

"That was your choice," said Tyler, taking the bottle of Evian the Filipino houseboy brought him, waving away the glass.

"Expand that thought," Bunyan said.

"Genius carries with it too much responsibility." He opened the bottle, took a swig from it. All the men watched, riveted. He took the bottle from his lips, wiped his mouth with the back of his long-fingered hand. "Your yellow just wants to play."

"Isn't he fascinating," Bunyan said. "Can my yellow play with yours?"

"Sure," Tyler said, and smiled.

"What color am I?" asked Hoover.

"Blue-violet. Very maternal. A drama queen."

"He's seen you act," Gil said.

"Not in the judgmental or pejorative sense," Tyler was quick to say. "Emotional. Someone who really loves getting carried away."

"It's been so long," Hoover said. "I'd almost forgotten."

"Look at his eyes," Bunyan remarked. "They're opalescent. Luminous. Translucent. Like the children's eyes in *Village of the Damned.* I do believe he can see through us."

"What color am I?" Norman asked.

"Violet and green, with a red overlay."

"What's that?"

"Rage," said Tyler.

"Well, if you'd just been through what he's been through," Bunyan said, "you'd have a red overlay, too."

"Can I get rid of it?" Norman asked.

"If you want to. But it involves forgiveness. First you have to forgive yourself, then you have to forgive whoever it is . . . "

"You ask too much," said Norman. "How come we've never seen you around?"

"I just got into town."

"Where are you living?"

"I don't know that yet."

"You could come live with me," said Gil. "We wouldn't have to get married, unless you're old-fashioned, or really mad about the Bel-Air."

"How many are you having to the wedding, Norman?" Bunyan asked.

"A hundred and fifty is all they can hold."

"Are you inviting Sarah?"

"I doubt that Miss Nash will be with us by autumn."

"Is she leaving the country again?" asked Bunyan. "We must warn Australia."

"I doubt she will be on the planet," said Norman.

"Yes, I heard she's been seeing Dr. Arnie, and it isn't for collagen," said Bunyan. "Apparently she's got some kind of nervous skin disorder."

"I think . . . she's been acting suicidal," said Norman.

"Oh, dear," said Roscoe. "Have we issued a *fatwa?*"

"She issued her own *fatwa,*" Norman said. "By her actions she put a price on her own head. In the Arab countries they do it for the glory of Allah. This is Hollywood. Power inspires the zealotry of a Muslim fundamentalist. Making it here is as good as being with Allah."

"Maybe better," said Gil. "Allah is so strict."

"So what are you going to do?" Bunyan said. "Have her *offed?*"

"Don't be absurd," Norman said. He was in the company of strangers, potential blackmailers. Not the boy, though. For some reason Norman knew he could trust him, knew that this was a young man with no evil in him, like an innocent in a Williams play, had Tennessee ever written one without sinister twists. Or, more aptly, like the boy in *Narcissus and Goldmund,* a property Norman was familiar with: he'd had coverage done on it as a potential vehicle for Brad Pitt. A Herman Hesse character, plucked like a starfish from the sand, here on the beach of Malibu. And just as he knew he could trust him, he also knew that the statement he'd unfortunately made to Sarah, that there wasn't a man he couldn't have, was no longer operable. But that was just as well, since Carina would be coming soon, and he was finally ready for commitment.

"So if you're not going to get a hit man, how can you be sure she'll be gone by your wedding?" Bunyan asked.

"I have every conviction that Sour Mash will take care of herself. Anyway, I could't find her if I wanted to. She's done a better job of hiding out than Salman Rushdie. Is anyone hungry?"

"I am," said Gil.

"I mean anyone who isn't always hungry."

"I could eat," said Tyler.

"I bet you could," said Gil.

"So if you're not an actor," Norman said hurriedly, "what do you do?"

"I have a master's in psychology, but I don't really want to practice. You only get to work with disturbed people."

Gil laughed. "I think I'm seriously in love with you."

*S*o were most of the people at lunch. But they all left him alone. Including Norman, who offered him the guest house at the back of his property, along with the promise that he'd never try to make a move on him. All Tyler had to do in return was run a few errands for Norman. Nothing demeaning. Just your general odd job, Norman said. In a town where a man could hire people to do his reading for him, there was no reason a rich, influential man couldn't get someone else to do his stalking.

By Hook or by Crook

*B*esides her love for Fitzgerald and a belief in the sanctity of the written word, Kate understood that writing was a kind of trust. Anne Frank had written in her diary that she wanted to go on living after her death, "and therefore I am grateful to God for giving me this gift, this possibility of developing myself and of writing, of expressing all that is in me." Kate wasn't sure where she stood on God, but she did know that being able to put words together well was a gift, one she thought she had. One she hoped she had.

So to squander a gift on something superficial and meaningless might be a sin, depending on where you stood on God. But, as Lincoln (or perhaps it was Will Rogers?) might have said: The good Lord must have loved the superficial man, or he wouldn't have made so many of them.

Still, as she got Lila Darshowitz out of her rancid dress, eased her voluminous flesh out of its confining undergarments, and helped her into the bath she'd filled for her at her hotel, Kate wondered if she wasn't wasting her time. Act of kindness aside, she wanted desperately to establish herself, to *be* somebody. Maybe some of her longings went a little higher; maybe she wanted, like the dead, practically sainted Anne, to express all that was in her. But she knew it was unlikely she could do that with Larry Drayco, no matter what she uncovered. So maybe the whole idea was a mistake.

She hadn't even started yet, and she was already having concerns about her conceit. Not *conceit* in its literary sense. Not in the sense they'd flung around the quad: an ingenious or witty expression, an extended metaphor, but *conceit*, as most people understood it: vanity. Maybe she had too high an opinion of her own abilities, imagining that she could give weight where there was only air. Find truth where there was only duplicity. Nobility where there was most likely just villainy.

"Let me know if you have to throw up again," she said to Lila now, moving the cheap plastic wastebasket closer to the tub.

"You're being so good to me," Lila said weakly, rippling some water over her voluminous breasts, sinking down into the bath just up to her chin, washing away the dried vomit. "Why are you being so good to me?"

"There are things I'd like to know from you," Kate said, straightforward again, finally. She knew there was nothing at stake with this woman, nothing she really had to lose, especially as she was already starting to sour on the project.

"Things?"

"About Larry."

"You from the *Enquirer*?"

"I'm not a reporter."

"What are you?"

"I write books. Or at least, I want to."

Lila sunk further down, the water just below her nostrils, her bloodshot, heavily lidded eyes so clouded over that their color was indeterminate. She studied Kate suspiciously, before coming up to speak. "You mean like that whore book?"

"I'm a serious writer. I mean, I hope I am."

"Some fucking epitaph that publisher left him. Did you read that piece of shit?"

"I only heard about it. I don't even know what it's called."

"*By Hook or by Crook*," Lila said contemptuously. "I guess Larry was supposed to be one of the crooks they meant, who run Hollywood."

"Wasn't he?"

"Not to me," Lila said. "Never to me."

"He was good to his mother," Kate said kindly. "Well, that's something."

"He wasn't really that close to her."

"*Her?*"

"Esther. She was very possessive. One of those mothers that couldn't let go, so he stayed away from her."

"You aren't . . . you weren't . . . ?"

"What?" She sat up in the tub.

"I thought *you* were his mother."

Lila sank down into the water, all the way under, so for a moment Kate was afraid she might be drowning. But she came up laughing, raucously, uproariously. "Honey . . . " Her gray-white hair, mottled with vestiges of a really bad yellow rinse that hadn't completely washed out, clung to her skull. "I'm his wife."

*K*ate waited in the other room while Lila finished bathing, trying to pull her thoughts together, sort out her confusion. The obituary had placed Larry's age at fifty-eight. The woman in the tub had to be in her seventies. Did men do that, too, manipulate the numbers, so people would think they were younger? She had seen photos of him, recent ones, released to the papers with the announcement of his death. He had looked good, vital, almost youthful.

"Maybe you better help me out of here," Lila said over the sound of sloshing from the bathroom. "I don't want to break my neck and give them that to write about."

Kate collected what towels there were. The quarters were furnished with minimal amenities, a cheap, slatted chest of drawers, two beds in the main room, catercornered singles that slid under wooden bookshelves. Made up and covered they could double as couches, so it could serve as a sitting room, someplace to entertain. As if anyone would genuinely be able to entertain in such a place, except for one of those quickie humps that could be heard through the thin walls, not unlike the one her neighbor was having right now. Maybe a professional, judging from the mechanical "Yes, yes!" that came at the end of the joyless thudding, accompanied by grunts.

The towels were the skimpy variety of cheap hotels, no absorbency to them, too small to go around Lila's massive frame. Kate helped her out of the tub, struggling not to be repelled by the rolls of flesh, the broken veins on the enormous thighs. "Are you up to dressing yourself?" she asked Lila.

"What do I need to get dressed for?"

"Does this place have room service?"

"I don't think so."

"You could probably use some coffee."

"Yeah, okay. Sure."

*T*he Park Sunrise was one of those low-priced, high-gloss motels on the Sunset Strip that called themselves hotels. There was a coffee shop with bright brass bad-taste modern chandeliers shaped like spikey solar systems with too-high-watt candlebulbs that made Lila look even older than her seventy-some years. "How old are you exactly?" Kate ventured. "If you don't mind my asking."

"Once you stop caring if you get laid you don't mind if people know," Lila said. "I'm seventy-two."

"How old was Larry?"

"The same."

"How old were you when you got married?"

"Eighteen." Her eyes got almost pretty for a moment, with vestiges of their probably once-bright blue, as she seemed to remember.

Maybe she'd looked really cute, Kate considered. Maybe underneath the flab and the years was the really snappy kid who had managed to capture him. Everyone seemed to agree, no matter how little they thought of his other qualities, that Larry had been sharp. Maybe Lila had been sharp, too. Sassy in an appealing way, different from the combative style she'd shown at the funeral, when there was nothing more left to lose.

"My parents had a furniture business," Lila said, as if it hadn't been her looks alone she'd had to offer him. Dowries, in the guise of a line you had to offer someone, not quite the law firm he could partner into on a higher level, but the proud credentials of the lower middle class. "It was a pretty big business. Booming. End of the war." She poured a couple of packets of sugar into her coffee. "Ended just in time, so he wouldn't have to dodge the draft or have his eardrum punctured like he talked about doing."

She stirred her coffee, looking into it like tea leaves containing the past, smiling as though she considered that aspect of him cute, original, early indications of the guy who was to learn to worm his way out of anything. "It was not part of his program to die in somebody else's fight."

"What was his program?"

"To conquer the world. I guess in his way he did. If you think Hollywood is the world, and a lot of people do. You really want to write a book about him?"

"Maybe."

"Not an expose?" Lila left off the last syllable, not adding the final *a* sound, as though she had never really heard the word, only read it.

"That's not my style," Kate said, not quite sure yet what her style really was, but knowing it would have to hold her own redemption in it, as well as Larry Drayco's. There was so much she wanted from life. There were so many little shadows of ambition and desire in herself she avoided looking at. Instead, she did what most people did when they started out: she ennobled her path before setting out on it.

Even when she spoke of her infatuation with Fitzgerald, she left out the part of his history she really coveted, besides loving him, cherishing his talent, saving him from Zelda. And that was the conscienceless enjoyment of life, selfish, with no other purpose than having a fine time. She would have happily encouraged him to run through Paris. Paris or the south of France. Isadora Duncan at the next table. The Murphys under brightly colored parasols on the beach. What an adventure they would have had together! And though she was sincere in her wish to have taught him that there *were* second acts in American lives, she would have liked to have been assured of a first act of her own. All it had been so far for her was a curtain raiser.

Lila sipped her coffee, holding the cup with two hands. "What did Larry do, besides the movies, and the bad stuff they've already written, that makes him worth writing a book about?"

"That's what I'd like to find out," Kate said. "Socrates said, 'The unexamined life is not worth living.' "

"No shit. Socrates, huh?" Lila lifted her coffee to her lips, with shaking hands, and took a swallow. "Well, maybe it wasn't."

"What?"

"Worth living. Look how he threw himself away on those people, on those drugs. Like he didn't really care about himself."

"But you did."

Lila smiled. "I was crazy about him. Always. Even when he took the money my father gave him to start his own furniture business and ran away to Hollywood. Even when he changed his name. Even when he married those other women."

"You weren't upset he divorced you?"

"He never divorced me," Lila said, and drank some more coffee.

"And you never said anything?" Kate said, after a stunned moment.

"Being a bigamist could get him in trouble. He made enough trouble for himself. I knew he'd come back. And he always did. Whenever they died, he'd come home to me, and I'd make him tuna fish sandwiches. He always said nobody made tuna fish sandwiches like mine.

"He'd come in his limousine, and it would wait outside. And we'd talk, and hug, and cry a little, and I'd pack him a few sandwiches for the plane. Even when he had a private plane, or the studio plane, he never left without a little paper bag, with *my* tuna salad in it."

"So you forgave him."

"I was never angry. Disappointed, sure. Hurt. Jealous of the women. But I was the one he loved, I always knew that. Those other women were for the guy he was trying to be. They were like the custom shirts he took to wearing, the ones with the pointy collars. They looked pretty snappy, but they didn't launder well. Anyway, they all died. Not that I wished it on them, but I admit I never shed a tear."

"And you didn't mind that he never moved you out of Queens?"

"I like Queens," Lila said. "It was Larry who needed to live like a king."

"Will you tell me the whole story?" Kate asked.

"Maybe one day," Lila said. "Right now, I'm hungover, and that always makes me reserved."

*I*n the far corner of the restaurant, in the last beige Naugahyde booth, a man sat hunched down, back to the room, elbows on the hard surface of the table, fists clenched against his cheeks so what little of his face peeked from beneath his porkpie hat and from behind his heavy sunglasses was obscured. He had known this hotel in the fifties, shortly after the death of James Dean, when Marlon Brando was thin and heartbreakingly handsome, and Natalie Wood was a reckless teenager no one ever considered would come to a tragic end. Vince Edwards had stayed here before he'd had a hope of a television series. Nick Adams, having flogged himself to the press as Jimmy Dean's best friend, thereby earning the eternal enmity of Linus Archer, who thought the title his, had set up residence here just before committing suicide. The act garnered him more press than he'd ever received from holding himself out as Jimmy's buddy. Even the then very young and appealing Tony Perkins commented that if Nick had known how much publicity his suicide would get him, he would have done it a lot sooner. Tony at the time of the comment was being groomed to be the romantic idol who would replace Jimmy Stewart, before *Psycho* typecast him as the weirdo he was to play for the rest of his life. He had made that remark to a very young writer secreted in the hotel by the man who was sitting now, back to the room, in the very last booth, with another very young writer he was keeping there for exactly the same reason.

Forty years had passed, and Rodney Sameth, though his technique as a director had changed—some said blossomed, some said diminished, some said disappeared—was exactly the same in this one respect at least: he had engaged an unknown, worshipful would-be screenwriter to write his next movie and promise not to tell anybody. For that reason, he was putting the writer up at this hotel, where nobody had ever bumped into anybody, since nobody came there unless they were very hard up, which nobody Rodney Sameth knew was, except the young writer.

The reclusive director, who lived in fortified seclusion on the Isle of Wight behind electrified fences and a frontline of attack dogs, had met the young writer at a party in Sameth's honor. The party marked the only event Sameth would have come back to America for: an honorary PhD from Stanford. The one area in which he felt incomplete, in spite of his constantly acknowledged genius, was education. Admittedly he had done more and better than anyone who had received a real PhD. But Rodney was at the time of his life when he realized, in spite of the fact that Billy Wilder had referred to him always as "Twenty-nine-year-old Rodney Sameth," that he was no longer twenty-nine-year-old Rodney Sameth. And there were still some things he wanted, that he wouldn't have time to do, like get a PhD.

He had taken a ship and a cross-country train to get to the ceremony, since he didn't fly. On the Isle of Wight he wore safety belts when his driver, who was allowed to go no faster than thirty-five kilometers an hour, took him anywhere, which he rarely did. There was nowhere, really, that Rodney wanted to go. He sent second units out to locations to get exteriors for his films, used doctored process shots, invented ingenious special effects in his private lab, and filmed all interiors, as well as many pseudoexteriors, on a huge soundstage he had built inside his compound. If the tropical trees in his movies looked like plastic, which they were, the critics seemed to overlook it, so glad were they to get another film from him. Such was his stature that the world, what little he wanted of it, came to him. This included studio chieftains and his lawyer, who had emphysema and now had to travel with an oxygen tank. The man was frail and eager to retire, except that Rodney insisted he stay his lawyer. There was no one else he could trust.

He had never trusted Larry Drayco, but admired the Phi Beta Kappa key he'd gotten from Yale. So as long as Rodney had to be in California, he'd gone to the funeral. It was the first time in decades he'd been back in Hollywood, the only real reason being to have meetings with this boy, who would not return to England to hide out with him, as he was close to completing his doctoral thesis. He was bright enough to do that at the same time he was working on the screenplay for Rodney's movie.

"I just don't understand what all the secrecy is about," said Morgan, the young writer. "Everybody knows you bought the Novotny novel."

"Lower your voice," Rodney said, in a controlling whisper. "If they hear the name Novotny, they'll guess you're talking to me. If they find out you're a writer, they'll think you're writing the screenplay."

"But I am."

"Shhh." Rodney hunched down further in the booth. "You agreed to do it on the quiet because you want to work with me."

"I do, Mr. Sameth. You're the finest director of your generation."

"Call me Rodney. And I want to work with you. When I read your screenplay, I thought, 'This kid writes the best dialogue of any writer in America.'"

"Thank you." The young man tried not to beam, but it was difficult. Praise was new to him. The academic world wasn't particularly comfortable with graduate students who might be able to succeed in the world outside. His teachers had been close-vested with their accolades, saving their compliments for his work on Keats, which would not get him jobs except at other universities. That he aspired to writing movies threatened most of them. Some suggested he should consider transferring to UCLA. Most had declined to read his screenplay, and the ones who had had taken forever and then said they didn't know enough about screenplays to comment. So the fact that arguably the most original director of his lifetime had read it the same night it was given to him, and immediately asked Morgan to come to Los Angeles—all expenses paid—to start writing Sameth's next film, was intoxicating. He had agreed to Sameth's stipulation he not tell anybody where he was going or why.

"You're saving my life, Morgan. Josip Novotny can't write dialogue to save his own."

"Then why do you need to say he's writing the screenplay?"

"Janet Maslin is only going to give me a good review in *The New York Times* because I've bought the work of an acknowledged literary genius. I'm not sure he even wrote his own sex scenes, or was really a Holocaust survivor. But it's not up to me to bust anyone's balloon. The world admires him. I can't say some graduate student is writing the screenplay because the genius can't. What do you mean, of my generation?"

It took a beat for Morgan to realize Sameth was back a few thoughts, still hanging on the rating of his talent. "Well, for those who are into Spielberg and Scorsese . . . "

"Never mind, never mind," Sameth said, whisking it away with a thick-fingered hand. "I'll take care of whatever it costs to keep you here till you finish, and some pocket money. Maybe even enough to buy a used car. That way you won't have to walk to Schwab's."

"There is no more Schwab's," Morgan said. "I asked. They tore it down twenty years ago."

"This town," Rodney said, and shook his head. "No respect for history. Not enough they leveled the Garden of Allah, where Dorothy Parker stayed, and Fitzgerald, and Faulkner. They have to take away the drugstore where Sidney Skolsky found Lana Turner's tits. It's all just real estate."

"So why do I have to stay at this hotel?"

"Because if you're anyplace else, somebody might see you, and then they'll know what you're doing."

"But I hate it here. The only thing missing is Norman Bates."

"You work fast. Look at all the pages you've written already. You'll be done in no time, and out of here. And when it's a hit . . . "

"You'll reveal it was me?"

"I can't do that. The Writer's Guild would have my scrotum. But I promise to give you full credit and Guild minimum on my next movie."

The young man, whose skin was pale by nature, made more so by spending most of his time in libraries and at the computer, blanched. "You only do one picture every five years."

"What do you care? You're young."

*B*ecause Rodney Sameth sat hunched down with his back to the room so no one could see him, even obscured as he was by the hat and glasses that served as a disguise, he couldn't see if there was anyone else in the coffee shop. Morgan was so engrossed in his own exhilaration-cum-disappointment, so hypnotized by his reverence for Sameth and the man's indisputable, if dark, charisma that he noticed no one else in the room.

It was an odd hour. The transients who slept late had finished their breakfasts. The monthly residents of the apartment-hotel, some of them elderly, some of them prostitutes, had finished their lunches. Three freshly-arrived-from-Iowa waitresses, overly made up, just a bleach job away from becoming Tori Spelling, they were sure, studied a map of Beverly Hills, trying to determine where 90210 was. Unable to locate it, they set out for Melrose Place. So except for two women in a booth near the cashier and the old cashier herself, who had played opposite Turhan Bey and been deeply in love with him until he lost all his hair, the place was virtually empty. The only sound besides Rodney's heavy breathing and the subdued conversation coming from the two women was the clatter of plates being cleared by the busboy.

"Enough socializing," Rodney said, and put a twenty-dollar bill on the green, pencil-marked check. "I'm keeping you from your work."

The two men got up and headed for the door. "I'll be back tomorrow morning for the new pages."

They passed the two women, the younger of them with her back to the booth where they'd sat. She looked up. *"Morgan!"* she cried excitedly, and leapt out of the booth, throwing her arms around him. "What are you doing in L.A.?"

"Nothing!" Morgan said. "Not a thing!" The man with him headed straight for the door, head down, hand covering his face, the back of his neck crimson.

"But I can't believe this!" She turned to Lila. "This is Morgan Craig. He's a friend of mine from graduate school! Lila Darshowitz."

"Enchanted," Lila said.

"This is like a miracle! I've been so lonely. Are you staying here?"

"No. I'm not staying anywhere. I'm not even really in town." He backed towards the door, sneakers squeaking on the linoleum.

"Hey, I'll never tell them you're playing hooky." She smiled at him, very white and wide, real connection animating her face and making her look fresher, younger, brighter. "Did you finish your thesis?"

"Not quite."

"Then how come . . . " Kate frowned suddenly, feeling his discomfort, putting his evasiveness together with the man who had hurried out of the coffee shop. She looked out the window, into the glaring sunlight. He was nowhere to be seen. "I'm sorry," she said softly and sat back down.

"It's okay," Morgan said, phumphering. "Really. Not to worry."

"I'm listed. Will you call me?"

"Sure. Sure. If I'm ever in town." He ran out of the restaurant.

"I guess you caught him with his boyfriend," Lila said.

"But he isn't gay." Kate looked genuinely flustered.

"Maybe he *wasn't*," Lila said, and drank the rest of her coffee. "But this *is* L.A."

*S*hit!" Rodney said, when Morgan found him, huddled in the parking lot behind the building. "Fuck! I might as well have put you at the Beverly Hills Hotel!"

"I would have liked that," said Morgan. He saw that Sameth wasn't smiling. "Don't worry. I didn't tell her anything."

"The same fucking English department," Rodney fumed. "Two literate people in the whole of Los Angeles, and Fate puts them in the same place."

"Fate has very little to do with it. I would have put me at the Chateau Marmont."

"Don't be a wiseguy. If you're saying it's my fault, I agree. I should have stashed you at my lawyer's. Maybe I should move you there."

"I thought he was in an oxygen tent."

"Exactly. He won't even know."

"Nothing's going to happen."

"What if she saw me? What if she guesses?"

"Nobody even knows what you look like."

"Of course they do." Rodney took his hat off, his hair glued to his skull from perspiration. He fanned himself. "I'm an icon."

*W*hen Tyler Hayden got back to the house in Malibu, there was a cold lunch waiting for him in the guest house refrigerator. A salad with sprouts, laid out appetizingly in the style of nouvelle cuisine, strips of red pepper making it into a happy face, sided with a plate of turkey breast, thickly sliced. There was a large bottle of Evian out on the table, since Norman knew he didn't like it chilled. Tyler took the two plates in one hand, as he'd learned to do during a brief stint as a waiter, a miniloaf of olive bread from The Godmother still in its bag and the Evian in the other, and pushed the screen to the deck open with his hip, letting it slam shut behind him. A wooden picnic table was set with a bamboo place mat, silverware, a plastic goblet that looked like crystal, a twin decanter of oil and balsamic vinegar, and a small vase filled with delicate flowers, miniature purple and yellow calla lilies, their slender necks drooping. He sat down and cut the crusty dark bread down the center, drizzled some olive oil on it, and started to eat. It was crunchy and flavorful, and felt good in his mouth, in spite of what was going on in his belly.

"So did you find where she lives?" Norman said, coming up the wooden steps from the back deck of his house.

"I found where she lives," Tyler answered in a monotone. "She's in Topanga Canyon. There isn't a number, but it's behind a really high hedge, about three-quarters of a mile in." He put his feet up on the bench in front of the railing. "I wouldn't mind living in Topanga Canyon."

"Then one day you will," said Norman, sitting down on the bench beside Tyler's sandaled feet. "Thank you."

"This whole thing makes me sick," Tyler said.

"You don't like turkey?"

"You know what I mean. The situation is sick, and you're sick, and being part of it is making me sick. You're not going to heal until you forget about her and let the whole thing go."

Norman leaned his red head back on the railing so his neck was against it and he could see the sky. "When I was a little boy, and I would drop a piece of food on the floor, my mother would tell me to kiss it up to God, and then it wouldn't be dirty anymore."

"You want to kiss Sarah Nash up to God?"

"I wish I could." He brought his head up sharply. "I don't want you to concern yourself with this anymore."

"Good," Tyler said firmly. That he was accepting what passed for Grace in Malibu, someplace really nice to stay, did not bother him. He genuinely liked Norman Jessup, and in spite of his power, Tyler could feel his pain, which served to reinforce his conviction that what most people considered power had no real force. But it did bother him that he might be part of some dark purpose here with Norman, especially since his reason for being on the planet was to bring light. He'd read that in his own chart. He had seven planets in his mid-Heaven, so his job was to illuminate. He just didn't know where the employment agency was that told you where to apply for that one.

"Carina wants very much for you to come into town to dinner with us."

He also liked Carina. He had been genuinely surprised by her serenity, the gracefulness with which she moved, the tender way she dealt with Norman. Tyler liked to think he was without judgment, but his mother had been extremely judgmental, and you couldn't help picking some of that up, no matter how spiritually independent you were. So it had close to astonished him that this flagrant homosexual had actually been drawn to such a feminine woman. It actually *had* astonished him, and once he integrated it totally into his consciousness, it thrilled him. Because it reinforced the truth that there was God even for gays, and so much for Jerry Falwell.

"You have anything to wear?" Norman asked.

Norman's mother and probably his father as well had been totally into judgment, and appearances. Tyler knew that. "What you see is what you get," said Tyler.

"We're about the same size. I've got a closet full of jeans with no holes in the knees."

"It took me a long time to get these holes exactly right. A lot of Dead concerts at the Oakland Coliseum. What if the spirit of Jerry Garcia came to look for me? How would he know me if I wasn't in these jeans?"

"Jerry's manager threw his ashes in the Ganges," Norman said. "He won't be coming to Beverly Hills."

"He was an ascended Master," Tyler said. "Alive, he could be in two places at once. God knows what he can do now."

"God knows. About the pants . . . "

"You either love me as I am—"

"I do," said Norman. "But I'd like you to do it for Carina. She's from another hemisphere, you know. A more formal one. If you don't want to wear something of mine, go to Fred Segal's." He took a couple of crisp hundreds from his pocket, with the new Ben Franklin imprinted slightly off center, and younger, without the glasses, as though America didn't even like to think of the founders as growing old.

"I don't want any money from you," Tyler said. "Room and board is generous enough."

"You could come work for me," Norman said. "You're sharper and more imaginative than any of the kids in my company. You could shimmy up the ladder in no time."

"I don't like what's at the top of that ladder," Tyler said, meaning it. He hadn't been exactly sure what brought him to L.A. Everybody said he was good-looking enough to be a movie star, and in an objective way, he knew that to be true. This was not vanity. He simply saw what was in the mirror and knew how women reacted to him, following him down the street sometimes, trying to think of a way to start a conversation. He could feel them behind him. Occasionally he would stop and turn and smile and let them get it off their minds. Sometimes he would even engage with them, take them for a cappuccino, and think, when they were smart enough, and physically appealing enough, that something might come of it. But usually they stopped short of the place where it could fly. Where they could fly together, because they understood where he was coming from. Nobody had ever really come from the same place except Diana, and she'd been sexually abused, something that never really got healed, so it was too hard to have fun, to be completely spontaneous. He'd had no choice but to end it, as work that had no joy in the process was anathema to him.

Still, knowing how attractive he was, reading the inane interviews of his contemporaries who had made it as stars, he had come to think from time to time that what society could really use was someone to admire who had more on their mind than slurpees. He thought what it would be like to date Uma Thurman, who seemed to have depth, and came from parents with enlightened credentials. He pictured his own indisputable sparkle at an opening with Gwyneth Paltrow, and then realized he was getting caught. He could not fulfill what he'd come to the planet to do unless he was free. Even *Premiere* magazine, which he read standing up at the open magazine rack in the Santa Monica mall, admitted Hollywood was a trap.

So he'd abandoned his impulse to give it a shot as an actor, even though there was no one in movies six three, golden-haired, straight-shouldered, barrel-chested, but slim-hipped enough so as not to look beefy, with eyes that were Orientally slanted and very pale blue, heavily lashed, able to see through just about anybody. And since he didn't want to get into a power structure where people were afraid, where mad queens could declare "Off with their heads" for no visible reason, he passed on Norman's offer of a job. A real one, in an office, not just shadowing some enemy.

"What's at the top that's so odious to you?" Norman asked.

"I'm not sure. But I know that people in your business are afraid. Fear can blow big holes in the imagination. And that would be worse than the ones in my jeans. Fear not, doubt not, rejoice always. You should make that into a placard and put it on the wall of your office."

"What do you want, Tyler?"

"I don't know. I'm trying to work it out. What I'd really like to do is inspire people."

"So you've said. In what way?"

"To be the best they can be. To see themselves as a little piece of God. Like they really are. Like you are, if you'd forget about Sarah Nash."

"Look. You don't lean on me, I won't lean on you." He got up from the bench. "You can wear those jeans to dinner."

"It wouldn't be respectful to Carina," Tyler said. "I'll borrow a pair of yours."

*I*n the end, he also borrowed a really nice shirt, brand new, that Norman had bought for him, but not offered, knowing that Tyler wouldn't accept it. But the kid had good taste, and found it in the closet where the jeans were hanging. Because they were going to Morton's, Norman had suggested offhandedly, Tyler might also want to borrow a shirt.

"What's Morton's?" Tyler was looking through Norman's jeans, and found the shirt hanging there.

In spite of how much he loved Carina, Norman hadn't been able to help thinking that the shirt was just the right shade of radiant light blue to go with Tyler's eyes. Old habits died hard, and none of them were really fashioned for fidelity. "It's where to go on Monday nights."

"You're such a victim," Tyler said. "So easily manipulated, in spite of your so-called power."

"So-called?"

"Letting people tell you what's the right place to go on a Monday."

"It was I who set that standard, decided it," Norman said imperiously. "People go there on Monday because there's a chance of running into me."

"Can I borrow this shirt?"

"If you like," said Norman, trying to sound casual, covering his exhilaration that still someone else had fallen into a snare of his devising, no matter how small or benign a snare it was. "It would probably look good on you."

Tyler tried it on, smiled at his reflection. "I like it. It's my color."

Actually, now that Norman examined his own feelings deeply, he felt, besides the feather-flicks of desire, fatherly. "From now on," he said, "they'll go there on Mondays because there's a chance of running into you."

*H*elen Manning had not really intended to sing at Larry's funeral. She felt genuinely bad that he had died, as she felt genuinely bad when anybody died. She was without rancor, or the wish for revenge, which made her almost as unique in her community as did her phoenix eyes, so labeled by Bunyan Reis, with whom she was dining at Morton's. She had sung because the song had reminded her of Larry Drayco on what was probably one of his best days. She'd been present for part of the scoring of his picture and seen how happy he looked that the song was genuinely wonderful. Remarked to her that it was really a world-class ballad. She'd heard in that instant that he would have liked to be, himself, world class. For all his affectations of breeding, his Phi Beta Kappa key, and the latest wife he'd married in a ceremony that had to have cost him a million with the rooms he'd redone in Vegas, the private jets to take everyone there, the orchids flown in to make a carpet for the bride to walk down, suites for all those invited with gift baskets in each one that included not just champagne and fruit and sweets but his and hers Tag Heuer watches that gave time and date all over the world, with a card that said "So you'll remember our perfect day," a day which had lasted just a little over a year—for all of that, Helen had known he wasn't that sure of himself. Even if he hadn't been caught embezzling.

Her intuition went deeper than anyone imagined, especially about insecurity. There had never been a room she was in where any man present looked at anyone else, and she still had to check the mirror to make sure she was really beautiful. So she knew in her heart, which was quite open and surprisingly good, in spite of the disappointments she'd suffered, that Drayco didn't have even the confidence she was supposed to. While they scored the song, she'd pressed his hand in an unaccustomedly affectionate gesture as he clutched his armrest. She felt the cold sweat, experienced a moment of genuine, deep affinity, perceiving how vulnerable he was. She understood that he would have liked nothing better than to be as unmistakably fine, even for a moment, as that song.

When she'd heard the song at the funeral, all that he'd been that he couldn't show, all that he'd wanted that he couldn't achieve, bubbled up in her, like sorrow. Longing for the things that eluded most people, that they pursued: prosperity, peace, the perfect love. The last still applied in her case, and it was that lack, that place of continuing emptiness and yearning she'd been moved by, as well as what she'd felt for Larry, when she'd heard the song. So she'd involuntarily started singing.

Her eyes were still a little red around the edges this Monday evening at Morton's. But the redness didn't diminish their golden-amber glow. They felt a little tired from the force of the emotion and the tears she'd shed. So she wasn't sure if the boy with Norman Jessup and Carina was as beautiful as he seemed.

She tried not to appear too interested or excited as he passed her table, igniting in her a palpable electricity, making the small hairs on the back of her neck stand on end. She hoped that Bunyan wouldn't pick up on it and say something bitchy. But he wasn't paying attention to her, chatting to the man on the other side of his banquette.

"His name is Tyler Hayden," Bunyan was saying. "True *sparkle*. Inside as well as out."

"You've been?" asked Wilton Spenser.

"I've engaged. Verbally and metaphysically. He's very into that. *Tellement* New Age-y."

"I'll be dead soon enough," whimpered Lester Rolph, the seventyish man on the other side of Wilton, to the thirtyish man opposite. "And you'll get everything, and then you can give it to him. Can't you just pretend you love me?"

"I do love you," said the younger man, not looking at Lester.

"And Carina doesn't mind that he's living there?" Wilton asked Bunyan.

"Then why do you have to see him? I'll be dead soon enough."

"He's straight as an arrow, so Carina doesn't mind," Bunyan said. "Did you see his eyes? Luminous. Like the children in *Village of the Damned*."

"I asked Elizabeth once," Wilton said, "if she'd seen *Village of the Damned*, and she said 'No, but I read the book!'" He chortled. "She's such a hoot!"

"I'm terribly sorry," said the maître d' to Arthur Finster, checking the reservations book. "But we have no table for you."

"That's bullshit," Arthur said, twirling one of his dreadlocks nervously. Morton's was the center of his universe on Monday nights, the capital of the need to see and be seen, to eat and not be eaten. "My secretary confirmed last Friday, and again this afternoon."

"Who did she confirm with?"

"Laurence." He gave it the French pronunciation.

"I'm so sorry," said the maître d'. "Laurence no longer works here."

"That'll teach him to book a table for you," Charley Best said, as he headed into the dining room, the buoyant Brandy on his arm, in a see-through dress with sequins strategically placed.

"I'll buy this fucking restaurant!" Arthur said. "*By Hook or by Crook* is going straight to number one."

"Funny," said Charley. "It smelled to me more like number two." Smiling, he followed the maître d' to his table.

"You're in particularly good company this evening," Wilton said to Bunyan, looking at Helen a little wistfully.

"Oh, I'm sorry," Bunyan said. "Do you know each other?"

"I don't think so," Helen said.

"That's right, you waited in the car." He held out his hand. "Wilton Spenser. A privilege."

"Car?" She shook his hand.

"Larry Drayco brought you by my place once, made a quick stop."

"I never went out with Larry Drayco," Helen said.

"Well, maybe he only said you were in the car so I'd give him a better grade," Wilton said. "But it's great to meet you. I really enjoyed your singing today. I didn't know you sang."

"Neither did I." She looked away from him. "Bunyan, that young man with Norman and Carina . . . ?"

"That way lies madness, my darling. You're old enough to be his mother."

"I'm thirty-eight," she said, angrily.

"Forty. I've seen your passport. He's twenty-five."

"No one has children when they're fifteen."

"Joan of Arc saved France at that age."

"Maybe she had no sex drive."

"I've seen you pursued by sultans," Bunyan said. "I won't watch you make a fool of yourself."

"Then look the other way," Helen said, and signaling the waiter, asked for a piece of paper. She wrote a short note and asked the waiter to give it to the young man with the Jessup party.

At the next table Lester Rolph was weeping. "You can't wait for me to die."

"You're boring me," the younger man said.

"What about me?" asked Wilton. "I only invited you because I thought you'd tell us tales about old Hollywood. Why can't you dwell on the past, like other people your age?"

Helen ordered a second coffee, lingering over dessert, making a visible effort not to seem to be waiting. Carina and Norman Jessup stopped by the table to say hello on their way out of the restaurant.

"I really loved your singing," Norman said.

She seemed not to hear him, her eyes on the young man, who did not look at her, but just kept walking. "I'll be outside getting the car," he said to Norman.

"Isn't he clever," she said, devastated, after they were gone. "He's playing hard to get."

"I'm afraid he isn't playing," said Bunyan.

Rats

There were rats in Beverly Hills. It was not metaphor, or something Kate could regard as symbolically Kafka-esque, although she did. It was the reality.

The brush that burst into flames in the surrounding hills in the dry ovens of summer, the ivy that trailed around the best manicured streets in the flats, choking the stately palms, sucking life from the soft violet-blossomed jacarandas, housed rodent hordes. Unsightly trucks from exterminator companies proliferated on the choicest streets, more visible than the resident Mercedes. Even the best exterminators refused to guarantee that the rats would not come back.

Kate knew there were rats in the guest cottage she rented on Burton Way. She could hear them rustling in the night. She was aware they were nocturnal, as ghosts were supposed to be nocturnal. Still she wished there was such a thing as ghosts, so she could open one of her latticed windows, reach out, and only be touched by an icy hand. Sometimes she would turn on the light by the side of her bed, and catch a flash of tail, a rush of fur on the wooden rafters of her cathedral ceiling. She wondered if they followed the habit patterns of the populace and would seize her by the throat while sleeping.

She asked her landlord to get rid of them. At first he denied they were there. Then he said she could always move. He knew he had her, like the rats might, by the throat. It was a Beverly Hills address,

77

cheap for the neighborhood, an exquisitely wrought little cottage with a winding staircase leading up to a bedroom loft, every inch of it unique and beautifully crafted, carved, inlaid with antique paneling, designed by one of England's leading decorators as a gift to her lover before leaving him. It had been in *Architectural Digest*. A copy of the magazine lay on the red-and-white inlaid game table. The landlord told her the noises were in her imagination.

But of course being a writer, her imagination was very vivid, and she could hear them all the time. The night of Larry Drayco's funeral, she heard what might have been a thunder sheet in an amateur production of *Lear*, so persistent was the noise, so full of rustling and crackling. She switched on the lamp, picked up the baseball bat she kept beneath her bed in the event of an intruder, the flashlight beside it in the event of an earthquake, and followed the sound down the winding staircase, to the kitchen. There was a walk-in pantry built cleverly into what would have ordinarily been a broom closet, and in it Kate kept the essentials that got her through her up-to-now uneventful life. She beamed the flashlight around. There was a case of bottled water—not Evian yet, because she wasn't in that category—a case of soft drinks and mixers in the event of the party she hadn't yet thrown, pasta, rice, crackers, and a large box of Raisin Bran.

The box was shaking. The rustle was more than a rustle now, a swishing, an audible chomping, as though something were biting through wax paper, participating fully in the whole-grain value of the contents. She looked at the baseball bat in her hand, the box on the shelf, and wondered how, exactly, she would do it. The shelf was a little high. What if she only antagonized what was in the box, didn't even succeed in stunning it? The entire box seemed to be doing a kind of dance now, some ritualistic dark Disney thing. What if it fell to the floor and whatever was in it ran out at her?

Dropping the baseball bat, she seized the box and ran with it to the refrigerator, opened the freezer portion on the top, shoved the box inside, and slammed the door. Then she ran back upstairs, switched off the lamp, and tried to go back to sleep, lulled into quiescence finally by the decelerating pounding of her own heart.

In the morning she did not even brush her teeth or go to the bathroom, but went immediately to the freezer and warily opened the door. The cereal box was overturned. The rat stood frozen on its hind legs, frosted eyes fixed on the door, front legs up in a scrunched position, as though someone held a gun on him, and he was surrendering.

The phone rang. "Baby!" It was her agent's voice. Mel had never called her *baby* before. In fact, he had never called her, only occasionally accepting her calls, one of them the one she had made to him in terror because there were rats in her house, at which time he had put her on hold. "Why didn't you tell me?" Mel was saying now.

"Tell you what?"

"About Grandpa. And the manuscript."

"What are you talking about?"

"Haven't you seen the trades?" he said.

"I'll call you back," said Kate.

"You better," he said. "Don't forget who was in your corner when you were nobody."

She ran to the mat outside her front door, where the trade papers were delivered, along with the *Times,* and took them with her to the bathroom. It was in the middle of the party column in the *Reporter,* along with photos of celebrities who'd been at Drayco's funeral. Her name was in bold print, with Perry Zemmis's, and her "grandfather," F. Scott Fitzgerald's, and underlined and in bold, *The Last Tycoon.* Perry Zemmis had bought the "sequin," it said in quotes, like he had been being clever. Like he'd been making a witty joke. But they'd spelled her name right, which, according to Tallulah Bankhead, and the theatrical histories she'd read that she remembered, was all that mattered. A little quiver went through Kate at the sight of her name in print, along with all the celebrity names. Bold. She experienced something greater than relief, as she felt the release of her urine.

It was only after she'd washed, brushed her teeth, put on makeup and done her hair, and dressed very well in case somebody called to take her to, or rather, "do" lunch, that she remembered the rat in the freezer. She picked it up with the classified section of the L.A. *Times* and put it outside in the garbage. And just before she left the house, she put the cereal back in the closet, in case there was another one.

*W*hen she awoke this annoyingly sunny morning, Sarah Nash had a hangover. It took her a while to realize she hadn't had anything to drink the night before and was no longer on drugs. She tried to assess what would make her feel so dragged, so totally lacking in energy. Then she remembered the funeral, and what had happened with Norman Jessup.

Automatically, she reached behind her ear, checking it for stickiness. The bastard. Guacamole. It didn't bother her so much that he had done that to her in front of everybody, as that he had done it to her in front of her. It was almost as though she had set herself up, so he could humiliate her. Like she had something to feel guilty about.

She picked up the phone and hit the second button, programmed to speed-dial her researcher in New York. "Chuck?" she said, at the sound of his "Hello." He hated being called Chuck. He was twenty-two years old and desperate to seem mature, and so longed to be addressed as Charles. But this way he would be put immediately on the defensive. So much of Sarah's life had gotten away from her, she seized what control she could.

"Oh, hi, Sarah," he said, the juice instantly squeezed out of him.

"What did you find out?"

"You only called me yesterday afternoon. It was Monday. All the theaters were dark."

"Not so the people who work in them. Couldn't you find anybody who knew that Paulo what's-his-name?"

"Nerys," Charles said.

"Well, at least you've done that much for me," she said, in a dismissive tone. He was on a small retainer, the most she could honestly afford at the moment, since her publisher was holding back her royalties in the event anyone else sued before the statute of limitations had expired. She hated to be forced to be on a budget. Numbers were loathsome to her. In spite of the money the book had made, between the hiding out and the IRS, she could not afford a business manager. So she had to keep track of her own figures, and that made her nervous.

As Charles did. He was another generation, full of the resilience of youth, when you didn't really need the resilience, because people gave you a chance. If she didn't keep him backed into a corner, he might go out and find some other job. And she needed him, much as she hated to admit it to herself, and would never admit to him.

"Do you have any idea when he and Norman Jessup stopped being lovers?" Sarah asked.

"Like I said, I haven't had time to connect yet with anyone who knew him. I got his name from the dance library at Lincoln Center."

"Well, that was industrious," she said, meaning it, throwing him a bone. "See if you can find some track I can pick up. I'll be there tomorrow."

"Tomorrow?" Charles said anxiously.

"I have work to do," Sarah said, not adding, as she didn't dare even think, that there was nothing for her to do here. No one who wanted her. No one she even wanted, sadder to say.

She clicked the receiver and hit the fifth programmed number: Wilma, her travel agent and friend. One of the few people she trusted enough to let know her whereabouts, in charge of arranging them. She asked her to make the plane reservation to New York, and see if she could get her a break at some hotel.

"Are you alright?" Wilma asked. "You sound a little played out."

"I have not yet begun to play!" said Sarah.

$\mathcal{M}$aybe when she was in her crib, people had been able to keep their eyes off Helen Manning. Maybe when she was an infant, the mother who so cloyingly telephoned her now daily, asking why she didn't call, had been able to resist little Helen, not giving her the love and attention and affirmation she needed, creating the narcissist that actors needed to be to be actors. But from the time she was in her stroller, not yet completely able to walk, she remembered people stopping to stare, and ooh and ahh, to twirl the white-gold curls, and lift the dimpled chin, and exclaim they'd never seen a more beautiful child. Once on her feet, she'd toddled her way onto the screen. After that it was a profusion of lights, and people whose job it was to look at her, and no way of her knowing that she wasn't actually the center of the universe. Not that she hadn't made an attempt to discover that she wasn't. Not that she hadn't read books, and gone to see therapists, to try and find the antidote for being self-centered, seeing so much of the disease around her that she wanted to immunize herself even though she knew she was already infected, probably a carrier. She had given her glow over to causes, and actually come to believe in many of them. And cultivated a garden, of flowers, and people, so there would always be something to putter around in that would make her lose herself.

But then there were the men, fawning, adoring, covering her with gifts, traveling to the other side of the world, where a few of them came from, to find things she couldn't lavish on herself. And in spite of the rush she always felt when the romance was new, or the marriage ceremony was performed, it never lasted. So for all her success, she felt failed. And now this boy, this very young, very beautiful boy, had untethered her from the one balloon that kept her afloat: the given that no man could resist her.

"Helen Manning?" Norman Jessup said to his secretary, on the intercom. He still had an intercom in his office because the whole world had become too high-tech for him. He longed for a time when Cary Grant would have felt comfortable, when a man could make an impression with style and wit and fine tailoring, and it wasn't all computerized, on-line, virtual reality, virtual talent, virtual life. "Here?"

"In the outer office," his secretary, Carol, said.

"Not anymore," said Helen, bursting through the double doors.

She was dressed, unaccustomedly, in Lycra. Designer Lycra, to be sure, but Lycra nonetheless, this woman who prided herself on being the antithesis of grunge, who castigated the Up-and-Comings for not respecting the eye of the beholder, as she said in her interview in GQ, the first female movie star to make the cover. A fitting breakthrough for one who still made gentlemen feel like gentlemen. Norman Jessup leapt to his feet at her presence, his basic good manners galvanized by the force of her entrance.

"Forgive the intrusion, my darling," she said, and, moving towards him, swept what would have been in better days a train, but was now just the air behind her Donna Karaned buttocks. She stood on sneakered tiptoe to kiss his cheek.

"It's never an intrusion," he said, as though she had done this before, which she never had. He was stunned, not only by the unexpectedness of her appearance, but her appearance itself. Besides the Lycra, she was wearing a square-necked, tight, funky black sweater which Norman knew was Alberta Ferretti, because Carina had one. But anyone else might have thought it came from the Gap. Neither he, nor anyone else in the industry that he knew of, had ever seen her in clothes that might not have marked the second coming of Barbara Stanwyck.

"I was just out for a jog . . . " she said, her wide-set amber eyes making a quick tour of his staff, who, in spite of trafficking daily with movers and shakers and stars, sat gape-mouthed at her presence.

"A what?"

"A jog."

"But when I invited you to have a run on the beach, you said it was bad for the breasts."

"Well, I've had them long enough where they are," she said, and smiled. "Can I speak to you alone for a moment?"

"Certainly," he said, and nodded. The young men all left, one or two of them awkwardly bowing to her as they backed out of the office.

"I wanted to ask you—" she started to say.

There was a buzz on the intercom. "Hold all calls," he said.

"But this is the travel agent," said Carol. "*The* travel agent."

"Oh," said Norman. "Excuse me a moment, Helen." He picked up the phone. "Yes, Wilma?" His brow furrowed. "What flight?" He wrote something down. "Thank you. Get one on the same flight for a Tyler Hayden. He'll pick the ticket up tomorrow at American . . . of course . . . the usual arrangement." He hung up the phone, seemed to refocus, looked at Helen. "Now what can I do for you?"

"Do?"

"You wanted to ask me something?"

"How are you, Norman?"

He seemed a little taken aback. "Well, I'm fine. How are you?"

"Fit as a fiddle," she said, and got up from the carved oak chair she had temporarily settled on. "Or, unless I do a little work on these hips, more like a guitar. Well, I know how busy you are. Thank you for seeing me."

"That's it?" he asked, confused.

"Can't one just show interest in a friend? Does everything in this town have to be about *self*, and needing something?"

"You never cease to amaze me," he said, and came around the desk to kiss her good-bye.

"Good," she said, and went home to call American Airlines.

* * *

*I*t took a bit of doing. She had to weep on the phone to the man on reservations, who told her for security reasons he couldn't let her know which flight Tyler Hayden was taking, especially since she didn't know his destination, or time of departure. But without revealing who she was, she explained he was her boyfriend, and they'd had a dreadful row. She actually said *row* because she knew from the one time she'd done a play, to not bad reviews, really, that the word had more dramatic resonance than *fight*. So forty or fifty sniffles in, he looked it up on the computer and told her Tyler Hayden was on flight 2 the next day to New York. She thanked him profusely, hung up the phone, and called her travel agent.

*B*ut it's a total fabrication!" Kate said to Wilton. They were in the Daily Grill in Beverly Hills, in the corner booth where no one could hear them, except maybe the O.J. attorney in the next booth.

"Keep your voice down," Wilton said.

"He's not interested in anything I might say. I saw him on Larry King. He has his own agenda."

"Everybody has their own agenda," Wilton said. "Why are you denying it? Don't you want to be a hit?"

"As myself," she said. "As who I really am."

"After you're a hit, you can be a hit as who you really are."

"Well, well," said Mel, coming over to their booth.

"Wilton Spenser, this is my agent, Mel Brynner."

"Why didn't you call me back? Did someone else make the deal for you?"

"There is no deal," Kate said. "There is no manuscript."

"Isn't she a caution," said Wilton. "Some people just aren't comfortable in the laps of the gods."

"CAA," said Mel. "You're going with CAA."

The restaurant was decorated in the sterile way of places that had nothing to prove, since the food was simple and good and the location convenient. It was filled to capacity with blue-suited men from law firms and talent agencies within walking distance, though few of them had walked. Most of them had treadmills, and/or were members of a health club, so a walk was nothing they took casually or for pleasure. The women present were not the Ladies Who Lunch crowd, those who had been spiritually dispossessed by the closing of the Bistro Gardens, but businesswomen of similar ilk, except with lower salaries. They were dressed in softer shades than the men, grays and olives and beige, but the cut of their clothes was serious stuff, often Armani.

"There's Victor Lippton, the new head of Cosmos," Wilton said to Kate.

"Where?" Mel asked excitedly, scoping the room. He saw him and then sat down in their booth.

"Of course you may," said Wilton.

"Huh? Oh," Mel said. "May I sit down?" Mel gave Victor Lippton a subtle gladhand, trying to catch his eye. He kept focused on him all the time he talked to Kate, or rather to her through Wilton. "What do you suppose her problem is, Winston?"

"Wilton," Wilton said.

"Why would she keep it a secret from me, who her progenitors were?"

"Hard to believe you're a Hollywood agent, using a word like that."

"It was in Jane Austen. I can't believe the career she's having." Eyes still on Lippton, he addressed Wilton, carom-shooting at Kate. "So why do you think she kept it from me? Did she think I wouldn't love her for herself?"

"Maybe she already knew that," said Wilton.

"Well, she's wrong. If I didn't care about her, why would I have taken the time to read those crummy little stories?"

Kate tried not to seem wounded. "I didn't even think you read them."

"Saving the big guns," Mel said. "Your grandpa—"

"He *isn't*."

"Why do you deny it?"

"Because it isn't true. He had only one daughter. Scotty."

"That was with what's-her-name. Zelda. You came from the kid he had with the gossip columnist. Sheilah Graham."

"What?"

"You don't have to do this dance with me, kiddo. I already got a

85

call from the *Enquirer*. Somehow they found out I was your agent. Out of loyalty, I told them nothing, except how talented you are."

"He didn't have a child with Sheilah Graham," Kate said.

"Don't tell me. I saw *Beloved Infidel*. I always knew they left something out."

"This is ridiculous," Kate said.

"I find it very entertaining," said Wilton.

"If you're as smart as you'd like to think you are, and I thought you were, or I wouldn't have taken you on," Mel said, "you'll work up a CV. A sample of your writing, and a short pitch on the Fitzgerald novel. I hope it has more balls than *The Last Tycoon*. That laid a really big one." He suddenly was on his feet, as Victor Lippton, gray suit matching his leonine head of hair, strode towards their corner.

"Victor!" Mel cried, hand extended. "Victor! How kind of you to come over. I wasn't sure you saw me."

"I'll be with you in a minute," Victor Lippton said to the O.J. lawyer, at the table where he had obviously been heading.

"Victor Lippton, say hello to Winston, and my new star client, Kate Donnelly."

"Well, *hello*," Lippton said, and held out his hand. "It's a privilege to meet you." His smile was quite wide, and sincere. "That's exciting about the manuscript. I'm sorry it's sold. How are you, Wilton?"

Wilton just smiled.

"I haven't closed the deal for her yet," Mel said excitedly.

"Really?"

"*That's* the truth," Kate said, caught between disgust and elation. Victor Lippton. The top power player of them all.

"We're having a screening tomorrow night of Arnold's new picture at the studio. I'd like you to come as my guest. You, too, Wilton . . . " Lippton hesitated. "And . . . "

"Mel. Mel Brynner. We met at the party for Eva Marie."

"A lovely woman. Proof that our industry can produce and sustain first-rate people with balanced lives." Victor Lippton had moved to Los Angeles only a few months before, after an entire young lifetime in the tobacco business, and had made his adoptive city and movies his primary connection, as though he had lived and worked there always. There was a formality to his speech, a studied grace to his proprietary effort at belonging, like Joseph Conrad's writing in his second language what nobody else could in their first. "Too many of the people who have written about Hollywood have come at it with bitterness. They don't see the heroes and heroines here. Your grandfather did."

"But then he was a dreamer and a drunk," Kate said. "And he didn't live here very long. So he didn't really know the place that well."

"We'll be at the screening," Mel said quickly. "What time is it?"

"Eight o'clock." Victor smiled at Kate. "I'll look forward."

$\mathcal{H}$ow could you be so disrespectful," Mel said, sitting down again, covering his face, as though he were grieving. He took his hands away. "Is that a way to talk about a grandfather? Calling him a drunk?"

"Well, he was. And he wasn't my grandfather."

"Look, kid." He touched her shoulder. "Yesterday I couldn't have gotten you a meeting at Cosmos with the twelve-year-olds they have running their development program. Today you got invited by the owner. Not the president. Not the CEO. The *owner*. We're going to a screening at *his* studio. At *his* invitation."

"I'm going with Wilton," she said.

"Thank you," said Wilton. "Can Winston come, too?"

"Look." Mel turned to Wilton. "She's new in town. She doesn't understand how it works. If she goes with me, I can close the deal right there, when he's up, feeling good after the screening."

"I'm going with Wilton," Kate said stubbornly.

"You're going to make me go with my wife?"

"I guess if you're going . . . " Kate said.

"Why don't the four of us go together," said Mel. "I'll pick you up at seven-fifteen tomorrow. What's the address? The place with the rats?"

"We'll meet you at the screening," Kate said.

"It was nice meeting you, Nell," said Wilton.

$\mathcal{W}$hat a jerk," said Kate after he was gone.

"He means well, I think," said Wilton. "They're all jerks. You just have to find the one with the best intentions."

"But why would a man like Victor Lippton do business with someone like that?"

"Because he represents *you*. And you don't have to hold Victor Lippton in such high regard. He has this incredibly beautiful and cultured wife, and he's forking a lunatic."

"How do you know?"

"She's my customer. Or she *was*. I had to get rid of her. She was calling me twelve times a day, in between calls to her astrologer. I had to put my phone on call block so she'd leave me alone.

"And he's just as crazy as she is, or he wouldn't be involved with her. He started to call me, too, to find out where she was, when she wasn't where she said she was, because she was trying to drive him crazy. I had to call block him, too."

"The most powerful man in town," said Kate, smiling, admiring.

"Not for me," Wilton said. "All he did for me was keep my line busy so my customers couldn't call. I don't have the time he does. I have to earn a living."

*T*he beautiful wife of Victor Lippton shopped only on Rodeo Drive, except for an occasional charity buy she threw to Barney's. The department store was flawlessly constructed, an architectural masterpiece, its interior as well appointed visually as the banks designed by David Foster and I.M. Pei in Hong Kong, where her father had been king, at least until the handover, and Money was God, as opposed to America, where Power was God, and her husband was emperor. It touched Chen spiritually that Barney's, though it was so airy and light it could have been a cathedral with counters, might be going under. So she went there to pick up something pricey for the next evening's event, knowing that she by herself could not save the chain, but tales of her buying there could send those who marked her movements into copying them.

Chen bought a gold lace Ralph Lauren, naked as lingerie, the costliest dress they had in stock, even though it wasn't one of a kind. And because the evening would probably be cool, and the nude look somewhat chilly, she bought a gold brocade Chanel jacket, tight through the shoulders, just covering what she had of breasts.

"And what is the name on the account?" said the saleswoman.

"Victor Lippton," said Chen.

The woman watching her waited until Chen was on the escalator going down. She picked out the same two items.

"And the name on the account?" another salesgirl said.

"Victor Lippton," she answered.

*B*ecause Wendy could no longer use her title, she stood in Bullock's Westwood puzzling over what monogram to put on her towels. Shopping for household things was totally alien to her. All her very young life she had lived at boarding schools, or in the home of her parents, or in the castle of her husband, where linens were provided. She had never been aware they weren't automatically part of the landscape, like grass.

When the marriage ended, she had no idea that anyone might actually come to her aid. Her parents had moved to a condo in Nice, which they'd bought from selling her childhood photos. A naked one in the bathtub had been peddled in a packet with the telephoto nude of Jackie Onassis on her private Greek island, first printed in Hustler under the heading "The Billion Dollar Bush," reissued with a black border to commemorate her passing.

So when the call had come from Samantha Chatsworth, who'd been, the few times they'd met, extremely warm in an English way, inviting Wendy to come to Los Angeles, she'd gratefully accepted. At the time she had thought it would be just for a visit. But everyone had been so kind, she'd stayed. Besides, it was warm. She'd spent most of her winters huddled, all the more since the indignity started to set in. She welcomed the improbable, almost constant sunshine of California, and the existence of undeviating, unsalaried loyalties, like Samantha's.

Samantha stood beside her now, along with the bodyguard the royals had given Wendy, as Los Angeles was a lunatic place, and the last thing they needed was a martyred dumped duchess. "Definitely the right color," Samantha was saying, looking at the lush weave of the royal blue.

"But what shall I put on them?" Wendy asked. "I'm not allowed to use the family name. I assume that includes the initials. And I don't want to go back to my maiden name." She tried not to think about her parents, tanning in the south of France, negotiating with Robin Leach for a tell-all interview, a piece of intelligence she had picked up from watching *Hard Copy*, which she promised herself she would never do again. "What shall I put on them for a monogram?"

"Why not just *W*, for Wendy," Samantha said. And the fashion magazine, she didn't add. Because if her plan materialized, the darling once duchess would be the queen of the fashion world, which she already was, but in a reluctant way. It was Samantha's plan to make it aggressive, unmistakable, marketable. Her allegiance was to *East* magazine, but she wouldn't have minded a leg up with Fairchild publications. One had to look to one's later years, especially when one hadn't been given stock in one's own corporation, which even the drudges at Time, Inc. had gotten. "And woman," she added. "Because that's what you're becoming. A symbol for womankind."

"I hardly think so," Wendy said.

"But it's true, dear. You're an inspiration to us all. Put on the planet to guide your fellow feminines, who might, without your presence, and the discernment you practice, not know how to conduct themselves." She was laying it on a little heavily, but the girl was understandably still shockingly insecure, and it was Samantha's chosen task to bolster, if they were to make money. "Cast out into the storm by a wicked landlord . . . "

"Oh, you musn't say that about him," Wendy said.

"You see, that's what I mean. Even after the way you've been treated, not a nasty word. You are a living example of loving kindness. A true Christian. Practically a Buddhist."

"I'm supposed to be on my lunch hour," said the salesgirl.

*T*hey ordered the towels with the monogrammed *W*, and went back out to the subterranean parking lot where their car was parked. A young woman with long legs got out of a black Saab and greeted Samantha.

"How are you, Miss Chatsworth?" she said.

Samantha hadn't the least idea who she was. She smiled an automatic smile.

"Kate Donnelly," said the young woman. "We met yesterday at the funeral."

"Sad," said the ex-duchess. "He was kind."

"Did you know him well?" Kate asked her.

"Oh, you're the granddaughter," said Samantha, connecting. The garage was one of those gray, underground, cement-poled places that gave those with collective racial fears flashbacks to the concentration camps where they'd never actually been. Tunneling up at one side into the sunlight, the rest was minimally lit, as though there were no real security problems thus far in this area of Los Angeles, at least. In the shadowy, obfuscated environs, the girl looked rather sallow, as Wendy looked less lovely than fame had made her. "This is . . . "

"Wendy." The once duchess held out her hand, her own name having been clarified for her with the decision about the towels. She would be simply Wendy, only Wendy, as Madonna was only Madonna, only the virtuous version. The one who struggled for the good of her fellow Ws.

"It's an honor," Kate said, and lowered her head a little, the upper-body version of a curtsey.

"Thank you." Wendy smiled. "For me, too." Now that she had bought her own towels, Wendy coveted a little more of what she considered independence: the spontaneity that Americans had. Not coming from set rules of behavior or prepared dialogue, but saying what seemed real, doing what felt open, like the hearts and hearths around her.

"We've got to be going," said Samantha briskly.

"Wen . . . dy . . . " Kate said charily, not sure it was right to address her so, even though she had implicitly been given permission. "You're so keyed in to style. What should I buy for a screening at a studio? They said informal, but I'm not sure what that means here."

"Have you got gobs of money?" Wendy asked, with unaccustomed bluntness, setting aside her protective coloration, the drab skipping about things that came with her former territory.

"Not really," said Kate.

"Well, then why don't I just lend you something?" Wendy said, deliberately ignoring Samantha's scowl. "I've got tons of clothes that would be perfect. For hospital openings, visiting orphans, bank celebrations, the occasional ship launch. Worn one time only. We look the same size."

"I couldn't," said Kate, flabbergasted.

"That's right," Samantha said. "She couldn't."

"But they'll only go to waste," Wendy said. "Please. Byron," she instructed the bodyguard, "give her my address."

"But . . . " Kate said.

"I'll expect you around four," said Wendy.

The company that had loaned Samantha the Silver Cloud had not seen their name in print in spite of all the press around Drayco's funeral, so they had taken back the limousine, until, they'd said, she anted up. Wendy was still nervous about driving herself in Los Angeles, as she lost concentration a lot of the time and drifted to the wrong side of the road. The bodyguard did not like to act as driver, since that wasn't what he was hired for. Samantha herself had a ten-year-old 190 E Mercedes, but it needed a new muffler, for which the Benz repair people wanted almost four thousand, just a little less than the Blue Book value of her car. The car still looked good, but as noise-sensitive as Wendy was, Samantha didn't want her irritated, as irritated as she herself was by Wendy's imprudence, putting herself at risk, letting someone unknown into her circle, around which Samantha had kept a very tight rubber band.

The car that waited for them was a Lincoln. The driver was Morton Schein. He had told Wendy he was at her service, and he meant it. "Your carriage awaits without, my lady," he said, with mocking grandeur, sweeping his hand through the air as he held the back door open for her.

"Thank you, Morty," she said, smiling.

"You're supposed to say, 'Without what?' " Morton said.

"Without what?" said Wendy.

"Without horses," he said, and laughed. "An old joke but a bad one."

Wendy laughed.

"Don't encourage him," Samantha said, getting into the other side. "You laugh at that, he'll start telling jokes all the time."

"I like jokes," said Wendy. "Not many of the people I knew told jokes. They just played them."

"You mean like shorting the sheets?" asked the bodyguard. "Putting frogs in your bed?"

"I didn't know she was French," said Morton, and turned on the ignition.

"How could you do that?" Samantha asked Wendy, fuming, not knowing how to show anger to fallen royalty, knowing she oughtn't to show it at all, but seething inside. "How could you offer clothes and give your address to a perfect stranger?"

"You knew her."

"I only met her yesterday," Samantha said, as the car pulled up the ramp into the blazing sunlight and they all put on their sunglasses at once. "And I didn't even remember her."

"You said she was Larry Drayco's granddaughter. She's just suffered a loss." Her voice was filled with an understanding of loss, compassion for those who had experienced it.

"Not *his* granddaughter. Fitzgerald's. The American writer."

"Then it's even more meaningful," Wendy said. "You told me I was put on the planet to guide my fellow feminines." As questionable as Wendy's intelligence might have been, as negatively publicized for the purpose of making the house look better than one of its tenants, she had mastered the gift of remembering speeches to the letter, since she'd been forced to make so many of them, and had had so many made to her. "To inspire those who might, without my presence, and discernment, not know how to conduct themselves. Certainly it should be that way with clothes."

"I intended for you to have a line of clothing, not to give yours away," said Samantha.

"But she seems quite a nice girl, and pretty. I would only have given them to . . . what do you call it here? Good Will."

"You would have been better off," said Samantha, raging inside, fearful of something she couldn't quite pinpoint.

*T*his would be quite comely on you," Wendy was saying, holding out a beige cocktail dress with subtle gold threads and a chocolate weave through it. "To bring out your coloring."

Byron sat nearby, his jacket open so his gun would be easily accessible, as Samantha had cautioned him to do, unable to be present herself, since she did still have a job. The apartment was decorated with upscale rental furniture that Samantha had had an interior designer friend pick out in a day, so Wendy would feel comfortable till the good antiques arrived from home, once the in-laws had conducted the estate sale. She had wearied of the suite at the refurbished Beverly Hills Hotel, where there were always reporters waiting in the lobby for the arrival of Claudia Schiffer, or the reported return of Roman Polanski, incognito, always said to be in the offing.

"But what if I spill something on it?" Kate was saying.

"Then you shall send it to the cleaners. It's yours to keep anyway. I shan't want to wear it again. I might remember where I'd worn it last." Her blue eyes misted, the whites showing underneath, melancholy, silent movie portentous. "What's your shoe size?"

"Seven," Kate said.

"How lucky. Mine, too. I have matching shoes. Well, not matching exactly. That would be, what's your wonderful American word . . . tacky?" She was on her knees in the bottom of her walk-in closet. "But coordinated." She sat back on her haunches, holding them out.

"I couldn't."

"Of course you could. And must. I even have the perfect purse." She stood now, foraging through her well-stacked shelves of purses. "Bags are very much in again, according to Samantha, largely because of how well I carry them." She held the appropriate one she had chosen by the handle, at her hip, clutched it to her side, looped it over her arm, demonstrating. "Isn't that fashionable? A little superficial and trivial of course, but that's what people think I am."

"But you're not," said Kate. "You're so thoughtful. Aldous Huxley said, 'In the end, all that matters is to be kind.' "

"Did he say that?" Wendy asked. "No wonder he had to move to California. It must be so reassuring to come from people with genuine gifts, instead of those who give them to restrict you."

Kate reddened. Another opportunity to tell the truth. Clear up the misunderstanding with this lovely spirit at least. But explaining was so complicated. And she had already seen what clout the ingenious lie had in this society, as opposed to the pedestrian truth. She had seen her own name brandished across slick trade papers, and from those onto envelopes of sleek invitations. It was as though deceit were the local fairy godmother, transporting you to the ball.

She was starting to imagine it might be possible in such an environment to be able to live with a falsehood. Might even be comfortable, like Wendy's shoes. So "What can I do for *you?*" was all she said.

"You can have a happy life," Wendy said, the corners of her mouth suddenly pulled down, as though weights had been attached to them. "Excuse me." She ran to the bathroom and shut the door.

*W*hen she got home, Kate tried on her new ensemble. It looked wonderful. Wendy had a perfect eye. Kate held the purse on her wrist, clutched it, let it fall from her arm against her hip, as Wendy had demonstrated. She opened the clasp. Inside was a letter. "My dearest darling," it read, in a masculine hand. "It hurts my heart to see you, and not be able to speak because of all those who might be watching . . . "

Kate's mind raced, imagining who it might be from. She read no further, but folded it over, set it inside an envelope of her own, reached for notepaper.

"Dear . . . " She hesitated, and then wrote, "Wendy. I cannot thank you enough for your generosity of spirit and material both. I shall feel proud to be wearing something so lovely, especially remembering its source, and try to sport it with a portion of your grace." She added a P.S. "The enclosed was in your bag. I return it, unread, in case you need it."

She messengered it with an arrangement from her local florist, and her telephone number. She had no expectations that Wendy would ever call.

*W*hen Kate was in bed, in the darkness, the rustling started in the pantry again. Sanguine now about it, she went downstairs, and beamed her flashlight on the cereal box. There was movement, chomping, shaking. She took it to the freezer and shut it inside, without thought, without hesitation.

And in the night when she couldn't sleep and heard more rustling, she got up and dressed, and went to the twenty-four-hour market on the corner of Beverly. She bought Corn Flakes, Raisin Bran, and Cocoa Puffs, in case one of the rats was a chocoholic. Then she bought a Kellogg's variety pack, a cellophaned assortment of different cereals, in the event smaller members of the family had individual tastes.

That it was becoming cold-blooded, premeditated, was something she excised from her mind. There were rats in the place where she lived. What she was doing was inventive, like omission of the truth with people who didn't particularly want to hear it. Like a novel one might write pretending to be someone else, if one wrote well enough, and had a really good story.

Setting out the cereals in a neat little arrangement in the pantry, she felt more inspired than censurable. Wasn't it your own comic darkness, really, that gave you dominion over things you couldn't see, but were aware had the power to harm you? Resourcefulness was the key. Wit was the power. Dark humor was the salvation.

Hearing the shadowy rustle in the silence, being frightened by it, but finding a way to deal with it by discovering the cunning shadow in yourself, was the answer. Somehow managing both to take on the adversary, put him in his place (she knew what she would find in the morning in the freezer) and to find that part of you that, too, was capable of darkness. Somehow making it into a joke. That was the best part. Even unwitting wit would do.

Here she was now. What she had become. A cereal killer.

A Stalker's Daisy Chain

$\mathcal{F}$light 2 for New York left LAX at nine in the morning. Tyler went directly to the gate, as he had no luggage but the small rucksack he was carrying. The attendant checked him in, and let him preboard. Although he wasn't traveling with small children, there was something so innocent about the young man. Big as he was, he seemed almost childlike, and the attendant wanted to take extra care of him.

So Tyler didn't see Helen Manning stumble up to the gate, loaded down with hand luggage, all the things she had considered at the last moment she might need and didn't want to lose in the event the plane went down. There were many who had offered to help her, from the driver of her car, to the porter at the curb, to those who checked her through security and marveled at what they saw in the X ray: hair blower *and* electric curlers, a cosmetics case filled to bursting with what appeared to be an arsenal of pills and medications, jewels enough for an auction at Sotheby's. Helen had declined all offers of aid, although she had never gone on a trip when there hadn't been at least two people to carry things for her, one of them usually a lover or a husband, the latter's status determining how many people there were to carry things for him so he could carry things for her. But this was the first time in all her life that she was in pursuit, and as he was young, and strong, and doubtless idealistic, he would want her to pull her own weight. So she started with her hand luggage.

"Here, let me help you on board with that," said three flight attendants simultaneously. Everybody laughed, including Helen, who'd been very close to tears because she'd never realized how much all that shit weighed.

They took it from her, and saw her to her seat. It was right behind his. Already she could recognize Tyler from the golden crest of his hair, a sign of infatuation she hadn't experienced since her thirteenth year, when they were schooling her at the studio as part of her contract, and she'd gotten a crush on the back of her tutor's neck.

"Do you mind sitting by the emergency door?" the flight attendant asked her, as he stuffed one of her bags, the one that wouldn't fit in the overhead bin, under the seat in front of her. "We might need your help during an emergency procedure. Is that all right?"

"Actually, I'd like it," Helen said, her mind going to the moment when the plane flipped down in the water and she had to be the one in charge of abandoning ship, opening the door, easing everyone past her. She would exchange a a meaningful look with him just before he slid down the chute. He would say, "I can't leave you like this," and pull her after him, so their bodies were entwined, pressed hotly together in that chilling moment before they hit the life raft.

She was already exhausted from the ordeal of packing, which always involved an oath not to take so much next time, and the carrying, and the settling into the seat, and the relief of seeing he was, in fact, on board, not to mention the fantasy of their being in a crash together. So as soon as she fastened her safety belt, she fell sound asleep.

Sarah Nash boarded the plane and saw who was sleeping beside her assigned place. "If you don't mind," she said to the flight attendant, "I think you'd better change my seat."

"You object to having to deal with the door in the event of emergency?"

"Let's just say that's it," Sarah said, not wanting to go into an explanation about what might happen if Helen awoke and saw who she was sitting next to. She had not been one of the most pilloried—nothing in Sarah's book being worse than what Kitty Kelley might have revealed, and probably had. But with various friends, Helen had joined in an *entente* less than *cordiale* not to have anything to do with Sarah. So waking up next to her might have caused a scene, and Sarah wasn't up for it.

"I'll be glad to change seats with you," said a fiftyish man, a look of renewal in his eyes, unconcealed joy at his good fortune.

"You're very kind," said Sarah, pleasantly, waiting till she was in the other seat and buckled to add, under her breath, "and optimistic."

*B*ehind them, in business class, Arthur Finster regretted now that he had not traveled first. His life was filled with little economies, most of them at the expense of other people. There were writers who, in their desperation, waived royalties for a quick advance, and saw their books become mass market bestsellers, the profits all going to Arthur. There were the subjects of the tawdry publications, who had also signed away all future claims in exchange for airfare and someplace to hide. And not least, there were the physical publishers, the printers, with their Central American presses, compared to whose factories sweatshops would have seemed Carnival cruises.

But this was the first time, since he had money, that he had stinted on himself. And seeing who was up there in first, he was sorry not to have flown the same. All the more so since it would have been tax deductible.

He was on his way to New York to do a TV show and find a lawyer. Any attorney with stature, anyone decent in L.A., was refusing to take him as a client. Not that he would have minded someone without integrity, a no-holds-barred sleazeball, like (he was nothing if not honest) himself. But as the world now understood, what the law was about was not justice, but lawyers. Juries voted not on the issue or the evidence, but according to which lawyer they liked better.

So he was sorry not to have flown first class, less so when the plane hit terrible turbulence and his primary concern became not who you spent time with socially, but who you died with. Jesus Christ. Helen Manning, of course, would get the headline. Sarah Nash coming in second. If the L.A. *Times* front-paged it, which they certainly would, he might not get any more than a mention one column down. "Also lost in the crash was Arthur Finster, the controversial publisher," it would probably say. "The despised publisher," perhaps. He didn't mind. As long as he was remembered.

But after a good, or bad, half hour of flingings and stomach-churning downdrafts, the plane resettled on its normal course. And all Arthur had to worry about was the show, and where to start to look for a shyster who seemed like a good guy.

*I*n spite of the fact that he had no reason to wait for his luggage, since he was carrying all he needed, Tyler stood by the baggage carousel watching Sarah Nash wait for hers. She bit her lips with a nervous continuity, so that at moments she seemed to have no lower lip at all. In the part of his heart that was not on the job for Norman Jessup, he felt genuinely sorry for her. Pity was judgmental, and made the one feeling it think he was above and apart from the other person. So Tyler tried very hard to integrate what he was experiencing into his own being, and feel compassion. But it was difficult to identify with someone who had gone out of her way to be unkind. And she had matching luggage, embroidered, tapestry, so she was really into the externals, the bullshit that had probably trapped her into becoming vicious.

*H*elen Manning was relieved to see that Tyler was not dashing off as she feared he might, with the jauntiness that came from having only one thing to carry, not to mention youth. Her limousine driver had relieved her of her hand luggage, and was waiting for her rest of her things. So she was free to saunter over to where Tyler was leaning, although sauntering was not easy with the height of her heels. She regretted not having worn the sneakers she'd bought for her foray into Norman's office.

"Oh, hi," she said, like it was a surprise, finding him there. "Aren't you that friend of Norman Jessup's?"

"Which friend is that?" Tyler said, his eyes still someplace else.

It moved her that he had the self-possession to look past her, at the same time giving her clear access to all that was inside him. From her vantage point, she saw depth, intelligence, sensitivity, and, almost more important, eyes that were more dazzling than her own. What would Bunyan call these, if hers were phoenix eyes? Tyler's were an intense blue, but pale, paler than blue topaz. Nor was there more than the slightest hint of green, so they weren't aquamarine. Really what they were was crystal blue, not precious enough to describe them, not rare enough. She wished she had Bunyan's gift for imagery and a knowledge of stones that were not semiprecious, other than diamonds, which wouldn't have done it at all.

And his smell was quite wonderful. Slightly toasty. Fresh from the shower that morning, clean, warmed in its own juice during the flight. Very much his own scent, inoffensive but male, reassuring. It reached someplace deeper than her nostrils.

"The one who was with him and Carina at Morton's," she said. "It must have been a Monday."

"*Must?* Because you, like everyone else there, are a victim of the 'shoulds'?" he asked, smiling.

"Victim?" she said, bristling, although she didn't know why, since she didn't really understand him. "Shoulds?"

"Monday nights," he said, and looked straight at her, the merriment undisguised, a tiny dimple appearing to the left of his generous mouth. "We should go to Morton's. The categorical imperative of a society with no philosophy."

"I was invited," she said, trying not to sound petulant.

"It wasn't an attack," he said gently.

"Well, I don't know if I'm glad or sorry. At least if someone attacks you, you know you're having an effect on them."

He looked straight into her eyes. She felt absolutely giddy.

"You have an effect on everybody," he said. "You don't need to have one on me."

She looked away, actually feeling herself blush. Blushing, for God's sake. Even when she'd been an ingenue, she hadn't been an ingenue.

"I gotta go," he said, and started to move past her.

She could feel his warmth, even without touching. "Can I give you a lift into town? I have a limousine."

"So do I. Thanks anyway."

"I could use a ride," said Arthur Finster, who was standing an eavesdrop away.

"Take a cab," Helen said, signaling to her driver.

$\mathcal{S}$arah Nash had called ahead to Tel Aviv taxi. It was a comedown, of course, from the days of the curbside limo, but a cut above a regular cab. And they always sent a good car for her now, with a woman driver, Carmen, a Cuban who also sold jewelry. All the way into town Sarah would try on rings and pretend that her hands were really lovely, instead of square and stubby-fingered. She would flash the jewels at herself, and try not to despise the men who had never given her any, reaffirm that she was completely independent, wanted no man in her life anymore, even one who would bejewel her.

"Where we going?" Felicia asked her.

"The Carlyle." She sat back and watched the sparkle in the darkness, the sparkle on her hands, the sparkle across the bridge, the pileup of lights that blinked and beckoned more seductively than stars. People still shook their fist at that city, figured they could beat it. For all its toughness, New York seemed to Sarah more innocent than L.A., because if you connected big enough, it forgave you. Welcomed you to its concrete bosom, asked you to all the best parties, gave parties for you, where the guest list was what passed for a meritocracy. A culture where achievement was honored, especially when you scapegoated another city. She would have moved there if it hadn't been so wind chill–factored in the winter.

Fortunately, it was spring now. As young men's fancies turned to thoughts of love, hers returned to revenge. It was just after six. Too late to set up any investigatory appointments for this evening. Maybe she would just have a quiet dinner in her room, telephone Chuck and make him nervous, and start her uncovering tomorrow.

*T*he Tel Aviv taxi crossed the 59th Street Bridge with a limousine behind it and a limousine after that. The unintentional caravan at last reached its destination. Tyler went in the Madison Avenue entrance to the Carlyle. Sarah Nash had her luggage unloaded at the side, where the doorman was, and the welcome that made it worth not getting a break on the price of the room.

*N*ow that she knew where Tyler was staying, Helen had her driver circle the block a few times, so she could phone from the car and make a reservation. They were fully booked, but after a weep to the manager, explaining she'd come to the city for the funeral of her father, he managed to make a place for her, giving up the suite he was holding for his dearest friend.

Being himself one of the few great gentlemanly toffs left on the planet, as nattily clad as he was jolly, the manager of the Carlyle, after dealing with the crisis on the phone, stepped behind the reception desk and saw Tyler. He tried not to react to the deliberately worn-through-the-knees jeans. But he did have a bad moment.

Then he looked at the name on the register, at the same time noting the great beauty of the boy, and remembered that Norman Jessup was paying the bill. So he thought, Oh, well. As Tyler himself often thought or said Oh, well, releasing it to the universe. First class hotel managers were every bit in their way as attuned to the mysteries as metaphysicians.

1 hate all this spying and sneaking around," Tyler said to Norman on the phone.

"*Hate* isn't in your vocabulary," said Norman. "I thought it was all about love and light."

"It can't be when you're being devious and manipulative. Let her go, Norman. The only way Sarah can really beat you is if you empower her, give her power over you. Let her go."

"Find out first what she's doing, and where she's going, and when I know, I'll let her go."

"I wish I could believe you," Tyler said.

"Visualize it happening," said Norman. "Affirm it. Claim it. Isn't that how it works?"

"Only if you're not making fun of it," said Tyler.

The ballet company at City Center was in rehearsal all during the day, the stage empty, the scenery for the evening performance of another ballet carefully pushed out of the way. Alexander Winsett, the choreographer, had a lot on his mind, more than enough, what with dancers leaving and dancers dying, and the New York City Ballet at Lincoln Center with its best program in years, and there not being the appetite or vast audience for dance there had been once. On top of all his other concerns, he was having to parry the intrusive thrusts of this Hollywood harridan.

He tried to take mental sanctuary in the sense of community and safety the group provided, as the dancers did, the balletic version of the spiritual *sanga*. But the dancers were on a break, and this woman was continuing to grill him as she had most of the afternoon, waiting for the moments when he stopped to think, in order to interrupt the flow of his thinking. Right now he didn't have the dancers' physical presence to fortify him, with the exception of one eager girl from Michigan, who continued practicing fouettés, a kind of virtuoso whipping pirouette, around the stage.

Winsett and Sarah were sitting in one of the empty rows. He was two seats away from her. But he still had the suffocated feeling she was on top of him.

"And you brought Paulo up from Brazil?" Sarah Nash was saying, holding her tape recorder out like a gun.

She had asked his permission to record their conversation. Assaulted by her persistence, the overwhelming number of phone calls he had received from her the night before, he had assented, thinking it might be for his own protection as well as hers.

"He brought himself up from Brazil," Winsett said. "Or rather, his company brought him. Capoeiras de Bahia. An inspired group." He had a towel around his muscular shoulders, soaking up the sweat he could work up even in his head as he directed the company's movements. They were rehearsing *Midsummer Night's Dream*, part Balanchine, part Winsett himself, a mélange that had set the purists screaming in advance. But he wasn't afraid of critics or the ballet community and its advocates, having lost so many friends in the past few years he knew not to be fearful of words or opinions. Still, this woman frightened him, with her scarlet Mohawk with its shaven sides, and her relentlessness.

"How old was he?"

"Fourteen."

"You really start them young," she said.

He tried to read her for facetiousness. "A dancer's life is limited," he said. "The knees usually go by forty."

"And you persuaded him to stay in New York?"

"That was his original hope in coming here. That an American ballet company would want him."

"Or an American ballet master?"

"I have accepted the fact that you are tenacious, Miss Nash. I won't abide your being rude." He started to get up.

"Please," she said, and reached with a hand to his arm, a gesture she supposed would comfort him. "Forgive me. I didn't sleep very well. I didn't mean to be discourteous. I'd much rather talk *to* you than to people who talk about you."

"Is that an apology, or a threat?" he asked.

"Both," she said, and smiled.

He sat back down.

"You did become lovers?" When he didn't answer, she softened her voice. "Look . . . besides being politically correct now, so you have nothing to be uncomfortable about, I have this enterprising assistant who spoke to a bunch of dancers, and they all said—"

"Yes, we were lovers," he said, suddenly old. His hair was thinning and grayish blond, the high forehead that in his youth had been taken quite correctly as indicating intelligence expanded now almost to brilliance. He had prominent cheekbones, slightly caved in underneath, and dark eyes that scanned her for danger, found it. He shifted in the chair. "Why don't you just talk to Paulo?"

"I'd be happy to, if I could find out where he was."

"He isn't in California?"

"No. One of the dancers said he stayed in New York. Weren't you guys in touch?"

"We had a falling out."

"Over Norman Jessup?"

"It doesn't matter what it was over," said Winsett. "We stopped being associates *and* friends."

"But the dance world is supposed to be pretty small and incestuous. You must have heard something about what happened to him."

"Not a word."

"And that doesn't strike you as odd?"

"Only if I was interested."

"Well, I'm really interested, and it strikes me as *more* than odd. It strikes me as highly peculiar that a man could disappear and no one has a clue where he went. Does he have a family?"

"They're all dead."

"Of natural causes?" Sarah grinned. "Only kidding. It just makes it so convenient, you know, nobody who might care about him being around to ask questions."

"Like you, you mean. Do you care about him?"

"I don't know him."

"Then why do you care?"

"I'm interested in Norman Jessup. Paulo left you for Norman, didn't he?"

"Will you ask her to please stop hogging the stage!" a young man in leotards called out to Winsett. "We know how earnest they are in Michigan, but she's not the only one who wants to practice."

"You'll all have the stage in a moment," Winsett said. "The break is almost over." He turned to Sarah. "As is the interview."

"He did leave you for Norman," Sarah said.

"I'm in the middle of a real crisis here. I don't know if you've been following what's going on with this theater . . . "

"Theater and ballet aren't it for me," Sarah said. "That's nothing against you. I have nothing against you. I'd just like to know . . . the reason he left you."

"If you don't care to understand the feelings of theater people and dancers, you can't possibly understand Paulo. We all have dreams. Paulo's were bigger than mine. He'd been a dance sensation when he was a child in Brazil. There was major play about him when he first got to the States. But it never really happened as big as he thought it would. And then he met Norman. I guess . . . well, to be the love of a great man is the next best thing."

"You consider Norman Jessup a great man?"

"Paulo did," said Winsett. "I have to get back to work."

"When he left you, they took a place together. Here in New York, wasn't it?"

"I have to go," said Winsett. "All right, boys and girls," he said and clapped his hands. "Hit your marks."

Some choreographer named Winsett," Tyler said into the pay phone backstage. "She recorded whatever they were talking about. She's leaving the theater now."

"Follow her," Norman Jessup said.

"Follow her yourself," said Tyler. "This is not my style. I've had enough of this secret agent shit." He hung up the phone.

*W*hen Tyler reached the waning daylight, Helen Manning was standing outside the theater. She was by the box office, her purse in her hand, as though she were in the process of buying tickets. Tyler sort of pursed his mouth, a residual expression from before he had become totally openhearted, and cleansed, and still disbelieved people, sometimes actually looked doubtful, maybe even cynical.

"What a coincidence!" she said.

"Oh, come on," said Tyler. "Like you're not staying in the same hotel."

"You're at the Carlyle? Imagine that!" When she was cornered, Helen spoke in exclamation points, as though scriptwriters of quality had never made their way into her awareness, and she was caught in the comic books of her childhood, no option ahead of her but a Batman sequel.

"I don't have to," he said. "It's the reality."

He was clearly making fun of her. Even if he hadn't been clear about it, if he were being subtle or enigmatic, she would have picked up on it. She had never been stupid, and was rarely foolish, as she was being now. Her own behavior shamed her, but not enough to make her walk away from him. "Is there a reason you're giving me such a hard time?"

"I'm flattered that you're interested," he said. "But it can't go anywhere."

Ordinarily she would have brazened it out, in the best tradition of brazening, calling him presumptuous. "Presumptuous pup!" would have had a nice Bette Davis ring to it. But he seemed so honest, in addition to the rest of it, a kind of melancholy around the edges of his observation, that she had no choice but to be sincere. "Why does it have to? Aren't you one of those 'in the moment' people? That's what Bunyan Reis said. That you're very 'be here now.' Can't we just be here now?"

He looked at her, with her sleek white-gold chignon, and her sleeker body, draped now almost loosely with a pale blue fabric that made her less intimidating than the black she usually wore, but still showed her body off to advantage. As if anything would not show it off to advantage, lush as it was, overwhelming.

Tyler had few doubts about himself as a man. But as a young man who didn't know exactly where he was going, and had just blown off what little security he had, he had no wish to vanish into this gorgeous woman who ate tycoons for breakfast. Still, he could afford to be generous.

"Okay, we're here now," he said.

"My name is Helen Manning." She held out her hand.

"Like you had to tell me." He shook it. "Tyler Hayden."

"That wasn't so bad now, was it?"

He could still feel her palm in his hand. To his surprise, it had been a little clammy. As though she might be as uneasy, as unsure about all this as he was. "Not bad at all," he admitted.

"The best Italian restaurant in New York is just a quick cab ride away," she said. "May I invite you to dinner?"

"I'm not hungry," Tyler said.

"Of course you are," she said. "You're a growing boy."

*T*he manager of Felidia's considered himself fairly centered. Julie Andrews ate there all the time and Al Pacino came in for pasta and roasted fish whenever he was in New York, so John knew better than to be impressed by stars. Stars were just like other people, except other people were inordinately fascinated by them. So stars had more reason both to feel important and to feel insecure, since at any moment it might be taken away. John's pulse never raced at the sight of a celebrity, nor did his breath stop, only occasionally quicken. Still, when he saw Helen Manning, and she actually threw her arms around him, it did make him break into an adrenaline sweat.

"I didn't know you were in town," he said, leading her to the table she preferred, which he remembered well, as he knew most of the dialogue she'd spoken on screen by heart. He pulled the chair out for her, seating her facing the front of the restaurant, so everyone else, as they came in during the dinner hour which it was still a little early for, could see what no cat had dragged in. "Are you in New York to talk about a play?"

"Oh, once on Broadway was enough," she said, smiling up at him as she sat. "I was grateful to get out with my skin still on."

"What are you saying?" said John as he subtly signaled for the wine list. "The critics absolutely adored you."

"They were kind," she said.

"And *you* were great," he said. "You look fabulous. Champagne or something delicious and Italian? On me."

"How thoughtful," she said. "Tyler? You prefer champagne or wine?"

"I'll have a beer," Tyler said.

"I didn't know you had a son," said the manager.

She took a moment to answer. "Well, it was either that, or save France."

Tyler studied her face, digested the comment, and laughed.

"Dom Perignon," said the manager to the waiter, and, smiling, left their table.

"That was really cool," Tyler said. "I imagined you took yourself a lot more seriously."

"Imagined?" she said. "You've thought about me?"

"Of course."

"Then why so elusive?"

"Do you read many fairy tales?" Tyler asked.

"I did. Do you?"

"Well, I studied Jung, and he totally believed in mythologizing, you know, man's need to relate to bigger pictures than himself. Fairy tales are a way of mythologizing, that's why they've lasted so long."

"Your champagne," the waiter said, and popping the cork, poured for her, eyes fixed on her glass, intently, demonstrating that who she was would not distract him. "And what kind of beer did you want?" he asked Tyler.

"Anything that isn't filtered through carbon," Tyler said.

"They don't tell us that on the bottle," said the waiter.

"You have draft beer?" Tyler asked. The waiter nodded. "That'll be fine."

"Fairy tales," Helen prompted as the waiter moved away.

"Well, there's this one about the Golden Princess, who's slept with demons. So every time she makes love to a man, she cuts off his head. She can't help herself. And I can't afford to lose my head."

Helen covered her anguish with a sip of champagne. "I haven't slept with demons," she said. "The worst they were was not as great as they seemed. And of course Ricky drank and became physically abusive, but—"

"Ambition, that's the demon," Tyler interrupted. "Life, like fairy tales, is all about good and evil. Light and darkness. A constant struggle to avoid the shadow side."

"You don't have any ambition?"

"Not for things you'd understand."

"Try me."

Tyler took a breath, closed his eyes. She was moved to see he was even more beautiful with them shut, his lashes golden, sweeping down to his lightly tanned cheeks, like painted angel's wings on the overdone ceilings of Venice.

"I'd like to give them some visionary information," he said, "those morons you run with." He opened his eyes. They looked angry now, a deeper blue, storm clouds gathering over a turbulent sea. "They're blind. No spirit, no insight, no compassion. It's fucking gross.

"No sense of God, or their obligation to that awareness. No perception of what they owe other people. None of them taking the time to learn about life, or purpose, their metaphysical responsibility to what they put out. Lost adolescents whose biggest accomplishment is not being on drugs." His words were coming in a rush now, blazing, tempered only by the softness of his voice, which had a slightly grated edge to it.

"It's not okay that lightweights are running the world. Steven Seagal. Quentin Tarantino. Undeveloped, unintelligent, racist, sexist, homophobic—but in a hip way—a moron who thinks he's smart. Oliver Stone. Knowing nothing of beauty, nothing about real inspiration, with no real enthusiasm. You know where the word *enthusiasm* comes from?"

"Not really."

"En*theos,*" he said, as the waiter set his beer down. "To be infused with God."

"You want to make movies?" she asked, bottom-lining his quiet railing, seeing only his passion. She was even now picturing his ferocity unleashed in bed. She would have liked very much to be infused with God, if it came in that package.

"There are only two great rituals left on this planet that bring people together. Rock and roll, and the movies. Those people are telling people how to live, when they don't know what life is about. All of them morons except Spielberg and Tim Robbins. They should give someone access who cares about what really matters, and you'll see what happens."

"I'd be glad to try and get you access," she said, and meant it, suddenly seeing herself as that Joan of Arc who might have given birth at fifteen, had she not instead chosen to save Hollywood. Through this boy, this beautiful, charismatic boy, who cast spells even in a restaurant on East Fifty-eighth Street, radiating something otherworldly, a world she longed to join.

The waiter was setting something in front of them that he said was a special offering from the chef. Ravenous as she had been a few moments before, she was now completely without appetite. Except for Tyler's face, his eyes, his words, the ardor pouring from the mouth she kept seeing on hers. Because she wasn't like the rest of them, empty, never seeking. She read books all the time.

"I'd be glad to help you," Helen said.

"They wouldn't take me seriously if you did," he said. "They'd think it was because you wanted me."

"Anyone would want you," she said, and looked at him the way she'd only been able to look at men onscreen.

"And anyone would want you," he said, gently. "If they didn't mind losing their head."

*N*orman Jessup's private plane left Burbank a little after seven. He tried never to be angry when he flew, since in spite of the luxury of having his own aircraft, the experience always provoked a little anxiety. So he tried to feel loving and calm, for balance. But besides the inconvenience of having to make an unscheduled trip to New York, there was also his deep disappointment with Tyler.

In fact, he loved the boy on a level he hadn't felt since he was a boy himself and wished he had a brother. Now, as a man, he had found through Tyler the never-acknowledged, even to himself, wish to have a son. He'd discussed it at length with Carina, who'd responded with a sympathy that bordered on relief. And she'd been staunch in her support of Norman's feelings, sharing, for the moment, at least, his outrage at Tyler's having hung up on him, forcing him to make the trip to New York.

It was, of course, a different kind of betrayal from Sarah's. But it seemed to Norman betrayal nonetheless. He called Carina once the plane was sufficiently on course so the pilot wouldn't crash from the electronic interference.

"I hate it that I have to make this trip," Norman said.

"I know," she sort of whispered.

"I can't get over Tyler's being so disloyal."

"It isn't disloyalty, darling. It's not like he's telling Sarah she's being watched. He just doesn't want to do it anymore."

"You're such a calming influence," he said. "No wonder I love you. Besides how beautiful you are."

"Why don't you just hire a private detective?"

"I couldn't trust them not to blow the whistle on me if anything happened to Sarah. I'd be opening myself up to extortion."

"Is something going to happen to Sarah?"

"I don't know yet," Norman said.

"Are you going to talk to Winsett, and find out how much he told her?"

"Probably."

"What will you do if she finds out?"

"She won't find out. She can't find out."

"But what if she did?"

"That's easy," he said, and sort of laughed. "The same thing'll happen to her that happened to Paulo."

*W*hen he and Helen got back to the Carlyle, the desk clerk informed Tyler that regrettably, he said, they had received a phone call from Los Angeles canceling his credit, and so, also, the room. "I believe this is yours," the desk clerk said, handing him his rucksack, and his book.

"Stay with me," Helen whispered, pulling him back into what privacy could be found in that well-lit lobby, what shelter the pillars provided, the clever little niches where nothing was but huge urns filled with flowers, gloriously arranged.

"No, thanks," Tyler said. "I'll find someplace to sleep."

"Sleep with me," she murmured. "Sleep with me."

"Potiphar," he said. "Song of Solomon."

"Pardon?"

"You're quoting the Bible," he said.

"There's one next to the bed," she said. "We could read it together. You could infuse me with God."

"I have to go," he said, and stooped to kiss her, lightly, just on the surface of her mouth. But it seared her soul, and apparently, her skin. When she awoke in the morning, her lips were blistered.

Special Occasions

In spite of the fact that the evening had been designated informal, nearly all the women present at the screening were dressed, if not to the teeth, at least to the collarbone. The outside world saw Hollywood as an unending black-tie occasion, premiere after premiere, dinner party after concert after museum opening. In fact, for a group called The Blue Ribbon, women from old Los Angeles society, grown up around Hancock Park, life was a lot like that, since they were able to support many charities, and charity events almost always came in black tie. But for the ordinary citizen, or even the extraordinary one who had made it into the insider realms, there were not that many chances to dress up, it being the season of spare and bare, crocheted halters for those who were lean and high-breasted enough, suede hip-huggers and designer jeans, slender bandeaus and low-waisted white pants from Armani.

So informal at Cosmos, owned as the studio now was by Victor Lippton, whose family could be traced back to the tobacco fields adjacent to Thomas Jefferson's, and whose wife was a symbol of chic, meant that everybody could overdo. Several of the women present wore cocktail dresses with jewel necklines, officially allowing them to wear necklaces, Indian pearls and cabochon rubies, carved emeralds and hammered gold, nothing as flashy as Oscar-time diamonds, but elegant past what they could have sported even had the Bistro Gardens not closed.

Chen Lippton, Victor's fragilely beautiful Chinese wife, her tiny hand threaded through his arm, made her entrance in a gold lace Lauren that looked like a slip, her breasts barely making a curve in the cup. Over her arm she carried a gold brocade jacket, which came at that exact moment, like a dual vision in a fashion show, through the other door, worn over the bony shoulders of a white-skinned redhead, clad in the same lacy dress, but with the cups rounded out by impressive breasts. There was an audible gasp as both women reached the center aisle at exactly the same moment, Victor Lippton not even raising his eyes to take in the measure of the usurper, but hurrying his wife to the taped section of the auditorium.

Kate Donnelly was so concerned with her own place in what she now recognized as a minor spectacle that she hardly picked up on their embarrassing moment. "Where are we supposed to sit?" she asked Wilton.

"Well, the cordoned-off rows are for the people directly involved with the picture, or the studio," Wilton said.

"Did you hear the one about the three-thousand-pound gorilla?" Mel asked, moving eagerly towards Kate, his back to his wife.

"You mean where does he sit? Answer: anyplace he wants to?" asked Wilton.

"That used to be the joke," Mel said. "Now they say it about Michael Crichton."

"Ha ha," said Wilton.

"There don't seem to be any fours," said Kate. "We'd better split up."

"Would you like to sit with my wife?" asked Mel.

"No. I never even wanted one of my own."

"Oh. Well, see you after," Mel said, sorrowfully.

They moved into one of the rows. Wilton shook hands with the bespectacled man sitting next to him. "How are you, Asher?"

"On page two hundred," Asher said. "Just at the point where the boys mulcted Warners."

"Mulcted," Wilton said, sitting down on the aisle seat. "Such a literary word, and so ugly. Why don't you just say 'fucked'? Everybody knows that's what the two of them did."

"We don't all have your gift for street language," Asher said. "Especially in front of those who look like ladies."

"Kate Donnelly," Wilton said, "Asher Pfaltz. The literary critic and Hollywood historian."

"Oh, yes," Asher said, and took her in. "You're the girl who claims to be Fitzgerald's granddaughter."

"She *claims* nothing," said Wilton.

"That's absolutely true," said Kate.

"One of the best-documented lives in modern literary history. My closest friend wrote the definitive biography."

"Are you and Herb still together?" asked Wilton.

"He's moved to Vegas," said Asher.

"For the waters?" asked Wilton.

Asher fixed Kate with his lashless black eyes. "How could you imagine you would get away with it?"

"Get away with what?" asked Wilton.

Asher's look turned to glower. "You should have picked someone more obscure. Nathanael West. You might've put that one over."

"What are you saying, you ponce?" said Wilton.

"She's no more his granddaughter than I am."

"Actually . . . " He looked at him carefully. "There *is* a resemblance. But you're a little too butch. Not *much*, but . . . "

"Very funny," said Asher.

"Look, Asher," said Wilton, expansively. "They don't document the illegitimate side. Nobody was more carefully watched than Clark Gable, and what about his child with Loretta Young? By the time that came out, no one even remembered who Clark Gable was."

"What are we saying here?" Asher asked. "Are we saying someone popped unrecorded?"

"Sheilah Graham," said Wilton.

"There *was* always that whisper," Asher conceded, and then inhaled deeply. "Well, it's nice to meet you."

"Thank you," said Kate. "It's nice to meet you, too."

"Don't go overboard," said Wilton, as the lights went down.

*A*fterwards, a little feast was laid, as elaborate as at most weddings. Kate still had a knot in her belly from the encounter with Asher, so she didn't take a plate. "Come. You'll need your strength," said Wilton, fixing one for her.

"Why haven't you taken my calls?" the redheaded woman wearing the same outfit as Lippton's wife said, furiously.

"Life is too short," said Wilton, turning his back to her, guiding Kate away through the crowd. "Excuse me."

"What do I need my strength for?" Kate asked. "The comedown that's inevitable? The humiliation? In my whole life I've never been a phony."

"You're young," Wilton said. "You have plenty of time."

"If this Asher was suspicious . . . "

"He's a pompous asshole," said Wilton.

"Who are we talking about?" asked Mel, elbowing his way towards them.

"Asher Pfaltz."

"Nobody listens to a word he says," said Wilton.

"That's true," said Mel. "He reads."

"And knows his literary history," said Kate.

Wilton made his way towards the beluga. The caviar was set in the middle of a great iced bowl, the label still on the outside of the jar. "He's the literate local version of the foreign press. You can lead him around by the hors d'oeuvres."

"Let's just forget the whole story," Kate said.

"Ah, there you are," said Victor Lippton. "I've been looking for you." He handed her a glass of champagne. "How did you like the movie?"

"It's fun," Kate said.

"Arnold doesn't take himself seriously," said Victor. "That's what makes it work."

"I don't take myself seriously either," said Jake Alonzo, coming into their circle. "But some things hurt me to the quick."

"I've never really figured out where my quick was," Wilton said.

"Like what?" Kate asked Jake, smiling.

"Like when someone doesn't call me back. I don't make that many phone calls."

"You called me?" Kate asked.

"Don't you pick up your messages?"

"Well things have been happening so fast, I haven't had time to call my service." True, they'd been happening fast, but only in the past forty-eight hours. Before that she had been so dispirited by the lack of messages, she'd gotten out of the habit of checking.

117

"Services are *old*," Jake said. "Why don't you get a machine?"

"Something going on here?" Mel asked, looking back and forth between the two of them.

"Not yet," said Jake.

"Have you read that script I sent you?" Victor asked him.

"It isn't for me," said Jake.

"We could make the guy more sensitive," said Victor.

"He's still a hired killer."

"Well, we could change that."

"Then you'd lose the plot," said Jake.

"The plot isn't that important," said Victor. "Maybe you should take a look at it," he said to Kate.

"Me?"

"You want to do something with her, don't you?" Victor asked Jake.

"Well, yes, but . . . "

"As I begin to understand this town, I see where it's often about the pressures of time." Victor smiled. "You know, Gather ye rosebuds while ye may. To the Virgins, to make much of time."

"I didn't realize there were any left in Hollywood," Wilton said. "Rosebuds I mean."

Victor continued, unheeding. "If people are going to spend six months, a year, working on a project, it might as well be in the company of people they like."

"Amen to that one," said Jake.

"I'll send you the script in the morning," said Victor.

"How do you even know I can write?" Kate said.

"It's like me and business," said Victor. "It's in the genes."

"Just smile and say thank you," said Wilton, pinching.

*L*ila Darshowitz woke grieving. Larry had not been a physical presence beside her for a lot of years. But she came up from dreaming with his breath on her cheek, and it was sweet, and they were young again. When she suddenly remembered he was dead, the absence made her truly bereft. That he was not in bed with her was something she had long ago gotten used to, stopped even thinking about. But now that she knew he could never be there again, the pillow seemed to have a hole in it, like the world did.

There were two open bottles of wine on the floor, the smell of it in the air, a small red stain on the carpet where she had probably tipped it, set it down sloppily. It was cheap wine, so she didn't think of reaching for it, starting her day with a hair of the dog. It was probably already slightly vinegary. "We have to let this breathe," Larry had said to her the first time he came back from Hollywood, where he had been to dinner parties. She could sort of hear him now, telling her about the breathing, one of a thousand affectations he had paraded in front of her, as though he needed to impress her, as though his merely being alive hadn't been enough.

"You elegant fuck," she said to his ghost, easing her swollen feet out of the bed. "I remember the time with the hamburger."

She went to the bathroom and more or less performed what Larry would have labeled her "ablutions." Then she dialed the phone, called the only person she sort of knew, who wanted to talk about him, or wanted her to. "Kate?" she said. "I remembered the time with the hamburger."

$\mathcal{T}$hey were in the coffee shop now, Lila and the girl who wanted to be a scribe, having breakfast. Lila had her hair in a bandanna, a babushka her grandma would have called it, a little cream foundation on so the broken blood vessels on her nose and cheeks showed less.

"It just seemed like a really good story for your book," Lila said. "You still want to do that book?"

"Sure," Kate said, like she wasn't.

"Well, it's a good story with or without a book," Lila said, because all she really wanted was a chance to talk about him. There was no one left alive who really knew him, except some failing friends from the young days whose feelings towards him were completely negative, who always gave Lila flack about the fact that she still cared. After all he had done to her, or failed to do.

"So we were in this diner in Brooklyn. He was maybe sixteen, and already he had this piss-elegance, you know. Like he studied people with manners who came from good families, read books about their lives, went to plays. Stood in the back of the theater because he couldn't afford to sit. Noël Coward. Somerset what's-his-name."

"Maugham," Kate said.

"So there we were in this diner, him and me and some of his friends, and he said in his veddy king's English, 'I'll have a hahmburger, rare.' So they brought the burger, and he took a bite and looked at it and snapped his fingers for the waiter. 'I said "rare," ' he said. 'This is medium.'

"So the waiter shrugged his shoulders and took it. In a couple of minutes he was back. And he set the burger in front of Larry. The bun still had the bite in it." Lila laughed, until tears were streaming down her face. "This big bite." She wiped her cheeks. "A diner in Brooklyn, and he sends it back. And it comes with the bite out of the bun."

"Did he know it was funny?" Kate asked.

"He always knew what was funny," Lila said. "He just couldn't see it about himself."

"So he took himself seriously?"

"Well, how else could he become what he became?" Lila asked.

Kate was half looking around, as though she, too, were clinging to another time, hoping her friend from Stanford might show up in the coffee shop again. But there were only the three girls from Kansas or Missouri or Iowa or wherever it was, the bleached, ebullient trio, bused in on a Greyhound and a fantasy, giggling and studying their *TV Guide,* a casting directory, a map of L.A., a prayer book to set the whole thing in motion.

"Did he leave you any money?" Kate asked.

"I don't know." Lila looked miffed, suddenly. "Why would you ask such a question?"

"I'm concerned," Kate said. "I wondered if you had enough to get back home."

"You're tired of me," Lila whined, like she was talking to someone else.

"It's just the practical realities," Kate said.

"You're tired of Larry, too." Lila's tone was accusatory. "You're just like the rest of the phonies in this town. You lose interest in something the minute you're not sure if it will do you any good."

"That isn't true."

"Don't tell me what's true. I know what's true. That's why he always came back to me. He said I was . . . what's that paper that changes color?"

"Litmus."

"Right. A litmus test for bullshit. I can see into you, little girl, and I see where you're not exactly the sweet person you pretended."

"Really?" Kate asked with honest interest, and some alarm. Maybe this blowsy, sad woman saw with her milky eyes what Kate could not quite look at.

"You're in it for yourself," Lila censured.

"Who isn't?" Kate said defensively. She opened her purse, reached for her wallet. "Maybe we should continue this another time, when you're feeling less . . . " She hesitated.

"Honest?" Lila said.

"Self-pitying," she said unkindly. "I don't owe you anything." Kate put a bill on the table and stood.

"That's right, you don't. But you owe Larry."

"I never even met Larry."

"But you like to think you're smart. And fair. You can't just walk away from him now. You can't just leave the record how it is, with those shitty articles and books they wrote about the money scandal. And now this crap with the prostitutes. He deserves better."

"Why?"

"Because there was nobody like him. He could charm the birds out of trees, even in places where there were no trees. Because he was brilliant, and he knew how to make things happen. Because there was nothing he wanted to be that he didn't become."

"Except a nice guy," said Kate.

"How do you know, you little *momser?* You said yourself you didn't know him. If he wanted to, he could have wound you around his little finger." She looked at Kate intensely, and the whitish fluid in her eyes seemed to clear. "What were you doing at his funeral, if you never even met him?"

"I have to go," Kate said. "You have my number."

"I certainly do," said Lila.

*O*nce, in between wives, in between pictures and pretensions, Larry had flown Lila out in his private plane to show her L.A. Nothing of the nightlife, of course, because they both understood without bringing it up that she would not be good publicity, and the business he was in was a lot about publicity.

But he had shown her the physical beauty of the place, passed on the overblown, overexposed Beverly Hills and Bel-Air and toured her through the hills and canyons of Pacific Palisades. He had pointed out the movie star mansions of this would-be Riviera with its Capri and Amalfi Drives. "Amalfi," he'd pointed out the sign to to her. "That's just below where Gore Vidal lives in Italy."

She didn't tell him she didn't know who Gore Vidal was.

They'd kept on going till they reached Santa Monica, and that had been her favorite. They'd walked on the pier, eaten corn on the cob, had their fortunes told. And he'd been fearless, himself, laughing the whole time, totally at ease, because nobody he knew who was anybody would be on the Santa Monica pier, trashy as it was, low class. She'd absolutely loved it. It was just like being in Rockaway.

She walked on the pier now without him, remembering that golden, butter-drenched afternoon. Somehow she had managed to connect with a network of buses that had gotten her to Santa Monica, although it took a good part of the day. The sun was at a leaving angle, like it was saying good-bye, almost down to the water. There was a bright orange radiance to it, the fire that came before it sizzled into the sea, as it did the day they spent there together.

There were five saloons in between the gypsies and the merry-go-round and the deep-fried shrimp. She stopped in every one, had a glass of red wine, and lifted it to him. In the last one she had three glasses, and forgot to make the toast, or let it breathe. Or let herself breathe.

And now the sun was sinking so low it gilded the sea. Half-blinded by the glare, the other half by the wine, she staggered towards the place she intended to jump from. She had not planned on leaving a note or anything, because who the fuck cared? Who would even note her absence, now that he was gone? Maybe her landlord, but she didn't much care for him. It wasn't like she needed to give notice. When she never came back, he'd probably have a garage sale of her clothes, sell the furniture, and get another tenant.

But all at once she came to a fence. A chain-link fence, with some half-assed apology on it, pardon the inconvenience kind of thing, we're building a better end to the pier. Frustrated and confused, she narrowed her eyes and struggled to see the completion date, as though planning to return to accomplish her mission then.

But even days away, much less months away, would be far too long. She wanted to die now. Maybe he was still just a layer above the sunset, and she could get to him before he reached his final destination.

So she turned back and looked for a way down to the beach. Hitting the water from the pier would have at least put her in shock. From the sand she would have to wander in and drown. But she had never been much of a swimmer. And there probably was a good undertow, the pilings of the pier creating their own dangerous currents, like the places they warned you not to go near in Rockaway, Coney Island.

She thought she had seen some steps down to the ocean. Recalled a glass lifted to the then still-bright day, where she'd noted through the window the slatted wooden stairs to the beach. So much sand in comparison to the beaches of her girlhood, three boulevards wide it had seemed to her, instead of the sidestreet widths you got in New York. She searched for the steps now as twilight silvered the air.

She found them and started down, gripping the wooden siderail. Seagulls squawked their gratitude for garbage.

A single set of lovers strolled arm in arm on the darkening sands. For a moment Lila saw in their slender forms, heads nodded inward, crowns meeting, arms entwined, who she had once been, how she had once walked with Larry. And she reached for them, as though she could touch them across the distance, and touching them, would be able to feel her vanished self, contact the flesh of Larry. And so stretching, she lost what balance she had, and fell.

*W*hen the phone rang, Kate was halfway through the script Victor Lippton had sent over, hopeful she would want to do it and rope in Jake Alonzo. Jake Alonzo himself had shown some signs of wanting to be roped, sending a single rose, wrapped with red ribbon around an answering machine. It was all too much for Kate, being courted for who she wasn't, what it was assumed she could do because of genes that weren't really hers. She'd written Jake a note to thank him, afraid to call him, but didn't know where to send the note. Still, she didn't imagine formal good manners were the mode in this town any more than honesty was. So she didn't worry about seeming rude to Jake, since she'd already seen that a show of indifference worked better than a beating heart would.

Besides, the script was terrible. She had called Mel by page fifteen and told him it was really god-awful. He'd said, "Good." The worse it was, he'd explained, the more impressively she could harangue the powers at Cosmos with what needed to be done. The fact that the writer could not write a sentence of believable dialogue, that the characters had no character, that the lead, a hired assassin, had no charm in addition to no psychic core were all, Mel insisted, plusses.

But it was like wading through quicksand for her to read that level of—could she even call it prose? So when the phone sounded, it was a reprieve. She was already grateful to whomever was on the other end, receptive, friendly. It took her a minute to absorb the fact that it was the fire department.

"Lady broke her leg, and maybe her hip," the man said. "She's still up in X ray."

"What lady?"

"Lila Darshovitz," he said, slowly, as though he were reading it.

"Witz," said Kate. "How come you're calling me?"

"Well, she's pretty . . . out of it. Drunk. Besides being in shock. We asked her who we should call, and she couldn't tell us. Just kept crying. We went through her purse and found your number."

"What am I supposed to do?" Kate said, imposed upon, instantly hearing how selfish she sounded.

"Well, we thought you might be a friend, or a relative. Do you know where we could find a relative?"

"Her husband is in the Westwood Mortuary," Kate said. Maybe Lila had been right about her. Maybe she wasn't as sweet as she pretended. How fast did that happen? Not even a full twenty-four hours on the fast track, and she sounded tough. Maybe the humanity didn't ooze out of you in this setting, it just imploded. "Will she be alright?"

"Yes. But she's going to need help. They've got her in emergency now. But she doesn't seem to have any coverage for hospitalization, or insurance for nursing care . . . "

"Can she travel?" Kate said, mentally putting her on the plane.

"Not for a while, I don't guess," the fireman said.

"Where is she?" Grudgingly.

The fireman gave Kate the address. As she was going out the door, the phone rang, and she let her new machine pick it up. It was Jake Alonzo, asking what she thought of the script.

*Y*ou hate me," Lila said from the back of the car, where the ambulance crew had positioned her, the broken leg in its splint raised to the back of the passenger seat. Fortunately her hip had turned out not to be broken. "You wish I had died."

"No I don't," Kate said.

"Well, I wish I had died. I went there to throw myself off the end of the pier, but the fuckers put a fence up. I was trying to get down to the ocean to drown, when I fell."

"Maybe you could sue them," Kate suggested.

"That's what they're afraid of. That's why they fixed me for nothing," she said. "Larry would have liked that, my beating the city. Except I'd rather be dead."

"Don't be silly," said Kate, not knowing what else to say.

"What reason do I have to be alive?"

She couldn't think of any. "There's the book," Kate said, remembering how only a few days before she'd had mercy in her.

"You're going to write it?" Lila asked.

"I'm going to try."

"Well, good," Lila said, a great whoosh of air coming out of her with the words, like a bellows. "I remembered some other stories."

"What's *momser* mean?" asked Kate.

"It means a person who doesn't deserve what they get," Lila said. "A bastard if you want to be literal. Usually it's a man, but I suspected you were one of those feminist people. So I gave you equal status. But if you like, I could call you a *courvah*."

"What's that?"

"A whore."

"Let's leave that for the ones who wrote the other book," Kate said.

$\mathcal{T}$he broadcast studio for the Ralph Robertson show was rented from a local New York station on East Seventy-first Street. Arthur Finster hired a limousine service to take him there. He made sure that the stretch had a phone in it, so he could call his office as he already had countless times that day, just in case he remembered anyone else who ought to be alerted he was on the show.

"And you'll call the producers at Larry King to watch?" he asked and ordered into the phone.

"They've already passed," the PR woman said.

"And Oprah?"

"We've called everybody," she said.

"And don't forget my mother."

"We called her."

"But you didn't tell her I was in New York?" Even as he said it, he slumped down deep into the seat, a counterspy, just in case anyone who knew her should see the limo. The windows were darkened, shaded, opalescent, giving him the protection of a rock star. But she could see through walls and bathroom doors, so her friends would only have to notice a limousine passing to know that Arthur was inside and hadn't been to visit her.

"Well, she knew where the show was broadcast from, so I had to talk very fast. I told her they were linking you up by satellite."

"You get a raise as soon as the book hits number one," Arthur said.

"It's number one in the L.A. *Times* next Sunday."

"Nationwide," he said. He hung up the phone.

$\mathcal{B}$ut what about the accusations of blood money?" Ralph Robertson was asking him. He was blond, with elegant posture and the clipped accent of Johannesburg, where he had lived until moving to the States and becoming, as he often said, smiling, on the lecture circuit, an African American. "What about the people who are calling you a vampire?"

"What about them? There will always be jealousy. The publishing business is notoriously stodgy, slow-moving. They can't help resenting how fast it's happened for me. How much money I've made."

"But these are people many of whom are a great deal richer than you. And they call you a blight on the industry."

"Free country." Arthur shrugged. "First Amendment. They can say anything they like, and I can publish anything I like. And readers like."

"Readers?" Robertson gave his famous chuckle, the only well-known laugh on the air that seemed to have a British accent. "This has been called a nonbook, by nonwriters, in what many are calling non-English."

"These girls have been through terrible ordeals," said Arthur. "They speak from the heart."

"Is that what they call it?"

Ignoring the barb, Arthur plowed on. "The writing of this book has been a cleansing for them, a kind of therapy, where they have learned the foolishness of their ways, and now will lead a life of spiritual values."

"Sort of like the *Confessions of St. Augustine*?" Robertson said.

"You could say that."

"But I won't," said Ralph. "I don't need mail from the Vatican. How do you feel about the death of Larry Drayco?"

"I feel bad when anyone dies."

"Especially reading about himself in your book."

"That is an unconfirmed rumor. Natalia, that's the former call girl who hung out with Larry, Natalia has already apportioned part of her royalties to a headstone."

"Really. I heard your authors don't get royalties. That you have them sign away all rights in exchange for protection."

"From what? They haven't done anything wrong."

"Then why is there a class action libel suit against you and the . . . what did you call them? Former call girls? Filed on behalf of some of the biggest names in Hollywood by Fletcher McCallum, the most respected attorney in entertainment law? The suit alleges, besides libel, invasion of privacy, and malice, that you have deliberately vilified celebrities in order to promote the sale of *By Hook or by Crook*. Linus Archer, Rick Flinders, Jake Alonzo—"

"Jake wasn't even in the final draft," Arthur said.

"But you circulated the manuscript before he was cut out of it, and circulation constitutes publication. Apparently what was said about him—"

"You should talk to Delight, the hooker who—"

"No graphic details, please."

"—who performed her specialty on him. Because of personal circumstances, she was not available for the polygraph test, so we cut that chapter out. But she will be willing to testify at a trial, should it come to that."

"She's in rehab?"

"Either that, or a convent," Arthur said, and chortled.

"You really have no guilt about this garbage?"

"I have no reason to feel guilty about anything," Arthur said, clearing his mind of his mother. "These women were desperate. They'd lost all sense of themselves, descended into drug dependency, had nothing to trade on but their rapidly failing looks. They were unfeelingly used in the lowest possible way by these men, who thought they were entitled to do whatever they wanted, because they were celebrities. Power players high in the Hollywood echelons. This book is an important social document."

"And the greatest gift of all," Ralph said, inhaling deeply, "is self-delusion." He turned to the camera, facing it directly.

"We have to go now, people. The book is called *By Hook or by Crook,* by five *former,* and I stress former, ladies of the evening. Our guest was Arthur Finster, the publisher, editor in chief, and C.E.O. of Harbinger Press."

The lights went down. "Sorry if I was rough on you," Ralph said. "But my viewers wouldn't like it if I seemed to approve."

"Hey," Arthur said, and trying to run his hand through his dreadlocks, stopped by the knots in them, leaned over and shook them out. "You showed the book. You said the title. I appreciate it."

"So this Natalia, the one who did Drayco, she's into S&M?"

"Not always," said Arthur. "Her real specialty is fellatio. But with her breasts. She has these gigantic jugs, and she presses them on the outside of the guy's cock and rubs, while her tongue—"

"I get the picture," Ralph said. "I thought it was Delight who did that."

"They're all versatile," said Arthur. "And of course they're fabulous with phone sex."

"Maybe you should leave me their numbers," Ralph said, "in case there're any ramifications from the show. I should have that for my lawyers."

"Certainly," said Arthur, and taking out his pocket computer, called the numbers up, and started writing.

*T*he treadmills at the Star-Crossed Health Club in Brentwood were all in a line, by a floor-to-ceiling mirrored wall. Those who walked them had the option of facing themselves or the TVs, a special engineer having outfitted them to roll in either direction. During the heavily trafficked hours of the day all the treadmills were in use, as were the StairMasters opposite. But now it was the dinner hour, and most members had completed their workouts, the lucky or manipulative among them having found someone to spend the evening with.

Only two treadmills were now in use, on the far side of the room. On one Victor Lippton marched at an accelerated speed, next to the treadmill trod by a striking, white-skinned redhead who had sweated through her designer workout clothes at curiously provocative places, one stain outlining her crotch, the stain beneath her armpits having spread to underscore her magnificent breasts. It was almost as though she had deliberately splashed herself in those places, which Victor Lippton now suspected she had.

"Don't tell me it was a coincidence, Alexa," he little more than whispered, looking around uneasily to see if they were being watched. Almost all the high-end places in town had unobtrusive security systems: the Hotel Bel-Air with its barely perceptible TV eye on the pool to make sure nobody drowned, the restaurants with cameras on their parking lots, some of the pricier supermarkets following suit. "You couldn't have just *chanced* on the identical outfit."

"Why not?"

"They didn't even come as an ensemble. You had to have watched her pick them out."

"Did not."

"Don't deny it. And don't speak like a child. It couldn't have just happened. You did it deliberately. There's no way it was coincidence."

"Why not? We have the exact same taste in men."

"I hate it when you get smart," Victor said, not really hating it, enjoying it really, because he liked to think she was as clever as she was passionate. It was one of the things he dared not discuss with the therapist who was counseling him and Chen on their sex life, or lack of it. He didn't really trust the therapist, because the therapist had read them some of the fan mail he received from the people he counseled on the radio. And also the therapist was screwing one of his patients. Victor knew that because he paid a private investigator to watch him, so he would have something on him in the event he ever violated Victor's confidence.

The patient he was screwing was the wife of another psychiatrist who was probably paying him less than the $150 an hour that Victor paid. Professional courtesy, they labeled it to each other. But he was paying him something, giving him a stipend while the bastard was fucking his wife. The detective Victor had on him had followed the woman to a cheap little apartment in Toluca Lake, one of those ramshackle compounds built around a pool where she met her shrink lover three times a week, to put horns on her husband. How he could have been stupid enough not to know when she didn't come home three nights a week until after eleven was more than Victor could comprehend. Medical degrees. Internships. Their own analysis, years of practice and a mandatory amount of insight, and the jerk still didn't know he was paying for his wife to get screwed.

Or maybe he did. Maybe it took the pressure off him, and he wasn't attracted to his wife anymore, like Victor wasn't attracted to Chen. Maybe it got him off to be paying the other guy professional courtesy rates for fucking his wife. What did Victor know, except that they were all crazy.

"You're deliberately trying to provoke a confrontation," Victor said to Alexa. "You're going out of your way to make yourself conspicuous so she'll notice you, and get what's going on between us."

"What exactly is going on," Alexa said. "A love affair? Or am I just your strumpet?"

"I wish you'd stop watching those old movies," Victor said.

"What else am I supposed to do, those cold lonely nights?"

"You could read," he said.

"I read."

"Something besides *W*," he said.

"You got me the subscription."

"Because I honor what is special in you."

"The surface," she said. "You want me to look as good as your wife, and then when I look as good as your wife, you accuse me of trying to make trouble."

"Aren't you?"

She turned down the speed of her treadmill, and slowly came to a stop. "I love you, Victor. The last thing in the world I want is to cause you pain."

"Maybe the next-to-last thing," he said. "When I give in to you and let you come to one of those evenings I know better than to let you come to, and then, instead of making it easy and pleasant you almost cause a scene—"

"I didn't even speak," Alexa said.

"One picture is worth a thousand words," Victor said, sweating profusely now, his words coming almost in a pant, rushed, breathless from his exercise. "And an outfit that is the same as the one a man's wife is wearing speaks volumes. Photo albums."

He was very red in the face. The hairs that poked from above the scoop of his T-shirt had little dots of pink around them, as though the pores on his chest were blushing.

"Are you all right?" Alexa said anxiously. It was true what he had said, that it was the next-to-last thing she wanted to cause him pain. The last thing she wanted was for him to die. Oh, God, what would happen to her if he died? She would have to work this treadmill forever, like some kind of mechanized Flying Dutchman, till someone else showed up on the treadmill next to her, and, captured by the bob of her breasts, released her, ready to treadmill in her place.

"I'm in my prime," he said, winded, as he slowed to a stroll. "I have everything in the world I want, a great company, great company in you . . . "

"But not all the time."

"I told you when it started that it could only be so much, that I was married to Chen for life. Even if I didn't love her, which I do, her father is one of the most powerful men on the planet. And I'm not talking the kind of power they honor in this town, or even in this country. I'm talking Asia. Americans have no concept of how things operate there, no interest, not enough foresight or widesight or whatever kind of sight it is that gets people out of their own belly buttons, or their own backyards. I'm talking about the ability to put whole countries out of business, whole businesses out of countries, shutting down newspapers if the man in charge doesn't like something that was written without even mentioning his name. Have you ever been to Singapore?"

"I'd love to go," she said, flirting, thinking it an invitation, his mind going much too fast for her. Their discussions, such as they were, never involved anything of a sociological nature except Donald Trump, and what had happened with Marla, which Alexa had prayed for at night, until that shuttle mission, too, had been aborted.

"Say something that ruffles the feathers of the senior minister of Singapore, and you're finished."

"They even cane you in church?" she asked, having absorbed one news item about a boy who did graffiti.

"Not that kind of minister," Victor said. "A political minister. When the plane descends into Singapore they remind you that having drugs is a capital offense. They could also remind you that having an opinion that is not shared by the head of state could result in your being driven out of the country. *If* they were being merciful.

"Well, that's who Chen's father is," he tried to explain.

"I thought he was a Chinaman."

"I was speaking metaphorically," he said. "That means it's a symbol. And we don't say Chinaman, we say Chinese."

"Even in Singapore?" She saw the expression on his face, and knew she was being thick. The only way to fix it was to make him even thicker. She jumped onto his treadmill and stuck her hand down the front of his shorts.

"Not here," he said. "Are you crazy?" But even as he denounced her with his words he blossomed in her hand.

And not letting him go even for the moment it took them to cross the floor like a vaudeville team, she led him, at point, to the ladies' room, and blew him in the toilet. Locking the door, of course, and covering his mouth with the hand that was free when he climaxed and started screaming, as she imagined him doing in Singapore, when they caned him for throwing his wife out the window, strict as the laws were about littering.

*C*an we have lunch tomorrow?" Sarah Nash asked Bunyan Reis. She had become a fairly accomplished shadower of those who did not want to be shadowed; bearding him outside his Sutton Place lair had been no problem at all. Bunyan was forever giving interviews in which he pronounced his writing and his painting extremely accessible. He would then add himself to the package, saying he continued to have his number listed, and his place of residence well known, in spite of what had happened to John Lennon. Of course his popularity in no way touched on that of the gunned-down icon, and his building had a much better security system than the Dakota. But she had waited outside till the moment she knew from his memoirs he went out to dinner, though no longer at the restaurants he loved, because almost all of them had closed.

Once she might have waited for him outside Lutèce or La Côte Basque, when both he and the restaurants he counted as his own had been in favor with his women friends, before he had betrayed them in print. But now they were shuttered, as the women were, coffined up, most of them. Living well was the best revenge, according to the maxim and the Murphys. But Bunyan had gone them one better. Living was the best revenge, especially after those who had dropped you had died.

The night was lightly misted, no sign of stars except in the sidewalk, those illusory little glistens in the asphalt that caught the lights from streetlamps. Sarah was literally cloaked in darkness, a soft black felt serape flung around her shoulders, her pale face unrouged, the only color visible the scarlet of the dinosaur back that spiked the top and center of her hair.

"Are you mad?" he asked Sarah. "Lunch with you?"

"You could bring your food taster."

"But your poison doesn't come in food, my nonadorable. It's much more insidious."

"I've never harmed you."

"That's only because you had nothing to gain, and didn't know me that well."

"We don't have to speak of anything you don't want to. And, in addition to the food, I have a little tidbit for you that will put you back in the gossip mainstream."

He was suddenly alert, helmeted, with a life jacket on, ready to ride the rapids of the rivers of scandal he had been so abruptly excluded from because he had blown a few hundred confidences, as Sarah had. In fact they were not unalike, except that he always dressed in muted tones, grays and silvers to match his eyes, and now his beard, and she was so frighteningly flamboyant, crown-wise. But they both had the same kinds of tastes, in calumny and young boys. "Tell, tell," he urged.

"At lunch, at lunch," said Sarah. "Where shall we have it?"

"Nowhere anyone can see us," said Bunyan, already excited. Positively Shakespearean it was, meeting in the antechambers, plotting the downfall of the liege. Not that he intended to harm anyone he cared for, though it might have been construed that way had anyone seen them together and then reported back to Norman that Bunyan was consorting with the enemy. Important to choose the place craftily.

Someplace that seemed friendly, but where no one worth their salt would go. Maybe the bench by the lake in Central Park donated by Leona Helmsley.

Incidental Music

*T*he minute Norman Jessup got to New York, he felt restless. It was a part of the city's consciousness, he understood that, a factor in what made the place so high energy. New York was crowded with events, as in other places cemeteries were with the dead. There were the museums, theaters, galleries, church programs, constant concerts. Even the homeless ranting in front of Lincoln Center were more articulate than many politicians in less fevered locales. So there was always something happening, and the feeling you might be missing it. It was an angst that was different from the loneliness or alienation you might experience anywhere else, the sense that life might be passing you by. In New York, it was. In parades, on skateboards, in marathons, on billboards, on the sides of buses, a constant stream of reminders that you were missing something, if only the ability to be still.

He felt lonely now, sorry he hadn't brought Carina. He was shrouded with nostalgia for the vanished Paulo, the laughter they had shared, the magical way the boy had of quieting him down, at the same time making the romantic adventure, which it had been, more intense.

Sarah Nash was out for the evening according to the switchboard at the hotel. Without Tyler's being there to alert him where she might have been or gone, Norman, for all his sense of command, had no idea what to do with himself.

So he went to the theater. It was, he decided by the end of the evening, like Columbus's heading for India and coming across America by accident. The play was a musical. He knew instantly who should star in the movie version, got it in a flash that made Madonna as Evita seem uninspired, which maybe it really was. Taking the world by storm in the movie version of *Pilgrims!*, a musicalization of Geoffrey Chaucer's *Canterbury Tales,* according to the program, playing the Wife of Bath.

Helen Manning. He could see her lusting and remarrying around the medieval sets, bruiting about her bawdy philosophy, taking on all comers spread-legged, in a manner of speaking, while still retaining the love of an audience. As unexpected as the sweetness of the voice that had come out of her at Drayco's funeral was the predictability of the fans' rooting for her, knowing it was not her fault but her virtue that she'd been fucked, this time in song.

"Has anyone got the movie rights?" he asked the director, cornering him backstage the minute the curtain went down, already halfway down the alley as he'd been with the first tap of handclapping applause. The man was strictly a New York type, *The-ah-tre,* so did not instantly react to Norman's name, something Jessup would find a subtle way of punishing him for, giving him the hope of a say-so in the movie, and then cutting him out of it abruptly, with not so much as a good-bye. Just an unreturned call to his agent.

"Well, there's talks going on with Disney and Fox . . . " the director, Lars Bernstein, said.

"But no deal yet?"

"No deal."

"Who can make the deal with me, now, this minute?"

"I can try and get hold of Ed Korbin, the producer—"

"Do it." Jessup handed him his cellular phone. "What kind of name is Lars Bernstein?" he asked, while the man hit the numbers, dialing.

"My mother was moved by Marlon Brando in *I Remember Mama.* How do I get it to ring?"

"Press send," Jessup said. "What about Jeff Chaucer. Can I talk to him?"

Bernstein looked at him blankly, then smiled. "Oh, I get it," he said. "Funny. Hello, Kit? Can I speak to Ed?"

The deal was made in as much time as it took to have the conversation. Norman felt elated, the way he always did when he knew he'd had an inspiration and closed it, even though he was a little bit quashed by the slip he'd made about the author. But what the hell. He'd seen the contracts on the first remake of *Hunchback of Notre Dame,* and they'd put a healthy per diem in for Victor Hugo.

He believed in destiny. Everything happened for a reason. Although it was Sarah Nash's darkness that had brought him to New York, the musical was the light at the end of the Midtown Tunnel.

And just in case he had any doubt in the world, when he got back to his hotel, too juiced up to sleep, he went into the Bemelmans bar, and there sat Helen Manning. "You won't believe this," he said, and sat down with her.

"Of course I won't," she said, downing the last of what appeared to be a stinger.

He snapped his fingers for the waiter. "A black Russian," he said. "And another of whatever it is for the lady."

She snickered. Apparently she'd had a little to drink, because it came out a snort. "Lady," she repeated, when she'd caught her breath.

"I've just bought something for you," said Norman.

"I hope it isn't jewelry," she said. "My insurance is *so* high."

"I've bought you a gem beyond price." He felt so warmed by his action that obviously drunk as she was, he touched her arm in a gesture that was as close as he could come to affection for the opposite sex, which in her case could not have been more opposite. "It's a musical."

"What?" Her eyes looked very nearly crossed.

"*Pilgrims,*" he said, leaving out the exclamation point in his intonation. "It's the musical version of *The Canterbury Tales,* by Geoffrey Chaucer. You'll be the Wife of Bath."

"Who's playing Bath?" she asked, lids half shut now.

"It's a town," said Norman. "*Tales* is the first true classic of English literature." He'd called his researcher on his cellular phone in the taxi back to the hotel, and was now up to speed. "A ribald, rollicking tale," he said, quoting the logo outside the theater. "And the Wife, or as it was then, Wyf, is a lovable bawd who takes to sex like . . . " He hesitated.

"A fuck to water," Helen said.

"I guess you could say that. The songs are wonderful. Ribald. Rollicking. You'll be dynamite in the part."

The waiter brought their drinks. She looked up through heavy lids, mouthed "Thank you," and drank without tasting.

"Are you upset about something?" Norman said.

"How perceptive you are," she said, slurring the sibilance.

"Well, whatever it is, this will heal you. It will be a new beginning for you. Helen Manning, musical comedy star."

"I don't sing," she said.

"Of course you do. I heard you at Larry's funeral."

"That was a weird moment."

"Unforgettable," he said. "You'll be fantastic in the part."

"I'm too old to make a fool of myself," she said. "On screen anyway."

"I'll pay you anything you want. Highest salary ever paid to a woman. Female Sylvester Stallone."

"Spare me."

"Name your price."

"I don't need money," she said. "I have more money than I'll ever be able to spend."

"There must be something you want."

She looked up slowly. "Well, there *is* one thing . . . " She seemed to jolt herself into sobriety. "You have in your employ a certain young man. Young, young man," she said poignantly, as Blanche DuBois would have said it if they ever made *her* into a musical.

*A*ctually, the idea of a picnic on Leona's bench, as appealing as it had seemed to Bunyan the night before, appeared ludicrous in the light of day. Especially with the homeless person stretched out on the bench, the paper bag with his beer bottle acting as his pillow, yesterday's *Daily News* warming his rather shapely ass. Bunyan called Sarah from the pay phone on the corner.

"We must relocate our assignation," he said. "Someone's taken our table."

"But I've already bought the sandwiches."

"Bring them with you," he said. "I have the perfect recipient."

They settled on a restaurant near the Algonquin, but not so close that they would run into anybody literary. Bunyan asked for a table in the corner, and sat with his back to the wall, like a mafioso, something he had learned from Mario Puzo. He signaled to Sarah when she came in, carrying her smart little sack from EAT, wearing her spikey hair.

"Have you considered hats?" he said, as she came to the table.

"No fashion commentary." She sat down.

"I didn't know there were ground rules."

"I said you didn't have to talk about anything you didn't want to. And I would appreciate it if you didn't comment on my hair."

"It's actually hair?" Bunyan marveled. "I thought it was a piece. Something Burt Reynolds might wear in *Jurassic Park Three*. The skull version of dentatum."

"I don't know what dentatum is."

"It's when men fear a woman's vagina has teeth in it. I thought that might be your way of offering head."

"Very witty," she said.

"Thank you. That's what I do."

The waiter gave them menus. Bunyan ordered wine, and Sarah asked for a Fanta.

"Tell me about Paulo," she said.

"Paulo who? Neruda? A great sense of humanity and horniness."

"That's Pablo. I mean the dancer Paulo. Norman Jessup's Paulo."

"Exquisite boy. Great talent, really. Not just another pretty face. Not just a dancer, either. He could have been a great musical star on Broadway. This is not gossip. I'm not telling you anything that would impact badly on Norman," he said, a little too quickly. "Norman's taste was flawless."

"Why didn't Paulo do musical comedy?"

"Paulo himself had esoteric taste. He worked out an audition piece to 'The World Is Your Balloon.' That was his favorite Harburg lyric. I mean, consider that English was his second language, that he didn't even start to speak it until he was maybe thirteen, yet he had the subtlety to appreciate Yip Harburg. The song was from a show of Yipper's called *Flahooley* that I don't think anyone ever saw. But Paulo loved the song, and he thought the writers he auditioned for would be touched that he'd prepared an obscure song from a failed show.

"But they didn't have the class or the style to know what the hell it was, so they talked all during his singing. Didn't even call him back. He was so disheartened, he never went to another Broadway audition."

At that moment a noted English actress recognized Bunyan, got up from her table, and swept over to greet him. She was one of the great standard bearers of British cinema, but Sarah couldn't call up her name, as she was neither Emma Thompson nor Helena Bonham-Carter, the only two Sarah had ever met personally, and so the only ones whose identities she could actually label, as the rest of them all sounded alike to her.

"Bunyan!" cried the actress, kissing the air a few feet away from him.

"What? Still alive, my Lady Disdain?" Bunyan said.

"I thought . . . " She smiled wickedly, revealing teeth that were bad, Swiss-cheesy, with little gray stains on them that looked like holes, a dead giveaway that she'd never done a film in Hollywood. "I thought *you* were Lady Disdain."

"I am Lord," Bunyan said.

"Of all you survey?"

"Why not? Are the Hesseltines in town with you?"

"Of course. Staying at the Plaza. Will we see you?"

"Here I am, now."

"He's brought Evelyn Waugh's grandnephew. You'd like him. A chip off the old block."

"Old, old block. The chip would have had to petrify by now." He turned to Sarah. "That's Roger Hesseltine's only claim to fame, long ago Evelyn. I'll never forget his tale of being with him in the steam-bath, and how red Evelyn's willy was."

"Red willies are always in fashion," said the actress.

"Apparently so are the grandspawn of literary figures," said Sarah, longing to be more conspicuous than her hair apparently made her. Bunyan had shown no inclination to introduce her. "There's a young woman just arrived in L.A. who's Fitzgerald's granddaughter."

"Geraldine's?"

"F. Scott's," said Sarah.

"American writers are greatly overrated," said the Brit. "Present company included."

"You've read Miss Nash's book, then?" asked Bunyan.

"I'm afraid not. Only yours. None of those boys, not Hemingway, not Fitzgerald could hold a candle to who we had. Huxley. Forster."

"Waugh with his willy," Bunyan said. "We'd better order."

"Please call." The actress stooped to kiss him.

It was only then that Sarah realized he'd never gotten up. "It was a pleasure to almost meet you," she said.

The actress minced away. "I would've introduced you," Bunyan said, "but I couldn't think of her name."

"Why didn't you stand up?" Sarah asked, as the waiter came to take their order.

"That would have been a sign of respect."

"I see," said Sarah.

"There's hope for you, then. I'll have the seared Ahi Niçoise," he told the waiter. "Rare."

"Same," said Sarah. "What was that about Evelyn Waugh's willy?"

"A hilarious tale. One I shall tell you if we become friends, which won't happen. But that's the kind of thing you should focus on, not personal, emotional history. Your book was a bore, really, because it told everything from your point of view, all your hurt feelings, which you tried to cover with bitchiness and gossip that was bloody around the edges because you were so wounded. Great gossip is detached, dispassionate. Like recipes. What good stories do you have to recount if you're ever invited to a truly sophisticated dinner party?"

"Well, maybe you could tell me the one about Evelyn Waugh's willy."

"Why would I tell you anything?"

"You really consider that dinner party conversation?"

"Well, fortunately, he had a very pretty one, even though it got quite red in the steam."

Sarah sipped on her Fanta. "When was the last time you saw Paulo?"

"Is this your check? Is your publisher paying?"

"No."

"But you're going to pick it up anyway."

"Of course. I invited you."

"We should have gone to Cirque 2000. But then *everyone* would have seen us. And of course it can't hold a chandelier to the old Le Cirque."

"Was Paulo bright?"

"Bright for what? Bright for a dancer? Bright for a Nobel Prize winner? Bright for a lamp that led Norman through the darkness?"

"Did he?"

"He had a genuinely sweet spirit."

"Had?"

"Has."

"He's still alive then?"

The waiter came with the food. "Oh, good, I'm famished," Bunyan said, and started eating.

"You didn't answer me."

"I'm eating," Bunyan said.

She watched him. Waited until his plate was almost empty. "You weren't disturbed . . . " It was a total shot in the dark on Sarah's part. But she figured that with his extraordinary sense of plotting, both in his work and in the parlor games he was famous for playing, Bunyan might have been party to any murder scheme, and helped it along. " . . . by what was done to him?"

To Sarah's intense satisfaction, Bunyan went ashen, and choked on a string bean. He drank some water, and appeared quieted. But his skin was still gray. "Who told you?" he said, finally.

"I have to protect my sources," she said. "Unlike some people."

"I always protected my sources," he said. "Nobody who loved me or confided in me ever had occasion to sue me."

"They just committed suicide," she said.

"I've had enough of you and your odious bitchiness."

"That's redundant," she said.

"*You* are redundant." He got up. "But fortunately, not to be so for long. Where is the tidbit you promised me?"

"You already have it. The detached, dispassionate morsel is that Sarah Nash knows what Norman Jessup did to Paulo."

"Give me that!" Bunyan grabbed the sack of delicatessen on the chair beside her and walked, at a running pace, really, out of the restaurant, his spectator shoes with their Fred Astaire holes beating a rapid tattoo on the peg-and-groove wooden floor.

He speed-walked all the way to Central Park, fearful he might have a heart attack, it was so far away from his usual stroll. But it was worth the risk, the pounding blood in his ears making him nearly forget about Sarah, how frightened he was of her, actually. The man was still asleep on Leona's bench, his shapely bottom rounded against the slats. "For you," Bunyan said, setting the sack near his face, where he'd see it when he woke, careful to wedge it between the man's nose and the back of the bench, so nobody would steal it. "And your beautiful ass."

$\mathcal{F}$or a while Perry Zemmis had been much like the departed Drayco, the good part of that hustler type, the man that went into every aspect of the entertainment industry and conquered it. But Drayco, for all his hipness and versatility, had never tried to get a foot in the music business, understanding that when you messed with those people, you ended up under the same part of the highway as Jimmy Hoffa.

Perry Zemmis, though, had a handle on music, an armhold on Berl Wilson, the prairie dog whose yelps were the most popular ones of the seventies. Perry had thrown him out of his office after Berl had made him fifty million, because tastes were changing, including Perry's own, and he'd never really liked the son of a bitch. Berl had been kind of slow to get it, since he was not too sharp to begin with and imagined there had been a mistake, and Zemmis was just kidding him, calling him a Nazi son-of-a-bitch cocksucker, just because he was blond and lived in Idaho. So he'd kept on calling. Sal, Zemmis's right-hand guy, telephoned Berl's publisher, and said, "Tell your boy not to call here anymore." That was about as gentle a way of saying good-bye as Perry knew.

Right now he was on the phone with Washington, as he usually was a couple of times a day, since he was becoming Our Man in Hollywood, the major entertainment link to politics. In the inner office two of his assistants were strong-arming a bookkeeper suspected of manipulating figures. From time to time the man would cry out, and Perry would have to cover the mouthpiece.

"I figure a fund-raiser in my garden," Zemmis said into the phone. "Everyone wants to get a look at it since we bought all the Henry Moores and the Rodins."

"But the senator has allergies," the woman on the other end said. "We wouldn't want to place him in a position of having to sneeze. It might seem a sign of weakness."

"I swear to Christ, I never changed any numbers," Bruiser, the bookkeeper, was pleading.

"Can you hang on a minute, Bitsey?" Zemmis said, pleasantly, and pressed the hold button. He went to the door. "Hold it down," he said to what might have been called his henchmen under different circumstances, but in Century City were known as personal assistants. "I'm talking to campaign headquarters."

"You could close the door," said one of the men.

"Then how will I know you're doing your job?"

"The same way you know I did mine," the bookkeeper wept. "You got the numbers on the page."

"They don't add up to enough," said Zemmis, "considering what the Abominable Snowmen took in."

"There were expenses. You okayed the expenses for the road trip."

"That did not include redoing four hotel suites, Bruiser," Zemmis said.

"You know what these groups do. They drug out of control and trash the place."

"It's your job to keep them in line. Or it was."

"That was never my job. My job is only to handle the money."

"That's how you keep them in line."

"Please," Bruiser mewled. "Ask them. They'll tell you I always played fair."

"How would they know, stoned as they are? Okay," Zemmis nodded to one of his assistants. "Give them a call, ask them to fall by."

He closed the door behind him, and concluded his conversation with Bitsey. Then he sent some e-mail to his adopted children, the ones who were able to read, playful stuff so that whoever was online, tapping in to check if Zemmis had the stuff to be ambassador should the election go their way, would see how paternal he was, how nonjudgmental, even if they were retardos and crips.

"You wanted to see us?" Yeti, the biggest of the Snowmen, his hair shagged down over his eyes to meet the tufts that grew on his cheeks, above and apart from his untrimmed beard, ambled into the office. He was followed by his sidemen, a drummer and an electric bass player carrying his instrument like a canoe paddle.

"Don't you guys ever wash?" Perry covered his nose.

"What do you want?" Yeti said. "We only came 'cause Bruiser was crying."

"I want to know what he did with the money."

"Spent it, I guess," Yeti said.

"Lucky for him you're on his side," said Zemmis. He took some papers out of the drawer and put them on his desk, one that had belonged to Kennedy that he'd managed to buy a few years before the Sotheby's auction, saving himself a bundle. "As long as you're here, your contract is up for renewal soon. We might as well get it out of the way."

"We're not signing," Yeti said.

"Not," echoed the drummer. The bass player struck a chord, but as the instrument was electric, and not plugged in, it made a feeble sound. Still, Zemmis got the effect it was meant to have, a chorus.

"You boys can go home," he said. "I'll talk to Yeti."

"Okay?" the drummer asked.

Yeti nodded. The two sidemen left.

"Bring Bruiser in here," Zemmis yelled.

*W*ithin a short time it was settled, an accord reached, signed by Yeti, notarized by a secretary who was also a notary, that Yeti would reimburse Zemmis's company for unauthorized expenditures on his last tour. The agreement had been made in the spirit of true fellowship, after one of Zemmis's assistants broke Bruiser's left kneecap, and Zemmis told Yeti what happened to the other kneecap was up to him. In spite of being unwashed and in many ways unfriendly, Yeti was, all the same, a musician, with the sweetness and generosity of spirit that usually characterized that breed. The best of them as well as the least of them understood that even when they wrote a good song, there had been Bach and Beethoven, so there was no point in a swelled head. Or in Bruiser's case, since he had always been kind, another swelled knee.

The receptionist called a paramedic to take Bruiser to the hospital. After he was gone, Zemmis, with his two assistants present, let Yeti listen to a conversation on the speakerphone with a guy named Bonafetti, who had worked for the DA in New York, confirming that they were going after the mob in the record business.

"Still, these people don't really give a fuck about you guys," Zemmis said, when the conversation was over. "Whereas, I do. So I really think you ought to re-sign."

The two assistants picked Yeti up by the ankles and dangled him from the terrace, twenty-two stories above Century Park East. "Jack

145

Benny used to live in the apartment building over there," said Zemmis, like a tour guide. "You can see his pool. I guess if you live long enough it makes sense to take a condo. That way you don't have to worry about keeping the place up. But maybe you won't get old enough to have those kinds of worries."

"Okay, okay," Yeti choked, so much blood having rushed to his head he could hardly get the words out. "Let me have the papers."

They brought him in and let him sit, giving him a pen. "Can I at least read it?" he asked Zemmis.

"Not much point," Perry said. "It's kind of an offer you can't review." He laughed at the pun he'd made, walked Yeti to the door of the office, and shook his trembling hand.

Right after that, Zemmis tried to call Kate Donnelly to tell her he was waiting for the Fitzgerald manuscript, but she wasn't home. He left a message on her machine.

I have these pictures from when he was a little boy," Lila said, opening a weathered leather album that Kate had helped her get from the bottom of her suitcase. "Look how beautiful he was. *Goldeneh* curls. Like an angel." She started singing. *"Die goldeneh hairelach. Die tsener vi Perelech."*

"In this picture he was a choirboy?"

"Shiksa," Lila said. "Jews don't have choirs. Goyim and angels have choirs."

"You said he was an angel."

"Not officially then," she said. "Maybe now."

"You believe in an afterlife?" Kate stretched her legs, silkily clad in panty hose for the important appointments she had imagined might be coming this day, semisprawled on the bed catercornered to the one where Lila half lay, making herself comfortable, as the older woman with her broken leg couldn't.

"Certainly," Lila said. "You don't go through all this shit and struggle to be a good person without there's a payoff."

"What if you're a bad person? Do you go to hell?"

"He wasn't a bad person," she said hotly. "He was smart. People are jealous of that, resentful, so they put labels on you."

"Like embezzler?"

"Everybody steals in business," Lila said. "Larry was just a little more direct about it. I need to go to the bathroom."

Kate helped her. The two of them were anxious, awkward. The newly acquired crutches supporting Lila's ponderous weight made the trip to the toilet an ordeal. The telephone rang, and Kate went to answer it.

"Mrs. Darshowitz?" A woman's voice.

"She's indisposed," said Kate.

"To whom am I speaking?"

Kate had to think about it for a moment. A friend? Not really. A passing cormorant looking for material? A good samaritan, involuntarily? But it was shame that she didn't care more that had made Kate go get Lila, as shame made her be present now. Guilt made her stay, guilt that she wasn't really concerned with the woman's plight. And a plight it certainly was, sorry and old-fashioned, a difficulty that would better have been set on some gloomy moor. Alone and aimless, deserted by a man who had seemed to love her, but loved a place with an empty heart more. "I'm sort of an acquaintance," Kate said.

"This is Anita Streng," the woman said. "I'm Larry Drayco's estate attorney. We've had a hard time locating Mrs. Darshowitz."

"How did you happen to find her here?" Kate asked, interested in the tracks that lawyers followed, interested, as it was turning out, in the tracks that everyone followed. It was all starting to seem such an elaborate tangle to her, truth, lies, revelations, and fire departments.

"One of the parking attendants at Puck's remembered her saying she was going there."

"He must have telescopic hearing," said Kate, who could herself recall only a barely discernible drunken mumble from Lila leaving the wake about where she was staying. But probably the boys working the lot were like moles in the Cold War, paid to keep extra alert, in their case by scandal mags, or *Inside Edition,* tips that could sustain them better than tips.

"When do you think she'll be able to come to my office?" Anita said.

"She can't. She's broken her leg. I just brought her back from the emergency hospital."

"What did you say your name was?"

"Kate Donnelly," she said, wondering if she wouldn't be better off making one up. It was, after all, a land of pseudonyms and acronyms, sounds that supposedly made things easier to remember, though she was starting to wish there was something that made things easier to forget, to hide.

She thought now about how she had felt only a few days before, perilously close to a panic in her longing to be conspicuous. Already she was starting to feel sentimental about being obscure. All her life she had been in places where people seemed concerned only with what she was: honest, bright, straightforward, anxious to learn, impatient to create, longing for affection, perhaps, but not so intensely that it superceded her wish to *be* herself. Herself, before becoming a part of someone else, identity in tandem. Herself as the not yet fully defined person she hoped to become, but filled with qualities those around her seemed to honor and respect, like honor and respect. Like aspiration. What she was had been all that mattered.

But here everything was *who*. Who you knew. Who had invited you. Who represented you. She wished she could say, it's *me*. I represent myself. I represent the vanished American dream: ambition and talent and yearning in a healthy young package, with a fresh face, and some leftover romanticism from my purported forebear.

"Would it be okay if I came over there?" the lawyer was saying.

"I'm sure it would be fine," Kate said. "She'd probably be glad to see someone who cared about Larry."

"I didn't say I cared about him," Anita said. There was a sudden hard edge to her voice, making it not so much unfeminine as unavailable, except for the job, except by the clock. "I said I was his lawyer."

$\mathcal{T}$he suit Anita Streng wore was well cut, severe, navy blue and right to the point, making her the match for any male lawyer. There were legs coming out from under the skirt, but they seemed there solely to carry her where she intended to go.

"He had a lady lawyer?" Lila said, her eyes not so much squinting as appraising.

Kate could study her watching and understand now what Lila was watching for. Had this been one of Larry's numbers? Kate was starting to sense the glands of the older woman, or whatever part of the body it was that generated suspicion, jealousy, all the emotions Lila claimed not to have registered.

Anita Streng made a slight moue of distaste. "We don't call—"

"A woman lawyer, excuse me," said Lila. "I suppose I should be glad he had such confidence in us." She included herself easily in the blue-suited package.

Or maybe that was spiteful. Sardonic. Maybe, Kate thought, it was a prick in the uppity balloon that appeared to be pulling at the young woman's nose. She was strangely pretty, her face deliberately drab, it seemed to Kate, a kind of combative lack of makeup, as if she were shoving her intelligence in the observer's face, daring them to make her bright blue eyes and thick beige-yellow hair more important than her brains were. In spite of good bone structure and impressive features, she had succeeded in neutralizing herself. She had turned beige. Her skin was the same color as her cupid bow lips. But you would not notice them unless you were studying them, so disappeared were they into her sandy pallor.

"How old are you?" Lila asked.

"Twenty-seven."

Lila sighed. "And you have your own firm?"

"I am one of the attorneys in Fletcher McCallum's office."

"I don't know who that is," Lila said.

"He's an entertainment lawyer. He represented Mr. Drayco."

"And most of the important actors and directors in town," noted Kate.

"Fresh out of law school, right?"

"I've passed the bar," said Anita. "And I *did* go to Yale. Where Clinton went. And Mr. Drayco."

"Excuse me?" said Lila.

"Yale. Where he got his Phi Beta Kappa key."

"Is that in New Haven?" asked Lila.

"It is," said Anita, setting her briefcase on the console.

"Yeah, I remember when he went to New Haven," said Lila. "He got involved in some musical, trying out out of town. He found that key thing in a pawn shop."

"I beg your pardon?" said Anita.

"You don't have to apologize to me because he fooled you," Lila said, grinning. " 'Every man is a hero to his fool of an attorney'; that was his favorite saying."

"I believe the saying is 'No man is a hero to his valet,' or 'Only a fool has himself for a lawyer,' " Anita said coolly.

"Well it's good you can straighten me out," said Lila.

The young woman opened the briefcase. "Do you have a VCR?" she asked.

"We can get one from the desk," said Lila. "It's ten extra dollars a day."

"I suspect you'll be able to afford it," said Anita, and pulled out a sealed envelope. "His instructions were to give this to you and that I be present while it was played."

*D*o you want me to leave?" Kate asked, once the VCR was installed and the tape was about to go on. As curious as she was about its contents, she would not have minded Lila's excusing her, letting her off the hook. Already she was feeling somewhat relieved, the burden of Lila Darshowitz shifting in her mind onto this blue-suited, gently officious young woman, paid to carry the load.

"Can she stay?" Lila asked Anita.

"It's up to you."

"Stay," Lila said.

There was a sadness in the way she said "Stay," it seemed to Kate, as though everything else had deserted her. Her youth, her lover, seasons, perhaps, that she had wished she could cling to, spring that had changed too quickly to summer, summer that blazed into fall. "Stay," she might have whispered out her window to the turning leaves on the trees. But they'd fallen all the same, plunging her into winter.

"Then we'll proceed," Anita said, and turned the tape on.

*T*he lighting was a little harsh. But on the screen there was a sur-prising softness about Larry Drayco, an unexpected sweetness. His hair was very light, cut short, so the eyes in the still-babyish face, round cheeks, tanned skin, looked large and very clear. His voice as he spoke was gentle, little more than a whisper, not as in the famous, uncontrollable rages he was noted for.

"I suppose you're wondering why I called you here today," he said, and then laughed. "No, I guess not." He looked straight at the camera. "Lila, I'm sorry. I hope I didn't go in any way that made things tougher for you than I already have.

"I'm leaving you whatever I have in the bank, my house and all its contents. But I don't have to tell you there are people waiting in line with claims against me. Some gonifs I beat fair and square who still took me to court, and won because I made the mistake of telling the judges to go fuck themselves. You know me, with people who think they're in charge.

"Plus there's the IRS. *And* the lawyers who are bringing this to you now. I owe them for the time in court—plus the other guys' attorneys' fees. Without me there to put up a fight, I guess they'll take pretty much everything.

"Herb and I do have a new picture coming out, and if it's a winner maybe the studio can be leaned on to give you some share. Darcy Linette is a decent woman, very active in charities, so maybe she'll realize that you deserve something. But I wouldn't hold my breath because she's got that whole fucking corporate bureaucracy to work through, and charity ain't their game.

"I wouldn't hold my breath." He repeated the words, and gave a gentle chuckle. His smile, like his voice, was curiously gentle, lighting up his face. "I guess that's really just an expression now.

"But I *am* able to leave you a little something that could put you in the catbird seat. This town, as you probably figured out by now, is all about power. I have something on a truly major player. The other item in this packet is an audiotape that should give you a three-picture deal, or a place on the board of his studio, which comes with a pretty steep stipend, as they say when they've been to Hahvahd." He pronounced it in the Bostonian manner, slyly, slightly contemptuously, as if he had, indeed, gone to Yale, and had traditional reason to look down or at least askance at Cambridge. "I don't know if you want to get involved in this shitty business, but if you do, this is your passport. Don't be intimidated by the fact that you don't know anything about making movies. They got clothes designers who connect with the right star, get them to feel dependent, and make themselves producers. Hairdressers who hoist themselves up by their clients' tresses like they was Rapunzel, climbing to the towers of power. So don't be shy. And don't take crap from anybody. You're worth all of them.

"Listen to the tape alone. As Benjamin Franklin said, three people can keep a secret if two of them are dead. As far as I know, since you're playing this tape, I'm the only one who qualifies.

"I wish I could give you something more concrete. You've been the only one in my life I could always count on—"

At this point Lila burst into sobs. Convulsive they were, wracked, as though she were vomiting tears.

"I'm sorry you couldn't say the same about me. But I really loved you, probably still do. I mean, even now, when I'm not there anymore. If I'm anywhere, I bet included in my package is how I feel about you. I hope that counts for something."

By now, Lila was wailing uncontrollably. The phone rang. Anita hit the remote control and stopped the tape while Kate picked the receiver up. It was the desk clerk, saying someone had heard screams, asking should he call 911.

"No, it's okay," Kate said. "We've been to a funeral." She hung up the phone, and the video resumed.

"Well, I'm outta here," Larry was saying. "Probably by now I'll be doing lunch with Orson Welles in that big Chasen's in the sky. I've got a lot I'd like to ask him. I really would've loved to be a great film-maker. But what can you do? You do what you can. I even would've loved to have left you with Rosebud. You know, some big mystery about what was really important to me. The thing I missed out on, grieved over losing. But I don't think even I know what that was.

"So all I have to leave you is the tape. May it serve you well. Au revoir, I sincerely hope."

The screen went dark.

*A*fter they were gone, after she had pulled herself together, and Kate had put a box of Kleenex where she had easy access to it, Lila played the audiotape. Anita had loaned her a small cassette player, and called an agency for her for home nursing care, which she was sure Larry's health insurance could cover, since Lila was still officially his wife. Otherwise, she said, the firm would be glad to sue the city of Santa Monica, on contingency. It seemed to Lila as close as that young goy lawyer could get to being warmhearted.

There was music on the tape. Larry with his sense of theatrics, his love of song, producing, staging, putting a curtain around whatever it was he was going to show. It wasn't until a little further in that Lila realized the music was actually happening wherever the scene was playing out, part of whatever was going on, the squeaks that she'd thought were bad violins the springs of a mattress going up and down.

"Oh, God, I love these," the man was saying.

"And I love that you talk in bed," said the woman, throatily. "Most men . . . " there were moist pauses " . . . don't like to talk when they're making love."

"Why?" he said, with difficulty.

"Because talking requires an answer," she whispered. "And you'd rather my mouth was doing this."

A pause. He groaned.

"Oh, Larry," Lila said. "You really going to make me listen to this?"

When it was over, Larry's voice came on the recording. "Honey," he said. "That was Victor Lippton, tobacco zillionaire, and new head of Cosmos, with his mistress, Alexa de Carville. Not *exactly* a poor person either. Her father invented a utility software that writes all kinds of letters for you, sold it to a giant corporation for a bundle.

"Richest of all is Victor's wife, daughter of a Hong Kong businessman whose enemies often turn up in Victoria Harbor. *If* the weights fall off and they turn up at all. So this is nothing he would like her to find out. Or take a chance on her finding out.

"Call him at Cosmos—it's in Culver City, the number changes all the time as the owners do, so call information. Ask for Victor Lippton. Tell his secretary you're Larry Drayco's widow, and I left him something."

*H*ow did he get it?" Victor Lippton asked, white-faced. They were alone in his office, which he had shown her with the automatic pride of very rich men who knew they didn't have to impress anyone, and

153

so impressed everybody. Four interior designers had banded together to make it an instant understated showplace, erecting it like a tent over a society wedding in less than two days. Carpenters and electricians from the studio had done the construction work, seamlessly, flawlessly, with unbelievable speed. That is to say, it would have been unbelievable, Victor had said, smiling benignly at the start of their meeting, had their futures, like the suite, not hung in the balance.

The offices jutted out like a ship's prow over the garden below, the corner of the main room at an improbable angle, finished with floor-to-ceiling glass. To be in that place, even in the wheelchair they'd brought her in, had given Lila a slight attack of vertigo, a condition that seemed to be shared by Victor once he heard the tape.

"I don't know exactly," Lila said. "Somebody he knew at the *National Enquirer,* probably. They were always doing exposes on him." She said it as she always did, without any kind of *A* sound, so it rhymed with noses, only having read the word. "After a while he started trading information, and you know Larry. He had a knack for making friends."

Victor Lippton guffawed. It was a nasty sound, artificial in its merriment.

"What I would ask myself," Lila said, "before I sent any more hate and mistrust to Larry, is how did they get under her mattress?"

He seemed not to register what she was saying. "Where's the original of the tape?" he asked.

"That's it."

"I suppose you made copies."

"I suppose you'd suppose that."

"So you picked up the finer traits of blackmail from your late husband."

"He was never a blackmailer," she said darkly.

"Then what is this?" He indicated the tape on the recorder.

"He wanted to leave me a legacy."

"What exactly do you want?"

"I'll have to think about it." She shifted in her wheelchair as best she could. "He suggested a three-picture deal, or a place on your board. But I don't know if that's my style."

"Cash?" he asked, his dark eyes narrowing underneath the leonine head of wheat-colored hair. "How much?"

"This town shit all over my husband," she said sullenly.

"I understand it was reciprocal."

"He was a decent kid when he came here. It was the place . . . "

"People like to blame the environment they live in when they can't take responsibility . . . "

"Don't give me that sophisticated crap. I'm a very simple woman."

"So what do you want?"

She was silent for a moment. "A monument to him."

"You're putting me on. We're supposed to erect a goddamned statue to a man who broke every rule, violated every ethic—"

"I didn't say a statue," she interrupted. "And I wouldn't talk about ethics if I was you. Or maybe we should play the tape again. Adultery. And you're not even in the military."

"I'm talking business ethics," he said, reddening.

"I got a flash for you, Mr. Lippton. Life isn't just about business. Maybe it seems to be that way here . . . "

"Hollywood is a microcosm of America," he said.

"I don't know what that means."

"A microcosm . . . " He assumed the stance he took when he addressed his board of directors with the annual report, inhaling air as though it were tobacco through slightly pursed lips. He exhaled the explanation. "A miniature of the big picture, a little model of what it's all about."

"You think America is about movies?"

"People want to be entertained. Forget their troubles, even if they're not interesting enough to have any. America is a company town. Sometimes the company is Eastman Kodak. Sometimes it's government. Here it's about pictures, so it's got a greater hold on the public. But every company has the same bottom line, and the bottom line is success. That's what this country is about."

"That's really pathetic," said Lila.

For a moment Victor was taken aback, as though it were his explanation she found unacceptable. "I'm sorry you find my theory offensive."

"I'm not offended," she said. "Nothing this town does can offend me. Not anymore. My only interest in Hollywood is already underground. And I want him . . . what's that word, when you want to make sure somebody is remembered?"

"Oh, he'll be remembered," Victor said.

"I mean *good* remembered."

"Commemorated," Lippton said.

"Yeah. That's it. Commemorated."

"How do you suggest we do that?"

"I'll have to think about it," Lila said, and smiled.

Last Lunches

Algernon Reddy awoke from a dream of death. It took him a moment to remember that it was life that was the illusion. Because he had full confidence in that precept, he had chosen to return to New York as his semifinal resting place, electing to die in an environment where man was assaulted with reality. Mugged, you might say.

Even cosseted as he was with the comforts his confreres had provided, safe in a very soft bed, with the hum of *Oms* from the meditation room downstairs in his ears, he could still hear the rumble of traffic, the slam of lids on garbage cans, the sirens. "I have chosen not to die in California," he'd said, on leaving, "because how could I tell?"

The pronouncement had been made a few days after Larry Drayco's funeral. As that man's death had been unexpected, and his own was imminent and predictable, he'd decided to make tracks. Attached as he was to the weather in L.A., to the outer peace that seemed at times to match his inner one, to the profusion of flowers outside the guest house that the last in a long line of heiresses had made available to him, he understood, as Carl Sandburg had said, that life was "a series of relinquishments." So he knew he had to let go of what made him, even in his pain, sensually comfortable, for the final relinquishment that lay ahead.

Friends who ran the meditation center in New York had been sadly delighted to welcome him. All had the same view of mortality, that it was but part of an infinite journey. Still, they hated to see him go. He had brought wild colors to the philosophy, as vibrant as those he had seen on his psychedelic trips, and his gift of words had made them almost visible, even to the spiritually blind.

Now he lay, or sometimes sat, dying, his last public appearance walking unaided having been at Drayco's funeral. The man had befriended him, as much as a man like Larry Drayco could befriend anyone who could do him no measurable good. They had shared a few quiet dinners in a vegetarian restaurant, as the producer made a perceptible effort to seem like he didn't wish he were at Matteo's. As though following Algernon's urgings that he open himself to his own spirituality, Drayco had actually made a trip to India and spent several days at Sayed Baba's ashram, where he watched him perform some of his miracles, and had come back a little calmer. Algernon had found himself feeling fondness for the fellow, a sentiment that did not diminish even when he found out that Drayco's real reason for the trek was the presence at the ashram of an Indian billionaire who was thinking of putting money in movies. Whatever got you there, Algernon had thought at the time, looking back at his own metaphysical beginnings, when, still known as "Ever" Reddy, he'd dropped acid because he thought it might enhance his fucking.

There was a table beside the bed that had on it medicines doctors had given him to dull the pain, or put him out of his head so he couldn't measure how excruciating it was; liquid cocaine friends had smuggled in from England where it was legitimate and freely administered to the mortally ill; plus a variety of psychedelics to make the passage easier and more interesting. The least of these was marijuana, which so attenuated time that Algernon had the illusion that he was living forever. Which, as he knew from heavier tripping, he was destined to do.

Because the house where he was staying had an official, tax-deductible spiritual label, it was filled with seekers, some of them residents, some transients, some there for the day just to chant or be still. All of them wanted interviews and audiences with Algernon. But his strength was measurably ebbing, and, as Self vanished, he became more selfish. The sense of playfulness had disappeared from his journey: he had sent away the young filmmakers who had been in attendance to record his departure. Of all those who wanted to be with him, the only one he wanted was the young boy—he could not help thinking of him as that even though he was a man—who sat beside his bed now.

The boy was golden-haired, golden-lashed, and golden-skinned, a remnant of his California bronze, as beautiful a creature, man, woman, or beast, as Algernon had ever laid eyes on. They had first met when Algernon gave a reading of his poems at the Viper, the Los Angeles nightclub where River Phoenix had OD'd.

"You are my final gift," Algernon said in a voice that was still surprisingly strong. "On this side, anyway. I am grateful to Destiny for bringing you to the Viper to see me."

"I didn't come to see you," Tyler Hayden said.

"Why, then?"

"I was looking for my peers."

"You don't have any," Algernon said. "It's you and everybody else."

He wished Reddy hadn't said that. Tyler suffered from pride and disliked it in himself, wanting very much to shed what seemed to him often to be arrogance, since he, too, knew how beautiful he was, and how smart. At the same time he could feel himself flush with pleasure, because that was the conviction he himself had had, that he was one of a kind. To have it confirmed by someone as brilliant and perceptive as Algernon came as a great relief, even as it burdened him with how lonely he would be.

"I'm fading," Algernon said.

"Can you see God yet?" asked Tyler.

"I see Him all the time," said Algernon. "I see Him in you. I hear Him in music. I taste Him in food. I feel Him in sex."

"Pretty irreverent," said Tyler.

"That's why I came," said Algernon. "If God didn't mean us to be irreverent, He wouldn't have created me. Or Jonathan Swift, making him a clergyman. It's the pompous and the pious who are an insult to Him."

"I wish you had been my father," said Tyler. "I wish it had been you who raised me."

"But I did," he said. "In the little piece of time we have known each other, this life, anyway, I have seen you grow like a spiritual fungus."

"Not a pretty picture," Tyler said.

"It is to me. But then, I've known some really great fungi."

They both laughed. Algernon winced suddenly.

"Are you in a lot of pain?" Tyler asked softly.

"I can't really tell. Maybe agony itself is a hallucination. A convincing one, I grant you. But passing, as everything is passing."

"I can't believe how lucid you are, with everything you're on."

"Well, drugs are mother's milk to me," said Reddy. "On the other hand, maybe I haven't taken everything I seem to have taken. Maybe I want the full experience as it is. Maybe I've only told my friends I'm ingesting all this shit to make *them* more comfortable."

"Is there anything I can do?"

Algernon closed his eyes, and thought for a moment. "Don't compromise," he said, at last.

"Have you?" Tyler asked. "Have you ever?"

"Well, to tell you the truth, in my youth, when I was a fabled swordsman, I from time to time shtupped a woman or twelve I felt nothing for, including lust."

"Why?"

"Ego. To reaffirm I was the best. To raise money for my foundation. You'd be surprised how many women there are who have too much money and feel guilty about it, and are desperate to go deeper, give their life significance, get laid. Fucking for me was no more than a smile is to most people. A way of manipulating."

"And you regret it?"

"I regret nothing. See that you do the same. Regret is a cancer, and I already have that covered."

"How about . . . " Tyler hesitated. "How about if you were drawn to a woman that you knew was a ditz, empty?"

"Why, I should fill her up," Algernon said. "Besides, an enlightened man doesn't judge."

"I don't have to judge. It's evident."

"That's very superior of you."

"I thought you said I was superior."

"I only said you were apart. Apart shouldn't put you on a perch, looking down. Is she beautiful?"

"Like nobody else," Tyler said.

"Then go for it."

It had been Tyler's hope that Reddy would discourage him. The taste of Helen's mouth, the expert softness of her lips, collapsing under his even while she ate them, had nearly made him stumble off his road. He had actually considered for a moment trying to do something commercially acceptable, like being a movie star. Or taking her up on her offer to give him entree to everybody. But he knew in his heart, which was as good as his brain, that people would consider him her Toy Boy. Whatever of inspiration he had to deliver to the unaware could not be passed on from such a position.

So he desperately wanted someone to dissuade him. His own father was not around anymore to talk sense to him, and even when alive had been easily intimidated, especially by people he deemed successful, which he was not. Tyler's mother was self-absorbed, never even noting how exceptional her son was, except when it reflected on her. His beauty was nearly lost on her, so caught was she in the most superficial of externals, like his failing to wear a tie. So to take on another narcissistic female after his struggle to escape the one he'd issued from seemed to him self-destructive and stupid. Especially as Helen Manning had undoubtedly had every man she'd ever wanted. Unique as Tyler held himself to be, and Algernon Reddy had just confirmed, perhaps all that made him really different for Helen, as simplistic as her thinking seemed, was the fact that he withheld himself.

Besides, he was scared. "I don't want to end up a man who's led around by his thing," Tyler said.

"Thing?" said Algernon, energized enough by outrage to raise himself on his elbow. "Am I to leave my spiritual estate to a man who can't say penis?"

Tyler grinned. "Why do you suppose they gave genitals such ugly names? Penis. Vagina."

"As beauty is in the eye of the beholder, ugliness is in the mind of the listener. There's nothing wrong with those words, unless you live in Orange County."

"You don't think lewdness diminishes our connection with God?"

"It only makes it stronger," said Algernon, and took Tyler's hand, his own fingers frail against the firm, healthy flesh. "If God didn't mean us to be sexual beings, he wouldn't have given us dicks."

Sometime late that evening, he died, still clutching Tyler's hand. They both knew that what Algernon was, what everybody was, was indestructible consciousness. He had talked of the bubble of his spirit becoming a part of the infinite ocean. It all sounded so correct that when the moment came, and the terrible gurgle issued from his throat, an actual rattle, and the man was gone, fled, gray-faced, nobody home, Tyler had a hard time with how final it seemed. Somehow he had not expected death to be what it was when looked straight in the face. He had not been present when his father died: his body was gone when Tyler came home from school. Death. That was really the right word for it, no matter how convinced you were it was part of a passage.

They had spoken, in part, about the afterlife, Reddy telling Tyler how it would be, what paths he would have to tread, what transitions he would go through, even the hospital wards on the other side he might be wayfared into for a while, to recuperate from his fleshly agonies. Tyler already knew all that Algernon told him, having read the same books and eaten the same kinds of mushrooms. But as he loved the man, and was struggling to learn complete compassion, he kept silent. He understood it was Reddy's greatest joy to teach.

He had wept at the last, as Algernon wept, the two holding each other, pooling tears, not because they believed he was dying in the true sense, but because their dialogue was temporarily coming to an end. Tyler never told him that the woman he was talking about was Helen Manning. He was afraid that, much as Algernon cared for him, he might call him a fool for even hesitating. A fucking fool, most likely.

*S*till, when he came away from the cremation, when they gave Tyler a share of the ashes Reddy had bequeathed him, along with the *aviso* to sprinkle them somewhere transcendent, and enough carfare to take him there, Tyler did not even think of Los Angeles. That is to say, he thought of it. He thought of Topanga Canyon, with its green arroyos; Leo Carrillo Beach sparkling mica gold; Point Dume, where towering, tufted cliffs overlooked a flawless stretch of unoiled azure ocean and the air was so crystal you couldn't tell a few miles away was smog. And he thought of the Self-Realization Center with its devotee-tended radiant purple flowers lining the hills, its Mark Twain–like white steamboat anchored on a still, silver green pond, with only the detached meandering of swans lightly riffling the surface. And he thought of the Hollywood Bowl on a Beethoven night. He thought of the fountains outside the Ahmanson. All places where Algernon might have felt comfortable, lifted, exalted.

But in Tyler's belly was still a little knot of fear. Because as one-dimensional as Helen Manning might have been, he suspected she was still more woman than he had ever had. Than anyone had ever had, probably, aside from the forty or fifty or maybe hundreds of men she had known.

*W*henever Jake Alonzo looked in the mirror now, he was pleased with what he saw. All his very young life it had sort of dismayed him that he was so flawlessly handsome. As the afflicted cried *why me?*, Jake wondered why he'd been chosen, what there was special about him that God, or Nature, or some positive freaking of genes had given him a face that made people stop and stare. He had been aware since early childhood that his older brother was retarded, that his parents were simple and ugly and cruel and often violent, that it was just him and his baby brother who, for some invisible reason, had been given a generous portion of beauty. When they walked through their dingy part of the Bronx, off Shakespeare Avenue, shopkeepers would offer them candy, soda, all the things you weren't supposed to take from strangers even when you knew them. The two boys were so exquisite, their dark tousled curls so shiny, their smiles so winning, they seemed princes in a neighborhood of thugs, and behaved accordingly. Jake was the older royal, the one whose kingdom it was destined to be, with the second in line, his little brother Max, trailing after.

Not quite as clever as he was good-looking, Jake at a very early age still had sufficient curiosity to find out who Shakespeare was that he got his own avenue, just as he'd learned why James Monroe deserved a high school. Impressed, and a reader, he'd started to study the Bard and, sponsored by his high school English teacher, found his way to an acting school run by one of the last great divas. She was a member of the Actor's Studio, a spiritual descendent of Stella Adler, and although in her fifties, still incredibly randy. She did not ask him to move in with her till he turned nineteen.

His parents had no idea where he was living, not that they would have cared. But his mentor was afraid they might make trouble. So he went back home from time to time to take his little brother for a soda. Adored as he was by the diva, and everyone in his acting class, and even casting people who were starting to fall all over him, there was nothing like a worshiping sibling. And Max would trail after him as he had all through their childhood.

"I gotta go back downtown," Jake told him, one autumn afternoon, when a tree that grew through the cracks in the sidewalk had amber leaves, all that the neighborhood offered of nature. The first time Jake had had a girl he'd been ten, and they did it on the concrete of the schoolyard at night, there being no parks in the vicinity.

"How come you don't let me visit you?" Max asked.

"They don't allow kids in my building." It was as good an excuse as any, and probably true. The building where the diva lived was a rent-controlled high-rise on Eighth Avenue. It was inhabited exclusively by theater people who signed up years in advance and waited so long for a vacancy that by the time they were ensconced they were too old to breed. Max was only twelve.

From the corner of his eyes, Jake caught a glimpse of an old school friend, now a banker for the Mafia, collecting money for numbers. The mob recruited from the graduating class of James Monroe as law firms did from Harvard and Yale.

"Yo, Red!" Jake called out, anxious to have his friend see how far he had come, or gone, actually. He wanted Red to take note of his clothes, which were well cut now, as custom-tended as his diction. "See you," he said to his little brother.

"But we didn't get a chance to really talk . . . " Max pleaded, as his brother cut across the street.

"You're twelve," Jake said, his back to him. "What makes you think you've got that much to say?"

"But . . . " Max started after him. Jake was on the far corner when he heard the screech of the brakes, and the impact.

*I*n class, they worked on guilt, how to incorporate it nonverbally into the subtext of a scene. He didn't have any problem using that. He would look in the mirror while shaving, and wonder why he was clock-stopping handsome, why he was the one left alive, why he was the one with a brain that functioned. What made the chips fall the way they did?

They found him for Hollywood. His press agent sent out releases about charisma. Several leading ladies who became his lovers threatened suicide, and the diva who'd launched him died.

Cocaine and booze were easier to come by than absolution. He was twenty-eight when he crashed into the tree.

*N*ow when he shaved and saw what was in the mirror, he was satisfied. He looked as flawed as he felt. Humpty-Dumpty. All the king's plastic surgeons. As good a job as they'd done, his face was slightly asymmetrical, the unrestorable nerve in his eyelid causing a slight droop over his right eye. The rosebud mouth, once so lushly feminine, was pulled at the corners. But along with the not quite perfect reconstruction had come acting bonanzas. He could now play the obsessed, the psychopaths, and that seemed somehow appropriate. If a woman loved him onscreen it was because she was needy, so her judgment was off.

It was not like that in real life, of course. Or real life as it was in Hollywood. Ingenues and the seemingly well were among the women waiting in line.

*R*ight now the woman across from him was Samantha Chatsworth, the West Coast editor of *East* magazine. The lunch they were having at an open-air cafe near the ocean in Santa Monica had been set under the pretext of an interview she was thinking of doing. So far she had taken not a single note. Since she was English, Jake understood it would take her a while to get to the point, dancing around her true agenda as the Happy Breed usually did.

"I was wondering," she said eventually, leaning back so her tightly coiled auburn hair touched the fringe of the white umbrella shading their table, "who you were planning on taking to the Oscars?" She was dressed in her New York chic: a sleeveless black sheath, pearl choker at her throat. It was totally inappropriate for the setting, where even the local lawyers taking their lunch breaks had their jackets off and only the waitresses wore ties.

"I haven't been nominated this year," Jake said. "I'm not sure I'll be going."

"But certainly you'll go to the parties and the Governor's Ball."

She was working her breadstick like a baton, twirling it subtly through the air as she spoke, conducting herself, quite literally, Jake noted, like a lady. What she really wanted was still a puzzle to him. She would certainly have her own invitations to the awards, people in power in Hollywood being intimidated by the press, especially when headquartered in New York.

But he waited, understanding the protocol. The British rarely asked anything even as straightforward as "How are you feeling?" for fear you might answer the truth, say something open, show a piece of heart that had blood in it, and then the questioner would have to cope. He knew from the gossip, and the vibes she sent out, that Samantha was not particularly interested in men. So she certainly wasn't trying to wangle his escorting her.

"I'm not much for parties," he said.

"But the Oscars aren't a party. They're a worldwide celebration. A billion people around the planet watching, riveted."

"What does that say about the planet?" Jake asked.

"Let me tell you about the specials," their waitress said. She was long-legged and brilliantly red-haired, her thick Scottish tresses snared unsuccessfully into a ponytail.

"I'm just going to have the chopped Cobb," said Samantha, dismissing her with a wave of her breadstick.

"Go ahead," Jake said, smiling at the big-breasted girl. "You can tell me."

"For appetizers there's a carpaccio of gravlax and scallops, very nice, on a bed of watercress or pepper-seared tuna with papaya relish and eggplant. For entree: halibut with a raspberry coulis, and the pasta special is penne with sundried tomatoes, roasted yellow peppers, and garlic."

"Who's your acting teacher?" Jake asked.

"How did you know I was an actress?"

"You're waiting tables in L.A., aren't you?" Jake said, and smiled. She said the name of a once almost-star.

166

"She's good," Jake said. "I did a movie with her. Give her my love."

"And you are . . . ?" the waitress asked him.

"Very funny," said Samantha, coldly. "I'll have the chopped Cobb."

She didn't come to the point until they were having coffee, a cappuccino for Jake, an espresso for Samantha. "Have you met our adorable Wendy?" she finally said.

"The duchess?"

"We're not supposed to call her that anymore. Of course she's more royal than practically anyone who's left, but don't quote me."

"Who to?" he said. "It's not my kind of conversation. Nothing that captures my attention."

"What *does* interest you?" Samantha asked.

"Aspiration," said Jake. "Longing for what can never be achieved."

"How frustrating."

"Not really. It's the struggle to be more that keeps us from being less."

"Very thoughtful," Samantha said, writing it down. "We must do a piece on you. I wouldn't have expected that."

"What would you have expected?"

"An interest in politics. Sports. Most men like to talk about sports."

"That's so they can go on for hours without revealing anything about themselves, who they really are, what they feel."

She seemed uncomfortable, actually looking away. "What a sensitive man you are," she said, although the revelation seemed to irritate her, apparently being more than she cared to know.

"Thank you."

"Would you like to take Wendy to the Oscars?" There it was.

"Not particularly," Jake said.

She looked surprised, literally caught her breath. "But you're not attached to anyone, are you?"

"Only to myself," he said. "And she's not exactly my cup of tea, as you might say."

"You don't even know her. She's an absolute darling."

"I'm sure. But darling doesn't do it for me. Not at this point in my life."

"What do you want?" asked Samantha, not meaning to be curious, but unable to stop herself. She could hardly believe it. This man, this *actor*, turning down the duchess. Even though he'd topped the short list of eligible, impressive locals who might escort her, he was still as common as clay. Talented clay, to be sure, but who did he think he was? "She's one of the most sought-after women in the world."

"Not by me," he said. "I'm flattered that you'd think of me, but—"

"Answer my question," said Samantha imperiously. "What do you want?"

Jake thought for a moment. "The part of a lifetime. A woman who loves me. To make amends for the wrongs I've done. To be all that I can be."

"You should join the army," said Samantha, furious, and, getting up, left him with the check.

*T*he horror was that now Wendy might go with someone inappropriate. The whole world was inappropriate, in Samantha's opinion, and the young woman was headstrong. Even in her wounded state, she was fiercely determined. It was all Samantha could do to shepherd her properly, an assignment she had given herself.

The first public event Wendy would attend since Larry Drayco's funeral, which didn't count, especially as Samantha had unsuccessfully attempted to dissuade her from going, was the Oscars. Who she went with would determine how the world would now perceive her. The only name on Samantha's list Wendy had responded to with interest was Jake Alonzo. And the man had had the nerve, the actual hubris, to turn her down.

"He's made other plans," Samantha told her now. She herself was unable to bear the truth. How could she tell it to Wendy?

They were in the ex-duchess's apartment on Wilshire, a low floor of a high-rise in case of earthquake. Unreality came with the territory, built in, like the assurance the building had sway, and if the big one came you'd be just as safe in a high-rise. Still, they had contracted for a lower floor, putting aside any thought that the apartments on top could just as easily collapse on you as not.

The room they were in had fabric-covered walls, a flowery chintz that gave the feeling of country. Wendy didn't want to feel confined when she rode her stationary bicycle as she was doing now.

"That's fine," Wendy said, a little short of breath. "I only said alright to him because I like his acting. I have no idea what he's like as a person."

"Surly and full of himself," said Samantha, still livid.

"Maybe I'll ask Morty," said Wendy.

"Are you mad?" She saw little dots of light in the air around her, swirling, the kind that preceded a migraine.

"Why? He's sweet. And you're the one who brought us together."

"So he could make your line of clothes," Samantha said. "Not your evening. For God's sake, Wendy. Think how it would look. The two of you together."

"He's taller than the duke."

"He's a Jew."

"You're not serious," Wendy said.

"You didn't know he was a Jew? Mortimer *Schein?*"

"Of course I knew that," Wendy said, and stopped bicycling, got down from the seat. "What I didn't know was that you were an anti-Semite."

"Oh, for God's sake," Samantha said impatiently.

"Exactly," said Wendy, and wiped the perspiration from her brow with a royal blue washcloth. "And let's not leave out His Son."

"Now, don't you go all unctuous on me," Samantha said, defensive anger being more powerful in her than her wish to maintain an important connection. "Some of my best friends are anti-Semites."

"I have no doubt." Wendy wiped the back of her neck. She had sweated through her workout clothes, a sample Mortimer had sent her of the model he was considering for marketing under their banner. It was pale blue Lycra and fleece, the color of her eyes. "The colour of your eyes," he had written in his accompanying note to her. "You see, I can spell in English." She could not help considering him a little adorable.

"Some of the most intelligent people in history . . . " Samantha went on, unable to contain herself. "T.S. Eliot. The founding father of literary modernism. There's a book by the Princess of Wales's own solicitor, proving that very point."

"That doesn't make it an endorsement. I never even particularly liked Eliot. 'I am old. I am old. I will wear my stockings rolled.' It gives one an aversion to age."

"You should have that anyway," said Samantha.

"Then I shall have to die young," Wendy said.

"Don't be so tragic."

"I was simply stating the truth. That's the only way to avoid getting older."

"I have a line to every important plastic surgeon on four continents. There's no reason you ever have to change."

"Yes, there is," Wendy said, and opened the door to show her out. "I don't want to be like you."

"You're making a great mistake," said Samantha, stepping into the hall. "There's no one you can really trust besides me."

"Then I'm in worse trouble than I thought," said Wendy.

*W*hen she got back to her office, Samantha patched a call through her switchboard in New York to the United Kingdom. "You'd better do something," she said. "It's more appalling than the equerry or the art collector."

*T*here was a gay underground in New York, just as there was in Los Angeles. There were those who gossiped and knew unrevealed truths about each other, even though one could presumably do no more harm now that everybody was out of the closet. Almost everybody, that was. Still there were advertising executives playing out their two-and-a-half-children charades in Greenwich. Politicians who kept silent because it could be used against them at the polls. But in the theater everyone knew, and everybody acknowledged. The red ribbons they'd worn for AIDS awareness were now matched by pink ribbons for breast cancer awareness, and pale gray for prostate cancer awareness, as if life-threatening illness had become less disease than fashion statement.

So Sarah Nash had little trouble turning up people who were willing to feed her information about Norman Jessup and the vanished Paulo and their tumultuous love affair in the days before homosexuality had been politically correct. "Yes, Norman was friends with Stephen Ryder," the young gay man her publisher had put her in touch with told her over lunch at Fiorello's, a noisy restaurant across from Lincoln Center. "Stephen of course was the first movie star to 'out' himself *after* he was married, and before it was politically correct. That's what makes him such an interesting subject for a biography."

"How's it coming?" Sarah asked, not really interested. But writers seemed to demand that one be curious about what they were working on.

"I'm becoming just a *tad* obsessed with him," Eliott, the young man, said with Woody Allen mannerisms. The glasses he wore were owlish, in further veneration.

"Well, you'd have to be if you're writing his biography."

"I mean, *really* obsessed. It's harder to get to know him, since he's dead . . . "

"I'd imagine."

". . . so I've started dreaming about him. Mostly he comes to me in red satin briefs."

"How is he hung?" Sarah asked.

"Fabulously," Eliott said, twirling his spaghetti. "I never realized he was such a hunk."

"And he was friends with Paulo and Norman?" she said, getting him back on track.

"They all lived in the same neighborhood when they were in New York."

"Where?"

"Turtle Bay. Stephen told friends he felt very special in New York because he lived near Katharine Hepburn. And he had a bill among his papers from a liquor store addressed to Cole Porter, that was marked 'Third Notice,' with these big red letters 'OVERDUE.' Apparently it blew over his fence when he was very young and doing a play, and he kept it because he found it so *droll*. Cole lived in Turtle Bay."

"You knew him?" She did not quite sneer at the use of the songwriter's first name.

"God, I wish. But he lived *eons* before I was born. Still, I know all his lyrics by heart. I don't know why they make such a fuss over Stephen."

"Sondheim?"

"Equal wit, maybe, but none of the humor, basically mean-spirited, except for *Forum*. And, of course, 'Send in the Clowns.' " He started to hum it.

"And Norman and Paulo lived in that neighborhood?" she asked, trying not to show her impatience. The theater interested her hardly at all, nor did twenty-five-year-old gays who spoke like insiders when they weren't and had contracted to write about movie stars they hadn't even known just to be able to interview people with whom the stars had been friendly. Her take on Eliott was sharp and accurate, backed up by information from a junior editor who'd been disgusted by the deal Eliott had gotten because he lived downstairs from a successful author with a powerful agent. There was just as much corruption in publishing as in the movie business, Sarah knew. But somehow it wasn't as fascinating to the public, so Sarah had no intention of exposing it. Besides, she'd have to get a publisher who wasn't in publishing.

"All you would have had to do is check the real estate records," Eliott said, picking up the brusqueness in her tone.

"I find you a lot livelier." She did not add that she hated doing regular research. That was what she had Chuck for. She was annoyed with him for not thinking of simply checking the residential house sales, sparing her this lunch.

"Well, *thanks*," Eliott said. "I was a little intimidated at the prospect of meeting you, but I *did* love your book. How come you didn't write about Stephen Ryder in it?"

"He was already ill."

"That was merciful," Eliott said.

"And people weren't that interested in him anymore."

Eliott paled. "Really?"

"Have you ever written anything before?" she asked, trying not to let the scorn she felt become audible in her tone.

"A piece for the *Voice*," he said.

"*The Village Voice*?"

"Yes." He was starting to sense how little she wanted to be with him. He looked chagrined.

"And you didn't know Stephen?"

"He died when I was still in college," he said.

"Oh, you went to college."

"You know," Eliott set his fork down, "I heard you were a bitch. But I had no idea."

"That doesn't surprise me. You don't seem to have many ideas of your own."

"What did I do to antagonize you?" he asked, shaken.

"Maybe I just don't like people who call themselves writers when they haven't written. Who get writing deals because of who they live near, not because of what they write. Maybe I don't like people who exploit the dead."

"As opposed to the living?" he said.

"That's right."

"Or maybe you just don't like gays," he said.

"Maybe," she agreed. "Would you like coffee?"

*W*hen lunch was over, as it had been the moment it began and she saw how little he would be able to tell her, Sarah went across the street to the Library of the Performing Arts at Lincoln Center. One of the few things in the world, alive or inanimate, that Sarah felt affection for was libraries. They had been the havens of her childhood, the place where she went for silence so she didn't have to hear her family argue. She avoided them now as she avoided peace, because they might put her in touch with herself. She was afraid she wasn't as bright as everyone thought because she was bitchy. To confront her own limitations was nothing she wanted to do at this point in her life. And so she left the research to Chuck.

But she also kept away from libraries because it broke what heart she had that they were going out of business. Computer nerds and technology boosters were becoming billionaires, while those who loved books had to deal with limited hours, days when the quiet sanctuaries didn't open at all, what with staff cutbacks and lack of funding. Some of the branches in the cities where she'd been on her book tour were closed altogether, never to reopen. She took it personally that the structures that had been her refuge and become her advocates in the career she had moved to when the movies closed her out were themselves now in danger of closing.

A kind of piety came over her as she ascended the steps, a sense of wonder that all that knowledge could be so enshrined, and yet in peril. She floated towards the stillness. The library edged just behind the Metropolitan Opera, a flat, square, three-story building. It was the only one in the fountain-centered complex that was less than architecturally interesting, as if music and theater and dance were more deserving than words.

There were signs all around telling people to watch their wallets. At the checkout desk, with its metal portal magnetically guarding against book theft, were caveats advising those with pacemakers that they might set off the alarm.

The inside of the vast, sterile building was well, if flatly, lit. Around her rose several stories of books, magazines, newspapers. Even from the ground floor she could see donated collections. And the sad, inevitable signs advising they'd be closed certain days, that the hours on the days they were open were limited.

"Could you tell me where the material is on dance?" she asked the not-so-young but still pretty woman by the card catalogue.

"Second floor," she said.

Sarah climbed the stairs. There was a bright-eyed brunette behind the second-floor desk, alert and cheerful. She had probably gone into library science for her graduate degree, imagining that libraries, and she, still had a healthy future.

"Where would I find material on dance companies from Brazil?" Sarah asked her.

"Back table," the woman said, pointing. "There's a catalogue. Listed alphabetically."

Sarah made her way to the giant book, and opened it to B. But it fell open first to A. At the bottom of the paged index was "AIDS, obituaries." She turned it quickly.

BRAZIL. The heading directed her back to the main desk.

"It says I get the newspapers from you," Sarah said.

"I'll need your ID."

She gave the librarian her passport, which she carried with her now like Kleenex in the event she was moved to flee. No place was a safe haven for her anymore, nothing felt like home. Be it ever so humble, there was no place like a departure lounge.

The woman handed her folders filled with newspaper clippings. Some of them were current; most of them yellowing and old. It was a while before Sarah found what she was looking for, from 1980: a review of the Capoeiras de Bahia, a dance company that starred the fourteen-year-old Paulo Nerys.

There was a picture of him, grainy and unsatisfactory. But it was possible to see how muscularly slender his young body was, the grace he had in flight. His legs were spread in a leap worthy of Baryshnikov.

On the third floor, among the closed stacks, she found the glossy photographs of balletic figures captured in interesting close-up by Martha Swope. There was a study of the young Paulo Nerys. A sudden surprising sadness came over Sarah, as when she had seen the pristine fields that were once Beverly Hills, commemorated in the pizza parlor that sat on them now. The beautiful boy in the picture existed no more, even if Jessup hadn't had him killed. Had he? How could someone have so completely vanished, unless that was the explanation? Had he contracted AIDS and, like so many of the dying, hidden away, adding shame and guilt to his ordeal? Whatever the explanation was—and there had to be one—the boy in the picture was vanished. If he was alive, which Sarah doubted, he wasn't that boy anymore.

Thick black hair flowed around his face, but not so freely that it obscured the high cheekbones, the wide imposing nose, the V of his chin. It was easy to see why Winsett had been smitten with him, why Norman Jessup had been struck. Especially with that look, not really a look. His eyes seemed loathe to look at the camera. So indirect, and so curiously guileless. A step back from guileless, really. Blank. A spiritual tabula rasa, as though one could write anything on that psyche that one wanted, so empty were those eyes.

Empty eyes. Sarah's mind meandered. Where had she seen eyes that were that strangely empty? Where had she encountered, close up, those vacant eyes?

Building Bridges

*A*s accustomed as he was to having a full staff to do legwork of any fashion for him, including stalking, it momentarily irritated Norman Jessup to have to hire a private detective. Especially as the man was going to be paid to find the man who had only just stopped doing Norman's stalking. But as there was nothing sinister involved, Norman figured the detective could do him no harm in the way of extortion or wanting a job in the movie business, the risk you always ran when you were Norman. He could not even address a ladies' luncheon, which he did only for his public image, without someone in a hat asking him to interview her nephew.

The detective he decided on was recommended by one of the security people at the Carlyle, a breed Norman trusted to be reliable as much as he did the manager and Bobby Short, who was currently doing a stint on piano in the Cafe. They sat in the darkened room where the entertainer played, and the detective murmured his credentials, but not so loud that it interfered with the music.

"It's okay, you come highly recommended," Jessup said, raising his hand to stop the recounting of runaway teenagers found, renegade fraudulent financiers stopped at the airport, and wives caught in flagrante. Only when the singer finished his first show and the lights went up did Norman tell the man what he wanted.

The detective looked slightly seedy, which put Norman at his ease, as the only private eyes he'd seen were those in films. Apparently this man had been to the same movies. His face was scratchily Humphrey Bogart, his overlarge head Bruce Willis, shaved, bridging the generations in a single overweight bound. Even though he'd been assured he had Norman's confidence, he still held out his ID and his license to carry a gun. Both had his name, Hallowell Vincent, and a thumbprint.

"Hallowell," Jessup said. "That's some moniker." He felt an actual lift in his heart as he used that word.

"Call me Hal," the man said. "You got a picture of the kid?"

There was the miniature album that Norman carried with him and put on his bedside table when he traveled to give him a sense of permanence. It had photos of afternoons at the beach. There was a recent snapshot of Carina, and one of a bunch of the boys, Bunyan, Gil, those who had been present the day he'd found Tyler. And one of that young man standing all alone, Michelangelo's David in cutoffs. Reluctantly Norman drew it from the plastic, not really willing to take the chance the former cop would get his prints on it.

But the man held it by its edges, like he was used to parents who might never see their kids again, so the photo would have to serve as a remembrance. "Beautiful boy," said Hal, and then, realizing what the scuttlebutt was, added, "I mean, healthy-looking. You got any idea where he might have gone?"

"Well, he didn't have much cash, so it couldn't have been far. He's probably still in New York."

"There are eight million stories in the naked city," Hal said.

"Excuse me?"

"It was a show. A terrific show." Hal smiled feebly. He had big teeth, tobacco stained. The smell of cigarettes came from his mouth, even though he wasn't smoking.

"I remember the show."

"Meaning . . . there's a lot of people. He have any relatives or friends here?"

"I'm not really sure. I know very little about where he came from. He made it an exercise to talk in the present. No history. A 'today' person."

"Personal habits?"

"He meditates. Sitting cross-legged with his thumb and first finger in a little circle while he 'Oms.' " Even as he attempted to sound contemptuous, the memory of it made Norman melancholy. He recalled finding Tyler on the beach in just such a pose, his buff young body all burnished dark gold and his eyes closed, their gilded lashes fanning down. He remembered the sound, the occasional chant coming from the guest cottage behind his beach house, something that would have annoyed him usually, but reassured him since it meant Tyler was home.

Even though he'd never made a move on him, he was caught by the boy. In the beginning he'd been so mesmerized he had actually followed him a few times when he'd left the beach, trying to find out what he did when he wasn't there. Before he commissioned Tyler to do the same with Sarah, Norman trailed him to see where he was going. Embarrassed, but unable to control himself, Norman skulked in doorways while Tyler took his walks through the Santa Monica mall.

"He likes to walk," Norman told the detective, trying to deal with how wistful the recollected picture made him. "Takes really long walks. Reads through the magazines at newsstands. Very pop culture kind of kid."

"There are eight million newsstands in the naked city."

"You got a car." He could hear himself talking a little tough, falling into the patois of the street guy he was speaking to.

"How tall is he?"

"Six three, maybe a little taller."

"Any identifying marks?"

"Wherever he goes, people turn around."

"I meant scars, blemishes."

"That's a kind of scar, don't you think? That you can't go anywhere without being noticed? I mean, I don't think he's even aware of it, but that's what happens."

"Why did he run away?"

"He didn't. I . . . well, I sort of threw him out."

"And now you want him back?" It wasn't really a question, but a statement, lightly larded with resignation.

"Not for myself," Jessup said, wondering why he felt he had to explain that. Probably out of the affection he bore for the memory of Bogart, who'd lived and died while everyone was still in the closet, and likely wouldn't have had any use for any of it, politically correct or no. Norman could visualize him grubbily putt-putting to Hawaii in an old fishing boat, ready to break up same-sex marriages.

"Okay. I'll get on it in the morning."

"Really early morning," said Norman. "He likes to get up around five and go on a walk before dawn." Once he had followed him on a silvery morning lit by a waning moon, wondering if maybe he had a lover somewhere down in Malibu.

"Well, he won't do that in New York."

"Sure, he will. He's fearless."

"In New York, fearless is stupid."

"He believes the universe is looking out for him."

"Well, it is now," Hallowell said, and stood. "I'll find him for you."

*T*he first thing Arthur Finster did on returning to Los Angeles was check the sales figures on *By Hook or by Crook*. Normally a spot on Oprah, if she held up the book and said anything the least bit favorable, sent the book to the top of the bestseller list. But there were no consistent demographics on the Ralph Robertson show. Still, it had been a hot interview: people called in to scream at Arthur for being a peddler of pornography, and one woman phoned in to weep that the text had saved her from a life of degradation and vice. Finster had arranged that call, of course, but wasn't sure she would get through.

"How many copies did we move since last Monday?" he asked his sales rep.

She checked the distributor's computer line. "A little over seven thousand."

"That can't possibly be all," Arthur said. "Millions of people watch Robertson's show."

"Not that night," the sales rep said.

He felt measurably depressed. There was just so much sensationalism available, even in Los Angeles, and he'd tapped nearly every vein. The only one he'd missed was O.J., and there were no new wrinkles to that.

"You want your mail and phone messages now, Arthur?" his secretary asked him.

"Anything interesting?" he asked about the mail, deflated and jet-lagged.

"There's one marked 'Personal and Confidential' that I didn't open."

"That was generous of you."

"You don't have to get sour with me just because the numbers aren't better."

She was his cousin. His aunt was a terror, worse than his mother, hell to deal with, so he couldn't fire her daughter. He told everyone he kept Joyce there because she was so forthright, the quality in her he secretly hated most.

"Here's the letter," Joyce said, and threw it at him.

He put it in his pocket, after checking for the return address. There was none. He was in no mood for an attack. His mind seethed with what amounted to yet another rejection, this one from the public at large. Appetite raged, but he didn't want to try any of the better restaurants, unwilling to chance further humiliation. In his early days in Hollywood he had gone to Ma Maison, the "in" place at the time, where executives would tremble if Patrick Terrail, who ran the restaurant, didn't seem pleased to see them. He had witnessed film potentates who had learned the movie trade at the knobby knees of Darryl Zanuck grow pale when they couldn't catch Patrick's eye. They'd been visibly fearful that they might not get a table, or be seated in the wrong room, or the portion of the yellow tented garden that wasn't fashionable. So Arthur knew he was observing an honored local ritual, to be intimidated by headwaiters who measured your rise and fall more quickly than box office returns. He'd had every intention of buying Morton's as he'd threatened to do when they turned him away, as soon as the book went to number one. Now it probably never would.

*H*e was in bed, wearing silk pajamas from Hong Kong which he'd planned on donning for his interview with *Esquire*, but they hadn't called back either, when he remembered the letter. He leaned over to the chair where his jacket hung, and reached for it.

Dear Mr. Finster,

I am a student at Beverly High. I read all your books. I admire you a lot. I read the story about you in Beverly Hills 213 *how you have so much nerve and initiative. I read that you aren't afraid to publish anything.*

I know there are already a lot of O.J. books, but here is the mystery that wasn't solved. What happened to the bag? The one O.J. was carrying that maybe had the knife in it, and the bloody clothes?

Well, what if I was to tell you I knew where that bag went? My dad was a friend of O.J.'s. He is always telling me I lack initiative. They said in 213 that's what you have plenty of. I know a lot of kids who's parents used to be friends of O.J.'s, and they all have stories about him. How about a book about the kids who's parents are friends of O.J.'s. Or used to be. I know one kid whose a waiter part time at Chin-Chin in Brentwood and he says O.J. orders take out, that he's afraid to come into resturants. We know a lot of anekdotes like that.

You better not call me at home. Its' a real dilema if I should tell you this stuff or not. But I admire your initiative and want some of my own. If you want to talk you can meet me at baseball practice at the field at Beverly High on Wednesday around four o'clock. Please don't tell about this to anybody. I play third base.

Yours very truely,
Richie Harnoun

Thrilled, Arthur looked at his watch. It was only Friday. How could he wait till Wednesday? A fresh angle: The Children of Friends. *The Apple Doesn't Fall Far from the Tree,* that could be the title. What a clever boy.

At the same time he got excited at the prospect, Arthur felt his first pang of compassion ever for O.J. Ordering takeout. Not willing to risk being turned away either.

Suddenly, he remembered how hungry he was. He reached for the phone, dialed 411, and asked Information for the number of Chin-Chin in Brentwood.

*W*hen Kate checked her new answering machine, there were two barked messages from Perry Zemmis, both from the same day. He had been calling her daily since the item first appeared that he had bought the Fitzgerald "sequin." She had never returned any of his calls. Once, when she picked up the phone and he was on the line himself, she had clicked the receiver, and told him her mother was on the other line from the hospital. As little as he seemed to respect anything, he was immediately browbeaten by the absentee spectacle of a mother, and jumped off the line. It appeared to be a town full of power players who feared the women who had spawned them, even when their mothers turned out to be their wives, as Lila Darshowitz had.

There was also a message from Mel, her agent; one from her mother, who wasn't in the hospital; Jake Alonzo; and, most unexpectedly, a call from Duchess Wendy. Kate had to play it a few times to make sure it really was Wendy. She spoke with a tremulous voice. Kate had to listen repeatedly to get the number right. Impressed and thrown, she put out of her mind the message from Jake Alonzo, and called Wendy's number. She needed a friend more than she needed a lover. Did he really want to be her lover? Could a duchess, even toppled, really want to be her friend?

"I wanted to thank you so much for the flowers, and your most kind note," Wendy said, and paused for a moment. "*And* the note you returned."

"You're more than welcome."

"Would you like to meet for tea?"

They settled on the terrace of the Hotel Bel-Air for a meeting place. There was an ex-president's wife at one of the balcony tables, and the fallen head of a studio at another, so the setting seemed perfect for deposed royalty.

"One doesn't have a lot of people one can trust," Wendy said, into a finger sandwich, so her words were partially obscured. But Kate heard clearly what she was trying to say.

"I understand."

"I wonder if you do," Wendy said, putting her sandwich down, looking at Kate with woeful eyes, the whites visible above the lower lids. "I wonder if you know how relieved I was when you returned that note. Relieved, and, to be frank, agreeably surprised. Many people would have sold it." She lowered her very soft voice even further as she said that, with a sidelong glance at her security person to make sure he wasn't eavesdropping. He was standing a few feet away, watching her, but not listening, engaged in a sidelong conversation with the security man for the ex-president's wife.

"I'm not many people," Kate said.

"That's why I called," said Wendy. She turned towards the wooden-latticed railing, so her face would be visible only to the swans, gliding on the artificial lake below. But the slight quiver of her chin was unmistakable.

"I'm very glad you did," Kate said.

When she turned back, there were wells of tears in Wendy's eyes. "Have you a lot of friends?"

"Not really. Certainly not in L.A."

"I had only one great friend here, and I'm afraid she's turned out to be rather small." A single tear slid down her peaches-and-cream cheek. She wiped it away with a quick, barely perceptible gesture, her hands expert at wiping away tears faster than anyone could see them. Her fingers came to rest on the arm of the wicker chair.

Without even meaning to, not knowing if it would constitute audacity, but unable to control the conciliatory gesture, Kate touched Wendy's hand. "I'm sorry," she said.

"Have you a big family?" Wendy asked her.

"I'm an only child," she said.

"I, too. That makes it lonely when you're little, don't you think? And your parents?"

"My father died. But they were divorced," Kate said, hearing how cruel the word suddenly sounded. Below them a florist had approached the white pillared gazebo, arms laden with white and apricot roses. Two assistants trailed her, carrying greens. The garden of the Bel-Air was famous for weddings, Kate knew from her forays through the social pages. She also knew it was Wendy's favorite hot-watering spot, the place where she often took tea. Right now the hotel was apparently setting up for another ceremony. Salt on Wendy's wound,

Kate thought, hoping that with her back to the proceedings, Wendy might not note what was happening. She might not see the sheaves of leaves being wound around the white-painted pillars, softening them with greens like streamers, pinning them with white satin bows.

"I feel it's a kind of bond, your returning the note. So forgive me if I seem impertinent."

"You're the least impertinent person I've ever met," Kate said.

"I haven't been on my own to make friends since O levels. I'm not quite sure what to ask. But I would like to know about you."

"Well, I only recently moved to Los Angeles. I'm a writer." She hoped that Wendy would know nothing of the Fitzgerald tale. Kate couldn't imagine that she read the trade papers. "I'm from Nebraska."

"Nebraska," Wendy said. "How wonderfully American. One can practically hear the wheat grow."

"What luck! Wendy!" A tall, lean, red-haired man approached their table. As he did, the security man stepped forward, checking Wendy's face for recognition.

"Binky!"

Kate took in the full formality of his gray three-piece suit, an actual weskit beneath the jacket, warm as the day was. His collar was starched, as his attitude seemed to be, his diamond-printed tie tightly knotted, the handkerchief that peeked from his pocket a not-quite-perfect coordination to the tie, the border of it red.

"I'd heard you moved here," the man said. "May I join you for a moment?"

"Of course," Wendy said. "What are you doing here?"

"But I live here," said Binky, pulling out the chair.

"At the hotel?"

"In Beverly Hills. Hello, you," he said, fondly.

"This is Kate Donnelly," Wendy said. "Binky Danforth-Smythe."

"Delighted." His smile was ready, but flawed, the teeth a little small, and not very white.

"Would you like some tea?" Wendy asked.

"I'm British," he said.

She signaled for another cup.

"I say, you're looking better than ever."

"Really?"

"Absolutely. You . . . I don't know . . . you've matured."

"Hardened," Wendy said.

"On the contrary. You look softer. Prettier, actually."

"You're flattering me."

"As a matter of fact, I am. But you deserve to be flattered. You've been really impressive."

"Stiff upper lip?" Wendy said.

"Well, in my opinion, it isn't you who's been stiff. You've made us very proud."

"You've married?"

"No, I meant all of us. The English."

For reasons she could not fathom, Kate didn't like him. The way he'd said "Hello, you" had made her the slightest bit bilious, a familiarity in the intonation that sounded distasteful as well as cloying. Maybe she was just being possessive, poised as she'd been on the brink of this unexpected friendship. She could feel Wendy's heart, how good it was, and cracked. Kate had thought so much about herself since coming to Los Angeles, been so caught in trying to advance, that the prospect of being able to help someone else had made her really happy. Self-absorption seemed to float on the local air, like pollen, afflicting everyone, even those who didn't know they were susceptible. She resented his having interrupted their getting to know one another.

"What are you doing that lets you live in Los Angeles?" Wendy asked, as she poured.

"I have a travel agency," he said. "Here's my card." He took one from his wallet, handed it to Wendy, saw that Kate was watching him. "Wouldn't want to seem rude," he said, and handed one to her. He turned his full attention back to Wendy. "Is there anywhere you'd like to go?"

"Into a hole, like Alice. Milk?"

"Nothing, thank you. I can think of better places. Puerto Vallarta, for instance. They're running an amazing special. I've been considering going there next weekend. Would you like to join me?"

"I don't think I can," said Wendy.

"Well, don't think," said Binky, and took a hearty gulp.

To Kate's unforgiving delight, it was apparently a little hot. She watched him struggle not to react.

"Well, hello!" Wilton Spenser said, jogging over to the table in workout clothes. There was a band around his close-cropped hair. Over his shoulder he carried a man's leather purse. He looked past Kate at Wendy. "No wonder you dropped me."

"I didn't drop you," Kate said good-naturedly, smiling. This was a more welcome interruption than Binky's had been, funny as Wilton was, outrageous. She only hoped he wasn't carrying any of his goods in the purse. "I've been really busy."

"So I see."

"Do you know . . . how do I introduce you?" she asked Wendy.

"Just Wendy."

"Wendy. Wilton Spenser."

"Chawmed," he said deliberately, and kissed her hand. "Is that alright to do if I don't drip sweat?"

"Behave yourself," Kate said.

"Well, this is really nice," Wilton noted. "All the royalty. Real royalty. Literary royalty . . . "

"Stop," Kate said firmly. "Wendy and I were just finding out who each other *really* is." She underlined the word with her diction, warning him with her eyes.

"I'm Binky Danforth-Smythe," Binky said.

"I would have known that without your saying anything," said Wilton.

"You've heard of me?" Binky asked, surprised.

"No. I just knew you had to have a hyphen. Oh, I've waited so long to meet a hyphenate, I thought the day might never come. And to think you're also a Binky!" Wilton clapped his hands together.

Binky made no attempt to conceal his distaste. He turned towards Wendy. "May I phone you?" He took out a small black book from his pocket, with a tiny gold pencil in its leathered loop, and handed it to her. She took it and started to write.

"Beware of men with little black books," Wilton said.

"Beware of men who carry purses," said Binky.

"I have to make a delivery," Wilton said, and kissed Kate's cheek. "Call me when you return to the common people."

"Is he some kind of grocery boy?" Binky asked condescendingly, watching him go.

"He's an actor," Kate said.

The three of them stayed on the terrace till people began to gather below, and the string quartet started to play. It was at the sound of Pachelbel that Wendy's eyes grew moist again. "I have to go," she said, getting up a little too quickly, all but running from the terrace restaurant, signing the check on her way towards the veranda, followed at a fevered clip by her security guard.

"She's very fragile," Kate noted, protectively.

"You needn't tell me about her," Binky said. "We've known each other since we were children."

She looked at him and tried to imagine him as a child so she'd feel better about him. There would have been just as many freckles then. The nose might not have been so pointed, downturned at its tip. The thatch of red hair had probably had a cowlick: it was plastered down now, pomaded. Somehow she had the feeling he'd been a nasty little boy, the kind that pulled at girls' braids, dipped them in inkwells. His eyes had likely always looked too close together, a signal to her of malevolence, as whites showing below the eye, as they did in Wendy, were a warning of doom. Marilyn Monroe had had eyes like that.

"She must have been a sweet little girl," Kate said.

"Yes, rather. Spoilt, though. Self-indulgent. We didn't like each other much as children. But she's really grown."

"In the physical or the California sense?"

"I have to go," said Binky.

*W*ho was the queer?" Wilton said, when Kate got home and called him.

"You think he's gay?"

"I'm gay," said Wilton. "He's *queer*."

"You thought so, too? He made me uneasy."

"What's happening with your career?" he said. "I guess since you were having lunch with the fallen duchess, you're pretty hot."

"She needed a friend," said Kate.

"We all need friends. But after the publicity you're obviously into the higher echelons."

Actually, Kate was amazed as well as appalled by the circles the hot air had lifted her into. She'd had a meeting with Victor Lippton himself to discuss the awful script. He'd been so impressed with her contempt for it he'd asked if there was anything else she wanted to do. She'd told him her idea about Larry Drayco. He'd dismissed it, holding out for the Fitzgerald story. "They all want Grandpa's book," she said.

"What you probably ought to do," said Wilton, "is write the unpublished Fitzgerald. You know so much about him, you could probably do it."

"That's fraud," Kate said.

"Linus was right. You are cute. 'Fraud.' What do you suppose this business is about? Who do you think started it? Short little men from Chicago who had to bring in people to show them what forks to use. Whose English was so bad all anyone had to do was talk with a British accent and they'd put him in charge. That was the way it was here in the twenties. And you think it's come that far? Look at how everyone slobbers over the duchess."

"She's really very touching," said Kate.

"*You're* touching. Still trying to be sincere. Look through your files. Maybe you can find his manuscript." There was a click on the line. "Oh, I hate that fucking call waiting. It's so rude."

"Then why do you have it?"

"I might miss something," said Wilton. "Hold on." He was gone from the line for a moment, came back. "I have to go. It's a customer."

"Aren't you embarrassed?"

"What? In this town? I feel proud to be a dope dealer. I don't hurt anybody. How many people here can say that? I wish I could hang out a shingle. I wish I had a son, so I could take him into the business. Spenser and Son. I'll call you."

"*W*hat I'd like to know is, how did that microphone get under your mattress?" Victor Lippton said. They were in Alexa's house in Benedict Canyon, the one she'd bought to make it easier for him, so he could stop on his way to and from the studio on days when he couldn't make it to the gym. She'd also taken a little pied-à-terre in Santa Monica, so if he got all heated up while doing his workout on the neighboring treadmill, they'd have someplace to go.

"It had to have been my maid," Alexa said. "The bitch. After I brought her whole family up from Guatemala."

"Rosa doesn't even speak English," Victor said, having gone through his own frustration with her on the telephone. He leaned towards that telephone now. It was a decorator French phone, ivory, old-fashioned, with a gold-surrounded dial and a gold cradle for the receiver. They had spent many fevered evenings with him on the other end, calling from his cell phone, with Alexa like an odalisque naked on this bronze satin sofa, as she'd described herself in minutest sexual detail to him, while she fingered her nipples and played with herself and drove him crazy. Even now, with his marriage on the line, and maybe his life if his father-in-law found out, just watching her undo the pearl buttons on her silk blouse to reveal a glimpse of the great pointed breasts in their lace embroidered sling clouded his mind, obscured the intelligence that had chaired a dozen boards, not all of them commandeered with his money.

"She knows enough to have gotten ambitious," Alexa said. "That happens as soon as they cross the border."

"But you'd have to be pretty sophisticated to know what to do with a tape."

"Probably someone bribed her to set it up."

"In order for someone to do that, they'd have to know you were involved with me. And you swore no one knew."

"No one but my astrologer."

"You told Serena?" Shock softened his erection.

"I didn't have to tell her. She saw you, conjuncting my Venus. She saw you before you even appeared. A handsome, powerful Gemini, with a beautiful cock." She started to unzip him.

"Never mind," he said, and stopped her hand. "Maybe they've hidden a camera."

"Oh, darling, no harm can come from the tape. All you have to do is give that Lila person what she asks."

"It's a travesty. To create a monument to the personification of what's foul in the film business."

"Maybe he wasn't all that bad."

"There's this young woman who's Fitzgerald's granddaughter, and she wants to write a book about Drayco, find his inherent humanity. Unearth what was noble about him."

"You see?"

"I'm trying to get her to write a screenplay instead," Victor said, letting her hands move over him, having calmed himself sufficiently to want her again.

"You're just such a mover and shaker," Alexa said, her head moving down to where it, too, could move and shake.

$\mathcal{N}$ow that Norman Jessup had a real detective on the track of Tyler, he was free to resume what had brought him to New York. Not free, really. Fettered. Unable to breathe easily, he could hear the air roiling in his lungs every time he thought about Sarah Nash. He had a flunky posted down the hall from her room between her and the elevator. Before she could leave the hotel, Norman would be alerted.

He'd slept in his clothes, the clothes he'd gotten especially for shadowing her: a dark sweatsuit with a hood, in case she went out in the middle of the night. But apparently she was more relaxed about her bird-dogging than Norman was, not even leaving her room until after eleven in the morning.

His limo followed her cab. To his kind of sentimental horror, he found she was heading for his old neighborhood, the place where he had once lived in a brownstone with Paulo.

There was something nostalgic about it, heading into Turtle Bay, remembering how young he had been. It was a beautiful street, even with the third world city that much of New York had become, the garbage that littered the sidewalks in front of the best addresses happily absent here. Slender little trees in a line down to Second Avenue marshaled the pavement, standing erect, growing from well-tended patches of earth, curled iron gates protecting the bases. Even as early in the spring as it was, small buds of green pimpled their branches, not quite at the point of bursting into leaves. Paulo on the brink of his blossoming.

Nostalgia gave way to anxiety as Sarah's cab stopped. She got out and looked at a piece of paper in her hand, checked it against the number of the house in front of her. What was she up to? The place he had lived with Paulo was almost down to the far corner, twenty or maybe thirty brownstones away. But she was starting with the first house on the block. Clearly she was checking out their old environs. Maybe she wasn't sure exactly which building it was.

As though in confirmation of his suspicions, Sarah rang first the bell on the house in front of her, and then, after talking to a man who seemed to be the super, moved to the next. But how had she even found out the street where Paulo and Norman had lived? He'd never bought the apartment, only rented, and then under Paulo's name. Not that many people had been invited to visit them, Norman having gone through a period of seclusion while in New York. Passion for and housekeeping with Paulo had been his main recreation while in Manhattan. He had saved all his bonhomie for California. Always he'd been a little fearful that someone might try and steal Paulo from him as he had done with Winsett. Over the boy's assurances of loyalty and equal—even greater—love, Norman had still thought it circumspect to keep their household closely sealed.

Reaching for the car phone, he dialed Bunyan Reis. Bunyan was the one in town who knew more gossip than anybody, including Liz Smith.

"My lines of communication must be down," Bunyan said. "I never even heard you were in town. You must have Draculaed your way in. Wearing a cape. Under cover of darkness. What brings you to our still in many ways fair city?"

"I've bought *Pilgrims!*" Norman said, as though success in the entertainment business were his primary motivation, which it no longer was. His principal goal had become revenge. But revenge flooded the head and the heart with heat, and he felt slightly chilled. Fear. What did she know? What was she finding out?

"Well, that's very upbeat," said Bunyan. "I was a little concerned that the wind might be out of your sails."

"Why?"

"The lovely Sarah Nash, I'm afraid, knows what happened to Paulo."

Panic gripped Jessup's throat. "How could she possibly?"

"I can't imagine. But she does."

"Nobody knows but the ones who actually did it." Norman could hardly breathe. "And you."

"May I be hanged by the testicles if I breathed so much as a word. You could have knocked me over with the proverbial feather when she told me."

"Told you?"

"She *knows*," Bunyan said, darkly.

"*What* does she know, you silly queen?"

"My, my," Bunyan said. "The pot calling the kettle African-American."

"Cut the wit shit! What did she say?"

"She said . . . " And here Bunyan paused. "I'm trying to remember the exact words. Yes. I think this is they. Most people would say 'this is *them.*' "

"Will you goddamn get to it?"

"She said, and I quote . . . " He waited.

"I don't know how you've lived this long," Norman fumed. "Why somebody hasn't killed you."

"She asked me if I wasn't disturbed by what was done to Paulo."

Norman listened to the pounding of his own blood in his ears. "When did she say that?"

"A few days ago. When we had lunch."

"You had lunch with Sarah?"

"I did it for you," Bunyan said. "I thought I could find out what exactly she was up to. It wasn't as if I gave her any information."

Norman slammed down the phone. It was a little hard to do with a car phone. The instrument fell from its holding niche on the side of the window to the floor.

"Norman?" Bunyan's squeaky voice cried from the carpet. "Norman?"

Norman pressed the button that opened the soundproof window between himself and the driver. "How do I shut him up?" he asked.

"Press end," the driver said.

"What a good idea," Norman said. "Take me back to the hotel."

*H*e waited until he was in his room and the doors were closed and nobody could hear to call Perry Zemmis. It was only nine on the coast, but Zemmis was still hungry, pushy, after twenty-five years of success, so he was already in his office. He took Norman's call immediately, like he'd been waiting for it, as he probably had for most of those twenty-five years.

"Well, I knew the day would come when you'd want to do business," Zemmis said. "You want to partner with me on the Fitzgerald book?"

"No," Norman said.

"You got my invitation to the garden party? I think he's a shoo-in, but we could certainly use your support, and if I make ambassador—"

"That's not why I'm calling," said Norman.

"Oh," Perry said.

"I know you're a guy who can be trusted to take care of business," Norman said.

"Well, considering the source, I am truly honored by that statement," Perry said fatuously. "I only wondered why it was taking so long for you to come around."

Norman waited a moment. "I want a contract."

"I'll have my lawyer write it up the minute we're off the phone. What's the contract for?"

"Not for. On."

"On?" asked Zemmis.

"I want a contract on Sarah Nash."

"Now just a minute. What makes you think I'm involved with anything like—"

"Don't fuck with me, Perry. I already have someone fucking with me. You handle this, and I'll get you whatever you need."

"Can I have that in writing?"

"We don't want anything in writing," Norman said. "You have my word. Whatever you want. The minute Sarah Nash is out of the picture. *Any* picture."

"Consider her on the cutting-room floor," said Perry.

People Who Live in Glass Houses

*T*he truth, of course, was that Sarah Nash knew little or nothing of what it was Norman Jessup was trying to conceal. But as the truth set some people free, fear of it enchained others. And a hunger for scandal, even treachery on a criminal scale, kept some going.

As she canvased Jessup's old neighborhood for the thread of information to weave into a rope to hang him, Sarah felt revitalized. Being feted or hated for what she had written, depending which coast she'd been on, had taken a great deal out of her. Once she had been a very attractive woman, fetching even, a British beau had said of her. But being disliked had toughened her expression, disliking had tightened her mouth, giving her a tendency to purse her lips as antipathy had pursed her spirit. Cocaine had coarsened her features, while the restoration of her nasal passages had left her nose slightly flattened. Champagne from celebrations in her honor when the book had been a hit broke blood vessels across her once-unblemished face. Now, there was a skeptical double line between her brows, a frown that was built in. Her dermatologist used collagen to fill it, but the pain of the needle, skilled as he was, had been so severe she thought it better to leave it alone.

Besides, other problems she had with her skin were more pressing than vanity. Vanity was for those whose lives and livelihoods depended on their looks. She had no conscious wish anymore to attract anyone who might consider her fetching. She was a writer now, contemptuous of those who felt imperiled by aging, even as she fretted and occasionally agonized over the eczema that had sprouted on her skin. No place that it really showed, like her face, but on her upper arms beside her breasts, and occasionally on them. No sooner would one small eruption be calmed by the salve that the doctor prescribed for her than another would come out someplace else.

Her masseuse, who was one of those New Age people, had given her a book called *You Can Heal Your Life,* by Louise Hay. Sarah didn't know which of the two women was battier, although she would never breathe a word to her masseuse, as the woman was sensitive and had a great touch. Even as she disdained the book, she couldn't help looking through its small encyclopedic listing of ailments and what caused them. Eczema, it read, was "breathtaking antagonisms." No shit.

Well, she would not go so far as to murmur any of the mantras that were supposed to counter the affliction. Her skin would clear up as soon as she put Norman Jessup away.

She rang the superintendent's bell on the next-to-the-last house on the north side of the street. Nobody so far on the block had known of the once-happy couple, though she had had the discretion to leave Katharine Hepburn's bell unrung.

The superintendent/janitor answered the door. "Can I help you?" he said. He was a wizened man with a fringe of gray and brown hair, wearing a dirty blue T-shirt, stretched-out jeans, and soiled sneakers. But his hands looked clean, so she offered hers, introducing herself.

"I'm trying to find an old friend," she said. "Did a Paulo Nerys ever live here?"

"The dancer kid?" the janitor said.

Excitement and relief washed over her at the same time; even as she felt one tiny mound near her elbow recede, another bloomed. "That's right," she said.

"Yeah. They had the back apartment, terrace and garden, him and his friend."

"Norman Jessup?"

"Yeah. Some kind of Hollywood producer, right?"

The worst kind, she didn't say. They could put all the rap they wanted on Larry Drayco, but at least he'd been straight. No matter how devious a man had been, he was still one up on a deviant. "Right."

"They lived here for around six, close to seven years."

"When did they move out?" Sarah asked.

"Winter, last year. I kept the apartment vacant for a while, in case they changed their minds and came back. They seemed pretty nervous about leaving, not sure what they were going to do. They were good tenants. I wasn't really in a hurry to get anyone else."

"Where were they moving to?"

"I don't know. Told me to deep-six the mail. If it was something looked urgent for Mr. Jessup, to send it to his lawyer. Some guy named McCallum. I have his address."

"No. I know how to get in touch with him," Sarah said, stopping him. "What about if somebody wanted to reach Paulo?"

"They didn't mention it. Paulo didn't tell me to forward his mail. He didn't say nothing. It was like that with those two. Jessup was a take-charge guy, so he always did the talking. They kept pretty much to themselves. Didn't make trouble, or have *those* kind of parties, if you know what I mean."

"I know what you mean," said Sarah.

"The kid was really quiet." The janitor half smiled. "I call him a kid. He was maybe a kid when he first came here, but I guess you could say he was a man when they left. He still looked like a kid, though. One of those tiny guys with a face you could never tell how old he was, you know what I mean?"

"I know what you mean," said Sarah.

"But neither of them ever made any trouble. Paulo, he was like . . . what's that big thing in Egypt that sits in the desert?"

"The sphinx," Sarah said.

"Yeah, right, the sphinx. Jessup called him that once in front of me. Told me that meant he was silent, but there was a lot going on underneath."

"I'll bet," said Sarah.

"But the day they moved . . . " He hesitated.

"Yes?" Sarah urged him.

"He was quieter than usual. He seemed sort of . . . I don't know. Scared."

"Was there ever any violence between them?"

"No. Nothing like that. They was the perfect couple, if that kind of thing don't bother you. It don't bother me. They didn't bother anybody. They really cared about each other. Like they say, whatever gets you through the night."

"Right," Sarah said. "But you have *no* idea where Paulo went?"

"Not a clue. He still gets a letter once in a while, from some university. I never know what to do with it. Got one last week, as a matter of fact."

"You don't still have it, by any chance?" She tried not to let her eagerness show.

"No. I threw it in the paper recycle bin, end of the block. Have to, or I catch hell from Miss Hepburn."

"She's still a feisty old lady," Sarah said, remembering an era of moviemaking that had ended when she was just a child. The memorable movies of that age gone, with nothing to take their place but blockbusters, mindless violence, and the occasional effort to create films with meaning, all the more dispiriting because of how little meaning there usually was. The truly great dinosaurs vanished, in their place the mechanical, computerized ones which were part of the blockbusters. "Last of a breed."

"They threw away the mold," the janitor said.

She thanked him for trying to help, waited till the door was closed before she literally bolted down the stairs, and breaking into a run, raced around the block like someone training for the marathon in the wrong shoes. She found the recycling bin. It was two car lengths long, black, taller than she was by a head, and deep. But standing on her toes she could see it was full. Maybe the letter was still in there.

She would have to find a way to get into it. Waiting until dusk she supposed would make sense. It might look more than odd in the daylight, what she intended to do.

She circled the bin, as an Indian might have a wagon train. Oops, she thought. A Native American. If there was one thing Sarah was selective about, it was picking her targets.

The private detective Norman Jessup had hired to find Tyler was no dummy. He dressed like a dummy, because he knew people were more comfortable when a man with his job looked like a cliche. Few people understood detectives were just ordinary guys who'd probably done police work in the past. His police work had been in San Francisco, where it was who you knew just as much as it was in Hollywood, only for less money. He'd considered having a discussion with Jessup about this, except he knew Jessup wouldn't be interested in his way of looking at things. The producer wanted him to find the kid, and that was the end of it.

Like the good investigator he was, he'd learned to know his new locale as well as he had San Francisco, studying it in the same way. He walked every block of Manhattan, feeling it, sensing where the bad spots were even without the confirmation of angry faces. He made a tour of the churches, the ethnic halls (the Bohemian National Hall being his favorite), and a lot of the crummier restaurants. And because there were always runaway teenagers, and finding them had become a principal source of income, he'd also checked out the Hare Krishnas, yoga studios, and various meditation centers. He'd come to call such places Soul Massage Parlors.

So the minute Norman Jessup talked about the kid Om-ing, Hallowell had some idea where to go. He had only said that stuff about the eight million newsstands in the naked city so Jessup would have some inkling how difficult the job was going to be, which it might have been, were Hallowell less savvy. First thing he did after their meeting was draw up a list of the Buddhist places. Out of deference to the clue Jessup had given him about the magazines, he did cruise around town checking out the major sidewalk newsstands and the coffeehouse portions of some giant bookstores, where the young cappuccinoed and read magazines.

But when morning came, he started making the rounds of places on his list. "Have you seen this young man?" he asked the people in charge, showing Tyler's picture

One of them, a towering bear of a man at the third place, an officially sanctioned offshoot of the nearby university, quietly reacted when he saw the photo. He was neatly dressed in western clothes that more or less contained his oversized body, and had one wild eye that seemed to travel to far-flung places even as he looked at you with the controlled one.

"What's he supposed to have done?" the big man asked Hallowell.

His voice was very soft, as though the sound of him came from a secret cave.

"Nothing. Somebody just wants to find him."

"Who?"

"Well, I'd be violating my client privilege if I told you that," said Hallowell. "But he's an alright guy."

"I like to try and see the good in everybody," the giant said, gently. "But I think it's up to individuals to decide who they want to see, and who they don't. I find it disturbing when someone hires a . . . you did say you were a private detective?"

"That's right."

"Somehow, I find the terminology odious."

"I used to be a cop."

"That's supposed to make me feel better?"

"Well, I was a good cop." Hallowell grinned, starting to feel easy in a way he hadn't been able to do with Jessup. The presence of the big man relaxed him, for in spite of his clearly being in opposition to whatever it was Hallowell wanted, obviously the man knew the kid. So it was a question of winning his confidence. "I know to a lot of people who were there in the sixties—"

"I was everywhere in the sixties. I am everywhere now. As far as I'm concerned it could still be the sixties." He was smiling, toying, but his crazy eye looked serious.

"So you consider me a pig?"

"I didn't say that," the big man said.

"I wasn't a cop yet. I was younger than this kid in the sixties."

"We were all younger than this kid in the sixties."

"Then you know him?"

"I see how young he is in the picture." He looked at it respectfully and handed it back to Hallowell. "If I see him, I'll call you. I have your card."

So the guy knew Tyler. He was protecting him. Maybe the kid was even staying there. It was one of those places where it was okay to flop, kind of a YMCA for the ones who found the established Judeo-Christian religions too confining. Many of them came to live at the center. An Om away from Om.

Hallowell's car was around the corner. He moved it and parked it across from the entrance to the center. He didn't have to wait long.

The boy came out wearing his backpack. Ready for a journey, it looked like. But they were always ready for a journey, these kids, all their possessions on their backs. Except he was also carrying something. A box.

Hallowell picked up his binoculars. A carved wooden box, with a leather strap around it so it hung from Tyler's wrist, like the old-fashioned way students used to carry books. He stopped and stood for a moment on the sidewalk. He squinted, as though the sun were in his eyes, which it wasn't. Then his glance moved directly to the binoculars, and he looked at them dead on, sought out the eyes peering through them.

He crossed the street to Hallowell's car. The detective put the binoculars down.

"You the guy asking questions about me?" Tyler said, leaning into the open window.

"Yes, I am." He held out his card.

"I already saw that," Tyler said. "What do you want?"

"A friend of yours was worried about you, that's all."

"What friend?"

"Norman Jessup."

"Maybe he should worry less and be decent more."

"That's probably what he was thinking," said Hallowell. "That's maybe why he hired me to look for you. Whatever it was he did—"

"He canceled my credit."

"Well, he's sorry."

"Not me. I wasn't that happy to be having credit where he sent me."

"He'd like to make it up to you."

"There's nothing to make up," Tyler said. "People are how they are. And things are the way they're supposed to be."

"He'd like to make them better. I'd have to guess it wouldn't take much for a man like Jessup to make life easier."

Tyler squinted again. "Your card said you were a private detective. Is it part of your job to make a case for him?"

"I get paid more if I deliver you," Hallowell said.

"That's honest. Where are you supposed to deliver me to?"

"He's at the Carlyle."

"I guess *his* credit is still good."

"You want me to drive you there, or you want to call him?"

"What if I don't want either of those options?"

"What's in the box?" Hallowell asked.

"A friend."

Hallowell hesitated. "Give Jessup a break, kid. He really cares about you."

"How do you know?"

"I thought . . . well, a couple of times he was close to tears when he talked about you."

"What exactly did he say?"

"I don't remember the words, but he was . . . full of . . . "

"Shit?" asked Tyler.

"Feeling, I was going to say."

"I think he's full of shit," said Tyler.

"I thought you people were so into forgiveness and not judging."

"Well, I haven't gotten there yet," Tyler said. "I'm not the guy in the box."

In the end, Hallowell persuaded Tyler to take a ride with him to the Carlyle. Jessup wasn't in his room. They left word for him at the front desk, and waited in the lounge adjacent to the dining room, with its semicircle of upholstered love seats.

"You want something to eat?" Hallowell asked. "I'm on expenses."

"Thanks," Tyler said. "So am I." He sat back and fingered the carved teak of the little box.

"Good friend?" Hallowell asked.

"The best."

"What are you going to do with the box?"

"Take it to someplace transcendent." He looked up at Hallowell. "You know what that means?"

"I wasn't born a detective," he said. "I read."

"Did you by any chance read *Ulysses*?"

"I tried to."

"Stephen Daedelus goes everywhere carrying an ash plant. It symbolizes his search for his father. I'm one symbol and one reality up on him. I found my father, and I'm carrying his ashes."

Hallowell felt a twist of pity. No matter how these kids tried to act like everything was no big deal, that whatever happened was cool and a part of the process, death was still a big deal. A terrible loss.

He studied Tyler out of the sides of his eyes. The boy was exactly as Jessup had described him. He had a kind of sparkle, Hallowell could see that. Women entering the lounge would halt for a moment on the top step leading down into the sunken dining room, as though they had forgotten something, or suddenly remembered. The old ones, the young ones, the ones in between, caught, every one of them. A few men paused as well.

Still, there was a hint of sadness underneath the young man's . . . what was it? . . . charisma. That was it. Charisma. A word they were always throwing around, but a quality that few people really had. Still, no matter how much light you gave off, losing your father was a dark one. "I'm sorry."

"Thanks," Tyler said. "But don't be sorry. He had a great run. Left a big trail. My only job is to find the place to put him." He fondled the box.

"Well, I guess that's where I come in," said Norman, from the entryway.

*Y*ou did a great job," Jessup said, shaking Hallowell's hand. "Your check will be in the mail."

"I'd ask for it now," advised Tyler. They had moved up to Norman's suite, overlooking what overlooked Madison Avenue. The view past the rooftops went clear to Central Park, greening in the sunlight.

"I'm okay with your sending it," Hallowell said. "Let me know if there's ever anything else you need."

Norman closed the door behind him. He turned to Tyler. "I haven't been very nice to you."

"I'd have to agree with that," Tyler said.

"But I want to make up for it." He walked to the window and looked out at the park. "I realize I was wrong to involve you with anything . . . unsavory."

"Thank you," said Tyler, and exhaled, kind of a whalespout blow of air, like he'd been holding it in for a long time. "It's big of you to admit it."

"I'd like to do something bigger. I'd like to undo New York and give you a trip to Paradise."

"Where's that?"

"Bali." Norman jumped on the name, even as he stretched it out, filling it with mystery and drama. "You ever been?"

"No."

"Ever thought you might like to go?"

"Who hasn't?"

"I'm thinking of setting a movie in Bali. I need someone to scout the locale. Take pictures. Look for great settings. Record how hot it is, find the clearest water in case we want to do underwater stuff. Check out the food, so I'm sure the crew will eat okay."

"Sounds like a really rough assignment," Tyler said.

"Well, it isn't following Sarah Nash, but it'll do. There's a hotel called the Oberoi, right on the edge of the Indian Ocean, as beautiful as any-place in the world. Palm trees. Moist, gentle breezes. I'd like you to go there, stay as long as you like, get a really good read on the place."

"What's the catch?"

"No catch."

"There's always a catch with you, Norman. At the moment of my greatest ecstasy, do I get eaten by a tribe of cannibals?"

"I guess I deserve that. But this time there isn't any downside."

"Bali, huh?" Tyler fingered the carved teak box. "That has to be pretty transcendent. I mean, a soul that wanted to sail from the top of the earth to a place in the sky, that might be a good jumping-off place, don't you think?"

"Better than perfect," said Norman, and took out his cell phone. "I'll book you a ticket."

*T*he baseball field of Beverly High School had an oil rig pumping at the far end of it, beyond which football practice was held in the fall season. The high-rise that cornered the field housed a hospital and a spate of medical suites. So patients visiting a psychiatrist, for example, could look down and see the children playing who had sent them there, all the while the steady flow of the wealth that charac-terized the community continued.

Peer pressure among the young to wear all the right clothes and use designer drugs had been present in the district for decades, along with the reputation for having the finest public schools in the country. Parents had long gone to great trouble and expense, sacrificing and often spending almost everything they had, to be able to live in a neighborhood that would allow their children to go to those schools for free.

With the fall of the Shah of Iran, real estate values peaked in the area, as well-behaved hordes of the Shah's friends, allies, ministers, retinue, and relatives, fleeing the Ayatollah, moved there and bought houses at inflated prices. As such a large percentage of the children spoke only Farsi, the language was introduced into the Beverly Hills school system, classes taught in it, and teachers engaged to bridge the two tongues and cultures.

By the time Richie Harnoun reached high school age, almost everybody had become assimilated, the first language of the children, in school at least, being English. In fact, the two cultures had overlapped so completely that the anguishes of Iranian adolescents had become exactly the same as those of native Angeleans. So Richie dressed as his buddies dressed, had felt bad as a little kid when his shoes weren't from Harry Harris, and felt bad now as a teenager when he couldn't shop on Rodeo Drive. His father, who'd been the young minister of law in Ishfahan, had studied for and passed the California bar, become a prominent Los Angeles lawyer, and tried to teach Richie real values when he had time.

But along with the cultural habits of the locals, the foreigners had adopted their priorities, and success in business always came first. So Richie's father was very busy, his mother had become quite social, his brothers and sisters were all going about their own affairs. Nobody but the maid went into Richie's room, and her job was only to clean. Her job became easier as the clutter of TV, CD players, amps, and speakers, complex electronic and computer equipment his parents had given him to keep up with schoolwork, disappeared. The maid never spoke of the equipment vanishing, the loss meaning nothing to her. The only meaningful loss was some of the mother's jewelry, for which the maid was blamed. In spite of her pleas of innocence, she was fired.

The little E tabs, the Ecstasy passed around in clubs, cost three hundred a pop; everyone knew the price of good cocaine. The problem for Richie, now that the maid was gone and there was no one to take the rap, was where the money would come from. It was in such a quandary that his eye had fallen on the article about Arthur Finster in *Beverly Hills 213*, which his mother read as though it held the truth of the Koran, even though the name alone misrepresented, the area code having changed to 310.

There had been a picture of Arthur along with the piece on him. He had not made the glossy status of the shining couple on the cover, usually people in their sixties who looked thirty-five. But Richie recognized him as soon as he came to the field, waited till his side was at bat to approach him.

"Mr. Finster?"

The whitish gray eyes looked absolutely firelit, they were so filled with excitement. "You Richie?"

"Uh-huh. I'm next at bat. Anyway, we better not try to talk while everyone's here."

They waited until practice was over to meet, sitting in the bleachers. "You got a great throwing arm," Arthur said.

"You really think so?" asked Richie. It had been a long time since his father came to a game. Although his mother usually attended and sat with the other women cheering, it wasn't the same as a man's recognizing what you had.

"A great arm. I would've liked to be an athlete myself, but I chose the life of the mind."

"I've read your books," said Richie.

"Yeah, well oftentimes you can't put your money where your mind is."

"I really liked them. Especially the one that the whores wrote. My mother hid it in the maid's toilet, but I found it."

"Good for you," Arthur said. "Now about your idea . . . "

"I know them all. All the kids whose parents are buddies with O.J. Or used to be. And they all have stories."

"When can we get together?" Arthur said eagerly.

"Well, first we have to hammer out a deal," said Richie. "I need to be sure you really have something to sell."

"The bag with the knife and the clothes. I know where it went."

"Yes?" asked Arthur, barely able to breathe.

"It's in my father's closet."

It was almost in Lila's pocket: a monument to Larry. The Widow Darshowitz had no sense of irony, didn't even really know the word. But she understood she had a bigwig by the short hairs, and that was the way you made an impression in this town. That notion pleased her so much her depression started to lift, even though she was in a wheelchair.

It was hard sitting in the antiseptic beige and chrome hotel room. In her own apartment there were print patterns everywhere, different prints on the pillows that angled on a print of another kind of couch, and little pots of flowers on the windowsills. So even in the harsh, gray winters of Queens there was plenty of color. Plus there were the magazines, the subscriptions Larry bought her that kept on arriving: W, like she was a fashion plate; *Mirabella,* like she was a today woman; *Vanity Fair,* like the thing that kept her alive was inside info about the death of Doris Duke.

Everywhere in her Queens apartment magazines were heaped up like she was a regular Collier brother. Somehow she had been unable to throw any away. They were reminders of Larry, piles of proof that he'd still really cared about her, thought about her, went to the trouble of mailing in the subscription blanks and wanted her to keep up with things. Perhaps at some point she might reenter what he'd called his sphere, a word he'd picked up about the same time he found the Phi Beta Kappa key. It was this fantasy of their getting back together that had kept her going—maybe him, too. Because in spite of how much she'd let herself go, nobody loved him like she did. Nobody loved him for himself, since nobody besides Lila knew who himself really was.

The screaming tantrums he'd thrown at his employees, the falling-outs he'd had with almost every major star, there'd never been a hint of that in their relationship. Only once in all the time they'd been together, at the very start of their dating when she'd laughed at something he took very seriously, had he shown the slightest resentment. With Lila he had always been gentle, spoken with such a soft voice, that even when he left her, she never heard him say good-bye. Maybe that was because he'd never said it. He just went to the corner for a newspaper once and never came home.

She wished now that she had the clutter of her magazines to warm up the sterile box of a room she was in. She thought of buying some, but that would have been greedy, since they were mounting up on her welcome mat at home in her absence. She hoped the super would have the sense to put them inside her apartment when he watered her plants, which she'd tipped him to do.

It was lonely in the hotel in the daytime. There was nothing to divert her from the dull ache in her leg and the one in her heart except television. She didn't really care for soap operas, and despised the way whole families were parading their messed-up sex lives on talk shows. It disgusted her that that was what the country had come to. Evenings were easier, because she had her wine, but never before six o'clock. People who drank in the day were alcoholics, and Lila wasn't one of those. The worst she ever was was a drunk.

Her days stretched long. She ordered her meals, brought by the bellman from the coffee shop, and ate without appetite, except dinner, when food was accompanied by wine. That writer girl Kate had brought her a case of Merlot from someplace called Trader Joe's. It was not a bad vintage, and had a slightly oaky taste. At least it did once she allowed it to breathe, as Larry had taught her, which she always did with the first bottle.

She saw there was only one bottle left in the case and picked up the phone, dialed. "Kate? It's Lila Darshowitz."

"How are you feeling?" the girl asked.

"A little thirsty," said Lila. "I wonder if I could trouble you to buy me another case of that nice Merlot. I'm sort of stuck here, and I'll pay you back."

"Don't worry about it," Kate said.

"Well, I do. I worry about being a drain on people. That's how it stayed so good with me and Larry. I never asked him for anything he couldn't give. Like loyalty." She snickered. "So what do you think? You think I could impose on you to get it for me? I'd ask my chauffeur to pick it up, but he's driving Anthony Hopkins to the airport."

Kate laughed. "I'll get it right away."

* * *

She arrived about forty minutes later. The bellboy, who looked older than Lila, his neck scrawny and thin above the traditional bell-boy collar, wheeled a trolley to Lila's room, set the case of wine on the floor, and thanked Kate for the tip.

"I'll pay you back," said Lila.

"Don't worry about it," said Kate.

"Will you join me in a glass? Of course, there wouldn't be room for the both of us." She laughed, a coarse but warm laugh, appreciating herself. She looked at her watch, and saw that in seven minutes it would be okay. The rules could be stretched when you had company. Expertly uncorking the wine, she poured.

"Here's looking at you, kid," she said, and clinked glasses. "*Casablanca.*"

"I know."

"That wasn't Larry's favorite Bogart. He liked *The Maltese Falcon* better. You remember how crazy Sydney Greenstreet goes when he's scraping the bird trying to uncover the jewels? 'It's a fake, it's lead!' "

"I remember."

"Larry used to say that was the movie business. 'The stuff dreams are made of.' But it's a fake, it's lead."

"It isn't all a fake," said Kate. "There are a lot of really nice people here."

"They haven't asked me to dine," said Lila, "so I wouldn't know. How much do I owe you for the wine?"

"It's my treat."

Lila narrowed her eyes. "Why?"

"I intend to exploit you."

"That means you want to use me, right?"

"Right."

"What for?" Lila said, and finished the glass, poured another.

"The book."

"You really going to write it?"

"I'm going to try."

"Larry always said nobody ever tries. You either do it or you don't. Give me a pencil." She pointed to the console.

Kate reached for the pencil there and handed it to Lila.

"Okay," Lila said, and dropped it on the floor. "Try to pick it up."

Kate got to her feet, reached down, and retrieved it.

"You see?" Lila said.

"Well, that's just an easy physical instance. The argument wouldn't hold with a difficult internal struggle."

Lila studied her. "You better have another drink," she said. "Or I better, so I can understand what the fuck you're talking about."

*T*hey finished the bottle.

"You said . . . " Lila noted, a little sloppily, "you said you didn't know him. So what were you doing at his funeral?"

"I wanted to brush shoulders with celebrity," she said.

"What exactly does that mean?"

"I wanted to get to know the glittering people." The wine had made her a little mawkish. She could hear how superficial it sounded, and disliked herself.

"But instead, you got saddled with me."

"Larry was right," Kate said kindly. "You're worth all of them."

"How do you know? Have you met all of them?"

"Not yet," Kate said.

"You will. You're young and pretty with a little round ass, and you know how to talk. Some people like that in a woman."

*B*y the time she left Lila's, Kate was caught. Without having heard Drayco's whole story, Kate had a strong sense F. Scott Fitzgerald would have made a fictionalized Larry touching and weakly heroic, for all his faults. Gatsbying to the last, or past the last, if there had been time after *The Last Tycoon*. The fabric a literary poseur could use to create the "sequin," if they were low enough to attempt such a thing, gifted enough to offer up a convincing counterfeit. Of course it would have to be flawed, as Fitzgerald's writing had certainly been towards the end of his life, what with the boozing, the surrender of what little spine was left, wallowing into his coddled relationship with Sheilah Graham. Grandma. Even as Kate's mouth curled up into a smile, she managed to be slightly appalled at herself, that she could not only conceive of such a thing, but, in the back of her mind, was already structuring the novel.

It was still pretty early, but already dark. Sunset Boulevard was lit with a strangely melancholy glow. James Dean stretched dungareed legs across the side of a building, cowboy hat tipped back at a slightly insolent angle, profile amused, defiant, like he already knew he would last forever, never growing old. Facing him, painted on the concrete side of another high-rise, Elizabeth Taylor rode Velvet to victory in the Grand National, her face childishly perfect, open, pre-sexual, none of the coming excesses or withdrawals, indulgences or denials, feasts or famines, loves or losses even hinted at. On a bill-board across the boulevard, moving panels flashed: "You're an Actor?" The slats moved like venetian blinds. "What restaurant?" Slatted again. "Life is harsh," it said. "Your tequila shouldn't be." The L.A. version of the eyes of Dr. T.J. Eckleburg, the eerie sign over-looking Gatsby's West Egg.

The stuff that dreams were made of. Except life was too short as it had been for James Dean, or life was too long as it seemed for Eliz-abeth, or life was too disappointing as it was for those who needed the tequila. A lure, a business, that had become as dark as the the-aters where movies were shown. That had shadowed Kate's own mind so she could view as a clever joke what the newly-arrived-in-Hollywood Kate would have fled in horror.

She was thinking that when she plowed into the back of the car in front of her.

"Oh, God," she murmured, first to herself, then aloud. "Oh, God." The car she had slammed into had braked for a red light she hadn't seen because she was so busy taking in the cheerfully grim paradox of the scenery. The hardest-edged predicament you could get into in Los Angeles this side of drugs was this one. She'd been drinking. She'd rear-ended somebody. They would test her breath, and then her blood. She'd be taken to jail. Who would she call? She didn't have a lawyer. Out of all the people she knew that she thought liked her a little, she could think of no one she could ask to help her. Mel would be out of the office by now, and she didn't have his home number; he hadn't yet made a deal for her, so real Hollywood inti-macy hadn't been attained. Jake Alonzo would probably not be home, and she couldn't call him to come to her rescue after not returning his calls. Wendy was a brand new friend, and elevated, not one you would bring into this kind of situation. Wilton would flee the moment she said she was calling from the police station. Her insurance company would probably cancel, and in Los Angeles you were dead without a car. Maybe she was dead already. "Oh, God!" she said again, realizing she hadn't given a thought to the people in the car she'd hit.

She got out and ran towards the driver. Let him not be crushed against the steering wheel, she silently pleaded. Let the one on the passenger side not be splattered on the windshield. Let their airbags have opened. Let them sue me for a phony claim of whiplash. Let my insurance company cancel me after paying them off so I can't drive and have to live the rest of my life in the Midwest. But let them not be truly injured.

The traffic was already making an arc around the two wracked-up vehicles. People were craning their necks for a moment, to see if it was bloody, then going on their way. Kate bent down towards the driver; he opened his window. The airbag that cramped him against the seat was open, so she couldn't quite see his face. "Are you alright?" she asked, frantically.

He leaned back, pushing against the billowing bag, so he could speak. "I'm fine," he said. She saw that it was Morgan Craig, her friend from Stanford.

"Oh, Morgan. Oh, God. I'm so sorry. Who's that with you?"

"Nobody," Rodney Sameth mumbled, muffled by the airbag, trying to sink deeper into its recesses.

"Oh, my God," Kate said. "Rodney Sameth! Are you alright?"

"I'm fine," he said, "fine. But I'm not Rodney Sameth. I just sound like him."

"You look like him, too."

"Well, I've put on a little weight. That happens to you when you live in France. All that butter. I'm stationed there. A member of the military."

"Are you okay?" she asked Morgan.

"I'm okay," he said, smiling feebly.

"I was hoping to run into you again. I'm sorry it had to be so literal." In the near distance she could hear the wail of a police siren. "I'll go get my insurance information, and you can give me yours—"

"It's okay," cried the man claiming not to be Rodney Sameth. "Not to worry. No real harm done."

"Don't you even want to see the back of your car?" she asked.

"Forget about it. It's a rented car. They have no personal stake—"

"What about my insurance record?" Morgan asked him, worriedly.

"I'll handle it, I'll handle it," said not-Rodney. "Let's just get out of here."

The motorcycle policeman pulled up to the place where the two cars sat enmeshed, and took out his report pad. "It's alright, officer," said the man in the passenger seat. "We've worked it all out. It's our fault. We're part of a funeral cortege, and we stopped short so this young woman inadvertently tapped us a little."

The officer walked around the car, and looked. "Jesus Christ," Rodney muttered, low, so only Morgan could hear him. "Jesus Christ. This is all I need. People will find out I'm in town and I've been in a wreck with an unknown writer. They'll put it together. They'll know you're writing the script. Police! Next they'll bring in cameras for E."

"Get a grip," Morgan said.

Rodney burrowed down into his chest, his ears disappearing under his collar, turtlelike. But his eyes still showed. He closed them, as though unseeing meant invisible.

"I'm so glad you're alright," Kate said to Morgan, waiting for the policeman to come back. What was he going to do? Check her breath? Arrest her for drunken driving? Put her in the tank, where she'd be held till morning and be set upon by lesbians? "I wondered why you didn't call."

"He hasn't been here," said Rodney.

"Do you by any chance know the name of a lawyer?"

"Helmut Rott," Morgan said, naming Rodney's attorney.

"For Christ's sake, the man's in an oxygen tent," screamed Rodney.

"But maybe his office can refer her . . . "

"The back of this car is fairly well smashed in," the policeman said, returning. "I better make a report."

"Please, officer. We'll be late for the funeral. The family's bereaved enough, without our showing up late." Rodney smiled at him. "Please let us just move on."

"What about you?" he looked at Kate.

She leaned away from him as she answered, almost bending in half backward, hoping he could not smell her breath. "Well, none of us wants to hold up the service."

"Okay. Go ahead," the policeman said.

"Thank you," said Rodney. "I shall write a letter to the chief of police telling him how far you men have come since the riots and O.J."

"That would be very nice of you, Mr. Sameth," said the cop.

"I'm not . . . " he started to say, then obviously thought better of it.

"I used to be in the business," the cop said. "I was an assistant cameraman on *Reverend Hate.*"

"I remember you," said Sameth, despondently. "You know how to uninflate these airbags?"

*A*fter he had helped Sameth out of the jumble and sent him on his way, the policeman went to a pay phone. As above reproach as he had been in the job that circumstance had edged him into when the lure of the lights and the grip of the Grip could not be counted on to feed a family, and as much as he had resisted anything that smacked of corruption, he still had a friend in the press. Nothing *Globe* or *Enquirer* of course, nothing he'd be paid for to ruin a man. Just an innocent local throwaway paper, where an old pal could use an item.

Thus it was that Rodney Sameth, reading *Beverly Hills 213* aloud the next weekend to his lawyer, Helmut Rott, who lay in an oxygen tent, came across an item stating the elusive director (himself) was secretly back in town. There was a twenty-four-hour nurse in attendance who managed to revive Rodney.

Burning Bridges

$\mathcal{R}$ichie Harnoun had been telling the truth. The missing bag, or at least one exactly like the one that had been described as missing, had indeed been in his father's closet. There had been so much tumult the night of the murder and the next morning and through all the incendiary episodes that followed, he supposed his father had just forgotten about it. To be a friend of O.J.'s at that particular time in local—and, as it turned out, national, and even worldwide—history, was to have a lot on your mind, as well as your answering machine.

Ibrahim Harnoun, Richie's dad, had been with his friend at the funeral, along with a select group of O.J.'s colleagues, including a movie director who'd used him in a bad film. The wife of the director had been one of O.J.'s staunchest supporters in the months that followed, since she had observed him in his distraught state at the service for Nicole. "I don't know," she was heard to say at an open-air lunch at La Scala in Beverly Hills. "He's such a terrible actor, I don't see how he could have put that on."

Richie had found the bag by accident while he was looking for some-place to hide the cash he had gotten for the sale of his CD player, since the maid cleaned everything, including the inside of his drawers and his bookshelves. He wasn't going to have the money long. He had a date with his dealer, a boy in the grade ahead of him, for the next afternoon. But his mother usually hugged him several times daily in a distracted way to remind him and maybe herself that he was important to her, and he was afraid maybe she'd feel the money in his pockets. Several of his friends had had run-ins with the local police and been frisked for weapons and illicit drugs. Each of them reported that it was not unlike having a going-over from your mother, only not as friendly.

He was afraid to look in the bag. He felt guilty enough about his own actions as a child of such an upstanding member of the community without adding to his burden by getting the goods on his dad. Upstanding. If the knife and the bloody clothes were in there, that would mean his father was complicitous or one of the words they had used on TV about Al Cowlings. Even after Richie had spent the money he'd worried about hiding (he'd Scotch-taped it to the back of his toilet, a trick he remembered from the video of *The Godfather*) and gotten out of his head on the cocaine, he'd been too scared in his spaciness to check out the bag.

Only as his desperation for money increased did he formulate his plan. He wrote the letter to Arthur Finster, and got the tacit agreement of his friends who needed money for the same reason, whose parents also had been close to O.J., to tell their parents' tales. Most of the stories were about gradual disillusionment with the once football hero, and eventual abandonment. Some, like the director's wife, were now about disgust. She had been one of those who helped put up the sign near the Burlingame house decrying "The Butcher of Brentwood" before going to Parent's Day at the high school. After Richie had written to Finster, he went to the closet.

The bag was gone.

The letter was already in the mail. Still, it wasn't exactly a lie, what he was to tell Finster on the athletic field. As soon as they'd closed the deal, he went shopping. Luggage on Rodeo Drive was way out of line, price-wise. Besides, it had been a simple black canvas bag. They would have one in the Mart, for sure, in downtown Los Angeles. All he needed was a couple of bucks, and a friend to go along with him, one who also had an O.J. story to tell.

*P*erry Zemmis picked up the phone and tried to think who he should give the contract to. What was really sad, he could not help thinking, was that George Bush had been right: there had been a kinder, gentler time. There had been a time when all a betrayed wife had to do was drop in at Roy Cohn's office, and presuming she was a good client, merely mention in passing, "I'm so sick of hearing about that woman." And the next thing you knew, men would be asking questions at the garage where the mistress had her white Mercedes convertible fixed, and life-imperiling things would happen. And the movie of the week the mistress had sold telling her story to try and stay afloat financially after she'd been cut off was sabotaged by the head of the agency that sold it. Eventually the woman herself would be bludgeoned to death, and the confused nance who was staying with her would be blamed, convicted, and sent to jail where he would die of AIDS. Oh, it had truly been a kinder, gentler time.

But now Roy himself had died of AIDS, so if you wanted someone or something out of the way, you had to take care of it yourself. What a world, what a world, as the witch in the *Wizard of Oz* said.

If you wanted someone dead, you had to be practically hands-on. No Roy anymore to mention your woes to and have them disappear. If Perry wanted that Kate person to give him the Fitzgerald story, he might have to strong-arm her himself. It really burned his ass, in a nostalgic way, that Roy wasn't around. Politics had taught Roy how to threaten without it sounding like a threat. Or maybe Roy had taught that to politics. There was much of that dead man's skill that Perry had yet to learn, and might never. But he had at least learned from him how to help an ally. Or someone you wanted for an ally. Norman Jessup in his corner. Perry could hardly wait.

He dialed a number in New Jersey and waited for the pick-up at the other end. "Chickie?" Perry said. "You ever read a book called *A Snowflake in Hell*? No. I'm not kidding. I know you can read. Well, here's your chance to become a literary figure."

*A*t the Mart in downtown L.A., Richie found a bag like the one that had been in the closet with no effort at all. Then he took the piece from the *National Enquirer* that he'd saved for more than a year and looked up the address of the Hoffritz store where O.J. had bought the knife a few weeks before the murder. The man who had sold the article to the tabloid wasn't working there anymore. But everybody knew the kind of knife of it was. The one with the serrated edge.

"Give me some money," he said to his friend Tony.

"Why should I pay for it?" he said. "It's your chapter of the book."

"I'll pay you back when we get our advance." There were still legal complications, according to Arthur Finster, since everyone involved except the kid who worked at Chin-Chin was a minor, so technically he needed parental permission for the contracts, which of course he couldn't imagine getting. Richie thought of asking his father what the legal way was for a minor to get a valid contract without his parents' permission, but senior Harnoun wasn't stupid, and as little attention as he paid to his family, that might start him thinking.

"You sure we're going to get it?"

"Of course I'm sure," said Richie, not sure. The hookers had just gone public with the fact that Finster had stinted on their payments, and the woman who'd been the "as told to" scribe for *By Hook or by Crook*, translating the sexually explicit illiteracy into what passed for writing, had done several talk shows complaining about how little she'd been paid and what a hard time she had collecting.

I'll need some of your blood," Richie said, when they were in his room with the bag and the knife and a big dark sweatsuit, size extra large, that he'd gotten on sale.

"What? You kidding me?" Tony said.

Richie had pierced his own palm with the tip of the knife, and was dripping on it and the clothes. "We'll need more than one type."

In the end they got four different kids, including Richie and Tony, to bleed on the knife and the sweatsuit, one more than they needed for victims and perpetrator, unless of course it had been a South American drug gang. But Richie figured if the DNA experts had so confused the jury, it would not be any easier for Arthur Finster, should he check.

I brought the bag," Richie said, when the door was closed to Finster's office.

"I'll put it somewhere safe," Arthur said, reaching for it. There were framed posters up on the leather brass-tacked walls, blowups of the covers of the books that had leapfrogged to popular prominence on the backs of those who could not defend themselves, including the brand new one just out about a drug-addicted, alcoholic former district attorney who'd lost a big case in San Francisco, an uncorroborated account of his ménage à trois with the homosexual city councilman who'd been murdered, and the murdered mayor, who'd been straight. It was having a brisk local sale in the Bay Area.

"Not till we get our money," said Richie.

Before he left that day, Arthur would pay him five hundred in cash, as an advance against his advance, and put him in a room with a tape recorder to tell his story. There were a lot of likes and you knows and basicallys on the tape. But deep in its recesses were words that struck ecstasy into Arthur, in addition to information about the father's friendship with O.J. and the appearance of the black bag. And those were, "My father's an associate in the law firm of Fletcher McCallum."

So an associate of the esteemed Mr. McCallum, Esq., was guilty of aiding and abetting in the most notorious criminal trial in memory. Why, in the wrong hands, a story like that could bring down an entire firm. The lawyer who had been his own lawyer and fired him as a client because he *disapproved* of the kind of thing he was publishing. The lawyer who had instituted and was handling the action against him. Ha ha. So much for Fletcher McCallum and the class action libel suit.

$\mathcal{F}$or the climb into the recycling bin, Sarah Nash had gotten into sneakers, an old pair of jeans, and a thin, funky sweater. She waited until twilight just so she wouldn't be *too* conspicuous. Anybody who saw her clambering up the hood of the old Buick next to the bin, gingerly leaping across the space between, jumping into the bin itself, her landing softened by the paper, might have thought her actions a little peculiar. But watching her forage carefully through the contents, those who knew New York would probably just dismiss her as a homeless person looking for soft drink cans to turn in for cash or food.

She had covered her attention-getting hairdo with a woolen ski cap that more or less did the job, although the spikes were so heavy with glue that they still sort of showed through, like five hard-ons. But freaky was pretty much run-of-the-mill now in the city. No one would bother her, out of apathy or fear she was one of the bona fide lunatics that roamed the streets since the laws had been changed so that the hospitals had to have permission from wackos to put them away.

She had brought a flashlight with her, a smart little thing she had picked up at JC Penney's in Santa Monica, someplace she only dropped into to get a parking validation when meeting with her lawyer in the building on the corner. The pocket flashlight was blue, very neat, an oval-shaped disc with a sliding top that illuminated when opened. There was a kind of slickness about it that pleased her as she went through the cast-off letters, the junk mail.

It took her a few hours to find it. The envelope was addressed to Paulo, postmarked in Baltimore a few weeks before, the return address Johns Hopkins University. She opened it.

It was a letter of inquiry from from a Dr. Aaronson. "It has been twenty months since successful completion of your surgery," he'd written. "We are doing a long-term study on the effects of estrogen on our patients, and would greatly appreciate your cooperation.

"Along with that, we are doing a co-study with the noted psychiatrist Dr. Harold Hoddingsworth on the long-term psychological effects of the procedure. Would you be willing to complete a questionnaire? Naturally no names will be used, and the confidentiality we promised will continue to be honored."

The questionnaire that accompanied the letter contained, among other inquiries, a request to know the frequency of intercourse, if there was any pain, and whether there was tenderness in the breasts. Sarah could hardly breathe. That she would have to wait until morning to call the doctor's office to verify her suspicions seemed truly a torture. In spite of what Jerry Falwell said, God must have loved homosexuals, or she wouldn't have had to spend such a difficult night.

And what, specifically, is Dr. Aaronson's field?" she asked his nurse on the phone.

"May I ask what this is for?"

"Well, he was recommended to my husband by our doctor. So I'm just double-checking that this is the right Dr. Aaronson."

"What is your husband's problem?"

"He's having a lot of trouble with his pee-pee," Sarah said, chancing it.

"Then you're calling the right man," the nurse said, pride of profession and allegiance coming through on the phone. "His field is urology."

"I see," said Sarah.

"Actually, he's a specialist in two fields. Urology *and* plastic surgery."

"Well, as Bette Davis would say, how very convenient."

"I beg your pardon?"

"Thank you for your help," Sarah said.

"Do you want to schedule an appointment?"

"I'll call you back," Sarah said, and hung up. "How very convenient," she said again, aloud, to herself, giving it the haughty diva's inflection. Urology *and* plastic surgery. He could change Paulo's penis and his face at the same time.

Everything but the eyes.

*T*he lovely Carina. Jessup hadn't killed Paulo at all, just had him altered. Made into a fashion model. The wonders of modern medicine. It was juicier than if he'd actually murdered him. Holy shit.

So when she'd said at Drayco's wake that Norman would have to turn Carina around to pretend she was a boy, Sarah had hit the nail right on the head. No wonder he'd shoved her in the guacamole.

"Oh, have I got a follow-up book for you," she said over lunch with her agent. They were eating at Michael's, a restaurant on East Fifty-fifth Street that had become fashionable for the book set, convenient as it was to the office of ex-publishing wives who'd gotten better jobs than the husbands who'd fired and divorced them, not necessarily in that order.

"What?" said the brightly blue-eyed brunette, who seemed a little soft, till she started talking business. "Tell, tell."

"No, no. Write, write."

"You're not going to let me in on it?"

"Not even you. It's so hot it could cook rock cocaine."

"I hope you're not doing that anymore," Lori said. She had changed the spelling of her name from Laurie, on the advice of a numerologist, and signed her letters now with a heart over the *i*.

"I'm not. I'm high on—"

"If you say life, I'll puke," said Lori. "I had to go to an AA meeting with . . . well, you know how you can't name who you've been to AA with, otherwise the Alcoholics are no longer Anonymous. Suffice it to say he's a well-known singer-actor and I'm selling his bio for landmark dollars. He'll confess himself in the book that he went through the entire production of . . . I can't tell you what musical it was or you'll know who I'm talking about . . . loaded. We went to an AA meeting in the Hamptons. Everyone there was so fucking positive, I needed a drink."

"I am not high on life," said Sarah, eyes sparkling. "I am high on revenge."

"It has to be about Norman Jessup," said Lori.

"Don't guess," said Sarah. "You'll find out soon enough. I've got an exposé that will make every scandal book about the Clinton White House read like the Bobbsey Twins."

"There's a rumor that that's who they are," Lori said.

*S*arah could hardly wait to get to her computer and write it. She booked her reservation back to the coast direct through the airline, not even calling her travel agent, she was so excited. Not one extra step. Just packed, took Tel Aviv taxi to the airport, buying a jewel from Carmen the driver on the way to Kennedy as a reward to herself, in advance, for the splash she would surely make with this one, and literally flew.

I suppose you think I was too easy," Wendy said, as she lay on her canopied bed.

"Easy is not exactly the word for it," said Binky Danforth-Smythe, lighting a gold-tipped cigarette.

"You think I'm a slut."

"I think that thinking is hardly involved here," he said, and inhaled deeply.

"It's just been so long. And I've been so lonely. They drummed Jeremy out of the corps and sent him to Hong Kong or somewhere. I haven't a clue even where he's gone."

"I doubt it was Hong Kong." Binky exhaled. "We have no more hold on Hong Kong. Nobody but the so-called People's Liberation Army has a hold on Hong Kong, including the people of Hong Kong."

"It only started with Jeremy because I was so lonely and humiliated. All those people writing books. My own parents selling the photos of me in the bath when I was two. Have you ever gotten mash notes from pedophiles?"

"I regret to say not," said Binky.

"So please don't think I'm easy."

"Easy? I couldn't even make you come."

"It's just that I was so nervous."

"Well, you have every reason to be," said Binky.

"What?"

"You're making a damned fool of yourself."

"With you?"

"With everyone. You seem to have forgotten how to conduct yourself in public, as well as private. The people you're seen with. It's a Disgrace." He gave it the emphasis that a literal fall from grace required. Or a shove, as it had been in her case.

"But you told me . . . you said how proud you were of me. How proud everyone was."

"I was trying to make you sound good in front of that intrusive American."

"Kate? Kate is hardly intrusive. If anyone in that situation was intrusive, it was you."

"What about that ponce, her friend with the reticule? You let yourself be seen in the company of just anyone. You're a dishonor to the nation."

"Oh, don't," Wendy said, and started to weep.

"Why don't you save it for Barbara Walters?" he said.

"Why are you being so cruel?"

"Do you have an ashtray? My ash is dripping."

"I'll get one," said Wendy, and got up from the bed. "My luck you'll set the bed on fire, and they'll find us here, naked, dead from smoke inhalation."

"Not a bad idea," he said.

"What?"

"To be dead." He reached for the ashtray she handed him, looked at the name on it. "Bistro Gardens," he said, flicking his ash. "Getting light-fingered in addition to everything else?"

"They were closing," she said. "Everyone the final day got a souvenir."

"I need to use the loo," he said, getting up, and went into the bathroom.

He came back a few moments later, still holding the ashtray. "Only genuinely elegant restaurant in the flats of Beverly Hills. Wouldn't you know they'd go out of business, with *those* people for a clientele."

"*Those people?*"

"Jews," he said.

"It just so happens, if they'd had them for a clientele, they wouldn't have gone out of business," Wendy said. "The reason they had to close was because a maître d' said 'You can smell them' about some Jewish women who were lunching there. The word spread like wildfire, and none of them would go back, or any of their friends, or their friends' friends. So the place was forced to close."

"How very unjust," said Binky. "To be boycotted for the truth."

"The truth?"

"They do smell."

"You are really vile," she said. "I wish you'd leave."

"Have you any tea?"

"We don't have to pretend to be civilized, after what you've said."

"Of course we do," he answered.

"This place is really quite cozy," he said, as they sat at the table in her breakfast nook. "At least you've done a first-rate job with the decoration."

He had a towel around him. She saw how pale and freckled his skin was, and felt ill. His penis, too, had freckles on it. She'd seen them as it emerged from the hanging foreskin, and tried not to be repelled. But through it all she had visualized those spots inside her, rubbing away, and gone totally cold.

The security guard had been sent away when the call had come from Binky. Seeing how empty the apartment was, even—or especially—with this man in it, Wendy felt truly isolated. She also felt foolish, as she'd felt from the moment everybody found out what a sham her marriage was. Including her. A world full of eyes that had once been admiring and envious fixed on her with pity, or loathing, depending which side of the fence they were on. She could not comprehend that her universe had turned into one that was gated, with her on the outside.

"This is lovely tea," Binky said, sipping.

"No need to chat," she said.

"Why not? Chat is good. It helps cover up the fact that you really don't have anything to say."

"You, meaning me? Or you, meaning one, which includes you?"

"You," he said. "What is that expression they have about men in America with no real persona? An empty shirt? You're an empty dress. Or, right now, an empty robe."

"I could throw myself off the terrace for letting you touch me."

"Not a bad idea."

"Is that why you came here? To drive me to suicide?"

"Nobody drives anybody to suicide," he said. "People commit suicide because they have no reason to live. What reason do you have?"

"How cruel you are."

"Cruel? I would say accurate. You haven't a bit of talent, your looks, such as they are, are going, your education was stunted, and you didn't have much of a brain to begin with. As they say in the fairy tales . . . " His voice grew all mincy, " 'What's to become of me?' "

"That's it, isn't it?" Wendy got to her feet. "They've sent you to drive me mad."

"Nobody drives anybody mad. People either have madness in them or they don't. From your comportment these past few months, I'd say it was probably in your genes. Actually being seen on the arm of a common tradesman. A kike in the bargain."

"I see," she said, coldly. "They heard about Morty."

"Morty," he said jeeringly. "You can actually speak of such a person with affection. Don't make an even bigger fool of yourself," he said. "May I have another cup?"

"You may have the whole pot," she said, and threw it at him.

*A*fter he'd gone, she lay on the bed. She felt queasy, the stickiness on the sheets a reminder that he'd been there, that she'd actually let him inside her. Bounder that he was, he was right about her. She was stupid. Stupid and unstable to let just anyone come into her life, into her body, because she was so desperate.

She'd started taking antidepressants to get through her ordeal, and they made her anxious. The anxiety was worse than the depression had been. She'd had to sneak to the psychiatrist to avoid the press as she'd had to sneak to see her lover. If he'd really been her lover. If he'd cared for her, how could he have disappeared after selling their story?

The doctor had prescribed a second pill to quell the anxiety. She went to the medicine cabinet, and opened it. Beside the two prescription bottles from her doctor was a bottle she hadn't seen before. She took it out of the cabinet and looked at it. It had her name on it, from a pharmacy she couldn't recollect ever visiting, from a doctor she didn't recall either. "Take 2 for sleep," it said on the label. Could she have been to a doctor she didn't even remember, just as she'd gone to bed with a man it turned out she didn't really know? Maybe she *was* going crazy.

"I'd like to speak to the pharmacist, please," she said into the phone.

"He's out to lunch," the woman said.

"Then I'm not alone," said Wendy.

She went to the mirror and looked at herself. It was true, what Binky had said. She was losing what looks she had. There were dark semicircles under her eyes, her hair hung limp and lifeless, her skin was mottled. The tabloids had made note of the fact that her thighs were going, and published a photo to prove it, taken by a hidden camera someone had at the gym. She'd had to start working out at home.

Home. It was no more home than the hole had been to Alice. Binky had asked her that day at the hotel where she'd like to go, and that was where she had told him. Into the hole, like Alice. Apparently she was already in it.

"Take me." It might as well have been written on the bottle. She opened the bottle, lined the pills up on the edge of the sink, and counted them. Fifty. Enough, she knew from the accounts of Marilyn's death, the ones that hadn't suggested the secret service had shoved something up her arse to finish her off so she wouldn't make any more trouble. Enough to make sure a country wouldn't be victimized by a woman dumped. Or, as they would have said in England, a woman Civic Amenity Tipped. What a place was Great Britain, that no one ever said exactly what they meant, so busy were they saying what sounded civilized.

$\mathcal{K}$ate had gotten into the habit of dropping in on Lila in the late afternoons, bringing with her herbal tea bags so the same thing wouldn't happen on the way home as had happened when she shared Lila's wine. As her affection for the woman deepened, which it did, she tried to get her, too, to change over to tea.

"I don't get great ideas from tea," she said to Kate now, as the younger woman started to pour a second cup. "I'll stick to my Merlot."

"You really think wine helps you get ideas?"

"I know it does. Or if it doesn't, at least I'm too drunk to notice. I'm not creative like you are, so I need all the help I can get. I have to come up with a real inspiration."

"Maybe I can help," Kate said.

Lila looked at her with narrowing eyes. "In order for you to help, I'd have to tell you the whole story."

"I can handle that," said Kate.

"You said you're going to *try* and write the book about him. I might as well give you the ammunition."

With that, she began to recount the true life saga of Larry Drayco. Included was everything he had told her, more than he'd ever told anyone, including the guru he'd seen in India and the psychiatrist he'd been to as part of his rehabilitation. In addition was everything Lila had found out that he hadn't told her, stuff about the other wives, and Jason Stone and Tim McClure, and the other women, gotten from a long line of secretaries whom she'd made into phone friends.

As accepting as Larry thought she'd been of his wanderings, as cool and dismissive about his behavior as she'd sounded to Kate, the fact was she'd been crazy about him. Really crazy. Agonizing over almost every moment he hadn't been with her. Needing to fill them in in her mind, so even if he hadn't been present, she'd know what he had been doing.

That way she always had something to do at night, besides drinking wine and wondering. That way at least she could be with him, in a way, knowing his entire story, as in "Jack and the Beanstalk," so she could follow him as he went out to seek what turned out to be not exactly his fortune.

Will the Real Larry Drayco Please Stand Up

$\mathcal{I}$t had not been just the Darshowitz that he changed. He had been born Laruschka, the son of Poles who had made it to this country just in time for his mother to spread her legs and deliver him to American citizenship. It made him proud for a while simply to be a Yankee Doodle Dandy. But he learned even as a boy that for him it was not enough.

To his parents, the streets had been paved with gold, just as the myths promised, at least in comparison to Warsaw. But Laruschka had been born with a silver spoon in his brain. Very early he started going to movies, where, in the dark, he could become anybody. *Little Lord Fauntleroy* was his particular favorite. Even as he came home from seeing it for the first time, he started to become uncomfortable with how common his parents were. "Laruschka, Laruschka!" his mother said, squeezing his cheeks between her big, calloused hands. She smelled of cabbage, the sweet and sour redolence that permeated their apartment on Fridays, penetrating the floor so it was even downstairs in his father's tailor shop. He loved cabbage. He loved her. But he already knew that the better life she'd come for and found wasn't as good as he could make it. He'd smelled the scent of lilacs on the blond girl who sold movie magazines, and it was preferable. "Larry," he said, as his mother kissed him, full on the puckered lips.

"Vass?"

"Larry," he said. "That's my name in English." The name would be cited once he hit big in Hollywood as having been after Laurence Olivier, later Sir Larry, later Lord O to his intimates, one of which Drayco longed to be. Olivier was the only major actor of any nationality with whom new Larry wanted to make a picture that he didn't. In spite of Drayco's claim that he'd been named after him, Olivier had yet to emerge as an actor of note when Laruschka was born. Indeed, he was probably not long out of diapers himself. A minor inconsistency. There were much bigger and better lies to come. Or, as Lord O might have put it, with the help of his best scriptwriter, "O, what a tangled web we weave, when first we practice to deceive," which, to Larry Drayco, meant making movies.

The girl behind the counter at the drugstore who sold magazines was named Pegeen, clearly a shiksa. He started hanging around there after school, thumbing through magazines so he could smell her. The combination of her scent and the shiny pages under his fingers, with their pictures of his favorite stars and their stories of how dashing and happy it was to be Douglas Fairbanks or how mysterious it was to be the Lady in Black, gave rise to his first public show of sexual excitement. He tried very hard to cover it with a magazine.

"Can I do anything for you?" Pegeen said, mischief apparent in her light blue eyes.

She was at least seventeen, an older woman, Gentile in the bargain. But he knew that he loved her, and she knew it, too, from the strain on his pants.

"You like movies?" he asked her, looking for a common bond, besides what she was making happen.

"I *love* movies," she said. "I go every Saturday."

"With your boyfriend?"

"I don't have a boyfriend," she said.

"That's crazy. You're so beautiful."

"You think so?"

"I *know*," he said. "I know what's beautiful." It was a line he was to use thirty-two years later on Ingrid Bergman, in a dark cocktail lounge in New York City, when they met on a script he wanted her to do. "I know what's beautiful. And you're the most beautiful woman who's ever been onscreen." "Isn't that lucky," Bergman had answered disinterestedly. "That's a line from *Saratoga Trunk*." By that time she had already had her fall from grace with the public, which was having trouble forgiving her for being a sexual woman. She had run off with Rossellini, had their children, been left by him, and had been grudgingly reaccepted by the American people, because she was unhappy. So the fact that she was cynical, even disappointed about what good her beauty had done her, and so detached as to quote Edna Ferber, instead of being flattered and original, as Larry hoped, was understandable. Still, she had dashed his expectations sufficiently that he cut in half what he intended to offer her to make the movie. He hated when people turned out to be less than what he imagined them to be. He knew he himself was less than he paraded, that his façades were true façades, with little behind them but hubris. But stars should have been better than that.

"You're pretty cute yourself," Pegeen said to the boy, her warmth wafting over the coldness of the counter.

"You mean it?"

"Try me."

"You want to go to the movies with me?"

"Sure," she said, even as his mind furtively raged on how he would get the money to take her.

He ended up stealing it from his mother. Maybe she would have loaned it to him if he asked her. But then there would have been all kinds of questions, like what did he need it for. Eventually she'd worm it out of him that he was taking a girl out. Then it would be "What girl?" And then it would turn out to be the Polish inquisition, which had to be tougher than the Spanish one because Jews hadn't been in charge of that. When she got it out of him, which she would, that it was a blond, blue-eyed Irisher, there would be hell to pay. It was easier to just take the two quarters, and another fifty cents in case Pegeen wanted an ice cream soda.

It turned out to be one of the finest investments of his life. All he had expected was a chance to maybe get close to her in the dark, smell her, put his arm on the back of her seat as he'd seen some older boys do, and let his fingers fall casually down a little, accidentally touching the top of her breasts. As it was, she asked him to get a box of popcorn. He worried about running out of money, in case she was thirsty after.

Then they got into the dark. "Why don't you hold the box on your lap?" she asked him.

He did as she said. She started reaching for it and eating out of it. Every time she reached she would press the box against him, and sort of jiggle it around, till she had some in her hand. Then she'd move the popcorn slowly to her lips, and put it in her mouth a piece at a time, slowly, taking it onto her tongue. He watched her out of the side of his eyes. By the time the box was empty, he thought he would go crazy.

But then, in the dark, never taking her eyes from the screen, she undid the folds of the box, and reached straight through the bottom of it. She opened his pants and took him in her hand, right through the open box. With him inside it, all swollen and hard. She whipped him up and down, like she was still just reaching in there for pop-corn.

"What's that on your pants?" his mother said when he came home.

"Butter," he said very quickly. "I spilled some popcorn."

They went every Saturday to the movie after that. They never discussed what Pegeen did. As time passed, she started holding the popcorn box on her lap when they were finished with his lap. She'd edge her skirt up in the darkness, and he'd reach through the box to her underpants. She'd move his hand down to the stickiness between her legs. And she'd move his hand to the hard little spot and he'd stroke it and rub round it with his middle finger till she convulsed and sighed. As he became more expert, he could some-times coordinate her finale to the one in the picture, when the lovers embraced. It worked particularly well with Gilbert and Garbo.

And they never said a word about it outside the theater. They met underneath the marquee every Saturday night. She wouldn't even let him walk her home. Nor did she ever suggest they see each other more than once a week. Being as fortunate as he knew he was, he didn't push his luck.

She quit her job and moved away without even telling him when he was thirteen years old, leaving no information with the guy who ran the drugstore how to find her. Larry thought his heart would break, and that his dickie would break off, he beat it so hard in his despair.

$\mathcal{B}$y the time he was a sophomore in high school, movies had clever dialogue. He went into the city to see plays, standing in the back, silently repeating the lofty words the actors spoke, pronouncing them as they did, mouthing them as he went back home on the subway. By the time he met Lila, he invited her for a "hahmburger." The third time he took her out, with a bunch of his friends to a diner in their neighborhood, he sent the hahmburger back because, he said, it was medium, and he'd ordered it "raeh." It came back with the bite still out of the bun.

They'd laughed a lot at that, Lila and his friends. Larry didn't see what was so funny. He got a little pissed off at her for laughing so hard and so long, a laugh that would erupt every few minutes as he walked her home.

"What are you laughing at?" he finally said.

"You sent it back!" she practically choked, doubled over. "Like it was the Stork Club."

"You think I couldn't go to the Stork Club if I wanted?" he asked, quietly furious.

"Why, sure you could," she said, not quite understanding the reason for his rage, contained.

"I could go anywhere I want," he fumed. "And I will. *With* anyone I want."

Just to show her, he didn't ask her to the prom. Instead, he invited the most beautiful girl in the school, a round-breasted strawberry-blonde, with legs that went up to her neck. To his delight and surprise, she accepted.

He had gotten a job after school as a delivery boy. With everything he had saved, he hired a limousine, rented a tuxedo, and bought her an orchid. He came to her building the night of the prom and rang the bell. And rang the bell. And rang the bell. Finally, a long time later, her father came out.

"I'm here to pick up Nancy," Larry said.

"She's out for the evening."

"What do you mean? She has a date with me."

"Not anymore," said her father.

$\mathcal{H}$e didn't go to the prom. He drove around Brooklyn in the limousine, as long as he had paid for it, looking out the window at the ordinary people, who envied him. The pain was so severe he could not even feel it. He saw her in school the next day, and didn't go near her or speak to her again. But twenty-five years later, when he had three pictures topping the box office simultaneously, he had his secretary make a number of calls and track her down.

She was living in the Bronx, which somehow pleased him, as it was a step down from Brooklyn in his mind. "Nancy?" he said, when he got her on the phone. "It's me. Larry Darshowitz, from Midwood High. Larry Drayco, I am now. Does that name mean anything to you?"

"No," said Nancy.

"I'm a movie producer. Perhaps if you don't recognize my name, these might mean something to you." He went on to list the titles of his movies, and the actors and actresses who starred in them, practically every glittering name in Hollywood. "There's a piece on me in *Time* magazine this week. I was supposed to be on the cover, but there was a shooting at some college in Michigan, so I got bumped. But there's a full color picture: I'm standing in front of my desk. It's twelve feet wide, carved teakwood from Tasmania. Do you know where that is?"

"No," said Nancy.

"It's in New Zealand. I made a movie there. I make movies all over the world."

"How exciting," Nancy said.

"So you got married?"

"Yes."

"Congratulations. What does your husband do?"

"He's a dentist."

"You have children?"

"Three. All grown up now. Two boys and a girl."

"Nice," said Larry. "So, Nancy. Let me ask you something. How come you didn't go with me to the prom?"

He never heard her answer. He wasn't really listening. His ears and his heart and his blood were pounding. He was so full of the fact that her life was nothing, and his was gold, and he was shoving it to her. He sent her a book of passes to a theater in the Bronx, part of a chain owned by one of his investors.

*T*he first time he made love to Lila was on her parent's couch. "Why don't you slip into something more comfortable," he said, in between the kissing, the furtive reaching.

"Why don't you?" she said, and guided him between her legs.

*O*f all the stars he worked with and loved, at least until the deal was signed, and the thrill was over, the one he had been hottest to get in a picture was Jason Stone. There was no bigger actor in the world, not ever, not Edmund Kean or Edwin Booth or Sarah Bern-hardt in her day. He'd had it researched. No one had ever trod the boards, as they said in the theatah, who was more magnetic, or made a greater impact. Jason had been beautiful and slender then, and women committed suicide as some of his children were later to do.

Larry sent Jason paints because he'd heard he painted. He sent him first editions because he'd heard he collected books. He sent him a pedigreed cat, because, as the note read, "I heard you like pussy." He found all his favorite eating places and ate in them, bribing one of the waiters at each place to call him if Jason came in.

He made official offers through Jason's agent. "Zack," he said, putting his arm around him as they ate lunch in La Dolce Vita, a gen-tle place for Los Angeles with-its, secluded booths and decent Italian food. "You let me have him for this picture, and I promise you you'll never have a bad day again."

It was a really lavish promise, especially since Zack, the agent, had recently had as bad a day as an agent could have in Hollywood. He'd come home unexpectedly at lunchtime and found his wife in bed with his most important client. He'd had to choose between them. Of course, he'd divorced her and kept Jason.

"What picture are we talking about?" the agent asked.

"Whatever picture he wants to do. I have three scripts he can choose from. Or, if there's something else he likes . . . "

"He likes Tim McClure," Zack said, naming the hot writer of the day. He authored westerns that a critic at *The New Yorker* had raved about, describing them as "mythic," sending every studio in pursuit. That is, once the studio heads read the reader's reports on the books, or at least the reader's report on the review.

"Everybody likes Tim McClure," said Larry. "His price has probably gone sky-high."

"Hey," said Zack. "I'm only trying to help you get Jason."

"Jimmy!" Larry signaled one of the owners of the restaurant, and pantomimed holding a phone to his ear. A waiter brought him a telephone, plugged it in by the plaque dedicating the booth to Frank Sinatra. Every good, important customer of the place had a brass commemoration on the wall over the red-leather-upholstered booth that would always be his, specially held if he called. Larry had his own booth, but he liked Sinatra's better. He dialed the number for the Writer's Guild, which he knew by heart, since they were bringing him up on charges for paying writers less than minimum.

"Representation," he said, when they answered. There was a click and some piped-in music.

"Agency," said a woman on the other end.

"Tim McClure," Larry said.

There was silence for a moment. "He's represented by Zack Arnold at MCA."

"Thanks," Larry said, hanging up the phone, and tried not to look like he'd been had. "I didn't know you represented writers."

"Well, I never did before, but this guy is really special."

"You want my balls in a vise," Larry said.

"Hey, sweetheart," Zack said. "Who trained me?"

"And this is how you pay me back?"

"What do you care? It's not your money."

That was true. Using the gentle charm he could always call upon when he wanted to, Larry would court virgin investors, rich people who knew nothing about movies, except that they captivated them. Men and women who were delirious at being introduced to the stars Larry knew at the Cannes festival, thrilled to be asked to the lavish dinners he would throw at the Hôtel du Cap. The majors were already wary of him, since he'd gotten the upper hand in deals even with his mentors. These were men who'd brought him into the inner circles, guided him, and, when he succeeded, offered him presidential and production chief posts at their studios. But those positions paid only salaries. As a freelance producer, he could pay himself whatever he wanted, take a chunk off the top before the picture even started filming, so whatever its fate or grosses, he, at least, was always ahead. So he took the road of the independent, and occasionally the ocean, on a yacht. And when one source dried up, he would study his list of the *Fortune* 500, write one or two or five of them on his very impressive letterhead, and arrange a meeting.

"So does he have a script for Jason?"

"I'll send it over this afternoon," Zack said, and did.

It was a great script. He bought it with money he had from an Israeli investor and a Saudi prince whom he never told about each other's involvement. He bought an original edition, signed, of *David Copperfield,* and took it himself to Jason Stone's house in the Hollywood Hills.

"Not home," said the maid, with whom it was rumored he had had a child. Down the cavernous marble hall there was the sound of a baby crying.

"*Donde?*" asked Larry.

"Mexico."

He called Zack Arnold. "You didn't tell me he was in Mexico."

"I didn't know he was in Mexico."

"When's he coming back?"

"Beats me."

"You fuck!" Larry hung up the phone. He bought a bottle of tequila, some chips and salsa, and went back to the house, and found out from the maid exactly *donde* Jason had gone.

He took a plane to Mexico City and rented a car for the long drive into the hills of San Miguel de Allende. It was a retreat even for people who weren't as reclusive as Jason Stone, so Larry figured he would no doubt be furious at being found. In all the time he had pursued him, they hadn't had a real exchange. Larry was intimidated by the talent and personal power of the man, and he kept his distance.

Besides, Jason was surly with all but his closest friends. Now, in San Miguel, a place dropped out of time, with art everywhere, and artists, and God in obvious charge of the art that was the mountains surrounding, Larry wondered how exactly he should approach him. Once again, he found out his favorite eating places, a little more limited in choice and distance from the casa than those in L.A.

The bar he found him in was not one tourists would frequent, even if they could find it, so off the beaten track that Larry literally had to climb there. The roads were rutted beyond ruts, with huge rocks in the holes. He was surprised the motorcycle parked outside the taverna had made it. Jason was seated at a carved wooden table in the corner, back to the room. He was with a woman.

Larry sat down, and when someone came, ordered a beer. The woman noticed him and murmured something to Jason.

Jason looked around. Then he turned back and put his head down on the table, the huge expanse of his shoulders collapsing in defeat. After a while, he got up and came over to Larry's table.

"Okay," he said softly. "You want it so badly, you can have it." He unzipped his fly and took out his penis.

There was later to be a privately circulated piece of film, one of the outtakes from *Last Dinner at Maxim's,* in which the director, Salvatore Guccione, told Jason to think of his character as "an extension of my cock." During one scene, where Jason was supposed to be fucking the leading lady in the ass with the help of a jar of Vaseline, his penis fell out of his pants and was captured on celluloid. Both Guccione's cock, if Jason was really the extension of it, and Jason's own were, according to those who bought the piece of film, very disappointing, at least in their flaccid state. But at the time he took it out of his pants as a gesture of surrender to Larry Drayco, it seemed truly monumental.

*A*nd hilarious. They would laugh about that incident later, during the brief, intense time they were friends. The screenplay by McClure became a movie that wasn't the winner Larry hoped. But he didn't really care that much anymore, because McClure's gifts weren't limited to the page. He had a coterie of women, each of them eccentric, striking, and ready for it all the time. Larry's first Hollywood marriage, to a powerful woman agent, had ended with her death some months before. He was lonely, and stir-crazy, the way you got on location. These women were out of their heads, and he enjoyed that in women, as long as they weren't bimbos or someplace anyone important would see him with them. As it was, the movie was being made in the desert near Taos, New Mexico. They would take him on two and three at a time, one of them tracing her tongue on his scrotum, while another one rode him, and a third one sat on his face, but not before holding up a big mirror so he could see what was going on down there. And sometimes Tim would join them and they'd back and front them. Larry would get into a rhythm so he could feel the friction of his new buddy's prick on the other side of the delicate membrane that separated them.

He had such a good time he ended up more fixated on Tim McClure than Jason Stone. He made about four pictures with the writer, all of them bombs.

$\mathcal{H}$is second Hollywood marriage took place at the Beverly Hills Hotel, to the daughter of the head of Marathon. His new father-in-law made him sign a prenuptial agreement, and then offered him a job as president of the studio.

"That's my gift to you," said Ernie Binderman. He was as close to aristocratic as a filmmaker could be, a man who had been in charge long enough to relax about his status and make it all the way to bona fide gentleman. Haute Hollywood was in full attendance. The bridal party's dresses were in deep shades of green to coordinate with the potted palms and the painted ones on the wall. The fifty thousand spent on floral arrangements had gone mainly to the sterling silver roses, which were wound around white trellises, set into crystal bowls, and trailing to the floor. The bridal bouquet was lightened by dainty bells of lilies of the valley. The designer of the bridal gown had flown in from Paris for the fittings and the actual occasion, bringing with him a new perfume he'd created especially for the day called Abby, the name of the bride. The scent was so subtle it hardly had a smell. All of the women present were given it as a gift, and all the men sniffed them when they sprayed it on, pronouncing it lovely, or sexy, except for the bridegroom, who said he couldn't smell anything.

A general amnesty on wounded feelings appeared to have been

declared in the town, in view of whom Larry was marrying. Even those he'd offended or bettered were there, at least the men in the top positions. There wasn't room in the hotel, even with all of its ballrooms and restaurants, for everyone Larry had affronted.

"That's really kind of you, Ernie," said Larry, fielding the offer of studio head. "And I hate to look a gift studio in the mouth. But you remember what they said about Selznick when he married Irene Mayer."

"The son-in-law also rises," Ernie said. "I remember. But you're already there."

"Thanks, anyway," Larry said.

"I just wanted you to know how much faith I have in you."

"Faith is different from trust, I guess," Larry said, and went off to kiss his bride, and accept an offer from another studio. He could still make more money as a producer, but he felt like chastening his father-in-law. He was smarting from the prenuptial agreement they'd made him agree to. Like he wasn't capable of delivering on a fiduciary agreement. *Fiduciary* was one of his favorite words. He used it in meetings all the time, to build up confidence. Not only in the sense that he was capable of entering into a fiduciary relationship, but also that he knew the word, like a lawyer. *Fiduciary* was second in his vocabulary only to *draconian*. He had read as a young man that a situation demanded draconian measures, and upon finding out how severe that meant the situation was, and that there had been an emperor involved, he chose it as the origin of his new name. Still, he thought his marriage to Abby called for nothing as draconian as a prenuptial agreement, since marriage itself was a fiduciary arrangement.

But as it turned out, he was just as glad that they had such an agreement, so Abby's money couldn't be counted as his. Because it wasn't long after that marriage that McClure took him to Vegas, where Larry had gotten hooked on gambling. He wouldn't have liked the civilized thugs he ended up owing, who now had lawyers as well as guns, to be able to move against Abby's bank accounts.

*T*he forgery and embezzlement scandal broke just about the time Abby got sick. "Why didn't you just ask me for the money?" she asked him, lying in her bed, all the fearsome medicines on the table beside her.

"Because I love you," he said. He really did. She was kind and pretty, and now that she was failing, her vulnerability gave her a pallid radiance. It really pained him that he'd brought grief to her. He was only glad Lila didn't read the trades. When this was all over, the lawyer crap, the trial, and maybe Abby, too, depending how strong she was—the prognosis was vague—he would have to make a trip back to Queens.

*H*ow does your client plead?" the judge asked.

"Guilty," said Gerald Morgan, Fletcher McCallum's criminal lawyer associate. McCallum's firm dealt strictly with entertainment law, but they did have a line to the best plea bargainers in town, just in case one of their clients went over the legal line, which many of them did. "With extenuating circumstances."

The lawyer then described the circumstances that were so extenuating in Larry's life: that he had fallen into bad company, gambled, gotten into debt, run through his personal wealth, accrued from . . . at this point, the lawyer gave a list of Larry's best-known pictures, including a glittering name or two who had starred in them. The judge looked not just impressed, but enthralled. By the time the lawyer got around to the fact that Larry had started using a little cocaine to get over the sorrow of his wife's now terminal illness, and had probably been suffering from a kind of temporary insanity, the judge had already softened. He sentenced him to two years probation, mandatory attendance at a narcotics support group, another for compulsive gamblers, plus public service, which would involve making two short features about the evils of gambling and cocaine, starring a well-known actor who was in a nearby courtroom pleading guilty to possession.

Larry made the movies. The judge visited the set.

*A*bby died shortly after. All who had been at the wedding came to the funeral. In addition there were foreign dignitaries who were friends of her father's and had been unable to attend the festive ceremony, but knew the importance of being at the sad one. Plus members of the press who had covered Larry's trial, been taken with his manner, and become his friends. Abby had been genuinely adored by the women of the community, as for all her privilege she had never been other than loving and generous to everyone, totally lacking in the competitiveness that characterized even the soft aspects of the town: clothes and mentions in Joyce Haber. Abby had given freely of her time and energy to charity, and unendingly of support and affection to her friends. So even those who thought Larry a swine came to the service out of respect for her, and considered revising their opinion of her husband because of her respect for him. Also present were a few new candidates from the fresh list of the world's wealthiest men, compiled by *Forbes* magazine, to whom Larry had written to find out if they were interested in investing in movies. And although he had resigned as the head of the studio from which he'd embezzled, he'd been offered the same job at Cosmos. "There is more than one Teflon president," Zack Arnold muttered to his wife, who still spoke to Larry although Zack did not.

So he was back on his feet again. The great men of the town came to make up the minyan that sat shivah. Their wives brought casseroles and pastries so that grief wouldn't weaken Larry after all his other troubles. As soon as a decent period of mourning had passed, he took a flying trip to New York to check in with Lila. Although she didn't read the trade papers, news of his conviction had made the national press, and there was a big story about the whole scandal in *Vanity Fair*, to which he'd bought her a subscription.

"You should never have started with those people," she said, cutting up celery for the tuna salad. "They made you have delusions of grandeur."

She pronounced it "grandoyer," but he didn't correct her. He considered that part of what was dear about her, just as he wasn't bothered by the radical change in her appearance. The deliciously upstart little blonde he'd married long ago was lost in her somewhere, like Livingstone in the Congo, her old features indistinguishable, except for her pretty mouth, and the straight-ahead words that fell out of it. Her once-bright blue eyes were nearly obscured by the flesh that heavy-lidded them. But she still saw truth, and spoke it, and he'd had enough sleek women.

"They're not delusions," he said, softly, but with some contention. As sharp as he considered her, she still didn't have a clue how big a man he was. There was nothing that could stop him now, except maybe a good deed.

$\mathcal{H}$e did one. In the beginning of Zack Arnold's career as an agent in Hollywood, Larry had taught him how to be a hardnose. Zack was a gentle man by nature, as Larry represented himself to be when the occasion called for it, or when he genuinely loved, as he did Lila. "You have to hang tough," he'd told Zack, the first time Zack had blown a deal. The expression had not yet come into popular usage. In fact, Larry considered he might have invented it when he found out from Tim McClure that hanged men got erections. At the time, Larry was having a problem getting one of those, since McClure and his women had shown him so much that was fancy he could hardly get excited by plain. So he had said, "That's really tough," meaning it seemed a terrible waste. Later he was to tell the titillating fact to Jason Stone, and Jason would agree to do another picture with him, playing a man who gets unfairly sentenced to death in the old West, but only if he could dangle with a visible hard-on.

"The condemned man ate a hearty beaver," Jason was to say.

But on the day Zack blew his first heavyweight deal, Larry helped him to totally revamp his thinking and, more important, his behavior, teaching him to "hang tough." They were meeting that afternoon, the two of them, with an actor who had just broken through as the number one box office attraction. Larry wanted him for a movie, Zack as a client. "We got to play good cop, bad cop," Larry said. "You bully him, I make you be gentle."

"I am gentle," Zack said.

"You can't show that to an actor, or he'll have no respect for you. You got to make him think you're capable of killing for him, like a woman likes to imagine. And then you kill him with a laugh. It's like est. They beat you up, starve you, don't let you piss, then tell you you're wonderful, and you belong to them. After you give him a really hard time, you make him laugh."

"I'm not funny," said Zack.

"I'll make you funny," said Larry.

They met with the actor. As they'd rehearsed, Zack came down on him very heavily, telling him he was blowing his future with lousy choices in scripts and lousy representation.

"I'm getting two hundred thousand a picture," the actor said, the sum at the time being monumental. The joke of the twenty-million-dollar salary for a star was still a *Star Wars* galaxy away.

"You should be getting four. What if you lose your hair?"

"Don't scare him like that," Larry said.

"He better be scared. He better be good and scared."

"You're talking about me like I'm not here," the actor said.

"You're not here. You're not here unless I tell them at the studio you're here. You're the Invisible Man. They don't care who actors really are. To them, you're whores. They bang you, and when they finish and you're all used up, unless you've got a great pimp, they don't even leave the money on the dresser."

"How can you talk so ugly to such a sweet guy?" Larry said.

"Sweet counts for shit, and you know it. You, as the great producer you are, don't offer a guy a script because he's sweet. You offer it because you think he'll deliver tickets."

"That's true."

"I deliver tickets," the actor said.

"And I deliver iron-clad contracts, so even if you slip, even if you don't show up, even if they don't make the movie, you still get your money."

"Is that true?" the actor asked Larry.

"He's the one who started that policy," said Larry, which was a lie, easy enough to check, but actors rarely did homework unless it was learning their sides.

"Okay," the actor said, finally. "I'll sign. There's only one thing that bothers me . . . "

"Yes?" asked Zack.

"I heard about your agency having connections to the mob."

"That's a vicious thing to say," said Zack, who knew that rumor was out there. "How could you think such a thing?" He unbuttoned his jacket. Hanging on the front of his shirt was a holster, holding a .45.

They all cracked up laughing. The actor sent a letter of dismissal to his agent and signed with Zack, becoming his first major client. After that there was Jason, and a raft of box office stars. And after that, Larry kept his promise to make sure Zack had no more bad days. When he became studio president, he appointed Zack European production head.

Zack outlasted him, keeping the post past Larry's disgrace, his seeming expiation, his move to another studio. And then Zack had a heart attack.

Larry flew to London. He had buried his second California wife, and he wasn't about to lose the best friend he had, even though they weren't speaking.

"I'm finished," Zack whispered, his arm connected to a network of machines, monitoring the life ebbing out of him.

"You aren't finished," said Larry. "I'm taking you to New York. I got the best heart doctor in the country waiting for you. We'll get you a transplant. If I have to, I'll give you mine."

"You don't have a heart," said Zack.

"Fuck you," said Larry.

"Up yours," said Zack.

Larry took him back on a hospital plane, chartered for the occasion, charged to his old studio, the one Zack worked for now. Larry was set to pay it if anyone made an issue, with a check he'd already written himself from Cosmos.

"I don't know if my insurance covers this," said Zack.

"Shut up and keep breathing," said Larry.

Zack needed and got a four-way bypass. "They took the veins from my legs," he said afterwards. "Can you imagine?"

"I offered them mine," said Larry.

"You got lousy legs."

"That's what the surgeon said. But I gave you some blood."

"Did they check it for HIV?"

"In your ear."

"How will I ever repay you?" Zack said, and started to cry.

"Oh, for Christ's sake," said Larry. "Who's asking for anything?"

"But I couldn't, even if I wanted to. The studio sent me a basket of flowers, with a notice my contract is up and they're not renewing."

"I hope somebody embezzles the fucks," Larry said.

"Who's going to give me a job? I'm damaged goods. I'm old."

"You aren't old," said Larry. "You're younger than I am."

"How old are you, anyway? You got a picture in the closet?"

"I'm making a picture. It's about this silly fart who thinks he has no future. And then this ghost comes to him on Easter Eve, and gives him visions, and he sees that he is the same as Christ, and he can rise again."

"You're kidding, right?"

"I'm kidding. But I am making a picture. And I'm making you associate producer. You're getting a hundred and twenty-five thousand."

"You don't have to do that," said Zack, and started to cry again.

"Don't tell me what I have to do," said Larry. "I know what I have to do."

The only problem was he forgot to pay him.

$\mathcal{W}$hen the process server came, at first Larry thought it was a joke. He had Fletcher McCallum call the lawyer whose name was on the subpoena as representing Zack to ask him what the hell was going on. Larry was too upset to call Zack directly. He couldn't believe it.

"Apparently you had a deal and you reneged," Fletcher McCallum said, his big jaw slightly receded, held with a carefully conscious underbite so his own clients wouldn't feel under attack.

"I didn't reneg," Larry said. "I forgot."

"It's three years ago," said McCallum. "With interest, that's—"

"Interest? I saved his life! He never even came to the set! I threw the salary to him, like a mercy fuck."

"But you didn't pay it. You had a deal."

"I saved his fucking life!"

"Maybe that was a mistake."

"You bet your ass it was a mistake."

"You better pay him."

"Over my dead body," said Larry.

$\mathcal{B}$y the time it got to court, it was four years later. Besides the additional interest that had accrued, there were the lawyers' fees. Then there were the lawyers' fees for Zack's lawyers that he would have to pay if he lost. He'd been ousted as the head of Cosmos by the Japanese, who'd bought the studio as though it were a golf course and brought in their own man to head it, a bully recommended by a man just out of rehab. Larry had returned to independent production and made three pictures that sank without a trace. He'd had such a hard time raising money for the third one, he'd actually had to forego his production fee, throw in what little he'd saved, and borrow more. In the meantime, he had married an Israeli heiress whose family cut her off for marrying him. He was bound and determined to show them he could keep her in her customary style. As a matter of fact, he exceeded it. He owed a couple of million.

The judge found for Zack. It was not the same judge who'd tried Larry for forgery and embezzlement. But it *was* his nephew. The uncle was in the courtroom, with an angrier look on his face than Zack, and a more pugnacious set to his jaw than Fletcher McCallum.

"I'm sorry, your honor," Larry said miserably. "But I don't have any money. I'm tapped out."

"Empty your pockets," the judge said.

Larry reached into them. He took out a small wad of low-currency bills, held together with his good luck money clip.

"Now turn your pockets inside out," the judge said.

Larry did as he was told. The key to his Mercedes fell to the floor.

"Is that a car key?"

"Yes, your honor."

"Give it to Mr. Arnold," the judge said. "With the money."

"But how will I get home?"

"You have a home?"

"It's heavily mortgaged," Larry said.

"Are those rings on your hands?"

"This is my wedding ring, your honor."

"You may keep that. What's the other one?"

"My class ring from Yale."

"Give it to him. You have a watch?"

"Yes, sir."

"Let me see it."

Mournfully, he rolled up his sleeve.

"What kind of watch is that?"

"A Rolex."

"Take it off and hand it over."

He ended up with a judgment against him for what he owed Zack, with a shitload of interest, the bill from Zack's lawyers, court costs, plus a bill from Fletcher McCallum for three hundred and eighty-five thousand dollars. He got another lawyer to sue McCallum for malpractice, and that lawyer ended up suing Larry for what he owed for suing McCallum. Larry's wife died soon after; her family took her body back to Haifa. Darcy Linette let him make one more movie at Marathon, as a kindness; it was later deemed unreleasable. McCallum forgave him his debt and the insult of the lawsuit, because in spite of everything, he'd always liked the little fuck and was sorry to see him with no springs on his legs for a comeback. The lawyer also understood the maxim that no good deed goes unpunished, and saw that Larry was a victim of the one clear moment of absolute humanity he'd had. It was a story Fletcher McCallum did not pass on to his sons, whom he was raising with the credo that the paramount virtue was integrity.

Larry Drayco was last seen in public at a memorial service at Beth Israel, given by the women of ORT, the Beverly Hills chapter of the Israeli organization, in his late wife's honor. No one at the temple spoke to him, and all those attending made a circle around him so wide it was as though Charlton Heston had come again to divide the Red Sea.

By the time the story was finished, Lila had had enough Merlot so she told Kate about the compromising tape Larry had left her. She hadn't meant to go that far.

But Kate promised her secret was safe, just as Victor Lippton's was, because she wasn't the type who would blackmail anyone.

"Neither am I," Lila said drunkenly. "He thinks I made a copy of the tape, but I didn't. He has the only one."

"Well, as long as he doesn't know that, he'll probably give you what you want."

"A monument," Lila said. "A monument to my Larry."

"What kind of monument?"

"That's what I'm working on," said Lila. "Let's open another bottle."

In the end, Kate broke down and had some. So she stayed a lot longer than she meant to. By the time she got home and found the hysterical message on her machine from Wendy, she was afraid it might be too late.

*W*ell, when Norman Jessup tried to make something up to you, he really did a first-rate job. Even though Tyler was ready to make the journey in his cutoffs and a T-shirt, just carrying his backpack and the box of ashes, there was a small, beautiful leather bag with his initials embossed in gold waiting for him in the limousine that took him to the airport.

Inside were some handsome batik shirts ("These are coals to Newcastle," read the note from Norman that was pinned to them. "You'll find much that you might want to wear in Bali itself. Although you'll probably spend most of your time naked.") There were also a pair of bathing trunks, shorts, some new underwear, cotton briefs, the kind Tyler wore that to the best of his knowledge Norman had never seen. Tyler realized now that he had probably gone through his drawers, looking at his drawers, or the choice wouldn't have been so appropriate.

"What the hell, Algernon," Tyler said to the box. "I can't get mad at someone for loving me."

"Are you talking to me?" the limo driver said.

"I'm talking to my box," said Tyler.

The driver gave him a look in the rearview mirror.

Outside the limo was the dismal architecture of the buildings alongside the expressway. Redbrick, piled-on high-rises housing existences that Tyler considered probably never became lives. His grandparents on his father's side had lived in such a place, and they'd just marked time till it was over, with no real concept of anything beyond, or probably even of anything during. He didn't like being judgmental; that was one of the things Algernon had told him he needed to work on. But to go through days with only the highlight of big-screen TV and the occasional great meal was a depressing concept. Just as the notion of measured days with a paycheck at the end of them was depressing.

He would have liked very much to be able to Walden it, hearing a different drummer. Be venerated when he was old for being a free spirit by students who sat at his feet and just listened to his words, or even to his silence. Live long after his life in the annals of thinkers who respected thinkers. Hang out with Reddy in the afterlife and have him tell Tyler he had done it exactly right. Then maybe introduce Algernon to his genetic father and have him straighten him out. But maybe his father knew now what a waste it was to struggle and have only earthly ambitions. Maybe his father had evolved on the next level to what he hadn't even attempted to be on this one. Or maybe his father was exactly where he had been, and would be pissed at Tyler for still not having a job.

"What class are you?" the driver asked, as they drove up the ramp to American Airlines.

Tyler looked at his ticket. "First," he said. There was a layover of several hours at the airport in L.A. before he boarded the flight to Singapore and Denpasar. During that time Norman had arranged for his passport to be delivered to him. His old one, dating from the time he still traveled with his parents, had lapsed, but Norman had handled it, had his office staff organize a new one, getting around the usual procedures. Tyler remembered a maxim from when he was considering being a philosophy major: "The wheels of the gods grind slowly, but they grind exceedingly fine." In Hollywood, it was rewritten that they ground quickly, even when all the wrong people were gods.

But what the hell. Or what the heaven. He was getting to take Algernon to Bali. What joys there would be in that transcendent finale, the box had no idea. Or maybe it did. Maybe it even knew what joys were waiting for him.

For a moment, as he boarded the plane, he thought he could hear a laugh coming out of the box.

Paradise East

Singapore Airlines, Flight 143, arrived in Denpasar, Bali, at four-forty in the afternoon. In Tyler's head it was two o'clock in the morning the night before. Crossing the international date line meant the loss of more than just one day. He had dreamed fitfully on and off through the journey, and was totally out of synch with himself. For one of the few times since he'd studied Jung, he had no idea what his dreams meant. They had been of goddesses and dancing gods, all wearing frightening masks. He was not sure if the images came from looking at brochures of Bali or having lived in Hollywood.

He was not stopped at customs, an escape that flooded him with relief. He hadn't known if there were regulations about bringing in the foreign dead. Still wearing his backpack, he clutched the teak-wood box, but let the driver from the hotel who had greeted him with his name on a chalkboard carry his leather bag outside to the van.

Relief turned to wonder. Wet, warm breezes fingered Tyler's hair. The mellow, moist air grazed the inside of his nostrils, a palpable sweetness touched his tongue. Paradise. For once, Norman Jessup had been absolutely straight with him.

A gold-scripted sign held by little stone gods with oversized grins, invitingly grotesque, stood at the edge of the hotel driveway. A towering shrine rose from a lotus pond on the right. In the rice paddies left of the entryway, kerchiefs on sticks waved in the heavy breeze, wind-driven wooden batons drummed against gongs to frighten away the birds. Impervious, the birds fluttered and swooped between and above and below the racket, diving for food, singing fearless songs.

Men in creamy white jackets and dark red sarongs helped Tyler from the van. They greeted him, setting his bag on the ground. Added to his joy at the beauty of the place was his clear perception that the people here, unlike so many in the place he'd come from, were happy.

Salmon and pink and gold bougainvillea clumped over thatched roofs. "Alright!" Tyler exclaimed.

"Welcome to the Oberoi," said a smiling, tiny woman, placing a garland of white, fragrant frangipani over his head, resting it around his neck. He could feel the cool of the blossoms against the heat on his skin, the sun already having toasted the base of his yellow-gold curls, where the barber had been allowed to clean it just a little.

*T*he Presidential Villa." The white-jacketed bellman pulled a brass ring on the heavy wooden double doors, and they opened. Walls of gray and white limestone surrounded the gateway. Hibiscus bunched between palm leaves, and lacy balls of bright red Japanese ixora bordered the spitting dragon fountain in the courtyard, brightened the dark sculpted Balinese lamps.

Beneath the main roof lay the villa itself. Tyler entered the bedroom. Alang alang poles, bamboo threaded with dried elephant grass, angled upwards on the cathedral ceiling, where it crested at a carved, floral center square. A teakwood four-poster, vines and flowers etched in its headboard, was built into the wall. A carved, cushioned step stool beside it, a freshly laundered white linen mat set on top.

Tyler handed the bellman some singles, part of the wad that Norman had stuffed in his hand when he said good-bye.

"That way bat-room," the bellman said, indicating another wooden door. He grinned. "Enjoy yourself."

"I think I can manage that," said Tyler, taking a piece of fruit from the bowl on a table by the couch. It seemed less a bowl of fruit than an offering, arranged like the pyramids of flowers that blessed the entryway. There were miniature pineapples, passion fruit, a fuzzy, spiked, round red ball that, he learned from the guide to Indonesian fruits beside the bowl, was called rambutan. Broken open—not easy—it yielded a soft, tasty center like a lichee nut.

Outside the glass double doors from the bedroom lay a second, inner courtyard with a private pool, turquoise in the sunlight. Beyond it, over a sequestering wall, was the sea. Even with the doors shut, Tyler could hear it gently roiling.

Stepping outside, he stood quiet, letting the sound of the ocean crash soft against his eardrums. Jungle colors splashed on his eyes. The fragrance of salt mixed with the sweet, heavy scent of tuberose. "Paradise," he said aloud, lifting the box. "Take a gander."

Sudden sorrow seized him, that his friend wasn't there in the flesh. Such beauty needed to be felt. Humanly shared.

He stepped back inside, set the box on a sideboard, and opened the door to the bath. There were two sinks of pale gray marble, one on either side, the space airily illumined by sun on a glassed-in atrium. By a circular pond in the center of the atrium stood a gray stone mermaid, fuchsia bougainvillea blossoms falling on her carven hair. In the gray marble floor was set a sunken bath, angled, reclining at its head. And in it, lovely breasts bobbing, lay Helen Manning.

"Hello, my darling," she said.

"Oh, well," said Tyler, and got in with her.

*T*here was a ferocity now to Sarah's writing, beyond the biting humor that so much of America had enjoyed with her first book. She was worse than a woman scorned. She sat at her computer breathing fire. And just to keep the dragon stoked, she decided to resume freebasing.

In the old days, before she'd cooled out and mended her ways, she'd been profligate with the cash she had, so she had someone come in and do her dirty work for her. That is, they'd taken care of all the preparations, brought her the rock cocaine, torch, glass pipe with bulb base, and some kind of alcohol. Then they'd start the whole thing going, cook the rock till the vapor gathered in the base, so all she had to do was suck it in and enjoy the ride. A very mellow high.

She'd freebased in hotels and on the road when she'd still been producing movies, in places where the problem was the vent in the room. Her ever-present fear was that someone would smell it. Usually she'd used the bathroom, with the water running, to hide the sound. Mellow as the high was, there was always paranoia lurking that someone might turn her in.

In her own house though, isolated, with so few people knowing where she lived, Sarah felt fearless. Especially since she was really going to get Norman. His wedding to Carina was only a few weeks off. It was her intention to make a deal with her publisher for the book, and then leak a chapter to the press the morning of the ceremony. So what the bride would wear, besides her veil, was a heavy layer of humiliation. The groom would be the center of a sensational scandal, what reputation he had tried mendaciously to salvage as a recovering gay destroyed. The perfect wedding gift.

But intrepid as she felt, she was under a time constraint. The pressure on her, and that she put on herself, was enormous. She really needed the coke. But she'd been out of touch with the druggies who, for some bucks and a shot at the smoke, had always handled the preparation.

So she called Wilton Spenser.

"I don't think so," he said. "I'm not in the freebase business. And even though we are not exactly close, I don't care to aid and abet you in your return to self-destruction."

"For Christ's sake, Wilton. You can't be a moralist and a drug dealer at the same time."

"Why? Is there a law?"

"You must know someone who's desperate enough to do this shit for me."

"Sarah," he said, "I don't like to look a gift user in the mouth. But the only really desperate person I know is you."

She hung up the phone.

Well, when she was finished with Norman, she'd find some way of getting even with Wilton. Right now she had to devote her concentration to the task at hand.

It took a while to round up everything she needed. She could no longer afford a full-time flunky to hold the torch, etc., for her. She was awkward, clumsy, the first few times she did it. But the beauty of cocaine was, once she'd done it, she thought she'd gotten it absolutely right. It was the same with her writing.

"I have about fifty sensational pages, plus an outline, and documentation," she had told her agent, Lori with a heart over the *i,* at lunch. She'd had her fly out, telling her it was too sensitive to talk about over the phone.

Sarah had set the lunch at the Hotel Bel-Air, where Lori was staying and Norman Jessup was to be married: the perfect irony. The glory of the day, the bright bougainvillea cascading around their balcony table, the fact that they were overlooking the gazebo under which the happy, bogus couple would be wed, added to the juiciness of the occasion. Sarah had no appetite. She'd done a little cocaine just before leaving her house. She was no longer afraid to get in her car when high, because like the writing, her driving seemed enhanced by the drug use. She put out of her mind that her long-ago friend Mama Cass had been convinced that she could eat and not gain weight when she used cocaine. She had died alone in a hotel room, choking on a ham sandwich. Self-delusion, Sarah was sure, was purely the domain of fat girls.

"Documentation?" Lori had asked. She was dressed in her New York-literary-agent-kicking-back-for-L.A. gear, jeans and an Ungaro sweater that the locals would have known better than to wear except in the evening, for no matter how together it looked, the day made it uncomfortably warm. She had also kicked back on her makeup, wearing it only on her bright blue eyes, because Helmut Newton was staying at the hotel and you never knew when he might consider taking a photo.

"Well, the publisher will want to feel safe, won't they?"

"Are we going to bring down another lawsuit on our heads?"

"I don't think this time he'll dare."

"Then it *is* Norman Jessup." Lori put down her spoon, held on to the sides of her tortilla soup as if it would give her ballast.

"No point in keeping you in the dark. I brought the pages." She handed Lori a folder.

"I can't wait."

"Only your eyes. You understand? No one else."

"What about Sean?" she said, naming Sarah's publisher.

"You're shrewd enough to make the deal with just a tantalizing pitch, aren't you? He doesn't have to see it."

"But for the money you'd want—"

"Are you losing your touch?"

"No, but—"

"No butts here but Norman's and his once and future beloved. I want his ass in a sling. And there's no way to do that but to keep this a secret till I'm absolutely ready."

"And when will that be?"

"May eleventh." The date of the wedding had been written about by several columnists, joining the struggle to get an invitation. Studio heads, agents, lawyers, stars, retired past masters of the deal now ranked their clout by whether or not they were part of what was fast becoming the industry's second biggest day. Maybe the first, if you didn't count the Academy Awards, which were past history for the year. Besides, an invitation to the Oscars could be maneuvered if you knew the right people: the Norman Jessup–Carina event couldn't. Maximum capacity for a wedding at the hotel was a hundred and fifty people. Invitations had been sent, and answered, nearly all acceptances. Usually there was a twenty-five to forty percent refusal, which Norman's social secretary had counted on. But that hadn't happened. So the event was already overbooked. Norman had again offered to build an annex for the hotel, but the new owner had again declined, since he was one of the richest men in the world and displays of wealth did not impress him. So there were still those who were waiting for a cancellation. Bigwigs were trying to set up movies that would put stars with invitations on other continents.

"That reminds me." Sarah lifted her hand, signaling for the restaurant manager.

The woman, a slender blond European of uncertain years, saw, smiled, and came over to the table. "May I help you?"

"Karla, I want to reserve this table for four o'clock on the eleventh of next month." The wedding was set for five. Sarah imagined that since the story would break in the papers that morning, she would need to hold court for a few reporters before the ceremony. And then she could look down on it, literally. She could watch the radiant bride stagger down the aisle created in the garden with white folding chairs, her/his dancer's legs buckling under her/him from the chagrin. That is, if she/he could walk at all. And Sarah could have a clear view of Norman's face, as he waited to receive his ha-ha bride. Bilious, it would be, or bright red, or maybe even black.

"I'm sorry, Miss Nash, but the terrace is completely booked that evening for a private party."

"They're not going to hold the reception inside?"

"They are. But they're anticipating an overflow."

"I see. Thank you, anyway."

"Another time, I hope." Karla smiled, and moved away.

"An overflow, huh," said Sarah, and smiled. "That's a new word for what they're going to get."

"Why don't you have a rival party at the Beverly Hills Hotel?" Lori asked.

"Don't be creative," said Sarah. "Just make the deal."

$\mathcal{T}$yler made made love to Helen the first time in the sunken tub. They made love on the floor, in the bed. They made love in the butler's pantry, the stall shower, the sitting room, on the courtyard balcony, and countless times in the pool. "That lousy Norman," Tyler said, about two weeks into the affair, when he and Helen were locked together in warm water. "I'll get him for this."

$\mathcal{T}$hey went horseback riding on the beach, in spite of Tyler's reluctance. "I didn't have your privileged childhood," he said. "I never learned to ride a horse."

"I didn't have a privileged childhood," she said. "I made a Western."

$\mathcal{T}$hey flew giant kites on the beach over Helen's objections. "I didn't have your underprivileged childhood," she said. "I never learned how to fly a kite."

"It wasn't underprivileged," he said, showing her. "We just didn't have horses."

$\mathcal{E}$verywhere in Bali there were kites in the sky, already aloft as the stars disappeared into dawn. Tyler knew that because he was having trouble sleeping, so he often went outside and lay on the chaise and studied the stars. He told himself the wakefulness was because of the difference in time zones. But they had been there many weeks now, and their bodies had adjusted. It was his mind that wouldn't get quiet. His mind and maybe his soul.

1 love you," Helen said to him every time they made love.

"Sure," he would say.

"You think I would go through all this if I didn't love you?"

"You mean the terrible ordeal of being in Bali?"

"I mean humiliating myself. Throwing myself at you. Making a deal to make a movie I don't want to make to get you here."

"That doesn't mean you love me. That just means you like getting your way."

"Can't I love you and like to get my way both?"

"It's a Scorpio island, Bali. Everything is sexy, intense, and self-absorbed."

"Including me?" she said.

"Especially you. It's the perfect place for you."

"Then let's stay here forever," she said, her tone suddenly wistful, melancholy.

*Th*ey went white-water rafting on the Ayung River.

"Are you afraid?" Tyler asked her, as they braced and bumped and held on.

"Not of this," she shouted. "At least I'll have a glorious death. 'She died white-water rafting in Indonesia,' they'll say. Better than 'She died shopping in Bloomingdale's.' "

One of the Japanese in another raft took her picture. "He knows who I am," she said. "We should have bought sunglasses with a funny nose."

"You have a funny nose," Tyler said.

*H*e went alone on the mission he'd come there for, to send Algernon on his final earth journey. Tyler had observed some local Hindu cremation ceremonies, discovered the best place to go. He put the ashes from the teakwood box in a golden coconut, as he'd seen the Balinese do, and carried it to the Yeh Ho, the most sacred river on the island.

He took off his clothes as the natives had done, and got into the river to swim with the coconut, sending it downstream. "See you." He waved.

Then in spite of all he knew, or thought he knew, and dreamed and imagined and hoped, he started to cry. Because ritual was so beautiful, and she was so beautiful, and life was so beautiful, and death, in its way, was so beautiful, you just couldn't help being moved to tears.

Sometimes, when she didn't have too much wine, Lila would dream very clear dreams of her man. They were young again, and he held her still-petite body in his arms, and kissed her neck and her breasts, and her then and always sweet mouth. And as the lovemaking became its most passionate, he would make her laugh. And even as she laughed he would burrow his head down, and make her come. She allowed only the memory of that release, not the release itself. Censoring her dreaming, she would not permit what her conscious mind considered unseemly in an old woman. How had that happened? wondered Lila as she woke. How did she get old? A few magazine subscriptions, and there went the years.

Then she would remember Larry was dead, the only state that didn't allow for transformation. Fat, you could get thin. Old, you could get wise, and outrageous. When you didn't give a fuck, and had nothing to lose, what could they do? But her husband was permanently out of action.

She still found that hard to believe. He'd come back so many times from what most people would consider the grave. She fantasied in suspended moments, in the hazy borders between wakefulness and sleep, or just on the brink of drunkenness, that he was only hiding out till the latest disaster blew over. She wondered why she hadn't insisted they open the coffin so she could have one last, sadly reassuring look.

This morning she woke from an uncertain sleep and called Kate to ask her to take her to the cemetery. Lila had been so angry at the funeral, she'd never actually prayed over him. Now that she remembered the minister, she got even madder that it hadn't been a rabbi. For all his pretensions, the affectations of wine that breathed, hamburgers sent back in greasy spoons, keys that came from intellectual societies he was never asked to join, class rings from schools he'd never been to, the one thing Larry had never dissembled about was being a Jew.

She wondered if it was too late to have some kind of service. She herself had not been at all religious, any more than Larry was. But they both understood that when the Nazis knocked they didn't ask if you observed or believed. They just knew what you were born, and that was the end of it.

Kate didn't answer the phone. Her machine was on, but Lila didn't much like machines, so she left no message. Instead she called the lobby for a phone book with the yellow pages. When the old bellman brought it, she looked up the temples. There was one with the same prefix as her hotel in West Hollywood.

*T*his is most unusual," the youngish rabbi said. He stood beside her at the not-yet-grassed-over grave in Westwood. The earth was neatly packed and shiny from a recent rain. Tender little tufts of green were starting to spring from the sod. "I wish I had been called for the actual service."

"So do I," said Lila. "That's why I asked you here now." She was out of the wheelchair, but still on crutches. She'd called her new friend Victor Lippton for transport. He'd sent his personal limousine to take her to the cemetery. She'd picked up the rabbi on the way, part of the reason he'd agreed to come.

He was probably around forty, darkly good-looking, with pleasant lines around his mouth that indicated he laughed a lot when he wasn't taking himself so seriously. "I do many show business funerals," he said.

"This was not a show business funeral," said Lila. "This was a funeral that wouldn't have happened if it hadn't been for show business."

"I see," the rabbi said.

"They buried him like a goy," said Lila. "They said words that meant shit."

"Please," the rabbi said.

"I'm sorry," said Lila. "I say what I mean. And what they said didn't mean doo-doo. Can you fix it?"

"I'll do my best," he said.

He began reciting in Hebrew, words Lila had never understood, but was always comforted by. As infrequently as she had attended temple in her life, there was something soothing about the sound of these men's voices. The low-pitched sounds coming from deep within their chests, breaking the cavernous silences with ancient prayers. Always, in spite of how little she had worshiped, she was moved. To Lila, the tone seemed to resonate not just with wisdom, laws, and long-ago kings, but with male protection.

When he finished his sing-song incantations, the rabbi put his arm around her. It was such an unexpected gesture, so achingly reminiscent of a kind of familiar touch she had almost forgotten, she started to cry.

"I'm sorry," he said.

"Don't be. It's been a long time since a handsome man put his arm around me, even if you didn't mean it like that. I enjoyed the feeling." She looked at the rain-slicked earth. "So when can we put up the stone?"

"Not for a year," the rabbi said.

"But a monument? That can be any time?"

"What kind of monument?"

"I'm still working on it," Lila said, blowing her nose. "But it's going to be a lulu."

*T*he travel agency run by Binky Danforth-Smythe was, according to the engraved card he'd given Kate, on the corner of Wilshire and Federal in West Los Angeles. It was an area Wilton didn't visit much, as most of his customers were in Beverly Hills, Bel-Air, or Brentwood. Any further out than that, they could come to his place. They did, usually at the end of the week or on the weekend, after he'd picked up the new supply. It came from Venice, from a house just behind Abbot Kinney Boulevard. Venice was the only other neighborhood in L.A. he considered worth visiting, and then only for business.

"I'd like to see Binky Hyphenate," Wilton said to the young brunette receptionist.

"I beg your pardon?" she said, her accent British.

"Mr. Danforth-Smythe." Wilton dragged the name out, so she knew he didn't confuse it with Smith, or any ordinary name.

"Whom shall I say is calling?"

"Mr. Wilton Spenser the Eleventh."

"One moment, please," she said, getting up from behind her desk, going into the inner office.

Wilton looked around. The office was a style he characterized as Early MCA: the walls hung with paintings of The Hunt, magazines angled neatly on a Sheraton table in front of a small sofa. *Yachting*, the top one read. The *Tatler* underneath. All veddy veddy. At the bottom was a *People* magazine with Wendy on its cover. "What's a Cast-off Duchess to Do?" said the heading.

"I'm sorry," the receptionist said, sticking her head out of the inner office. "Does he know you?"

"Not in the biblical sense," said Wilton. "Tell him I'm a friend of Wendy's friend Kate."

The door closed. And opened again. "I'm sorry," she said. "He's in a meeting."

"Really?" Wilton said. "I didn't know he was in the movie business."

"Pardon?"

"I'll wait." He sat down. "Is there a back way out?"

"No."

"Good."

After a few minutes, the intercom buzzed. She picked up the phone. "No, he hasn't," she said into the mouthpiece.

"And he isn't going to," murmured Wilton, flipping through the magazine.

"Very well," she said, and hung up. "Mr. Danforth-Smythe is very sorry, but he has to rush out to a luncheon."

"I'll rush out with him," Wilton said. "What I have to say won't take more than a moment."

"I see," she said, and went back inside. In a moment, the door opened. "Mr. Danforth-Smythe will see you now."

"How gracious," said Wilton, and went inside.

Binky stood behind his desk, his freckled skin looking slightly flushed. "Oh, yes," he said, seeing Wilton. "I thought that's who you might be."

"So good of you to see me."

"What can I do for you?"

"You can allow me to make amends," said Wilton, sitting down in the chair next to Binky's desk. "I'm afraid I behaved rather badly at our first meeting."

"Not to worry," said Binky, still standing. "I know how you Americans are."

"You do," said Wilton, indulgently. "Well, you're good to put up with our behavior. Don't you wish we could all be more like our cousins across the sea? *So* civilized."

"You're a friend of Kate's? She was that woman with Wendy?"

"Right."

"How is Wendy?" he asked cautiously.

"I don't think Kate has heard from her for a while. Anyway, let's not talk about out-of-fashion people. I'd like to talk about us."

"Us?"

"I want to be friends. I don't know that many people of your caliber, and I do do a lot of travel. I would love to have a new agent, as we say at unemployment."

"I'll be glad to do whatever I can," Binky said.

"Whew." Wilton exhaled noisily. "I was so afraid you might not take me on. Well, thanks." He got up. "And cheery-bye. I'll be in touch."

"You can give my secretary all your information. Credit card numbers. Frequent flyer, etc."

"I'll do that," he said, and started out the door. "Oh, I almost forgot." He turned. "I brought you a present."

"You did?"

"This office is so convenient to the post office. I brought you the new Marilyn Monroe stamp."

"Most kind," said Binky.

"Do you happen to have brochures from the QE II? I've been thinking of taking the round-the-world voyage. The one that's coming up soon?"

"My secretary will send them to you."

"Oh, the money's burning a hole in my purse. I'd so love to see them now."

"Miss Simpson," Binky said into the intercom. "Could you give the gentleman the QE II brochures on his way out."

"I'd really like to make the commitment right this minute, otherwise I might chicken out. One must travel when the impulse hits one."

"Quite right."

"Will you take my check?"

"Of course."

"Good," Wilton said, and sat back down. "How much do you want?"

"Well, it's a very costly cruise, depending on what kind of accommodations you're talking about . . . "

"The best," Wilton said. "Outside cabin. Posh. Port outbound, Starboard home."

"Not many Americans would know that's what that stands for," Binky said. "I'm impressed."

"Will ten thousand do it?"

"More than enough for a deposit," Binky said happily.

Wilton wrote a check. "May I have a receipt?"

"Certainly." He started writing on his agency invoice.

"I'm *so* disorganized. I have this business manager who sorts out all my receipts and bills. Would you mind if we mail it to him?"

"Not at all," said Binky.

"You have an envelope? I'll just make it out, and we can send it right now, and then I know it's taken care of." He took a pen from his purse and addressed the envelope Binky gave him. "You have a stamp handy?"

"This one you just gave me."

"I don't mean to be an Indian giver."

"Perfectly alright," said Binky.

"I'm sorry to impose on you, but I'm allergic to glue."

"I thought the new stamps are self-adhesive."

"This is the old-fashioned kind. Do you mind?"

He watched as Binky licked it.

I'll just wait for him to go where he's going, and then escort him," Wilton said into the pay phone in the underground garage. "How is Wendy?"

"She's going to be alright," said Kate. "But it was a close call. What did you give him?"

"Three tabs of LSD," Wilton said.

$\mathcal{T}$he police came to Roxbury Park in answer to an anxious mother's call. "There's a naked man wandering around the children's playground," she said.

It took them a few days to determine who Binky was, as it took him a few days to determine who he was. The only thing he had with him when he was picked up was a man's purse, with a card inside he insisted wasn't his. "I don't know what it was doing there," he sniffled, when he could put words together. A clever reporter from the *Los Angeles Times,* who happened to be at the station that day, found out they'd booked a suspected pedophile for indecent exposure. The reporter also learned that the suspect was carrying the card of Wendy's ex-husband, the duke.

$\mathcal{M}$aybe we could stay till there are no more kites flying in Bali," Helen said.

"It's not going to happen," said Tyler.

"Why are you so stubborn?"

"One of us has to be sensible."

They were sitting in chairs by a table on a secluded part of the beach sprinkled with marigold petals, torchlit, candlelit, a heart drawn in the sand around them. The hotel had prepared a Romantic Dinner, a specialty of the Oberoi. This included an elaborate meal, and a printed menu that said, "Romantic Dinner."

The table was draped with a red batik cloth that matched the umbrella protecting it. Red hibiscus and cut palm decorations were strung from the umbrella's yellow fringe. There was a coconut centerpiece mounded with marigolds and hibiscus. The colors of yellow and red flowers merged into the candle glow.

A waitress handed them their special menu. "Shall we have wine?" Helen said.

She was wearing green, his favorite color on her. He had said it once and would not repeat it, because she'd started wearing it all the time.

She twisted a silver ring that he had bought her on the beach with the symbol of Bali on it: earth, water, and fire.

They had cold bouillabaisse salad filled with plump jumbo shrimp, scallops, and squid, a lemon ice, followed by garoupa, a meaty white fish garnished with tiny potatoes and vegetables. "Baby carrots," she noted, eating one. "Now they'll never grow old."

"Give it a rest," said Tyler.

"I can't," she said, and looked at him, her eyes honey amber in the candlelight. "It just seems so foolish to end it."

"We have to end it before it's over, or it'll be too late."

"What makes you think it will be over?"

"Because it has to be. You'd never forgive me."

"For what?"

"For not being as much as you are."

"You're more."

"Not in the eyes of the world."

"I don't care about the world."

"Of course you do. You don't care about it now. Here. But Bali is fantasy."

"Not for the people who live here."

"You couldn't live here."

"I could. And would, in a minute."

"And what would you do?" he asked.

"I'd be with you."

"And what would I do?"

"You'd be with me."

"It isn't enough," Tyler said.

"I wouldn't be enough for you?"

"I didn't say that. It's just . . . " He put down his fork. "You can stop doing what you're doing if you want, because you've done it. I haven't found out yet what it is I'm supposed to do."

"You're a dreamer. A seeker. A poet."

"Who hasn't written poetry?"

"You can do that here."

"It's a cover," said Tyler. " 'What does he do?' 'He's a poet.' Artists and painters all over this island. Young, pretty boys with their rich, older women."

"So it gets back to that. I'm too old."

"That's not it at all. You're the youngest person I know. But you're famous. Important. If I hung out with you, that's all I'd ever be. *Her* boyfriend."

"That would be enough for plenty of people," she said sullenly.

"And already has."

"You bastard." Her eyes filled with tears.

"I'm sorry," he said. "You're making me say things I don't want to say."

"Then don't say them," she said.

"But you need to understand. My mother was a today woman before it was fashionable. She didn't mean to be more successful than my father, but she was. And he caved. He couldn't measure up. She never forgave him. She loved him, but she never forgave him."

"I'm not your mother. And you're not your father."

"But I could be if I don't become anything."

"You already *are*. Why do you have to *become*? Why can't you just *be*?"

"It doesn't work like that, and you know it." He lifted his champagne-filled glass. "Let's just celebrate the moment. To the most beautiful—"

"I can't bear that it's going to end."

"Don't think about it," he said. "To the most beautiful woman in the world."

"Who will be the loneliest," she said.

"Stop being such a drama queen," he said, and leaned to kiss her. The umbrella tilted and the hanging palm caught the flame of the candle and started to burn. A high wind whipped it, and in moments the whole thing was ablaze. They were beating it out with napkins and hurling water and, finally, sand. She was screaming and laughing and shouting, "Some romantic dinner!" Finally, they got it under control.

And then she was sobbing, sitting on the sand. He knelt beside her, and held her. "Stop," he said.

"*I'm* a drama queen," she wept. "What are you? Making things end. Setting the whole scene on fire."

"Fire is Shiva," he said. "The god of destruction. But in Bali fire is transformation."

"I don't want transformation. I want things to stay the same."

"They can't," he said. "They never do." He smiled, and handed her a Kleenex. "Have you ever made love on the sand?"

"It's very gritty." She blew her nose.

He lifted her in his arms, and carried her back to the villa. And they made love, like most people, on the bed. When it was over, he soothed her tears and stroked her into silence. He kissed her, and gently ran his fingers over her till she slept.

Then he went outside and lay on the chaise and looked up at the stars. There seemed to be more of them here, as he'd noted from the first night he'd seen the sky of Bali. For all that he knew of constellations, for all that he'd studied, and understood, of skies made darker by city lights, garbage, smog, still the stars in Bali's skies shone brighter, still there seemed to be more of them. Maybe there were bigger and better stars in the southern hemisphere than in the northern. He could pick out Venus, and the Seven Sisters. But besides those he knew, he was sure he could see a different constellation than appeared in any other sky, a great flying unicorn with huge wings and a giant horn. A creature of fantasy, of course, but fantasy was okay in a constellation. It just wasn't good when you didn't know yet who you were.

He went back inside and lay beside her. Her skin had a luminous sheen. It looked pale gold in the moonlight, the glow from the mermaid in the atrium. His hand rested on the silk surface of it, while he lay back and tried to sleep.

Outside, the wind whistled, howled, and whispered by turns. And what it whispered, he could make out distinctly, he was almost sure, was "Fool. Fool. Fool."

But maybe it wasn't really the wind. Maybe it wasn't even his imagination. Maybe it was Algernon.

And the Winner Is . . .

$\mathcal{S}$o this is what I've decided," Lila said. "I'd like you to build a statue."

"I see," said Victor Lippton.

He had come to the Park Sunrise out of deference to her still physically compromised condition. She was now in the care of his personal physician, as he wanted to help her get better as quickly as possible so she could get back to New York and resume her normal life and he could resume his. The doctors had taken off her cast, but she was still using crutches. Besides deferring to her incapacity, Victor had been raised well, and she *was* old. In addition, he imagined his secretary was starting to wonder why he was getting so many calls from Lila Darshowitz and, more importantly, why he was taking them. Nobody in the town, the industry, had more power than Victor Lippton, with the possible exception of Norman Jessup, two men who instantly picked up the phone on hearing each other's names. But those were the exceptional calls that they responded to at once, along with those coming from the women they loved: Chen, in Victor's case, Carina in Norman's. Victor had told Alexa not to call him anymore, even on his cell phone. "Don't call me," he'd actually said, "I'll call you."

"I have here a list of sculptors who would be acceptable." Lila handed him the index of names Kate had helped her draw up. This included a few suggestions of her own, culled from all the years of reading her au courant (an expression she knew from *W*) magazines. "But I'd like to interview them before making a decision."

"Naturally," Victor Lippton said.

"I have some ideas what I'd like the statue to be. Concepts, I guess you'd call them. I have pictures of him from when he was young. I like to remember him like that."

"I'm sure."

"Terra-cotta would be nice. Or bronze. He looked better with a tan."

"And where—" Victor's coffee went down the wrong pipe, and he sputtered a little, trying not to choke. They were in her boxlike room. He'd brought a picnic basket, prepared by the personal chef who made lunches for him in his private dining room at the studio. Lila had called and said she'd made her decision, was ready to talk, and wanted to "do" lunch. She had been in the city long enough to understand that nobody ate it. There was cold chicken, finger sandwiches, jellied madrilene in little crystal bowls with plastic covers, a bottle of wine which Lila said she'd love to try once she'd finished her presentation. "And where," he began again, "would you like this statue to be?"

"On the lot of Cosmos," she said. "Your studio."

This time he could not control the choking.

"He was the president there once," she continued, leaning over to pound him on the back, "so it would be, like you say, fitting."

"I don't—"

"Don't try to talk," she said. "Don't you hate that, when something goes down the wrong way? But I want a really nice spot for him. I wouldn't be happy with the parking lot. Maybe that lovely patch of grass just below your window, so people could see it from high-line executive meetings." She looked concerned at his struggle for air. "Maybe if you took a piece of bread . . . "

"I'll be alright," Victor said, and waved her offer away. He took an audible gulp of air, swallowed, and got the choking under control.

"You were very kind to go to all this trouble," she said, looking in the plaid-lined Nieman Marcus basket. "What's this?" She held up one of the little crystal bowls.

"Chilled consommé madrilene."

"Really? I've heard about that, but I've never tasted it. I'd like to try it."

He took off the lid, and handed it to her with a silver spoon. She tasted.

"Beef Jell-O," she said, making a face.

"Maybe you'd enjoy the chicken." He held out a piece on a customized plastic plate.

"Thank you," she said. "So is it agreed?"

"Very well," he said.

"I think I'd like some wine now," said Lila. "So how's your windpipe?" she asked him as he poured.

"Fine, fine."

"And another thing . . . thank you," she said taking her glass, and sipped. "Like everybody else, I watch the Academy Awards. Larry felt bad that he never got one. You know, the year his really good picture was up, there was that little trouble . . . "

"The forgery and embezzlement," Victor said.

Lila nodded. "So they didn't give it to him. They have that one they sometimes give posthumously?" She pronounced it "post," like the office, and "hum," as though it were a song, with emphasis. "That one after what's-his-name, who played Doctor Christian? God, I loved that show."

"The Jean Hersholt Award?" he managed.

"Did you ever hear that show? No, of course not. That was before you were born. Radio was probably before you were born. What do you think?"

"That's the humanitarian award." He was barely able to speak. "Let's not make this a complete travesty."

"What's that?"

"When you laugh at what deserves honor."

"Well, laughing was what Larry did best."

"I will not be a party to it," Victor said. "You can go ahead and expose me."

"I don't want to hurt you," Lila said. "Or anybody else. I just want Larry to have the recognition he deserves. How about that Irving Thalberg one?"

"For Lifetime Achievement?"

"You're not eating," Lila said.

"They would throw me out of the academy for daring to suggest it. Larry Drayco, for God's sake. To even mention him in the same breath as Irving Thalberg . . . "

"Then maybe he should have his own name," Lila said, holding out her glass for a refill. "His own award. Maybe you could introduce a new one."

"The Larry Drayco Award," he said, pouring a glass of wine for himself, drinking it very quickly. "For spitting in the face of an entire industry."

"Well, you wouldn't have to put it like that, exactly," Lila said. "He *was* an original."

"It's true," Victor said, and poured himself another wine, and drank it like it was medicine. "He had chutzpah."

"That he did," said Lila, and clinked her glass against his.

"And he *was* indefatigable."

"I don't know what that means."

"It means when you never give up. I will say that about him. He never gave up."

Lila took a deep breath. "That's two of us," she said.

*T*he day of the Norman Jessup–Carina nuptials dawned bright, if not exactly clear. That came as a great relief to the catering staff of the Hotel Bel-Air. They had been up since the early hours of the morning preparing, the Latinos among them running out periodically to light candles so it wouldn't rain. There was a storm front off the coast that they had been listening to reports of with more than trepidation. Though they were prepared to tent the garden by Swan Lake for the ceremony and the vast lawn next to the giant sycamore for the reception, a wedding was never the same when it was soggy. Rain is considered a blessing by Hindus and Jews, but nobody was exactly sure what religion Carina was. They did, however, know that Christian Lacroix was in the hotel, having been flown in from Paris for the final fittings, and he was as close as many of the brides in the area could come to having a pope.

There was a suite set aside just to hang the bridesmaid's dresses. The fashion press had written in advance about the designs. For the bridesmaids, it was mixes of fondant pink, pearl gray, and silver fox. For the matron of honor, Mrs. Victor Lippton, it would quicken to rose pink sashed in mauve and green. The ring bearer, a four-year-old descendent of one of the founders of Paramount, would wear quicksilver velvet, short pants and jacket, and carry a pillow of gray satin, matching his ruffled shirt. The flower girl's dress would be a six-year-old, full-skirted version of the bridesmaids'. She would strew mauve rose petals on the silver carpeted aisle. That would tie it all together esthetically, according to the art director Norman had brought in to orchestrate the affair. The wrought-iron lamps siding the garden, like the stairs leading down to it, would be strung with wide, mauve satin ribbon. Each bow was to hold an arrangement of mauve roses, lilies of the valley, and cymbidium orchids, matching the bride's bouquet, which would trail to the ground, not quite as long as her train, to be held by two boys from a nursery school reputed to be funded by Michael Jackson.

The bride's dress was the very one that Claudia Schiffer had worn at the climax of the St. Laurent collection in Paris, a slightly less glittering occasion. It would be a swirl of white and gray and pale pastels. Everything was so well planned, it would doubtless go without a hitch, except for the happy couple, wrote a local wag who hadn't been invited.

But as coolly organized as the catering staff was, having handled any number of important and splendid weddings, there was a specialness about this one that had everybody slightly on edge. The overflow, anticipated to be close to a hundred, was to observe the ceremony from the balcony of the terrace, where they would also dine. A microphone with a special amplification system had been set up by one of Jessup's production technicians so no one would miss what was said by the man officiating, or the "I do's" uttered by groom and bride. Still, with everything taken care of, there remained some clouds in the sky.

Brides were usually nervous. What the hotel offered for weddings, besides excellent service, an exquisite setting, and first-rate cuisine, was a unique air of tranquility that calmed the most jittery. This morning, however, even the caterer felt a need to pull herself together. She retreated to the herb garden while the busboys went to relight their candles, praying that the weather would hold. "Happy the bride the sun shines on," the caterer repeated, eyes closed, like a mantra. "Happy the bride the sun shines on. Pretty please."

$\int$arah Nash had lit no candles, not even black ones. Instead, she sat all night at her computer, ready to cast her own personal dark spell. For the perfect wedding gift, the coup de grace. She had almost everything she needed now to ruin him. On the pages she was ready to print out was the punch line she intended to release to the press, the tale of Paulo's tail. Rewritten in her own inimitable, venomous style was the heading: "Penis into Venus." She would staple it to the Xerox of the letter from the urologist/plastic surgeon from Johns Hopkins. She had not yet even hinted at this perfect piece of evidence to her agent Lori. Sarah had given her only enough ammunition to enable her to make the deal.

"It's set," Lori had said, in their last conversation. "Two million with the paperback."

"That may not be enough," Sarah had said.

"It's high in this market. And of course everything's contingent on your having what you said was proof of what happened to Paulo. We're all dying to hear, especially me. Tell, tell. Did Jessup kill him?"

"I'll fax it to you the morning of the wedding," Sarah said. "Just before I meet with the press. I have a breakfast date with a reporter from the L.A. *Times* and the entertainment editor of CNN."

"Entertainment?"

"Some people find the odious entertaining. 'Foul deeds will rise,' taking the people who do them to the top, especially in Hollywood."

"Put that in the book."

"I already have."

"If he's such a villain, aren't you afraid? If he did away with Paulo, what's to stop him from doing something to you?"

"He wouldn't dare," Sarah said. "If anything happened to me, everyone would know who was responsible."

"Then write away, baby."

She had, and was. She looked at the clock. It was seven-thirty. An hour and a half till the breakfast revelation. So caught was she in her rage that she saw none of her surroundings, except for the keyboard on her computer and the searing words on the screen. Just across from where she sat were sliding glass doors that led to her patio, flush with purple morning glories opening to the day. In the center was the pool, dark blue in the early remaining shadows cast by the huge leaves of the giant philodendron as it stretched up, entangling itself with the palms.

Driven by time and the acid juice of her vendetta, Sarah experienced nothing but her sense of urgency. If only her hands had the speed of her brain. Well, maybe she could accelerate the creative process.

She went to the closet to get her freebasing paraphernalia.

$\mathcal{G}$ood morning," Norman said, carrying a breakfast tray, setting it on the bed.

"You think of everything," Carina said, stretching.

"Yes, I do." He went to the glassene curtains softening the ocean view and pulled the string to open them. "I even ordered the perfect day."

"It's cloudy."

"The better to photograph you by." He sat by Carina on the bed. "By the end of this morning, all our cares will have vanished."

"I didn't know we had any cares."

"Well, just one. Sarah Nash. For the ultimate wedding gift, I'm giving you her head on a tray."

"You aren't serious."

"A friend of Perry Zemmis's is taking care of it. Tonight Sarah Nash sleeps with the fishes. Or Jimmy Hoffa."

"Are you crazy?" Carina said. "If anything happens to her, they'll know it was you."

"Not if they never find her."

"You must cancel. You'll bring a curse on our marriage."

"This isn't Brazil."

"Call him *now*," she said, and picked up the phone. "Call him this minute and call it off, or I'll call off the wedding."

"The world is coming. It's the event of the decade."

"Except the bride won't be there."

"Paulo—"

"Now," Carina said, holding the phone out to him. "Do it!"

Reluctantly, he took the phone.

$\mathcal{A}$rthur Finster had ordered a new tuxedo. That he wasn't invited to the wedding was beside the point. There would undoubtedly be security, but he'd already found a place up the road from the Bel-Air, on Tortuoso Way, where he could park unobserved by the attendants. From there he could skip through the camellia garden that bordered the hotel grounds to the north, make his way under the bridge, and come out slam, bang, right at the edge of the whole affair. As unruffled as the swans.

Many had been the places he didn't really belong. He found a poignancy to that thought, a kind of middle-of-the-road seventies folk song, John Denverish, as the tailor fitted him for the last time. The wedding wasn't until five, eight and a half hours away. There was plenty of time for the last-minute touches that might be needed, although it seemed a perfect fit, especially for one who had never fit in.

For all his intrusiveness, Arthur had not yet been quite this intrusive. But today he was taking on the giants. Today he was David vs. Goliath & Co. All of them, or certainly most of them, were due to be present at the wedding—most importantly, Fletcher McCallum.

"You look like a million dollars," said his tailor, putting pins in the sleeve of the one arm that was shorter than the other.

"Fifty million, to be exact," said Arthur, checking himself out in the full-length mirror, naming the sum that had been in the subpoena, the class action libel suit the celebrities had brought against him. Represented by Fletcher McCallum, whom he intended to serve with a subpoena for a lawsuit of twice that sum. It would be quite a scene as he crashed the wedding, serving as his own process server. The mystery bag would be over the shoulder of his customized tuxedo. Fortunately, the bag was black, so he wouldn't look *too* schleppy. He owed that doff of the hat to O.J., anyway. Whatever else he might be guilty of, he at least showed good taste.

It was Arthur's plan to make his way to wherever McCallum sat and kneel behind or beside and whisper an urgent suggestion that they meet in the men's room. Once there, and without further ado, he would tell McCallum what he had on Harnoun, an associate in his own firm. He would tell him that the goods had been provided by Harnoun's own son, Richie, along with testimony that the bag was the one his father had come home with the night of the murder and dumped in the closet. And then Arthur would say aloud what he had already rehearsed to himself countless times: "Why, in the wrong hands, Fletcher, this bag could bring down an entire firm."

"You going to take the tuxedo in that bag?" the tailor asked.

"No, thanks. I'll just eat it here." He laughed aloud at the antique joke. "Humor was never my strong suit."

"Or your tuxedo," the tailor said.

Arthur froze him with an icy stare. "Just fix the sleeve," he said.

*V*ictor Lippton drove Lila to the airport himself. His wife had asked him where he was going that was so important, when it was a weekend and they should both be relaxing before the wedding. "I have to take somebody to the airport," he'd told her, as he dressed.

"Who?" Chen asked. Her hairdresser had come to the house, and was washing her hair in the special basin she'd had installed, like the one in beauty parlors.

"Nobody you know," he said.

"Why don't you just send your limo?"

"I want to make personally sure she gets on the plane."

"She?" Chen said, as her hairdresser shampooed. "Are you seeing another woman?"

"I'd have to be crazy," he said, and kissed her lightly, while the hairdresser momentarily suspended his activities.

*T*here was a wheelchair waiting for Lila at curbside, and two special attendants. Victor was having her flown to New York on the company jet.

"You're certainly going to a lot of trouble," Lila said, as the car pulled into the loading zone and he signaled the attendant.

"It's the least I can do," he said. "You're a most unusual woman."

"A lot of wives are unusual. It just takes a smart man to notice. And, of course, he has to see beyond the end of his member."

"I'll bear that in mind," Victor said.

*W*ell, two million dollars. That should allow for some needle-pointed pillows. Everywhere she'd gone in her life at the height of her success, Sarah had noted the subtle little comforts of the very rich. Fine clocks on mantelpieces, fine wines on tables, Matisse and Renoirs on silk fabric walls. The countless extras you could live without, but why should you have to? The first thing she intended to do the minute she signed the contract and got her first payment was track down her old "secretary." She wanted to find the thin little guy who'd always done the shit work for her, run errands, rounded up boys from the beach, gotten the coke, kept the bulb bottom clean, and lit it.

Even as she went to light it now, she was angry at the indignity she was subjected to, forced to do all this by herself, aristocrat that she had become, a regular literary blueblood. After all, she had pulled herself out of this swamp by her own intellectual bootstraps. She'd only hurt people who had hurt her, and that had been almost everybody.

Two million, plus whatever she'd get from foreign sales. No movie, of course. But there was always merchandising. Maybe she could do a little Paulo/Carina doll, with genitals that tucked in.

Thinking about all that, she lit the torch and aimed it at the pipe, leaning in eagerly for a pull at the smoke that wasn't even there yet. Her hand was shaking in her eagerness and impatience. She hadn't slept all night, and her focus was off. The tip of the flame caught the spike at the front of her Mohawk, and with the aggregation of glue, it ignited. Before she could fully register what was happening, her head was on fire.

Screaming, she looked for something to put out the blaze. But the pain was so severe she could hardly see. She ran towards the sliding doors to the pool. They were latched. In agony, she crashed through them. As the glass shards pierced arms, legs, face, and throat, she fell, sizzling, into the water. Her blood fanned out dark red on the surface of the pool.

*T*he music for the wedding started long before the first guests arrived. The small combo that played behind the gazebo, though they would switch into classical with flute, viola, violin, and cello for the actual ceremony, were now noodling some light, spontaneous jazz. The musicians had themselves elected to begin early, since chances were there would be moguls from the music business, and it was still the land of You Never Knew.

For the cocktail hour after the couple was joined, the combo would move underneath the porte cochere by the reception on the lawn, where they would be joined by another member of their group for incidental music. Then, when the party moved inside for the dinner, they'd be joined by four more members, giving it a big band sound. Norman had told them to keep it low volume, since most of the guests liked to talk.

The threat of rain had definitely passed. The sky was slightly overcast, but the clouds were wispy, the dark ones having moved out to sea.

"Thank God," said the caterer, looking up at the sky as she stood by the table at the entrance to the garden, setting out calligraphied name cards.

"You really think there is one?" asked one of the bartenders, who was also an actor, and had been admonished under no circumstances to give any of those present his card.

"Well, just look at the sky," said the caterer. "How can you doubt?"

*V*ictor Lippton, crossing over the covered bridge leading to the entrance, overheard the above exchange. His wife was already inside, having come early to be with the women and get into her gown. And (deep exhale) Lila Darshowitz was in the air.

So he really did have to go along with the thought that there was a God, after all. He'd never given much credence to religion, although he'd followed its tenets, observed what he had to so as to please his family. But looking down now on the mirrored surface of the pond, seeing how serene it all was, how beautiful the setting, how relieved his heart was now that the little pull was gone from his soul, along with the duplicity, Victor did have to acknowledge that in all probability a Divine Intelligence was at work, no matter how bizarre its messengers. Lila Darshowitz. God worked in mysterious ways.

*T*he O.J. tour bus started just down the street from Mezzaluna, where Nicole had eaten her last meal and Ron had waited his last table. People were still coming, although in reduced droves, many of them wearing the hats and T-shirts they'd bought in Disneyland, their previous stop. Lunch was a separate item from the tour itself, which drove past the now out-of-business restaurant, went down to Bundy and the actual murder scene. The chicken-wire fence that had been put up by police to keep the huge numbers of gawkers in line had been taken down, and those selling strawberries and oranges on neighboring corners had moved their hawking elsewhere with the thinning of the crowds. But there were still enough who came to see and relive or redie that evening to have the company run a profit.

From Bundy, the bus went to Rockingham to circle O.J.'s mansion, the very house in which the former football player, television pitchman, B-movie actor and one-shot Oxford lecturer had held a fundraiser, attended by two of the jurors who had freed him, including the one who had said that domestic violence had nothing to do with murder. The route the bus took was via Bristol Court, where a woman lived who had known O.J. and once thought him incapable of murder, but changed her mind and joined the group who wanted him out of Brentwood, and was trying to ban the bus in the neighborhood.

The bus tour had run into a little trouble with the lessening of heat around and interest in the story. Those who went on the tour were no longer content to stand outside Nicole's condo for considerable periods of time, just taking pictures and exchanging opinions about the logistics of how who got killed, in what order, why there were no screams, what would happen if dogs could talk. Nor did they linger anymore outside Rockingham, hoping for a glimpse of O.J., since everyone in the country, and, indeed, around the world, had had more than enough glimpses of O.J.

For a while, when the restaurant was still open, the bus owner had considered having the tour include a lunch at Mezzaluna, but the restaurateurs had not been interested in making it an official tourist attraction, nor could the bus company get them to agree to a cheapie meal. As a desperate measure, they had the driver double back to the Ben and Jerry's where Nicole bought her last ice cream, the one that was found half-melted by police. Nobody could remember the exact flavor she'd had, so they'd let the people on the tour order whichever one they wanted, and included the single scoop cone or cup in the price of the tour.

Still, the whole excursion lasted less than forty minutes, and even with melting ice cream people were dissatisfied. So the company decided to take the bus on an extended tour to include other famous homes, feeding on the general hunger for inside information about stars, which people imagined they could get from seeing the outside of their houses. Outsight, it might be called, supposedly providing a glimpse into what made celebrities tick—or, in O.J.'s case, ticked off.

Thus it was that the O.J. tour bus, following the route of the Movie Stars Homes' map, toodled this balmy Saturday on St. Cloud Road in Bel-Air. And thus it was that Arthur Finster, happy as an outcast lark, careering around curves on his way to crash Norman Jessup's wedding to Carina, instead crashed head-on into the O.J. tour.

Seating was free, there being no bride's side or groom's side since Carina had no family, Norman had only his mother, and everyone in attendance was presumed to be a friend and supporter of both. So except for the elder Mrs. Jessup, who was ushered to a seat down front by one of the groom's men, Bunyan Reis, people could sit where they wanted to, depending on when they arrived.

Rodney Sameth arrived early, as he was leaving right after the ceremony for the Isle of Wight, and wanted to show respect for the proceedings. He'd had no choice but to agree to attend once his cover had been blown and it was printed that he was in Hollywood. "Rodney!" Perry Zemmis said. "I didn't know you were still in town."

"I'm not," he said. "I'm gone."

"We're all so excited about your new movie. It's been too long since we've seen a Sameth original. How do you make them so good?"

"Because I do them with integrity," Rodney said. "And because I don't live here."

Wendy did not intend to get there the same time as Samantha Chatsworth. But she had lived in this New Age world of California long enough to understand there was "Meant to Be," or "Beshert," as Mortimer Schein, on whose arm she was, called it.

"Such a lovely day," Wendy greeted Samantha, in her best we-British-don't-say-what's-on-our-minds manner. "Such a pretty dress."

"It's Lacroix," said Samantha. "He's doing the clothes for the wedding."

"Mine is Schein. I believe you know Morty." They moved down the stairs together. "Oh, but of course. You brought us together."

"It was only for the clothes line," Samantha said, her voice strained.

"Well, as they say in California, sometimes you think you're doing something for one reason, and it turns out to be totally for something else. Oh, Morty, look at the gazebo. What beautiful flowers."

"Sterling silver roses," said Mortimer Schein. "My favorite. I'd like to cover you with them."

"Well, then you will," said Wendy.

"Excuse me," said Samantha, trying to hurry.

"Isn't the gazebo gorgeous," mused Wendy. "Can you imagine a lovelier setting for a wedding?"

"No," said Samantha, caught in a slow-moving, very polite crush down the stairs.

"What a shame we can't get married here, isn't it, Morty?"

"Not really," he said. "You're going to love our temple."

"We're marrying in his family's temple. That way we can be underneath his mother's chuppah. They brought it all the way from Poland. They're Holocaust survivors."

"I see," said Samantha.

"I certainly hope so," said Wendy. "Are you alright?"

"I'm fine," Samantha said.

"Morty, do you have a quarter?"

He reached into the pocket of his pants and handed one to her. "Here," Wendy said, and gave it to Samantha, smiling sweetly.

"What's this for?"

"You might want to make a call."

$\mathcal{K}$ate had come with Jake Alonzo. She had finally returned his call, gotten him past his irritation that it had taken her so long, explained that she had been involved with a story. Soothed and more eager than he probably would have been had she responded to his interest sooner, he had invited her to be his date for the wedding.

"They should have gotten married months ago," he said, moving her down the aisle. "That way you wouldn't have taken so long to go out with me."

"That isn't the reason I waited."

"No? You weren't holding out for a big event?"

"I'm not that kind of girl," she said, and smiled, and pressed the tip of her right index finger into her cheek, forcing a dimple, so he'd know the words were a jest.

"What kind of girl are you?"

"I was working that out. That's why I waited."

"What conclusion did you come to?"

She looked at him carefully. "I can be had."

"What a relief," he said, and putting his arm around her, pressed her close, moved her face against the hollow of his throat.

"Hard to believe you came with him when you could have married me," said Linus Archer, from behind them.

"I'm not ready for marriage," said Kate. "I have things to do."

"I liked it better when you were all in the kitchen," Linus said. "Barefoot and pregnant."

"How about tied to a tree?" asked Jake.

"That's a dirty lie," said Linus. "We're going to get that Finster fuck. How come you didn't come in on the class action suit with us, Jake?"

"People like Arthur take care of themselves," Jake said, and taking Kate's hand, pulled her into one of the rows.

"What did they say about you in the book?"

"You'll find out for yourself." He took her arm, and they sat. "So what's with the unpublished manuscript your grandfather left you?"

"I've been trying to work out what to do about that, too." All around her were notable people, literally aglow in the late afternoon sunlight, the women glittering with beads, well-sewn sequins, and jewels, the men haloed with the subtle radiance of power. Many of them nodded their heads in greeting to her now. Some of them smiled. Wendy leaned in to kiss her. Darcy Linette, whom Kate had never actually met, raised her hand in greeting, and put it to her ear, as though it were a phone, and mouthed "Call me."

"What's to work out," said Jake. "It's a lost Fitzgerald. You owe it to the world to make it available."

*H*elen Manning was wearing green, a gown made from three sarongs she'd bought on the beach in Bali with golden threads woven subtly through the fabric that matched her hair. Tyler, holding her arm as they made their way down the stairs, held it very protectively, at the same time being careful not to grasp.

"You're the most beautiful woman here," Tyler said, softly, not quite in her ear.

"I'd rather be in Bali."

"Let it go."

"It, or you?"

"Both," he said. "You promised you wouldn't do this if I came with you. No whining."

"I didn't mean to whine. But why can't you be with me?"

"This path . . . " He indicated the rose-petal-strewn walkway, but his eyes looked far off, mystically taking in the entire arena that was Hollywood. "If I stay on this path, I'll never reach my perfect goal."

"And that is?"

"I don't know yet."

"Maybe you never will," Helen said. "Maybe it's only because it's unattainable that you think it's perfect."

"Could be. But we're talking about you."

"Right," said Helen, brightening.

"You're a great woman. And you're ready now for the person who really deserves you. The one who's smart enough, and successful enough, and rich enough, and funny enough, and famous enough, and deep enough."

"And where am I supposed to find this paragon?" she asked.

He looked at her for a moment with everything he felt. "It's you."

*T*he musical group behind the gazebo segued into traditional wedding music. The gentle lull of Pachelbel rolled across the lawn and the people sitting there like an affable wave.

Above the sound, beyond it, Fletcher McCallum thought he could hear the wail of a siren, and tried to close it out. He remembered the moment when he was still in law school and there'd been an accident ahead of him and how, as he ran to the mangled cars in the road ahead, his first thought had been not "Is anyone dead?" or "Is anyone hurt?" but "Who's liable?" And he'd understood in that moment that he'd made the transition from human being to lawyer.

It was a transformation he did not judge in himself, but simply acknowledged as part of his road. For all he tried to pass on to his sons of integrity and caring and compassion, he understood he was not there for justice or right, but for his clients. It helped, of course, when their cause was just, because for all his composure, he was a passionate man when it came to an issue. And it was really much more civilized to string a man up by his thumbs in a court of law than to kill him.

Still, it was a flaw in him, he considered, that even at a moment like this, with the glory of the greenery, the beauty of the crowd, the flowered crown on the white gazebo, the serenity of the setting, the peaceful glide of the swans, the grandeur of the music, his attention should be caught by a siren. He wondered whether it was fire, emergency illness, or accident. But then the groom's men began to assemble in front of the gazebo, and he brought his attention back to the proceedings.

*S*o what's the story?" Jake asked Kate.

"The story?"

"Your grandfather's story."

"Well," she began. "It's about this Hollywood producer. And he cheats, and lies, and even steals, but all through his life, there's this one faithful woman who loves him and never forgets him. She's there for him. And he always comes back to her."

"I love it," said Jake. "I absolutely love it. What's it called?"

"*West of Paradise,*" Kate said, capitalizing it with her breath.

"A real Fitzgerald title," he said.

"I thought so, too," said Kate.

"So what happens?"

"Well . . . he does everything imaginable that's amoral and terrible, but he always survives. And then he does a kindness for a friend, and that's the thing that finally destroys him."

"That's pretty cynical," Jake said. "Fitzgerald was a romantic."

"Well, we all have to grow up sometime," said Kate.

"I guess . . . " Jake said.

There was a rustle behind them. The flower girl came down the aisle, strewing rose petals on the silvered carpet. She giggled as she did so, and threw some of them at one of the onlookers she apparently knew. Behind her, the ringbearer came, with a gold ring on a silver satin pillow. He looked very serious, his eyes intent on the ring.

"It sounds like a great role," Jake said.

"I imagine it will be," said Kate.

"I'd really love to play it. When could I see the manuscript?"

"Probably in a couple of months," she said.

"Why so long?"

"I'll have to transcribe it. At the end of his life he was very drunk and probably ill, so the writing is hard to make out."

"Well, I guess I'll just have to wait. But I'm excited. I mean, *really* excited. I can hardly sit."

"Well, it's okay to stand," said Kate. "Here comes the bride."

Afterword

The statue of Larry Drayco stands beneath Victor Lippton's office at Cosmos. It is a huge bronze head, with a very big grin on its face and oversized teeth.

The Academy of Motion Picture Arts and Sciences turned down the idea of a Larry Drayco Award. But a special dinner was held to honor him, which satisfied Lila Darshowitz, who attended the event. The dinner was at the Beverly Hilton, and it was such a success that it was decided the dinner would be held every year, as a way of raising money for the Writer's Guild. Larry's biggest debt, not counting what he owed lawyers, was fines he owed that union for not paying writers the Guild's prescribed legal minimum. The award was to be given posthumously to the producer himself and accepted by Lila, for tenacity, courage in the face of seemingly overwhelming odds, and, though it was not put into official language, chutzpah. But the first time turned out to be the only time it was presented, as they never found anyone again who had Larry's nerve.

Asher Pfaltz, Hollywood historian and the town's most erudite book critic, pronounced the novel *West of Paradise* a "devastatingly brilliant literary find, more devastasting for the loss not only of writers like F. Scott Fitzgerald, but readers of an age that was bent on self-improvement." He went on to quote a colleague at *The New York Times* who had noted that in Fitzgerald's time people "read great writing because, like all good art, it was thought to improve the character of the person, to aid in the general bettering drift of the American dream." Pfaltz then cited Horace, in his *Ars Poetica,* that good writing should both educate and entertain, and concluded that *West of Paradise* succeeded, although it had not yet been selected for Oprah's book club.

The film, a screen adaptation by Kate Donnelly of the Fitzgerald novel, was produced by Norman Jessup in association with Perry Zemmis, and released by Cosmos Pictures, starring Jake Alonzo. In spite of more than respectful reviews, it did very little business since it had no special effects.